BREAKFAST WITH THE DIRT CULT

BY

SAMUEL FINLAY

For my family and friends.

And for Alpha Company, Second Platoon.

Joe Takes a Holiday

The young man stood in front of the neon-lit building and grinned. Its marquee crackled with a predatory magnetism that stirred up something in him; something far down in the depths of his maleness, forcing him to swallow the nervous lump in his throat. It was not the first of such places he had been to in his three years of service, and like the others, it made all the old familiar promises to fulfill his every desire. There was something wonderfully wild about those establishments, which to him, was worth wading through the black lights and compromise. There was a spark of mysterious possibilities in the sticky Montreal night air that made the young man the human equivalent of a chambered round with the safety off.

He was happy for the warm sensual buzz from the wine he'd had with dinner. The Cabernet had been just enough to loosen his inhibitions a bit while not diminishing his sharpness. There was a cockiness now in the way he wore his black polo and charcoal gray trousers that had been absent from his posture in the life from which he'd obtained a brief parole. He tingled with joy as he felt like a better version of the man he was back in the States. He couldn't remember feeling so free, and he had savored playing the role of the man-about-town as he'd gone tear-assing all over the grand old city and indulging his senses. One last pleasure remained.

He stood poised to murder one of his principles in cold blood. In spite of the long-blurred remnant of his Baptist upbringing. If he lived through the upcoming deployment and finally found his way to freedom again, then he'd really go nuts. He remembered the words his buddy Benamy had said to him before his Pass to Budapest long ago. It was there that the young man standing under the neon sign had met a girl named Aliz, and she had taught him a hard but invaluable lesson.

"Come on, man," Benamy had advised in Bosnia with his Kentucky accent dripping off his words. "I understand havin' standards in the States, but here in The Boz' you should have sex with any woman who'll stay still. You're actin' like the pussy's all *sancticized* and shit. You should let your standards float away like a balloon, and when you're on the plane back home you just reach out and grab them back. The stratosphere is filled with released standards."

He entered and paid the doorman, who in turn led him to a small table. The young man scanned the room and realized that Private Heinz had dropped the ball on this one. Yes, the room was scattered with beautiful, scantily-clad women. Yes, there was a stage with a brass stripper pole that was as shiny as sin, where a delightfully leggy brunette member of the local talent bent over to display her flawless undercarriage. However, that was all there was. This was no brothel.

Still though, it was a strip club, and that was something. Tension melted from his shoulders and he took a relaxed breath. People could talk all the shit they wanted to about strippers, but at least you knew where you stood with them. You could respect them. Strippers were God's Chosen People. There was an integrity about them and what they did, and all parties went in knowing the rules of the game, and enjoyed the bittersweet narcotic of mutual disposability. The negotiating of its price was all up front and out in the open, unlike the regular nightclubs and bars where bitches postured like beasts in heat on the Serengeti yet spouted the *"I'm just here to dance with my girlfriends / I'm not sure what I want right now"* lines they regurgitated from whatever piece of Clit-Lit they had just read. He figured he might be able to proposition one of the girls on the clock so he decided to stay. He also decided he needed a drink.

He got up from the table and took a seat at the bar next to a blonde in an elegant black cocktail dress of an Audrey

Hepburn cut who chatted casually with the barmaid during a break from trolling the room for marks. To him, the girl in the cocktail dress stuck out like a sore thumb among the other strippers there to the extent he smiled with amusement and shook his head. She exuded a hedonistic wholesomeness that gave her the effect of looking more like his date to the Junior Prom, rather than a hardened veteran of a stripping vocation. He redirected his attention to the barmaid and said, "*Bonjour. Pardon moi, mademoiselle. Parlez-vous Anglais?*"

"Yes, I speak English," she replied with the token sexy French accent. "What can I get you?"

"I'd like a Rum-and-Coke, please."

The barmaid turned to get his drink and he continued to think over a plan of action to salvage the situation.

"Oh my God!" exclaimed the blonde in the black cocktail dress with surprise. "You read *The Globe and Mail!*"

"Today I do," the young man replied. On his first trip to New York City he had developed the habit of carrying around a newspaper, and since then it had become one of his personal SOP's when by himself in a city. It was something lightweight to pretend to read so that he didn't look pathetic when he stopped somewhere alone. "It was the closest one to hand they had in English. I'm Tom Walton. What's your name, Miss?"

"Amy. That's some accent. Where are you from?"

Walton tried hard not to show his surprise. A world full of strippers with names like Destiny, Essence, and Ariel (there were a surprising number of Disney fans and former little girl princesses in the stripper population) and here was one who kept her real name. He focused back on answering her question and replied, "I'm an American. From Oklahoma."

She smiled widely. "You're a long way from Oklahoma, Tom. What brings you up here?" She tilted her head slightly, awaiting an answer.

The barmaid returned and set down the drink. Walton gave her a courteous nod, and while he held her gaze, he said, "*Merci.* By the way, could you set the lady up again with whatever she wants?"

"Aw, thanks," Amy said as she hit him with the Prom Date Smile. "I'll take a Scotch on-the-rocks, please."

Walton's eyes widened in astonishment for a second, and the corners of his mouth turned up merrily at the petite girl's choice of poison. What a dame. "Goddamn, darlin'. You're a hard woman to drink that shit. I'm impressed."

The barmaid exchanged smiles with them and came back with a fresh drink. "Thank you," Amy said politely. "When I first started stripping I was a lightweight, but after you spend a couple months with guys buying you drinks, you build a tolerance. I tried Scotch one night, and I was like, 'This is *so* good!' So, you were about to answer my question."

Walton grew a shitty grin. "Well...look, Amy, this is gonna sound like a total pick-up line, but I'm in the Army. I'm an infantry soldier stationed down at Ft. Drum, and I'm here to have some fun before we go to Afghanistan."

"You're absolutely right, that does sound like a total pick-up line. But you're serious?"

"Yes, I am."

She set her hand on top of his and Walton's pulse throbbed at the warmth of it. "Okay, just so you know, I'm no Progressive Conservative or anything, but I'm pro-Army. You guys are so brave."

"I don't know about that, but it's nice of you to say so."

Walton had never given Canadian politics a moment's thought, but sitting in the strip club, he got the impression that it was a pretty confusing enterprise. That the Liberals were probably watered-down Communists seemed to be a universal phenomenon, but he wondered what the hell a Progressive Conservative was. The phrase seemed contradictory. He figured they were probably something along the lines of really laid-back Democrat/Republican hybrids who said *"eh?"* a lot. The whole "Progressive" thing certainly didn't score any points with him. The inherent smugness in the word pissed him off. It seemed a hell of a lot like a civil religion; as though no man cometh unto the future but by it. The "Conservative" part didn't do much for him either. He took a sip then gave her a smile. "So do you go to college around here, Amy?" Strippers always seemed to be single mothers or college students.

"Oh, no. I graduated from university last year. I stick around though because I love Montreal and I've got a lot of friends here." She looked around with mild annoyance at the crowded club and leaned forward to be heard and draw him into her bubble of intimacy. "It's kind of loud down here around the stage," she said. "Would you be interested in going upstairs?"

Fancying himself as a bit of a stripper connoisseur, Walton was impressed by how naturally she could toss the hook and make him want to be caught. He hadn't seen a girl of this caliber in some time. The off-Post strip club didn't have much of a roster. The last time he'd been there, a stripper with a pot belly and a leg brace had asked his friend Lunchbox for a dollar and had held his hat for ransom until she got it. Walton figured Lunchbox had been lucky to settle cheap with that one. If she'd have fallen on him, he could've gotten hurt. "Certainly. Now, I don't mean to be the Ugly American, but how does it work here?"

"We go upstairs, and for a price, I do a private show for you." What began as The Prom Date Smile evolved into one far more wicked that promised to eat him alive but assured him he'd enjoy every second of it. Her warm tone then switched to no-nonsense in a jiffy. "There's *no* contact, though."

He agreed with a wink and followed Amy upstairs to a balcony where a number of low platforms lay spaced about. Two were already in use, one of which held a pair of girls with tight young bodies writhing together like snakes. Amy led Walton to a chair in front of a platform in the corner, and once he was seated, she smiled and began to disrobe. He grinned and remarked as jauntily as he could, "I'm afraid I don't wear underwear, darlin', so I apologize for any unsightly bulge."

Amy laughed without restraint or pretense, and in doing so, something ominous clicked in Walton. With her laugh, she ceased to be a hired hand in his eyes and became a real girl.

Her cocktail dress slid from her body and caressed her hips as it fell almost weightlessly to the platform, joined thereafter with delicious slowness by her black silk undergarments. The light from the dim club clung to her fair skin like a luminescent scent and Walton took a moment to burn the image into his brain. Her long curly blonde hair flowed down to two perfect pink-nippled breasts that stood with a natural enthusiasm rather than hung, above a slender waist that drew the eye down to hips supported by a real honest-to-God set of walkin,' talkin,' dancer's legs.

Amy's lithe young body was not that of the hot girl who takes her clothes off for money. It belonged instead to the girl who you wished lived next door, who in her heathen innocence had the decency to make sure the windows were always good and open when she changing her clothes. The Lord God A'mighty had hand-crafted her out of a bunch of sleek feminine curves all living together in perfect harmony. She looked soft; Walton figured she was soft in ways he'd never heard of. It even extended to her smile, or maybe all the rest came from there in the first place. It emanated a spritely, joyously pagan quality.

However, as drawn as he was toward the shape before him, his attention kept wandering back to her eyes. They were hazel. They were alive and aware, and couldn't have been more unlike the many mercenary ones he'd seen in places like this over the years, belonging to women who locked their souls away when they put on their stilettos.

Amy moved her body in a slow playful manner that made Walton want to leave his chair and do something that would probably result in a first-class ass-kicking, but he stilled that impulse for another one.

"Look, darlin', you don't have to do a bunch of that shit." His words from Budapest returned to him and he measured them out as slow and steady as he could manage. "I'll tell ya what, Amy. Let me make you a proposition. While we're up here, you work for me, and my only requirement is that you be honest and happy. You seem like an interesting girl. I'd rather you tell me a little about yourself."

She arched an eyebrow quizzically, and when she saw that he meant it, asked, "What would you like to know?"

"Well, let's say you're on an island by yourself for a month. You live in this *Swiss Family Robinson* style tree house. It's got a captain's wheel and everything, and when you turn it, the roof opens up and you can sleep under the stars. All your food is prepared by a gourmet chef and it's air-dropped in. There's even a theater on the island that has all the latest in sight and sound technology and The World's Most Comfortable Chair. However, you can only bring three movies. If it's a series of movies like, *Star Wars*, the James Bond movies, or *Anne of Green* fuckin' *Gables*, that series counts as one. Now, you're by yourself, so don't have to impress anyone, but you're there for a month, so you'll probably want something with some stayin' power. So, what would you bring?"

As she gave herself over to the wheels turning in her mind, she ceased her stripper-posturing and sat Indian style. "I'm not sure I can pick just three. Definitely, *Mulholland Drive*." She continued to ponder the answer, then suddenly changed like quicksilver and exploded. "Wait! I know one! I really got into *Fight Club* recently. I loved that whole Nietzsche-esque way of looking at things. You know, aggressively living your life in that whole, 'take no prisoners,' kind of way." The last she said with a tough squint while putting up her dukes challengingly. "It was so visceral too, what with all the violence and all."

Walton imagined a nude girl fight club. He bet the fights would end up looking a lot like the performance of the two lipstick lesbians on the platform. Everybody would be a winner.

The fantasy threatened to pull his full attention, so he reached out for more conversation. "Speakin' of Nietzsche, have you ever read *Hero with a Thousand Faces*? Well, my man Joseph Campbell has this sort of Unified Theory of Mythology. He poses that all myths tell essentially the same story, this Mono-Myth; the Hero hears the call of adventure and strikes out on a quest into the unknown and faces trials all along the way in pursuit of somethin'. I got a hold of that shit in college, and I wasn't the same. Joseph Campbell set my brain on fire. If you dig that sort of thing, you should give him a go sometime."

"Oh my God!" she said leaning forward excitedly, "I'm such a sucker for that shit; you know, the whole Hero-Cult thing. I think that's fucking awesome. Do you read a lot?"

"Are you kiddin'? I'm the bookworm of my platoon." He watched the light of interest and approval warm her face at the opportunity of having a chat with a fellow book-lover, and Walton thought he'd press his luck, courtesy of his Budapest Strategy. He let a portion of the hunger he felt for her shape his features, took a slow breath, and declared, "*Illa puella amanda est*."

Amy turned her head in a gesture of vague recognition and asked, "What does that mean?"

"It's Latin for, '*This girl must be loved.*'"

"You know Latin?"

"A bit. I took some in college. It's pretty atrophied now. About all I remember are pick-up lines to try to impress girls with. My Latin professor was this old dirty bastard who used to tell us that when he was a student they used to say, 'Latin is a language, as dead as it can be. First it killed the Romans, and now it kills me.'"

"Oh, no doubt. Having to memorize all those conjugations and declensions is the worst." She then began to bob her head from side to side in time with her voice as she tediously chanted, "*Hic, Haec, Hoc, Huis, Huis, Hui…* "

The naked blonde with the pretty eyes and mind-numbingly beautiful body had just begun declining the Latin pronoun *Hic*. It was all he could do to join her in finishing the cases, and laughing with her at the end of it.

Amy had officially blown Walton's mind.

He ordered another round from the waitress and they talked passionately about books, movies, their Signs (she was a Pisces, he an Aries) and the families and friends they had left behind them in their old lives. Halfway through their next drink he noticed the two girls in the lesbian act still gently attacking each other in the best of ways while their client, a balding man of middle years, watched intently as though there would be a test later. Walton noticed Amy playing the voyeur as well.

"Those two certainly seem to like each other."

Amy continued looking at the girls with a smile. "Yeah, you can't beat the lesbian show."

"I don't know about that, darlin'. I think you're the best thing out tonight," he said, and tossed her a leer when she turned to preen at his compliment. "You look uncomfortable in those shoes. Why don't you take them off? You know, show us some toe."

"You don't think they make my calves look sexy?" she asked coyly as she posed a leg.

Walton dished her a mock sneer. "It ain't that. Believe me, you don't need them to be sexy. I just think if I was a chick, I wouldn't want to wear high-heeled shoes. Take 'em off and relax a while. Sit a spell."

She untied the straps on the black high-heeled shoes, setting them off to the side, then pulled her legs into her chest, wrapped her arms around them, and tilted her head to rest it on her knees. Wearing nothing now but French mani/pedicures, she wiggled her toes and smiled.

"See, Amy, isn't that better?"

"Yes, it is. Do you have a foot fetish or something?"

"No, I have a beautiful girl fetish."

Amy's smile deepened, and then she returned to sitting Indian style. As she moved, Walton let his eyes roam her body. "My God, darlin', you're magical," he commented with aesthetic passion. "Serious. It's like, hard to think right now over here."

"I like it when you call me *darlin'*. It's so sexy," she said as she let her fingertips lazily trace her legs. She smiled knowingly at where she caught his eyes momentarily lingering, enjoying how powerless she had rendered him with such little effort. She mercifully stopped teasing him and went back to just sitting. "But thank you. You're way too kind." Her tone then became scholarly, which Walton thought an amusing contrast given her lack of clothes. "But seriously, what's humanity's obsession with the vagina?"

"I don't know," he answered, happy at her shift from the usual paint-by-numbers stripper seduction techniques to just plain talking. He suspected there was something very special about the unrepentantly positive girl that set her apart from the usual mattress-fodder types. "I guess 'cause it's the heart of creation. It's the mysterious nothin' from which all life springs."

She laughed loudly, the pure happiness in her voice filling their corner of the room, counter-balancing the soul-eroding decadence running amok upstairs like a candle in the dark, and Walton closed his eyes for just a moment to let the world revolve around that sound. It sparked a dangerous feeling in the back of his mind that he had met this girl before in some long lost yesterday and tonight fate had finally returned her to him.

A quiet pause asserted itself and the two looked at each other. He took the plunge. "Look, Amy. I'm gonna let you in on a little secret, and I hope you ain't offended. 'Cause that's the *last* thing I want to do. I came here thinkin' this was a brothel, and well . . . I wanted to be with a girl before I left for Afghanistan. You know, that ol' chestnut. I'd like it if it was with you."

Walton braced himself for consequences and repercussions. He glanced around for the back exit out of the corner of his eye and hoped he could make it past the bouncers, many of whom looked like boxers. Knowing his luck, they were probably Québécois nationalists who were *très* anti-American. He wondered how he'd explain being arrested after getting his ass beat in a Canadian strip club to The Brass. There would probably be lots of push-ups involved. Even though he assumed Amy must be propositioned by clients on a regular basis, mentioning that he'd been looking for a brothel was probably a bad tactical maneuver on his part

Amy, however, didn't seem fazed in the least. She took his declaration like a champ and smiled sweetly, then she reached out and touched his leg. "I would love to be your pre-deployment fling," she said, "but I've got a boyfriend. He's a piece of shit and he cheats on me, and I'm probably going to leave him soon, but I don't think I want to cheat on him." She tilted her head again inquisitively. "Why don't you have a girlfriend?"

Walton wryly arched one of his heavy eyebrows and replied, "Darlin', for one thing I'm ugly, and until I joined the Army, very broke. Neither of these qualities appeals to women. Also, it never seems to be the right time. The Army kinda dominates everything in my life and if I don't play along and walk small, I lose money or go to jail. We're also either training all the time or gettin' deployed to some Third World Shithole. Then, there's the work itself. I feel like I'm always havin' to take shit off of someone, and I can't imagine trying to be a man in a relationship with that in the back of my mind, you know? Like I'm never really the man of my own life." He then made a play for levity and grinned. "Besides, when I like a girl I go retarded for her to distraction."

Another pregnant look forced itself on them and Walton saw something visibly click in her mind. The aftermath of an instantaneous decision washed over her face so suddenly that it scared him. It felt to Walton as if she had just whimsically decided the fate of a world, and perhaps she had.

"Okay," she said, "I'm going to give you my number and I want you to call me tomorrow after one o'clock. I have tomorrow off, and I want to show you all around Montreal. Will you call me?"

He answered her in his head before she even asked. He produced a small green notebook and wrote down her number. She noticed the quotes he'd collected from the guys in his platoon and she added one of her own; some song lyrics from a group known as The Tragically Hip, who evidently were all the rage in Canada.

He was in a race against time. Walton continually checked his pocket watch to see how much time he had left with her. He tried to wring out every little nugget of information from her brain, almost as if on some level he believed that if he got enough of her thoughts and opinions he would have *her*. She was a drug. To fight the torrent she inspired in him, he tried to ignore her body and look her in the eye and concentrate completely on what she said.

Walton was so intent in his focus that his other senses were almost entirely absorbed by his ability to hear, like some sort of Fakir mysticism or Zen-like trance. His plan soon backfired, and her voice began to fondle his brain. Never before had the Canadian accent been so sexy. Had someone told him a week prior that the Canadian accent could inspire ravishment, he would've had a hard time wrapping his mind around the idea. Now, he was a believer. Hers was more subtle than the TV stereotype, though words like *about* still flirted with *aboot*, and *sorry* oozed into *souwry*. Once she even dropped an, *eh?*, and he'd had to give her hell about it, thus prompting her to throw a few sentences at him where she mimicked his *y'all's*, *ain't's*, and his inability to end a word with the letter *G*. For a few minutes their conversation became an etymologist's wet dream. Then, when Amy began speaking French at Walton's request, with that warm lively tone of hers, he just about died right there in the titty-bar. Fortunately for his mother, though, this wasn't the place from where he was to go on to his eternal reward.

After they spent their allotted time together, she dressed and they went back downstairs. She performed the first song in her set to *Heard it through the Grapevine*. (Walton had mentioned his tendency to try to get strippers to dance to Marvin Gaye as a general rule, and Amy surprised him by picking the track. She had said she loved to have fun with her choice of music and that once she had even stripped to *The Gambler*. Walton let himself have fun with that imagery and would have given his right hand to have seen it. A girl who looked that good naked and liked Kenny Rogers made Walton reconsider what he'd been taught as a boy. Maybe God really did love him and have a plan for his life.) He smiled and stared at her eyes the whole time. Almost. She was naked, after all.

When she finished her set and began collecting the money that the men had laid out for her, Walton felt a flash of repulsiveness. Though he had seen this portion of the transaction too many times to remember, it suddenly became revolting to a degree he had never felt before, not even the first time he'd gone to such a place. There was something inherently wrong about the act of this ex-ballerina kneeling as she collected the money that lay on the stage. The men watched her with heat in their eyes as she deflected it all with a gracious smile and laughed in a friendly fashion at their last-ditch attempts at banter before she made her exit.

A wordless, primal frame of mind took hold of Walton, overriding the craving that brought him there and held him still; this was wrong, all of it, and she didn't belong here. As she neared, he felt ashamed that he was no different than any of the other drones seated in their lust-induced idiocy around the Queen Bee on the stage. He was just as guilty as the rest of them. (And, he reminded himself, no one was putting a gun to her head and saying, "Strip or else!") Then again, he thought, it *was* worth every dime and more to see her in her skin.

She paused when she got to Walton. Though she still had up the walls of seduction and control which she used to rule the room, the openness that she had momentarily shared with him returned as they locked eyes, softening her features. She leaned over him from the edge of the stage and drew close to his face. Her hair cascaded over his head, creating a barrier between the two of them and the rest of the world that made everything suddenly dark and warm. Her breasts strained to touch him. Her breath tickled his ear as she whispered, "Thank you, Tom. Now don't forget to call me, okay?" then left a kiss on his cheek.

In the morning he woke up laughing, and after a late breakfast and some sightseeing, he called her and left a message. He watched a bit of a Bruce Lee movie in French and boiled in anticipation for her call. He decided he would try to get her to cheat on her boyfriend.

Until that day, Walton had prided himself on what was left of his integrity in regards with women. Throughout his life he had occasionally found an opportunity with a woman who'd had someone and he'd always refused because he didn't want to have being the Stunt Cock on his karma. He had largely avoided Filler Relationships because he didn't want to have to deal with a commitment or baggage, and was afraid of hurting or using someone. He had liked knowing he could control some of his impulses. After having met Amy, however, and finding out that she was soon to be leaving her boyfriend, he decided to take off the white hat.

She finally called and told him to meet her at a tavern on Rue Sainte-Élisabeth at nine o'clock, and gave him suggestions for what to do with the day. He left the hotel and saw the Mosaiculture Exhibit by the harbor and walked along the water feeling at ease around the people there in a way he never had in America.

When the sky darkened with clouds bearing an afternoon shower, he ducked into the nicest restaurant he could find for lunch while looking out the window and laughing at other people getting rained on for a change. After the rain passed, he left and wandered around in what was left of the steamy afternoon, meandering through a jazz festival and a multitude of eclectic shops, then at last, walked to meet her at the bar.

He stepped through the door and his eyes fixed on her just as sure as the turning of the Earth. She hadn't noticed him come in and he took the opportunity to watch her for a moment, not wanting to disturb the scene. If springtime ever wore a skirt it'd look like her, he thought, and the normality of it all strangled the small voice reminding him that in her other life she was a professional tart.

Amy had bound back her sun-kissed hair with a clip and had pulled up the long sleeves on the red cotton pullover blouse that whispered secrets about her figure beneath it. Her toned legs flashed out of a pleated, navy, mid-thigh length skirt, giving her the appearance of an off-duty Super Girl as she sat on her barstool reading a newspaper. No doubt, *The Globe and Mail.* There was a dynamic sense of grace and restrained action in her physicality; like a ballerina playing tennis before a bar fight, that manifested itself in the way her eyes occasionally glanced around, the way she drank her bottle of beer, and the way one of her sneakers never quite stayed still, swinging like a pendulum to an enthusiastic tune played by an invisible world of magic, as though a new adventure was hiding in the corner and she'd be damned if she'd miss it on her watch.

She beamed when she finally saw him and gestured for him to take a seat. "Hi, Tom! I was afraid you'd stood me up," she greeted. "I told the bartender and I was like, 'What the fuck?'"

As he approached, Walton gave the pub a quick scan and smiled at her taste in watering holes. It had an Old World European feel to it that reflected the warmth and charm of a more elegant time. He took a seat at the polished wooden bar, ordered a beer, and while the bartender popped the top, He looked Amy in the eyes. "There's no way in hell I could do that, Amy. In fact, earlier, when I was waitin' for you to return my call, I was afraid you'd forgotten about me."

"No, I was just busy running errands. Here, scoot closer and tell me about what all you did today. Did you see the Mosaiculture Exhibit?"

He drew his chair nearer to her and told her of his afternoon sight-seeing. They talked of Montreal and the cities they'd seen, and the others they would like to someday visit. They expressed their desire to taste life as fully as possible which saddened Walton and made him envious of her freedom. He bitched to her about the Army and how it controlled everything in his life from his hair cut to requiring his piss, given under the eye of a Meat Gazer, to see if he took drugs.

"Okay, that's one thing I was wondering about," she broke in with a hand on his arm. Walton wondered if they taught girls that hand-on-the-arm maneuver in school. It seemed like gentling a horse. "What is the States' policy on drugs?"

"They're pretty much against it," he replied. "If The Man finds it on you, your ass goes somewhere to spend your time makin' big rocks little."

"That's crazy. Here, it's no big deal. Taking them is a rite of passage. Like 'Shrooms. Here, everybody does 'Shrooms. I've done 'Shrooms, my boyfriend did 'Shrooms—here, watch this; even the bartender did 'Shrooms." She turned and called the bartender over. "Hey, let me ask you a question. Have you done 'Shrooms?"

The man nodded.

"See? What'd I say?"

She briefly compared recipes for 'Shroom Toblerone with the bartender, then looked back at Walton. "I want you to meet my roommate and get high so you can get kicked out of the Army and come live in Montreal."

Walton sighed and nursed a vivid fantasy. "I wish I could, Amy. You've got me half-tempted to go AWOL. I'd love to spend all kinds of time gettin' high with you and your friends. Among other things."

She broke eye contact with him, looked down, then after meeting his eyes again, she squeezed his hand and said, "Look, Tom, I want to apologize in advance for deciding not to 'do anything' with you on account of my boyfriend."

Alas, poor Walton could gaze upon the Promised

Land, but he could not cross the River Jordan. He sank inside, but managed to come up with a dirty grin just for show. He figured that was just his fucking luck to wind up with the only quasi-virtuous stripper in all of Montreal. "Don't apologize, Amy. I respect you for takin' the high road. If you should change your mind, though, keep me posted."

"I will, but I really don't want to come across as slatternly. I told my roommate, 'If I don't cheat on my boyfriend with the American soldier, I'll be good all summer.'"

Walton drank a deep consolation sip of his beer and wanted badly to put that to the test. He decided to play the sensitive "Aw Shucks, Ma'am" Card, and subtly let a fraction more of his native accent coat his words. "Look darlin', you're talkin' to a guy who's a big fan of you gals and what y'all bring to civilization. I figure with you being a cosmopolitan kinda girl, you ought to have some advice for a guy interested in being a better man to women." He gave her hand a faint squeeze of his own, looked her in the eye as if he were going to try to crawl in, and softened it with a smile.

"Advice on what?"

"I don't know. Whatever comes to mind."

She took a sip and looked up, thinking for a moment. When she had her answer, she looked back at him with mischievous eyes and said, "Don't waste a woman's time."

"Hmm. I'm gonna have to think about that." Walton heard a lot that was unsaid in her tone. There had to be a way to use that. Maybe he could play on something in there to attack the boyfriend from an angle.

"Women hate to have their time wasted," Amy reiterated. "And as a man, you should never do it."

They soon left at her suggestion and walked the streets of Montreal. After a few blocks, she grabbed his hand and led them across the intersection at a trot. While they ran hand-in-hand Walton heard fireworks go off in the downtown sky and he laughed out loud at how clichéd it seemed. He had read in the paper that morning that it was Canada Day, but he couldn't help but feel as though the display was just another thing to imprint his time with her in his brain. In a fit of delirium, he squeezed her hand as they ran.

Once they made it across the road and resumed their normal pace, he let go. As he did, Amy folded her arm over his, pulling into him, and said, "I hate it that the world is like it is. I hate it that you and all your soldier friends have to go Over There. It's not fucking right!"

Hearing Amy say that, and sounding like she meant it, was one of the nicest things any girl had ever said to him. He hoped to hell that he wouldn't fuck up things too badly. "Check it out, Amy, it's no big deal," he replied. "I volunteered, and so did my buddies, and I'm gettin' out as soon as I can. There's NCO's (Non-Commissioned Officers) in my platoon, though, who've been deploying all over the world their whole adult life, and they and their families pay a heavy price for that. That's what ain't right."

"You see, that's what I mean. Say, what are your thoughts on women in the military?"

Walton was leery of pissing her off but he decided to take the bait. "I think there's a place for them—this is where I piss off the semi-feminist in you—but I don't think they belong in the Combat Arms. It ain't that I don't think y'all are tough; far from it. I've known some girls who could probably kick the asses of a number of the guys in my company, but I don't think y'all are built to carry weight like we are. I won't even get into the hygiene issue.

"There's also somethin' I saw in the three months of Basic Training, and lots of times since then, when we'd be out in the field for weeks on end, or deployed, or havin' Cabin Fever in the barracks when the winter gets bad; guys forced to live close together without women in their lives on a regular basis turn into pissed-off cavemen. They ain't got nothin' to channel their procreative—Frank Herbert used the term *procreative* and I think that word's much more nuanced and true to life than the sterile and sciencey word *sexual*—energies into, so they get all pent up and start doin' all kinds of crazy shit. You know, being destructive, engagin' in high risk behavior, forming packs, that sort of thing. The shit's like *Paint Your Wagon* meets *Lord of the Flies*.

"As a dude, this sort of thing sucks, and it's shit for the civilian world because it can lead to things like gangs and serial killers and what-have-you. But for the infantry, that shit's cash money. Men who want women, but can't have them, will jump at the chance to fuck shit up till they can be with some. They're lookin' for a reason to fight. And that's what you want in a grunt. Realizin' that made me see the genius in the way our civilization set things up.

"Then there's the whole sexual politics thing that ALWAYS happens when you get guys and girls together. One time down at Ft. Polk we were doin' some training for The Boz' and my buddy Malone came upon this guard tower on a night patrol. Come to find out, this young chick corporal from the National Guard was up in it, fuckin' her older male First Sergeant. From what I've seen, that seems to be the way it goes. Girls wind up hookin' up with guys who outrank them, or PT studs—"

"Just a second," Amy interrupted. "What's 'PT?'"

"Sorry. My life is inundated with acronyms. 'PT' stands for 'Physical Training.' A guy who's really strong and fast is good at PT, and more often than not, looks all athletic and what-not. Those kinda guys make women *sauté* their panties, and chicks will claw each other's eyes out to be humped by 'em. Hence, 'PT stud.'"

"Oh. Okay."

"Anyhow, it seems to me that girls in the service tend to hook up with higher-ranking guys or PT studs who look like they're carved out of rock, either to get out of havin' to do shit, or to be the belle of the ball, or have fun, or whatever. Then the guys who ain't gettin' laid get pissed, and rightfully so. Discipline and unit cohesion go to shit. And I won't talk about the stuff my brother in the Navy said about the Lesbian Mafia. Either way, marksmanship, push-ups, sit-ups, and running, are one thing, but biology and sex is somethin' else. You don't sass Mother Nature. 'Least not for long. You stand at Parade Rest and say, 'Roger that, Ma'am!' and drive the fuck on with your bad self to the next objective.

"Now, you tell me; if you need to get together a group of people to kill 'n break shit on your behalf 'cause your survival is at stake, who do you want to send downrange? A bunch of cavemen in the physical prime of their lives with piss and vinegar in their veins 'cause they're *'lonesome, ornery, and mean,'* or a bunch of dudes and chicks tryin' to re-live High School drama with M4's 'n shit?"

Amy listened to his rant, and after considering his position, asked, "Okay. But what if you had a daughter? And one day she comes to you saying, 'Dad, I want to join the infantry like you did.'"

"Oh, I'd be proud of her. But I'd fight her. And I'd win."

"Yeah, but what if it was something she really wanted to do and felt like it would make her happy?"

"As her father, I'd be a damn sight more concerned about her survival than her happiness. After all, this is *war* we're talkin' about, Amy. People killin' and dyin'. A girl marchin' around in a beret and carrying a rifle, and gettin' fucked by PT studs, and feelin' 'empowered' is all fine and dandy till she gets blown the fuck up and her brains are paintin' the road and her ovaries are scattered all over some Third World Shithole, or she gets captured and gang-raped in the dirt from hell-to-breakfast.

"Anyways…on a personal level, I'd rather see a man

21

die than a woman." He felt a shock of embarrassment at his statement, but could do nothing about it. He decided to change his tactics. "Have you read *Dune*?"

"Are you kidding? I rationed water for months after reading it."

"Did you read any of the sequels? Well there's a character who's Paul Muad'Dib's son, Leto II. There's this passage where he says…" Walton continued to making his case via the *Dune* series for the things nature had obviously instilled within men and how thousands of years of history had shown how they are most effectively channeled for civilization.

Amy finally grew frustrated with the talk of war and death, and passed judgment upon the entire natural order, stating, "Well, it sucks! You know, I read this article once about why Quebec has so many good-looking people. It said that many of the ugly ones died while the good-looking ones dodged the draft in World War II. Hold on for a second."

She produced a joint from her purse and lit up in a doorway. The breeze on the wet summer air caught the sweet burning smell like incense in a holy rite. Walton was mesmerized by the way she transformed a conventional act into performance art without meaning to. When the joint burned to her satisfaction she said, "This way. I'll show you my park."

Walton ogled Amy from the corner of his eye as they strolled. She'd make Helen of Troy want to dyke out. Every feature on the living porcelain of her face screamed at him for attention, from the tiny scar above her chin to the outline of her cheekbones. He almost broke out into a sweat from want to touch her nose. It was the most fascinating one he'd ever seen. It was both patrician and cute, and the way it accented her face, eyes, and the spirals of her long golden hair added up to something vaguely Cate Blanchett *a la Lord of the Rings*.

The bright feminine soul that was fit to burst out of a body made for sin made him think back to the myth of Hades abducting Persephone. That was the way to go about it with a gal like this, he thought. Keep the bullshit to a minimum. Go Old School. He fought down the wish that courtship rituals were still what they were ten thousand years ago or so. He'd have scooped her ass up, ran like hell, and if the Devil himself tried to stop him, The Dark One would get a kick in the pills for his trouble, and that was the red-hot gospel.

They walked on a gravel path that crunched rhythmically beneath their shoes and chatted quietly as they passed under the green arms of trees while crickets chirped in the dark. Walton felt years of negativity slide off his back and he made it a point to walk through all the puddles he came across that had been left by the summer shower. He stopped after laughing at a remark of hers and wrote it in the damp earth with a finger; "*Montreal strippers are all beautiful and don't do Cocaine.*" Eventually, they arrived at her apartment.

Amy's apartment was feminine without all the usual girly effects. Sort of a minimalist, bohemian, Mary Tyler Moore affair. A poster for *The Hours* hung in the kitchen and crammed bookcases lined her living room walls. When he commented on them she replied, "Thank you. If a guy is going to be my lover he has to be a bibliophile."

She showed him pictures of her family and her boyfriend, forcing up the guilt he had been trying to forget, which left him feeling like an intruder. She told Walton the guy's story, and he wondered why she would stay with a man who would cheat on her. Why didn't she leave his ass cold? He wondered why he would cheat on her in the first place. When she told him her boyfriend was a vegetarian, Walton rolled his eyes. That figured.

He then remembered she was a stripper. He suspected she kept The Vegetarian out of the convenience of having a steady male presence in her life to laugh with, go out with, and be held by, and since there was no way in hell that any self-respecting man would commit to a woman who stripped and flirted with other men for pay (and enjoyed it), she probably had a hard time finding a guy who'd put up with her lifestyle.

The Vegetarian probably cheated out of jealousy, or to get back his pride, or simply because he could. Then again, maybe they genuinely liked each other, or had, but not enough to inspire them to change their ways. Walton became enveloped with a momentary wave at disgust at the convoluted situation and how fucking absurd life was at times. He just wanted to be in this room with this girl; no longer a soldier, and her no longer a stripper.

He thought about Amy as the bright-eyed little girl she no doubt had been and he tried to imagine the path that had led her here. She had mentioned growing up in a divorce, and he couldn't begin to conceptualize how that must have hurt her (especially given how much it sounded like she loved her family). Between the fallout of that and the boys who had been drawn to the blossoming woman she was then becoming, bringing with them the hormonal rush of attention and the baggage of bad heartbreaks, she had probably learned the hard way never to let her guard down around men again. Maybe she had decided to be tough, never get too involved, get all the attention (and money) she could, hold all the cards, have all the fun, and never *ever* be anybody's victim.

In a nutshell, the capricious girl had *High Risk* written all over her. She was a lost young woman going through her Roller Girl Phase, and chose to have her frivolity do her work for her in the way reserved only for the beautiful, charming people of the world who seemed to know secrets other mortals didn't. The world belonged to her and her kind. She broke all the rules, and rather than doing it from some bullshit predilection to anarchy, she did so simply because it was *fun*.

To make matters worse, while he had tried to keep himself free of entanglements over the years, she had gone in the opposite direction and would probably never really respect him because of the disparity in their experience. She was practiced with the opposite sex, made a living manipulating them, and gave him the impression that she didn't hear the word *"No"* much. She was obviously irresponsible with the people in her life to the point of cruelty. The fact she was there with him behind her boyfriend's back proved it, and it led Walton to wonder what innocuous doe-eyed alibi she would pass off on The Vegetarian after he became a memory at the end of the evening. If she told him at all.

Even if he magically got his wish, and he was out of the Army and she was done with professional nudification, Walton figured he'd eventually wind up as just another beau she was playing House with and get sent on the same goddamned ride as The Vegetarian.

She'd get bored one day, harden her heart, and instinctively start a manhunt like she was doing now, whether she would admit it to herself or not. Then there would follow the choreography of the come-to-Jesus meetings with her girlfriends that always resulted in them advising that whichever girl was in the hot seat was too good for whatever bastard was the flavor of the month, that they had never liked him anyways, and she deserved better and should dump his sorry ass and upgrade. Then, whenever the girl inevitably decided to follow their advice, they would all clap like delighted little girls and properly commence the bitchfest.

Next came the cheating phase with the getaway Fuck-'Em'-'n-Chuck-'Em Guy, and finally, socking him with the greatest hits from the sit-com playbook, telling him out of the blue one day things like, "It's not you, it's me," "I love you but I'm not *in love* with you," or "I think we should go on a Break." Girls seemed to live for that shit. It was like shopping. But for dick.

(*A Break*, as listed in *The Thomas Paul Walton Dictionary:* "A chickenshit modern way of getting out of a relationship in order to fuck other people while keeping open the option to go back to the Comfortable, Swell, Fella/Gal.")

Of course, she might just pull a Marshall Tucker Band Special and not even say good-bye at all. Girls sometimes liked to do that maneuver also. That way they didn't have to look anyone in the eye and feel responsible when they pulled the trigger on a relationship any more than the politicians who sent people off to war, or the do-gooders and moneyed interests whispering in their ears.

She was, in many ways, the epitome of the very girl he'd tried to avoid. Walton would never be able to trust her. Not if he had a goddamned lick of sense.

And yet...

When he looked beneath the surface of the things she said, he saw things that were so arresting they kept him from turning heel and running like hell. Though she no doubt had the standard female-issued quota of crazy and selfishness, she also seemed to have a caring, gentle soul and there was no malice in her. She had the positive air about her of someone always on the look-out for something worth liking. She went after what she wanted and said to hell with the consequences (unlike him, with all his restraints he held onto which often made him feel small and hypocritical or led to self-righteous martyrdom. She was too busy *livin'* to fall into that trap).

On the flip-side of that, she also alluded to the need to have an abundance of solitude and sometimes pushed away the people whom she cared for the most. She knew the species of loneliness borne of having nothing stick to her while simultaneously carrying so many thoughts and experiences that they sometimes threatened to make her

26

fold. Both were terrified they might just find the very things they wanted. She wanted to run just as badly as he did.

It suddenly startled him how alike their jobs were. Both were in gender-specific arenas specializing in a product; hers, the potential of sex, his, potential violence, and when you thought about it, each of the dynamic actions came from opposite ends of the same fundamental impulse that drove human history. Everything else was just advertising.

Walton wanted to cross the distance between them, look her point-blank in the eye, and tell her he *knew* her and had waited his whole life to meet her, or some such bit of douchebag idiocy running non-stop through his mind while he stood there in her living room. It was just as well that he didn't, he supposed. She had probably heard it all before.

He shook his head in an attempt to derail his thoughts. He was mind-fucking himself and needed to lighten the hell up. He wondered how normal guys could go about this sort of thing without thinking. He knew he was letting his pathetic need to connect carry him away. This was the very reason why he tried so hard to avoid proper attachments with women. Occasionally, rarely, one crossed his path that he wanted more than a soldier could dare to allow himself. Women came with strings, regardless of what the chic ones said or wrote. Every relationship, every marriage and divorce, started with the "We'll just have fun right now and see what happens," moment. He had done a fair job so far, but he had the feeling in his guts, though, like when he knew he was about to fall out of a fast run, or back when September 11th had hit right as they were about to go to Bosnia and he'd known that the world had just changed, that this Amy was something else. She scared him.

A video tape on the top of the TV caught his eye (Canada being behind the American technological

27

power-curve in the summer of 2003). "You rented *The Dirty Dozen?*"

"Uh-huh. I remembered you saying last night that it was one of the best war movies ever, so I picked it up earlier today. You know, you make me think of Jimmy Stewart in *Rear Window.*"

"I'm not sure I take that as a compliment, Amy. Jimmy Stewart ain't exactly a paragon of masculinity." This of course was a lie. If serving as a bomber pilot in WWII, having The Duke as a buddy, and romancing actresses until you married a gal and stayed with her for forty-some-odd years wasn't manly, then Walton didn't know what was. Having grown up watching his movies, Walton greatly admired the actor. (He was particularly fond of *Harvey, Shenandoah,* and *The Man Who Shot Liberty Valance.*) He saw men like Mr. Stewart as emblems of a nobler era, but he wanted to avoid getting tarred with the wholesome "Nice Guy" brush if he could help it. He knew all too well where that led. Nowadays, barbarians were in more demand than gentlemen, and a man had to play the game accordingly if he wanted to win.

"Oh, but he is!" Amy countered as she stepped forward to ardently defend her position. "He's this jet-setter photographer always 'lookin' for The Shit,' as you'd say. You've got to see it sometime."

She showed him her bedroom, and as she displayed her picture of Trudeau with Castro and an Impressionist print of a little girl at ballet, he immediately wanted to try to finagle her down to the low bed with the orange comforter. However, there was something about the vibe in the room that made him suspect he'd be pushing things too far and too fast. As much as his lust for her was burning a hole in his pants, he liked her, and didn't want to scare her off. He decided to be patient and see if an opening presented itself.

"I have some books I'll give you when we get back

from some places I want to show you," she mentioned as they gravitated back to the shelves in her living room. "I should throw in a copy of *The Sun Also Rises*. It seems kind of appropriate. You could wear it over your crotch to stop bullets in case you ever get shot at, that way you can avoid being impotent like Jake was."

"Jake was impotent?"

"Oh, yeah. Since it was back-in-the-day Hemingway couldn't write about that stuff so he made references. You know, like that bit about the steers. Also, there's all that romantic tension between him and Lady Brett, but they don't ever do anything."

"I'll be damned. I totally didn't pick up on that. I guess subtext is sometimes lost on teenagers. But no, Amy, don't worry about giving me books."

"I insist, Tom. Let me give you some books."

He decided to not get into a contest of wills. "Alright, then. Thank you. And I'll be sure to send you a copy of *Hero With a Thousand Faces*. From Afghanistan, no less."

She smiled and his blood ran hot.

They left and burned up the night wandering around her city. The sound of live jazz, blues, and rock cover bands exploded from the confines of the open-air bars and provided them with a soundtrack. Walton's ballroom dance lessons returned enough for him to grab the hand he held and send Amy into a turn that led into a grinning moment of dancing on the cobblestone street. They eventually wound up at a bar and put the finishing touches on a well-developed buzz.

"You should be here for winter," she demanded more than suggested after a cigarette. Though she'd handled the joint like a pro, the cigarette came across as a prop for a role that didn't suit her.

"Hell no," he replied, in spite of the world she had just brought to life in his mind. "When I'm out, I don't aim to spend another winter above the Mason-Dixon Line."

"I love that. *Mason-Dixon...*" She let the words hang in the air as if she was tasting them. "You're so Southern. That makes me think of that novel by Thomas Pynchon, have you read it? I love winter. I guess it's that whole Jack London, heroic struggle of Man-Versus-Nature thing."

"*Winter.* We've got this place on Ft. Drum where we do urban warfare training called OP-6Alpha. It gets so fuckin' cold there that it makes a man forget his fear 'a Hell. The wind comes barrelin' down the place so hard that it makes your eyes and nose watery, then freezes them. Fuck winter! I reject winter! I'm wagin' a one-man war against a whole damn season! How heroic is that?"

Amy laughed, then leaned forward and extended her pinkie. "I'm going to make a pinkie-swear with you right here and now, Tom Walton; *when*, not *if*, you return from Afghanistan, you must come up here and I will have a mad passionate affair with you. And if for some God-forsaken reason I'm still with my boyfriend, I'll hook you up with one of my friends."

Finally, the breach point opened!

"It takes a better man than me to refuse that, darlin'." Walton extended his pinkie and they locked fingers. He looked her in the eyes and tried to hold onto the moment for dear life.

In that instant, Thomas Walton committed himself to a solemn cause just as important (at least to him) as the war against faceless terrorists to which he was bound. The poor bastard knew, like a man who knew he would be hung with the dawn, that he would be a fool for this girl.

He would somehow live through the goddamn deployment. He'd save himself for The Great Affair. He'd throw his very *will* into a connection with this girl. And after that, who knew? Maybe she'd even be finished checking the stripper block by then.

They left after a few drinks then meandered through the park again. She eventually decided it was getting late.

They stopped at her doorstep and Walton suddenly hated his life so fully and completely that he wanted to howl at the moon and break things worse than he ever had during the binge-drinking sessions in the barracks. Barracks? Did that world still exist?

"I had a great evening, Tom."

"So did I. It's gonna be tough goin' back to Drum. Thank you for hanging out with me and showin' me the city."

"No, it was my pleasure. Well, I guess I better go up and get your books. I'll call you a cab."

He murmured a thanks and she went upstairs, returning a moment later with a plastic bag containing three books.

Amy smiled and drew near for a hug. As it began, Walton pulled her into him and slowly tightened his arms around her. He could smell the fresh scent of her skin beneath the faint whiff of shampoo and burnt marijuana. He reveled in the feel of her warm trim body and tender breasts against his chest. For a moment. They pulled away from each other and she gave him a kiss on the cheek.

"Don't forget," she said.

"How can I?" He gave her a smile in spite of a sudden sadness. "You made my whole trip to Canada, darlin'."

She smiled again, reaching up to squeeze his arms, then climbed the stairs under his gaze without looking back.

Walton waited alone on the sidewalk for the cab while the city slept. He supposed he should be pissed with himself for his mission failure, but his heart wasn't in it. Instead, he thought about the girl at the top of the stairs that a part of him feared he may never see again.

Second Platoon

No shit, there he was; Ft. Drum, New York, March 2002…

Walton stood rigidly with the rest of Alpha Company in front of the lean weathered man with steel gray hair. Though Walton often had a tough time taking the Army seriously, he had been on the business end of First Sergeant Wade's Copenhagen-drenched ass chewings too many times not to render his propers to the man whom he suspected was Darth Vader and Lee Marvin's neglected love child.

First Sergeant Wade looked over the formation of soldiers standing at Parade Rest; *his* soldiers, whatever the officers might say, that stretched across the company area in orderly camouflaged squares and announced, "All right, A Co., we finally made it. *Hooah?!*" The older man actually permitted himself a rare smile that distorted a face that seemed to have been forged for the sole purpose of reigning down blue-eyed judgment on all not wearing the small diamond-shaped device centered on a formation of chevrons and rockers on their collars as he did. Sometimes, even those who did weren't safe.

"Y'all did a good job in Bosnia, but don't fuck it up by trying to make up for six months of not drinkin' in one night. If you drink, don't be fuckin' driving. Don't go swimming in the Black fuckin' River. If any of you actually do get lucky, use a fuckin' condom. Specialist Bastick, take it easy on my door frames in the barracks. They haven't been used in a while, so when you bring your fat chicks up, you need to grease them first. I better have every swinging dick back in formation come Monday, 'cause the train ain't stopping. Bosnia's fuckin' over. You heard The Battalion Commander. We're gonna go back to doing actual INFANTRY shit again and not this pussy-ass

32

peacekeeping bullshit. I better not get any phone calls, A Co., telling me to come in and pick your sorry ass up from the MP station. If I do, I'll crush your fucking balls. Now let's go the fuck home. Company, Attention! Platoon Sergeants, take charge."

Sergeant Sparn saluted the First Sergeant, then pivoted crisply to face Second Platoon, somehow making turning around look potentially violent. The stone-cold killer of an NCO had just gotten off the trail of a three-year stint as a drill sergeant before Bosnia and carried himself like a black G.I. Joe. He also never lowered the volume or command presence of his voice. "Y'all heard the First Sergeant. If you drink, don't drive, if you fuck, use a rubber. There better not be any fucking phone calls. Any questions? Squad leaders, take charge."

Second Platoon's Second Squad Leader, Sergeant Bronson, then saluted Sergeant Sparn, walked to the middle of his squad with his world-weary, ex-football jock posture, and looked every one of his men in the eye. "My wife is up," he growled in his gravelly Virginian accent. "If I get a phone call 'cause 'a some dumb shit you did, I'll fuckin' kill you. Just try me." He gave them a moment to let his usual battery of impending torture sink in and walked away.

Within ten minutes, Walton was sitting with a beer in each hand on his buddy Malone's green velvet couch that looked as if it had been stolen from Miss Kitty. The Joes (lower enlisted soldiers) from Second Platoon boozed and smoked their raucous way around the room with an anxious vibe, unconsciously afraid of being alone after six months without privacy or solitude, and for the first time since his Pass to Budapest, Walton felt like he could begin to relax.

The violent throes of a life-altering, uterus-smashing, coma-inducing female orgasm filled the barracks until Walton could feel the sound through the couch and the building begin to tremble. One of the soldiers in Third Platoon had fired up some porn across the hall and turned the volume all the way up on his titanic sound system. A knot of Barracks Rats gathered around it like a fire, while others ran, walked, fought, cheered, and sang while still in their uniforms, with booze so thick in the air you could taste it, and all carrying the same Cro-Magnon sexual intent that a blind woman could see was a hair's-breadth away from being rape on a leash, and would compel the girls of Watertown to keep the soldiers at arms distance, and their mace handy. Alpha Company was home and the party had begun.

The Battalion became a great big quivering hard-on.

Though still fresh from a deployment, The Brass feverishly ached to be in The Shit, whether it be in Afghanistan, Iraq, the Sudan, or the Land of the Oompah Loompahs, and they couldn't push the NCO's to train up the Cherries for combat fast enough. This was Blood on the Moon, the dawn of the Trojan War, the Charge of the Light Brigade, and Ninety-Nine Red Balloons Going By with John Wayne riding down from Heaven, hell-bent-for-leather, on a steed made of fire and righteous what-not. Hot damn, sweet Jesus, there was a war on by God, and everyone wanted a piece before they ran out.

Immediately after The Battalion returned from Leave, The Brass started restructuring the unit to make it Combat-Effective, and their dynamic vision and clarity of purpose made Walton's life a very frustrating and confusing place. The first change that rolled downhill was the beginning of the loss of his friends, and this affected him deeply.

His buddies in the platoon who were soon to ETS (Exit The Service) were placed in a separate squad that no longer participated in the platoon's affairs, and might has well have taken up residence on another planet. Walton was happy for them and their upcoming parole, but he couldn't make himself not feel sad that he'd be left behind.

The time was coming when he'd never again be able to walk down the hall and pass the off-duty hours in conversation with Oversnach from Reno about books, music, and philosophy; drinking over movies and memories of girls from the Nineties with Malone and Hanes; analyzing McCann's effortless ways of pulling women, or walk in on Atnode drunkenly film himself vomit into their shared toilet with his perpetual rooster-like spike of blonde hair and rant over his three loves: Satan, porn, and Taunting Tanya the blow-up doll, with whom he had an on-again/off-again relationship.

Like a crazy Army version of *Invasion of the Body Snatchers*, Walton occasionally woke up to find some pod-hatched Cherry in the place of a face that he probably wouldn't see again for years, until one day he no longer recognized his unit. He was glad he still got to have Benamy and Lunchbox around for about another year or so, but he was always aware that the Old Second Platoon, and what it had meant to him, was dying, and he was about to be alone, stuck in a world between dumb-ass Cherries and bi-polar leaders, and it was a toss of the dice as to which would probably get him killed first.

Then came the training.

Though The Brass had planned The Battalion's schedule almost to the hour, order was just a pretense. Everyone in a uniform was on a runaway train, bound to some hard-to-spell question mark filled with pissed off Muslim extremists, and it was all they could do to hang on. Though Walton liked to think he was intelligent enough to see the big picture, he still lived in a perpetual state of wondering whether or not he should shit or go blind.

He held the rank of specialist, which was to say he was a high-ranking Joe. Walton still had to do chores like the

Cherries, endure the occasional smokings (pain applied by way of intense sessions of calisthenics), and generally have no privacy to speak of. It also meant that when an NCO was away on training or out with an injury, he had to fill in as a team leader, a job with responsibilities for which he felt ill-prepared. When the NCO returned, however, Walton had to go back to scratching gravel with the rest of the peasants.

Three weeks into the rebuilding phase, God lent credence to His existence by taking out Second Squad's fat obnoxious Bravo Team Leader, Sergeant Roper, with a back injury during a field exercise. Sergeant Bronson promptly told Walton to "Get tough or die," then charged him with taking care of Sergeant Roper's bastard Joes.

Two days after Walton's tenure as Substitute Team Leader began, Alpha Company went to the woods to teach the Cherries the fundamentals of field craft and basic fireteam react-to-contact drills. Walton found managing other soldiers in the field to be unnerving to distraction, and he lived in a constant pathological fear that he was doing something wrong. However, being on that side of the equation taught him something new every minute, and had things continued as smoothly as during those first few weeks, Walton would have been a happier man. But they didn't.

The sun shined through the windows of the hallway leading to Cold Storage, and Walton was mildly pleased with himself. Within the past two weeks he'd been filling in as team leader in Sergeant Roper's absence, he had been busy.

In addition to road marches and runs, Alpha Company had pushed to get all its soldiers qualified on their weapons, which meant staying out in the cold rain until the Joes entrusted to him shot "Expert" and policed up all the spent brass. Though training the Cherries hadn't been pleasant, it had filled him with a sense of accomplishment.

"You wanted to see me, Sergeant?"

Sergeant Bronson's face looked like the Devil on Sunday. "Yeah, why the fuck is there rust on Opie (Private Oppenheim) and Desilva's spare barrel?"

"I don't know, Sergeant."

"They got five minutes to fix that shit, and it better be fuckin' clean." He walked away and a threat was heavy in his voice.

Walton stared down at Desilva and Opie, who looked like they were trying to will themselves through the floor. "What's the fuckin' deal with the rust?"

"Specialist, I gave it to Desilva—"

"No, I thought, it was your—"

"Shut up. On second thought, I don't care. Just get it fuckin' clean."

Walton helped the two clean the 240 Bravo and its spare barrel. He inspected it and reported to Sergeant Bronson, who told him to have them turn in the weapon, and then smoke them.

After the Close of Business Formation, Walton sat drinking beer and watching a movie with Malone, an ex-comedian who couldn't have been Short-Timing more if he'd tried. He was due to ETS and go back to Staten Island in the summer. Malone looked over at him and said, "You seem to be turning into quite the team leader."

Walton grimaced with embarrassment. "Yeah, right. I'm fuckin' up all over the place."

"That's not what I hear. Bronson came in my room earlier today and went over to the window and said, 'Check this out, Malone; Walton's fuckin' those Cherries up!' I looked outside and saw you making them do front-back-go's and shit."

"My favorite was the rocks," Walton grinned. He'd decided to go Master Yoda on their Cherry-asses. "They didn't seem to like those."

Malone smiled. "It was definitely a crowd pleaser up here. Bronson was cheering you on and said he wants to make you a team leader and that you'd make a good sergeant."

"Damn. That means a lot from him. Anyway, those two knuckleheads had it comin'."

Walton's boots made an obscene noise in the mud as he made the turn at the bottom of a hill in a six-mile road march. He almost lost his balance and flailed wildly, but righted himself with a grunt that sounded like something that should have come from an animal. The second his feet were planted, a wave of heat needled his body and the dull pain in his back and shoulders began eating his mind again.

His rucksack alone bulged with over fifty pounds of gear, that when added with his LCE (Load Carrying Equipment) and rifle, became a weight that had stooped his posture since the second mile. He made a jumping motion without his feet leaving the ground and tugged downward on the rucksack's straps. The movement lifted it from his shoulders, buying him a second to adjust it while he took a deep breath and pretended it wasn't there.

The sudden activity caused his mind to temporarily live wholly in the present and he took stock of the tangled trails that scarred the coarse woods of Ft. Drum. The air was still moist, but the sun already carried with it a lusty heat. He lowered his eyes back to the ground and imagined himself on the deck of an ocean liner under a salty blue sky with his latest porn starlet crush.

His attention was soon broken again as Sergeant Bronson's voice cut the air, ordering, "Brickham, come here."

Private Brickham lurched awkwardly toward the squad leader under the weight of his ruck.

Sergeant Bronson pulled Brickham off to the side of

the gravel path. "Let me see your ruck," he said quietly. He quickly inspected the ruck and its straps. "What the fuck? Heslich! Walton! The AG (Assistant Gunner) gear ain't packed right on his ruck. But you know what? It ain't his fault. He's a fuckin' Cherry private and don't know any better. Y'all aren't. You want to let these soldiers go out all fucked up, then fine. Now, I'm gonna fuck you up. Heslich, swap rucks with Brickham."

Sergeant Heslich did as ordered and immediately wilted under the weight.

"Now get the fuck back in formation."

Sergeant Heslich exchanged an exasperated look with Walton and the two walked back to their places in the formation. Though Brickham wasn't one of Walton's temporary Joes, Walton offered to start up a rotation with Sergeant Heslich in which they would swap the ruck periodically. Sergeant Heslich agreed with a look of relief, and when Walton stepped out of the formation with him to put it on, he immediately felt like someone had kicked his ass. He had no idea the tripod and spare barrel for the 240 Bravo weighed so much or that its weight could be distributed in such a bizarre fashion.

After he had the freak-show ruck situated on his shoulders, he turned to the formation in misery. He could think of no way to deal with the situation but to make jokes. He took off toward the formation, and as he passed Private Dechico, he said, "Make way! Pappa's got a brand new bag!" Walton then began to hustle to the front as he sang, "*Boom shaka laka laka*," like in the movie *Stripes*.

Sergeant Bateman (who was soon to be leaving for Special Forces Selection) played along and asked, "What kind of training are you doing, Walton?"

Walton looked over to him as he shuffled and answered, "*Aaarrmy training, Sir!*"

He heard a commotion behind him, and turned to see Desilva, falling back.

"I got him," Sergeant Bronson said, and Walton faced forward with a bad feeling as he settled into forty-five more minutes of torture.

The muddy gravel path eventually narrowed to a deer trail, and the long formation of men consisting of two columns merged as a hand signal made its way back. The trail led up a steep hill and ended at a shallow, grassy ditch.

Walton let go of his daydreams as he neared the formation area back at the barracks. He noticed Sergeant Bronson standing with murder in his eyes and a shamed Desilva near tears. Desilva apologized to them all individually as they walked by.

On his way upstairs, Walton passed Sergeant Salino from Supply. After a quick hello, the NCO asked him, "Did you see Bronson?"

"Roger, Sergeant. What was that all about?"

"I don't know, exactly. We were doing our road march, and when we passed him, he was yelling and pointing at Desilva and saying, 'I see a dead man walking! I see a motherfucking dead man walking!' The First Sergeant had to tell him to calm down."

"Damn." Walton didn't think that boded well for him. He smiled at the affable sergeant, and said, "Well, I'm gonna drop this shit off. Take it easy, Sergeant."

Walton trudged upward on the barracks' stairs. The weary sound of his booted footsteps belonged to a man far older than his twenty-four years. It gave the listener the impression that a mule had taken possession of the young man's body. In the sound was nothing but the brute animal impulse to move his burden just one more step. Then another.

He silently cheered himself on as he neared the second floor. He was almost to his room. The tough part of the day was at long last over, and the thought of finally getting to ground his shit urged him onward. He smiled with joy as bead of sweat dripped off his brow on to the gleaming white tiles of the polished floor.

Once in his room, Walton shucked his gear, stripped off his BDU (Battle Dress Uniform) top, and sat with a tired soul and an aching back in the silence of the stark white cinder-block walls as he privately enjoyed the release from his olive drab burden. He scrubbed his fingers through his brown hair to scratch at the indentions in his scalp made from the webbing of his K-Pot and sighed. While heat radiated from the wet stink of the brown T-shirt that clung to him, he began tending his feet with a contented smile. He liked the ceremony of foot maintenance. For him, it was an infantry soldier's sacrament; taking off his muddy boots and wet socks, drying his feet, checking for blisters, applying foot powder—

The door suddenly banged open, admitting Sergeant Bronson with Private Desilva. Sergeant Bronson threw Desilva's ruck at Walton's feet and ordered, "Look inside that motherfucker and tell me what you see."

Walton loosened the straps and peered inside. He shook his head and looked up to glare at Desilva.

"When have you known rocks to be on the fuckin' packing list?" asked Sergeant Bronson.

"Never, Sergeant."

'That's right. Congratulations, Specialist Walton, that's *your* fuckin' ruck today. If I see you, you'd better be wearin' it. Oh, no, don't look mad at him, *team leader*. That's your job to check that shit. By the way, you get to supervise the grass-cutting detail." He sneered at Walton for a moment before turning to leave.

When the door closed, Walton took a moment to get a good look at the private and enjoy imagining what it would be like to rip out his windpipe. It would be good to kill the Texan, he mused. Maybe then he wouldn't have to listen to the private snore in the bunk next to him. When he felt composed enough, he asked with increasing volume, "Desilva, what the fuck did I say yesterday? Did I, or did I not, tell you to pack whatever you wanted, so long as it weighs fifty pounds, BUT NO ROCKS!?"

"Roger, Specialist."

"Then why the fuck are there big-ass rocks in here?"

Desilva shrugged his shoulders in sheepish ignorance, and Walton plotted digging his thumbs into the private's eyes this time. Instead, he put on fresh socks and boots, then cinched the ruck down on his back and left the room to get the lawn mowers ready. The pain began raping his brain like it had never left.

While he went about the business of getting the mowers ready and assigning them to the Joes on the detail, Walton mulled over it all, as if there were any kind of sense to be made. Watching his two minions listlessly mow the grass, he shook his head at the situation and snorted a cynical laugh. This shit had sure as hell hadn't been in the brochure.

Even though he'd majored in History back in college, he'd still thought that being a soldier would be different. More noble somehow. Sergeant Stalox, his old platoon sergeant back in The Boz' had told them in a speech before he'd been transferred, "You know, I first joined back in '79 with all these thoughts of the Napoleonic Wars, and the Civil War, and all that shit, and I thought war craft was glory. But I found out it wasn't. It's work. Dirty, ugly work." That was no shit.

The ruck continued to gnaw on his back. It was going to be a long day.

At lunchtime, Sergeant Bronson entered the room and took a seat on Walton's couch. He gave the soldier a flat look and asked, "Why don't you have your ruck on, Tom?"

Watching how Sergeant Bronson had walked in like he owned the place reminded him of the first words the man had ever said to him. Walton had just gotten to the unit and had been nervously packing his ruck for the field exercise the next morning, when the older man had stormed into the room, grabbed Benamy's chair, and sat down across from him. He'd stared at Walton point-blank and told him, "You don't know your fuckin' job."

Sergeant Bronson had looked at Walton's specialist rank, which he had been given by the Army for enlisting with a bachelor's degree instead of sweating it out for a year and a half on the line like normal Joes did, then continued with a drawl, "I'd rather have a dumb motherfucker that'll do what the fuck I tell him to, than some smart motherfucker who'll get people killed because he *thinks* he knows what the fuck he's doin'. But if you keep your mouth shut and pay attention, you'll fuckin' learn."

Walton figured the more things changed, the more they stayed the same. "I took it off to go across the street to get somethin' for lunch, Sergeant."

Sergeant Bronson shook his head, then lit up a cigarette. After he breathed out a lung-full of smoke, he informed Walton, "You ain't through with it yet." He then pointed to The Ruck of Woe. "That's a learning aide to help teach you not to trust a private."

Walton laughed bitterly. "I understand that now. Yesterday, when we were gettin' them ready for today's road march, I specifically told those assholes, 'no rocks.' When I inspected that shithead, he was packed up with a legitimate packin' list and everything."

Sergeant Bronson sighed almost imperceptibly. "He was? I didn't know that." A tension passed out of him as he changed gears. "Well, do what you want to him. Just don't kill him." He then shook his head again. "What do you think of those Cherries?"

Walton furrowed his brow. "They're better at PT than the group me and Benamy came in with, and they seem smart enough, but they're immature. In all honesty, though, I don't like 'em. They just look like more work."

Sergeant Bronson grinned and made an expansive gesture with his hands. "Welcome to my world!" he said triumphantly. The NCO visibly schemed. "Yep. I'm gonna bring you over to The Dark Side, Tom."

"You'll fail, Sergeant. Those Cherries may be more fucked up than Who Shit the Shower, but at the end of the day, Joe gets it done. I'm a fan of Joe, even if he gives me a case of the ass."

Sergeant Bronson let a menacing pause follow Walton's words, then said, "I'll remember you said that the next time one of those shitheads does some dumb shit that makes me have to fuck you up." When he saw Walton's derisive smirk, he returned it with one of his own as he got up to leave. "Like it or not, motherfucker, I'm in there runnin' around," he said as he pointed to his head. "Whenever you hate someone, you'll hear yourself thinkin' things the way I say them."

"Maybe, Sergeant," Walton countered. He decided this was as good a time as any to broach a scheme he'd been concocting. Second Platoon just wasn't home anymore. "Anyhow, I'm thinkin' of dropping a 4187 for Germany. What do you think the chances are of me gettin' it?"

"How many years you got left?"

"Two."

"It's unlikely. You need three to go there now, and from what it sounds like, you'll probably get locked in to wherever it is we're goin'." Sergeant Bronson then grinned malevolently. "You ain't gettin' rid of me that easy."

The Cherries were like children, and always had to be watched, and often punished. Sometimes they fucked up to the crazy extent that it almost seemed like they wanted to suffer, and this bred an odd phenomenon in the team leaders. Some of them came to revel in doling out smokings. They would be sitting around bullshitting, then one would say, "Well, I'm gonna go fuck up my Cherries," then casually get up to leave, and you just knew some poor unsuspecting bastards down the hall were about to get it.

Second and Third Platoon had a few semi-rabid NCO's floating around who would do so more than necessary, but for the most part it was seen more as a toughening phase that junior leadership had to go through, or that a guy had just gotten promoted and was temporarily insane with his new authority. Other times it was simply a case of a guy demonstrating to his Cherries the direction of the power dynamic, or punishing negative behavior without crushing a kid's career with paperwork for an infraction due to youthful stupidity. Either way, it would taper off when they had gotten their point across.

First Platoon, though, had a clique who got so into the sadism that it looked like they were auditioning for prison. They were the sort who would fuck up their boys wholesale to the point that soldiers in the company could barely walk around and get anything done for all the skinny kids sweating their asses off and scrambling their way through push-ups, flutter-kicks, side-straddle-hops, electric chairs, front-back-go's, monkey-fuckers, and various other exercises that were staples of the gratuitous smokings they caught in the hallway.

Walton had never really gotten used to seeing that sort of thing being done. The way he figured it, smoking soldiers indiscriminately was poor Joe Management; if you beat a dog all the time, it never knew when it deserved it. Granted, he'd do it if one of his temporary Joes had done something stupid and had earned a dose of pain, or maybe in a playful, teasing-a-kid-brother kind of way, but there was a line and he didn't want to cross it.

However, he knew that smokings and the discipline they enforced were important. Without discipline and a hierarchy with teeth, an army became a mob. He hadn't yet been in The Shit, but he figured it was one mean ol' honkey-tonk, and if a Joe had to get strong by doing wrong, so be it.

At the end of one week, a Cherry went AWOL, one got a DUI, and First Sergeant Wade caught yet another sleeping during the duty day. Sergeant Sparn subsequently called a team leader meeting for the platoon. Walton took solace that none of the idiot Joes had been his, but that didn't stop him from sitting like he was a kid in trouble.

"Why are the Joes fucked up?" Sergeant Sparn demanded in a tone that none of the team leaders dared answer. "Hmm? I'll tell you why. You team leaders are fuckin' up.

"We're going to combat soon, men. A year, maybe less. These new privates got no motherfuckin' discipline, and that's gonna get people killed. And it'll be because of y'all. They know they can get over, and that's the wrong fuckin' answer. They should fear you. You should be assholes and ball-busters. They should hate you, and hide from you when you walk down the motherfuckin' hall."

Sergeant Sparn looked them over with a cold stare. Walton thought it was a testimony to the man's character that he had been an object of explosive hilarity in The Boz', yet presently came off as so intimidating that a room full of NCO's didn't dare say anything. Toward the end of the Bosnia deployment, Sergeant Sparn had a boil in his ass lanced and had to go around with a tampon in his tailpipe. The medic had once pulled it out of Sergeant Sparn's asshole while the platoon had been staying in the same building. Without warning, Sergeant Sparn had bent over with his pants down and had bellowed in his drill sergeant voice, "Pull it out slow, Doc! Awww daammn!" The medic had looked like he was pulling a rabbit out of a hat. Walton had laughed so hard at the episode that he was pretty sure he'd risked an aneurysm.

Sergeant Sparn continued, saying, "The team leader is the shittiest job in the Army because you are directly responsible for the success or failure of a Joe. Squad leaders have the hardest job, and privates are there to just suffer. You need to start understanding that Joe is the enemy. *Joe is the motherfuckin' enemy!* Joe ain't got shit else to do but get you in motherfuckin' trouble." He pointed upstairs. "Right now, he's fuckin' off up there, and he ain't scared of you. I expect to see some boots in Joe Ass, or I'll find some new fuckin' team leaders."

The next week, Walton looked around in disgust at the room he shared with Desilva. The joint was a pigsty. Though he wanted to cut the private some slack considering that Desilva had to share a room with someone who outranked him, Walton was losing his patience with the boy. He was beginning to see the wisdom of Sergeant Sparn's words. Walton told the private, "You need to clean your fuckin' side of the room. It looks like ass."

"Roger, Specialist. Oh, before I forget, here's a copy of my appointment slip." Desilva dug in his pocket, removed a piece of paper, and handed it to Walton.

"What did you have to go to the clinic for?"

"I got The Clap."

"Does your girlfriend know?"

"Yeah, she's got it too. I either got it from her or this chick who gave me head."

"Could this affect her baby?"

"I don't know. I don't think it would."

Walton shook his head. He really wished he didn't have to share a bathroom with the kid. "Alright. We've got the Equal Opportunity class at thirteen-hundred. Don't be fuckin' late."

"Roger, Specialist."

"...So we've established that goddamn sexual harassment isn't tolerated by the Army," Sergeant Sparn explained from the front of the dayroom. All of the enlisted personnel of Alpha Company sat in attendance.

"But let me ask you a question. Who here likes it when the girl goes down on you? Come on, raise your hands.

"WELL, YOU'RE FUCKING WRONG! That is considered sodomy and is punishable under the United States Code of Military Justice!

"What about fuckin' a chick in the ass? You know, throwing it in the pudding?

"YOU'RE FUCKING WRONG, *HERO!* The Missionary Position is the only authorized position under UCMJ!"

When the laughter of the room calmed down, he began again. "Why is it, that when you're doing a chick Doggey Style—you know, you're all in the shit, and if you've got leverage—you got your leg over the shit—anyhow, why do we feel the need to slap the ass? I mean, she's giving up the pussy. Why slap her?"

Once Sergeant Sparn began accepting questions about the Army's Equal Opportunity Policy, some of the boys began commenting amongst themselves about women. From his seat next to Walton, Benamy expressed a desire to secure some female companionship for himself, stating, "Man, I need to get a freaky bitch."

Sergeant Sparn heard the comment and looked at Benamy. He shook his head and advised, "Oh no. You don't want a freaky bitch. Hmm-mmnh. You wanna get a bitch and *make her freaky*. That way, she's freaky the way *you* want her to be freaky. Yeah! Giddiyup!"

It wasn't always training and oppressive misery, though. On weekends when they weren't in the field, the soldiers crawled into a bottle and lived there until they had to start de-toxing before Monday. Sometimes, they'd skip the sobering up aspect altogether on account of it cutting into their drinking schedule, and on the subsequent Monday morning, the PT formations of hung-over soldiers were careful not to run next to open flames lest

48

New York catch fire. After September 11th, they felt as though the state had been through enough. It was the patriotic thing to do.

Walton was no different, and did his drinking with both fists. After months of catching all the shit that went both ways between the Leaders and the Led, Walton now understood why most of the NCO's seemed perpetually drunk when they were off-duty. He needed booze to function, and it was important that he got his regular doses. Sometimes, though, it didn't numb him like it had when he'd started *really* drinking as a Cherry, and it instead dug out various bits of pain from his skull.

After one particularly nasty week finally found the decency to die, half of Second Platoon occupied one of the primary off-Post dive bars as soon as they could change out of their uniforms. Walton rolled out with the advance party and sat at the bar having a drink with Hanes, who was returning to California in a few weeks.

A young woman with dishwater blonde hair suddenly appeared and squeezed in between them. She smiled at Walton and introduced herself as Krista. A few minutes later, she pressed her bottom against his leg and rubbed it in time with the music, earning his undivided attention. She tugged on his arm hair, raked his skin, then ordered two rounds of Tequila. She handed one to Walton and said, "Here, lick my lime." Walton complied and they downed their drinks. "Let's have another," she demanded, then began to grind against his leg with increased pressure and a Come-On, Getcha-Some grin.

A hard voice growled behind Walton. "We're going."

Walton turned around to see a living statue looming over him. He foresaw in The Magic Eight Ball in his mind that the signs pointed to: *You Are About to Get Your Ass Kicked by This Crazy Bitch's Boyfriend.*

The Statue glared at him, and Walton didn't let his pride keep him from showing a bewildered expression.

The glare swiveled to Krista and lingered there. Walton watched the storm of emotions in The Statue's eyes, and beneath the anger there was pain. The poor fool was caught in the bear trap, and Walton began to feel like the situation at hand was an episode of *Cops* just waiting to happen. The girl turned and immediately walked away with The Statue without uttering a word.

Walton turned and looked at Hanes, who busted out laughing. He shook his head and went back to drinking.

He shifted his focus to the dance floor. Girls cavorted on it (with many crowding greedily onto the higher altitude of the DJ's stage to posture for status), while guys stood around the perimeter watching them like they were at a Junior High dance.

Walton wondered what it was about women that fueled their incessant need for mass attention and manipulation. A barmaid had once told him, "Every girl is a stripper," and from where he sat, that was King James Gospel. The big difference, though, was that with strippers and whores you knew what they were after, whereas the women in the club looked normal, yet God only knew what lies their smiles concealed. Being kind or decent to those girls would be taken as a sign of weakness.

A few couples danced in the buffer area between the girls and the men who watched them, yet most of those were girls with other girls. The rest of the females stood in adolescent cliques holding drinks they didn't buy, and generally relishing in their power. They were a pile of deception and the truth was not in them. Walton felt a familiar spike of wry contempt and couldn't hide his sneer if he'd tried.

So this was the glorious cause for which the feminists had fought. They'd struggled for, and won, a world where men were seen as the problem and women as the solution. Women were deemed inherently "right" and needed a man "like a fish needs a bicycle." Men, however, were pigs, and were perceived as semi-functional retarded pariahs without a woman. A woman's sexuality was good and healthy; a man's, toxic and perverse. A woman could commit a wrong and the chattering classes would come out of the woodwork spouting Marxist bullshit to frame her as the victim rather than the perpetrator. A man, though, was guilty until proven innocent.

Oceans of ink and thousands of hours of television had made it abundantly clear that a man was expected to make his woman's happiness his top priority because she *deserved* it (or he wasn't a real man). If someone demanded that a woman reciprocate such devotion by putting her man first, however, legions of man-hating shrews would have screamed, "Misogyny!" and argued that whoever believed such politically incorrect heresy was trying to "set back the women's rights movement," and was guilty of trying to return The West to the Fifties or "the Dark Ages," or whenever it was that they deemed the height of barbarity.

As the gender solely responsible for the birth of future humans they could abort at will, zealously exclaiming slogans about their bodies and their rights. (Most American girls didn't like anything to come between them and their potential to buy stuff, have fun, and acquire status. For them, this passed for heroism. Being the heart and soul of a family they'd helped create, or simply giving a damn about something that didn't revolve around them or "Women's Issues," not so much.)

Men had no such luxury. They were deemed the disposable sex. When men turned eighteen they were required by law to register for the draft. If sent downrange to kill, get maimed, and perhaps die on behalf of what was left of the nation-state, talk about rights or the sovereignty of one's own body went out the fucking window. (Walton had once read the phrase, "surplus male population." No one wrote things like that about women. The underlying assumption being that the souls of men, if they had any at all in the eyes of cultural elites, were of far lesser value than those of women.)

Even medicine had been weaponized. People donated proudly for the cure of breast or ovarian cancer, but few gave a damn about men with tumors in their testicles or prostates. The same was true of parenthood. A girl wanting to "have it all" by being a single mom could seek to adopt, get knocked up, or go the spermcicle route and be considered a champion of progress. (Because she "didn't need a man." The Celebrity-Industrial Complex had told her so! Except of course, for her Uncle Sam. She also needed someone watch her child while she was busy focusing on her career. That, and it was nice to have a man around to lift heavy objects. And to perform household maintenance. And to deal with burglars and potential rapists. And to understand that in the event of an emergency, he was to forfeit his life for her and her offspring, because chivalry had died for some reason.)

However, if a single man dared to step foot into an adoption agency in the hopes of providing a home for a child and raising it as his own, he'd be suspected of being a pedophile. (Men weren't recognized as possessing any life-affirming instincts whatsoever. The very word *paternal*, which was once used to denote the strong qualities of a father, was now used as a slur. Fathers were now deemed unnecessary for civilization, save for their ability to hand over money and resources to women. The West had been conducting a scorched-earth war against its men, and husbands and fathers had been primary targets of longstanding. As for its single young men, it just ignored or vilified them. Unless of course they were entertainers or athletes.)

Women were authorized to make a man's life a living hell. A woman could hit a man, verbally abuse a man, and if she was feeling really empowered, go full-on Bobbit on a man, and it was acceptable. The second a man so much as raised his voice to a woman, though, he stood a chance of pulling the entire American legal system down on his Y-chromosomed ass.

Hell, women didn't even have to recognize the social convention of being nice to the people around them. They could go from rude to outright cuntishness and swear it was them projecting strength and independence. They could let themselves go, behave badly, and if they were unwanted it was the fault of men and the "unfair expectations" put upon women by The Evil Male Patriarchy.

However, let a man get laid off from his job. Or worse, let him not be exciting enough, or simply display some flaw on their list, and see how fast a woman started eyeing the door. (Because amusing them was all that mattered.)

Women could perform below standard or avoid authority and responsibility all together, then bitch that there weren't more women in charge. Activists tripped all over themselves to see that women "shattered the Glass Ceiling," yet for all their talk of gender merely being a social construct, the precious snowflakes didn't seem all that eager to establish female hiring quotas for the hard labor world of blue collar work. (Because those jobs weren't sexy. They were physically crushing, and women wouldn't get to the opportunity to play dress up at them, or circulate around high status males like they could at office gigs.) Men lived shorter lives and worked longer hours at more dangerous jobs, and with the exception of the occasional good wife, women didn't lose sleep over it.

As if all that wasn't enough, women also *still* got engagement rings, *still* got the custody of the kids, *still* got alimony, *still* got in for free, and it was *still* alright if they used their beauty and fuckability to get whatever they wanted. And they were *still* the gatekeepers of sex.

If asked if they thought it was right and just, the bitches on the dance floor would probably answer in a tone thick with righteous entitlement something to the tune of, "giving guys a dose of their own medicine," or that they were "just making up for centuries of male oppression." If they really wanted to go for the throat they'd say something like, "You're just mad 'cause you can't get laid." (Because men they didn't see as fuck-worthy occupied the lowest status possible, and they were to remain silent and invisible. Such men weren't permitted to have concerns and grievances, let alone hopes and dreams. They were to know and accept their places as sub-human pussy servants, or else.)

Walton thought it ironic that there the guys stood, soldiers in the most powerful army in the world, and between all the Joes in the bar they had the potential to level the place and take who and what they wanted, yet the dancing girls held all the cards. The uppity fucking slags had no idea what went on in the world to maintain their safety and material comfort. It looked so goddamn easy for them. It all belonged to them in the end, and the guys were…powerless. Equality; there was no such animal. Feminism could suck it.

Walton fought to see through his self-pity, yet every deployment brought with it real life instances of some of the wives back at home fucking Jodys with wild abandon, emptying bank accounts, breaking-up, and taking the kids. Occasionally, they even sent the deployed soldier a video of the significant other getting the shit railed out of her half-to-death by some Stunt Cock.

And in every bar on or near Post (including this one, he'd wager), there was at least one wife there of some poor dumb soldier risking his ass in some Third World Shithole, and she was out to end the evening by grabbing two fist-fulls of sheets and burying her face in a pillow with her ass in the air (because of *her needs*, no doubt) and didn't feel the least bit bad about it. Maybe she'd even be pregnant with the soldier's baby. That happened more than he felt comfortable knowing.

In the beginning, women would get all caught up in the testosterone swagger of the soldiers and the feeling of protection and potential violence that came from them. Then reality would set in. The ones who had either the sense or good luck to hook up with an officer would more than likely try to use their bodies and their feminine wiles to land a ring, thus securing themselves a man with money and benefits, but more importantly, endowed them with the suggestion of vicarious rank that came from being wedded to a man who had authority over other men. Walton was sure he could pick out the officer's wives or girlfriends on Post with nigh one hundred percent accuracy. They were the ones with an almost regal bearing and pride of their assumed superiority and responsibility.

The women with enlisted soldiers and NCO's evolved into something different. They found out fast where their men were in the pecking order and it never went down easy. Bitterness soon took root, and where the officers' wives walked with pride, many of the others often made their way with varying degrees of veiled contempt.

Sergeant Bronson had seemed to understand and accept all this with a bizarre measure of philosophical grace. One time before a class, some of the boys had been in the dayroom wondering and worrying aloud about the possibility of their girlfriends or wives cheating on them when they deployed. Sergeant Bronson had sneered and shook his head, then said, "Listen at you motherfuckers sniveling like a bunch of goddamn little girls. Look here, gentlemen. They're *gonna* cheat. They *all* cheat. No matter how much that bitch says she loves you, deep down, she *don't*."

Walton then recalled the numbers of soldiers that he'd heard had hooked up with whores in Budapest while wives and girlfriends had been unaware, and every Monday morning brought with it the pseudo-water cooler stories about someone humping some drunken slam-pig while their woman was elsewhere. He concluded that the whole damn human race was a fucking mess. Everyone ran around not knowing what they wanted. Except for wanting to be wanted; to have power over the Other, rather than the Other themselves. That, or maybe it was just the blind, unrestrained pursuit of Dopamine. He mentally shrugged and ordered a fresh round that died young. Then another.

The dim bar, with its pulsing Eighties music and packed crowd eventually became tolerable to Walton. He felt the tug of the hypnotic call of the booze and surrendered to its spell. He attacked the dance floor and approached two girls dancing together. He grabbed the hand of the better-looking one and twirled her around, spilling half of his drink on her back, yet the drunken girl continued to dance with him undeterred, slithering her crotch on his thigh.

He drunkenly blinked and was at the bar. Two girls pranced and postured on it with thongs staring proudly above soft but firm young asses fighting to escape the oppression of denim. Each poured a bottle of an indiscriminate alcohol into the mouths of any who wanted it. Walton partook from one and held up a dollar bill in the hopes of encouraging her to flash some flesh.

A secret wish for a better life suddenly struck Walton dumb, and he was back in Bosnia. One day at an orphanage near the city of Tuzla, the platoon's leadership had been busy conferring with the staff inside while the orphans themselves had swarmed the humvees in amusement and curiosity. A little boy had run up to Walton's window, right off the bat, yelling, "Hey, G.I., gimme Pepsi! Hey, G.I.! G.I., gimme dollar! Hey, G.I...fuck, ass...fuck, shit! . . . Hey, G.I . . ."

The crazy little boy had then commenced to grab the kid next to him with the frantic enthusiasm of a coke-head, and proclaimed, "He suck my dick!" as he'd pushed the unsuspecting boy toward his crotch. The kid was wily, though, and had escaped.

Regardless of his failed effort to embarrass his friend for social capital, Crazy Boy had moaned, and the children had gone into a hysterical fit of laughter at his routine. Judging from their behavior, it had been obvious that Second's visit hadn't been the orphans' first rodeo with grunts. Crazy Boy had known his audience.

Suddenly, a voice belonging to a little girl with a fierce accent had commanded, "Be quiet!"

Upon seeing the boys spout vulgarities at the soldiers to get a laugh and maybe a soda from them, the little girl had set down the baby she had been carrying on her hip, and had stormed up to them with a vengeance. Her black hair had been arranged in a shoulder-length bobbed cut and she'd worn a simple hand-me-down dress that looked as though the churchwomen who ran the orphanage had put great care into to keeping it clean and mended. She'd approached them like the miniature embodiment of righteous indignation. "Be quiet!" she'd demanded again. "You make us look bad to the soldiers! You're bad!"

The suddenness of her attack had stolen her a moment of silence from the stunned boys. She'd drawn near Walton's window and had apologized, saying, "I am sorry, soldier. Those boys are bad." The mob of children had looked abashed in pockets, but Crazy Boy had continued to valiantly act the fool to the amusement of his friends. The little girl, though, had put on the appearance of ignoring him and guided away from her face a lock of hair that had fallen into her eyes during her assault. "What is your name, soldier?"

"My name is Walton." She had repeated his name awkwardly with a smile, trying to make sense of the unfamiliar arrangement of the sounds. "What is your name, Miss?"

"I am Ivana. Do you like Tuzla?"

"Yes, I like Tuzla very much."

"Where are you from?"

"I'm from a place in America. Near the middle. Do y'all like school?"

"School suck my dick!" Crazy Boy had declared to the heavens with all the passion of having waited his whole young life to say those words.

"I SAID BE QUIET!" Ivana had yelled at the boys with an authority and fervor that this time had caused them to physically step back, but still failed to completely erase their eye for mischief. (Though he'd felt bad about seeing children use that kind of fucking language, Walton had admired their defiance. Their very lives were a middle finger to the war that had tried to keep them from existing. In The West, they'd have been lucky not to have wound up as abortions under similar circumstances.) Ivana had seemed satisfied with her Sisyphean efforts and composed herself. "I am sorry these boys are bad. I like school."

Walton had grinned at the good fortune of meeting such a squared-away little girl. Who knew they still made those? "That's good! If you stay in school, Ivana, I'll bet you'll grow up into a smart woman. Maybe someday you'll help run Bosnia and make it better." He'd hoped his friends hadn't heard him sounding like the PSA's at the end of a *G.I. Joe* episode. He'd never hear the end of it.

Crazy Boy had pushed back to Walton's window, ready for round two. "Girls cannot run the country!" he laughed. Susan B. Anthony could kiss his Bosnian ass.

"They can in America," Walton had countered with a stern look and tone in an effort to turn the tables again and keep Crazy Boy's youthful recklessness from breaking Ivana's spirit. He'd hoped that he'd someday have a daughter just like her. Although, a kid like Crazy Boy would keep a dad from ever getting bored. (Walton had

58

thought he was a good boy, but just needed a dose of the belt and to have his mouth washed out with soap, as had been the prescribed treatment in the Walton household.) "In my home, they are in charge of many things." Ivana had beamed triumphantly and Walton's heart had melted. Crazy Boy had wanted to call bullshit. "But first they have to go to school and learn a lot."

Walton had hoped they'd make it, and felt there should be a better world for those children. They were just too damned high-speed for this one.

With the faces of tough Bosnian orphans in his mind, Walton looked up at the unrestrained female *Id* coming out to play in the vain young women strutting on the bar like prostitutes as the result of the Slutification of the American Female, thought about himself sitting at their feet, and felt ashamed. He wanted to burn the fucking place to the ground and salt the earth.

His Grandma Gladys had told his mom as a girl, "You are known by the company you keep. If you hang around with white trash, you'll be known as white trash," and his mom had passed the strict warning on to her boys. (Being poor didn't justify trashy behavior in her book. Grandma Gladys had been of the Old School.) There was trash of every persuasion at the bar and he was right there with them. Walton had a hard time accepting through the brain cell holocaust that he was actually glad his grandmother wasn't alive to see him. He wouldn't have been able to look her in the eye.

If this was "progress" then he didn't want it for Ivana and Crazy Boy. Toynbee had called it; "Civilizations die from suicide, not by murder." Him, the floozies, the drunks stumbling around or fooling with their cell phones; they were all decadent as fuck. So much for the glory of consumerism, universal suffrage, sexual liberation, and U.S. hegemony. Americans had learned how to make false gods out of just about anything. And it was killing them. If the U.S. of A. didn't wind up as the Whore of Babylon, it wouldn't be for lack of trying.

He couldn't order another round fast enough.

Second Platoon was dead. Long live Second Platoon.

It is a widely known scientific fact that a vast majority of Ft. Drum remains unchanged since the Cretaceous Period, and that the Indians who sold the land that Ft. Drum sits upon to the White Man hundreds of years ago got the better end of the bargain and still laugh about it amongst themselves to this very day. After rain-filled months of living out of their rucks and running around in the woods in faces caked with camo-paint like a bad wet hallucination, it was in that primeval setting that Walton realized that most of the Cherries had become proper Joes, and that his artificial family had taken on its latest incarnation. This awareness first struck him during The Battalion Live Fire Exercise.

Sergeant Bronson's voice detonated with anger at Sergeant Heslich and his team. It filled their section of MOUT (Military Operations in Urban Terrain) City. "Why don't you call that room clear and mark it so we can get this fuckin' shit over with, you goddamn motherfuckin' morons!"

Walton laughed with Specialist Tener as they sat on the concrete slab with their backs against their assault packs and the antennae from their radios sticking over their shoulders. Tener was the FO (Forward Observer) for the mortars section and had been attached to Second Platoon since they'd returned from The Boz'. They had adopted him as one of their own, seeing him as a member of Second, rather than just some random-assed FO. During his time as substitute RTO (Radio and Telephone Operator) for the platoon, Walton had grown fond of the young black man and his mellow, dry sense of humor and friendly disposition. They both enjoyed a good laugh, especially if it was at some other poor bastard's expense.

They had been in the field thus far for three days. They had stepped off on the first day carrying almost a hundred pounds of gear and equipment per man for a seven-mile road march. Once at their destination, they had set up positions and got what rest they could.

The next day had been spent with the team leaders training the Joes, while the rest of the NCO's toured MOUT City and their target buildings. The third day found them training as a platoon at clearing rooms and moving from building to building.

"Heslich, what the fuck's taking so goddamn long?"

"There's a door that's tough to get through!" Sergeant Heslich answered in frustration.

"Motherfuckin' shit, if that was me, I'd just knock the goddamn door off the hinges," bragged Sergeant Bing, a diminutive NCO from Kentucky who had been an eighteen-year-old PFC (Private First Class) when Walton had been a Cherry. He was soon to be transferring to the 101st at Ft. Campbell.

"Bing, you don't even have enough ass to open the motherfucker," quipped Second's new platoon sergeant, Sergeant Cade, as he cleaned his ears with the tips of his glasses. "Let's wrap this shit up." Like his predecessor, he too was a former drill sergeant fresh off the trail, but was as white as Sergeant Sparn had been black, and carried a touch of Minnesota in his voice. He smoked whenever possible, earning him the secret nickname, "Smokey," within the first week, which the platoon occasionally used behind his back.

Sergeant Bronson shook his head. "They say Jesus died for all Man's sins. Today, Joe pays for all the stupid shit he's done to me. I'm just in one of those moods." Movement caught his attention and he yelled, "Hey! You don't kill that chipmunk! That's our only form of entertainment!"

Dechico stepped away from the animal.

"Let's just kill Joe and bury him. That way we can say they all went AWOL." Sergeant Bronson sighed and lowered his tone to an even more beat-up level. "Man, I'm fuckin' tired. I gives a fuck. If it wasn't for this check-the-block bullshit, I'd be happy sleepin' out back on my ruck. Even if it was in the motherfuckin' rain with fish swimmin' 'round my balls." He turned to Walton and asked, "You goin' out when we get back?"

"I 'spect so, Sergeant. If for no other reason than Katie. I'd like to touch her in a special way." Katie was a barmaid who worked at one of the off-Post dive bars. She appeared to be made out of cuteness. Every swinging dick who walked in the bar while she was on the clock looked at her with lust in their hearts and a situation in their pants.

Sergeant Bronson smirked, and said, "I'd like to touch her uterus...*with my dick*." He redirected his attention to his squad and yelled, "Heslich, I got a crazy idea; how 'bout y'all do it like I fuckin' showed ya!"

They spent the next day practicing react-to-contact. In a thunderstorm. Though Walton was happy that he didn't have to do it, he thought the radio antenna on his back resembled a lightning rod entirely too much to be good for his physical wellbeing.

At long last the main event in the exercise arrived, and all the companies, platoons, and squads which composed The Battalion converged on MOUT City for a coordinated, multidirectional attack on the Op-For (Opposition Forces) who were out to defend the city to the last man.

What made this exercise a bit more fun was that everyone was using their MILES gear. The soldiers had fitted their weapons with adapters so they could fire blanks, and the discharge would fire a laser mounted on the barrel. If the laser hit a soldier wearing the MILES harness on his chest or the Halo on his K-Pot, the sensors would whine, and the soldier would be fictionally dead or wounded.

After hours of road marching and waiting for all the platoons to make it to their starting points, The Battalion Commander's RTO finally gave the go-ahead to start their final assault in the week-long exercise, and Walton passed it on.

Sergeant Cade nodded, saying, "Thanks, Professor," then knelt down between the gunners and put his hands on their armored backs in a fatherly fashion. Sergeant Cade was partially deaf, and though he pitched his voice low, it suddenly seared through the wooded night that was darker than ten feet up a coal miner's ass as he ordered, "Alright boys, light 'em up!"

PFC's Brickham and Castor immediately opened up their two 240 Bravos that lay mounted atop steel tripods, as their AG's fed them ammo. They despoiled the midnight world with fully-automatic simulated war, killing combatants wholesale in the large building which Second had to seize.

Walton couldn't see much due to the thick brush and the moonless, clouded night except for the illuminated objective and whoever was within a few feet of him, even with his NOD's (Night Operational Devices). The voice in his ears coming through the hand-mike he had rigged to his K-Pot with a piece of 550 cord, spoke to him through the fight. He hated having that damn thing in his ear all the time, but he liked being in-the-know. "Roger, Six, we've established the support-by-fire, over," he answered into the mike, then continued shooting at a sniper. He estimated a quarter of the platoon was already dead from the whining of the MILES gear around him.

"Have Third and First Platoon made it in yet?" asked Lieutenant Hamner, Second Platoon's latest officer.

"Roger, Sir," Walton replied. "They've got their target buildings and are pressin' on, but they've taken heavy casualties."

"Tell 'em we're going in to secure the buildings near our support-by-fire. Let's go."

Walton called it in and Lieutenant Hamner and Sergeant Cade led what was left of the platoon into the chaos.

Then it happened.

Dechico grabbed a sniveling Private Bladner and threw him over a concertina wire obstacle, and in that moment, Walton got excited again about being in Second Platoon. He realized the Joes could fight and were playing the exercise like it was real. It put something in the air that was contagious and he caught the fever with a grin. They threw themselves into the battle with complete abandon, and from there on out the assault became a cluster-fuck of a symphony as Second fought like shithouse demons as they molested their way through the Op-For and whatever the assholes had cooked up to slow them down.

While trying to not get shot, yet staying within shouting distance of Lieutenant Hamner, with whom Walton had to constantly give and take information, things turned into a dreamlike blur; Second's remnants ran across the street under fire, then leapt through an open window...Private Bajez chewed up men with his SAW (Squad Automatic Weapon) from a doorway...Sergeant Cade led the platoon into the next building, got in the front of a stack, then led it into a room with four fireteams behind him...Sergeant Bronson taunted a sniper lurking in a window from behind his optics just before his M4 barked a controlled pair...Benamy's team crawled out of a window, one man at a time, while Sergeant Cade yelled instructions at Brickham and Castor's gun teams...

As the mock fight raged, Walton felt the fever fuel his actions as it propelled the survivors through MOUT City. His position as RTO prevented him from being the first man into the room, but he still jumped in a stack and helped clear buildings one room at a time. With each room it increased, building up within him and those around him until they tore into one room, and then another, addicted to the mystery of what was on the other side of the door and the hope that rode shotgun with the fear that there were enemies inside.

After clearing a room in a multiple-storied building, Walton realized that the sounds of contact echoing through the city were now sporadic, and that there wasn't any radio traffic. There was no longer any organization at all because everyone in charge was dead. He noticed that it was just after five o'clock in the morning.

The stack he'd been working with stepped out into the hallway, only to be held up by another team standing outside of the next door. He saw Sergeant Bing was leading it. "What's stoppin' us?" he asked.

Sergeant Bing continued to look at the doorway. "They got a motherfucker in there that we can't see."

Walton saw an opportunity for sleep. "Tell ya what. I'll go in first to draw fire, and y'all be right behind to hit 'em."

"Alright."

Walton waited for Bing to nod, then rushed into the room blasting the second he saw anything resembling a person. Three muzzles shot him from behind covered positions.

"You're dead," said the OC.

"Damn." Walton tried to keep the happiness out of his voice. He found a corner and went to sleep.

The Battalion sat arrayed on a field near a gravel road in neat columns awaiting the deuce-and-a-half trucks after the enlisted soldiers had worked for an hour picking up spent brass casings in the aftermath of The Battle of MOUT City. Second Platoon was no different, and sat napping against their rucks or lying in the grass. They luxuriated in one of the few days where they'd had sunshine and swapped stories like it had been an actual fight.

Sergeant Bronson laid on his stomach while a soldier from the mortars section named Hayden used his fists to knead out the knots in his back. "Goddamn, I love a motherfuckin' massage," he mused. "There ain't a day in the world I wouldn't give my old lady a massage, 'cause that usually leads to gettin' laid."

"Yeah, unless she falls asleep," Hayden added.

"That's how I get laid."

Espinoza, a wiry specialist from Long Island by way of Ft. Hood, opened his eyes at the mention of sex. "Oh man, when I get back, I'm givin' my girlfriend The Field Load! She loves it when I nut in her after a long time in the field."

"Yeah, and while you're gone I'll piss in your spaghetti sauce," Benamy mumbled beside him. The two were new roommates and spoke in taunts.

Espinoza turned his head to look at Benamy, and pointed his index finger at Benamy's face. "Motherfucker, you touch that sauce and that's the end of you! Hell, I'll get The Yeti after your ass again!"

"Man, I'm so glad I didn't fuck The Yeti," said Dechico. "The fact that I didn't hit that shit redeems me for fucking that black baby's mama who has a kid and a tattoo of her husband who's in jail." The young Italian PFC from Rhode Island had no qualms about putting it to a bar floozie or barracks whore, but he had drawn himself a line in the sand. He put Walton in mind of a cousin of Winnie the Pooh's from New Jersey who had "connections."

"It's called 'novelty,' gentlemen," Sergeant Bronson informed. "Fat chicks, midgets, paraplegics . . ."

Third Squad's leader, Sergeant Sandlin, walked up and nodded in cocky, debauched approval. "I think ol' Sergeant Sandlin might have to take a spin by the battered women's shelter," he said as he rubbed his hands together in anticipation.

"*Sarge*...the battered women's shelter is the best place to pick up chicks," Sergeant Bronson affirmed. He then shot a look directly at Walton. "You want me to let you in on a secret, Tom? It ain't the clothes you wear, or the car you drive, or the money in your account. You want to get a woman, you just gotta make a bitch feel like she's the only person in the world for ten minutes."

The triumph of the MOUT City exercise was short-lived. The tempo of the pre-deployment training was unrelenting, and Second Platoon continued to experience growing pains. Most of the squad leaders were ordered away for various specialized training schools, and with them went many of the buffers that helped maintain the delicate equilibrium in the platoon still struggling with developing its new identity.

"Alright, fall in on your shit," Sergeant Cade ordered without dislodging his cigarette. Alpha Company had just returned from the field, and Sergeant Cade had ordered Second to clean and prep their equipment over the weekend for a Monday inspection. He stood at the head of the ranks and files of the platoon's neatly arranged gear with a checklist.

Once the soldiers came over to stand near their gear, he began his inspection. He rifled through Benamy's equipment, then looked up at the soldier. "There's dirt in your canteen cup," he said holding the offending object.

"It was clean, Sergeant, but it's been out here on the ground for a while for the layout."

"Uh-huh. Check's in the mail, the sun was in my eyes, and I promise not to cum in your mouth." Sergeant Cade continued examining the gear and shook his head angrily. "What the fuck! Did you even clean your ruck?"

"Roger, Sergeant."

"You see this shit? That's trail dust!"

"I thought we were just supposed to knock the dirt off, Sergeant."

"Well you thought wrong! You're a team leader, Benamy, you should know better! This is bullshit! Is everybody's fucked up like this?"

Sergeant Cade moved on to a private and rummaged through his kit. He threw down an assault pack in disgust. "Yep, it's fucked up too! Tell you what; you've got till the end of the day to fix this shit, or I'll have the whole goddamn platoon doing front-back-goes!" He stalked away, and the substitute squad leaders called for their Joes.

Sergeant Roper (who had been waiting to reclaim his team once they'd returned to the barracks) looked at the Joes smugly. "Front-leaning-rest position, move!" The squad assumed the position. "Start fuckin' pushing!"

The squad began doing push-ups. Walton subtly glared at the NCO when he wasn't focusing on his movements. He had no doubt that Roper was in league with The Bad Man; the sinister metaphysical entity who had plagued Second Platoon since its inception. (None of the soldiers had actually *seen* The Bad Man, but that just showed He excelled at employing effective cover and concealment. The Bad Man worked in mysterious ways.) Roper hadn't led his team in the field for over a month due to his back flaring up. He hadn't been required to lay out his gear, or had even been aware of the new standards for equipment inspections. Walton suspected the man just wanted to feel the power of asserting himself over lower-ranking men.

As he endured the smoking with the rest of the Joes, Walton fed on his hatred for Roper and the system that put men like that over him. And he despised himself for following along with it.

Months evaporated with more training, as well as an obscene amount of formations and inspections as the new senior NCO, First Sergeant Nolen, replaced First Sergeant Wade, and Captain Cordova became Alpha Company's CO (Commanding Officer). Within no time, the unit racked up a slew of DUI's on the rare occasion they weren't in the field. The Brass subsequently pushed new regulations down, further curtailing the freedom of those in the barracks, thus causing even more DUI's under the stress. The cycle of repression and hedonism went round and round. (Some changes, though, had been welcomed, Walton found. Due to his back, Sergeant Roper had been sent to ride the desk as the training room NCO, taking with him every joke about abortion and pedophilia devised by man. In addition, the core sergeants of the platoon had returned.)

With feet of snow falling constantly and nowhere to go on the weekends, the boozing took on Olympic limits as Cabin Fever dug in. Drinking became their religion, and they all gathered together in their Spartan rooms to drink themselves into a coma and ride out the primitive rage of shared loneliness and the frustration borne of wearing a leash of regulations.

A cabal of Second Platoon congregated weekly in Sergeant Bronson's room after work on Friday, and the weekend began as if they were acting from a script. The soldiers stacked cases of beer by the door, put on the familiar drinking songs, and sat bitching about unit politics, women, or just shared silence. As they drank, they grew louder and more animated, then in a magic instant, the mundane erupted into mania with a dark undercurrent of violence. At that point it was game-on, and all bets were off. They blasted music, broke bottles and furniture, and fought to within an inch of the loss of life, limb, or eyesight.

One week, The Brass declared that Alpha Company could have no more than a six-pack of beer in their mini-fridges, and Walton hurried across the street to buy his limit and some frozen food. He re-entered the barracks as he had a thousand times before, climbed the stairs, and as he neared his room, he heard the voice of Sergeant Gage from the CQ desk call out, "Hey!"

Walton turned and saw the NCO storm down the hall as he continued to yell. "Hey! You can't come up that way!" Sergeant Gage was from First Platoon, and he zealously looked down from the authority that had come with a new set of sergeant's stripes. "You have to walk around! You can't come up through Bravo Company's door. Didn't you hear the First Sergeant put that out?"

"No Sergeant," Walton lied. He had heard the First Sergeant say that, but it seemed stupid to not take the shortest route to go across the street. "Well that's a lame rule. Tell ya what. Let me slide this once. I won't do it again."

"No, you've gotta go back down and come up the other way."

Walton clenched his jaw. He looked at his door as it silently taunted him from ten feet away. He shook his head with contempt and retraced his steps until he was back outside then came up the designated route. He didn't yet want to return to his empty room (Desilva had left for the weekend to be with some empty-headed Sausage Wallet he'd met at a club) so he knocked on the door of someone who'd understand.

Benamy opened the door, fish-lipping a cigarette and still in his uniform, with a Mountain Dew in hand and blaring *The Sound of Silence* behind him. (Benamy had vowed to learn all of Simon and Garfunkle's lyrics back in The Boz'.) Looking at Benamy, Walton saw a dirty old man stuck in a chain-smoking, twenty-year-old Kentucky boy's body. The corners of Benamy's lips turned up in a smirk and he greeted around the cigarette with mock continental dignity coupled with a defiant Southern accent, "Well, well, well. Thomas Motherfuckin' Walton.

We meet again. How's the motherfuckin' ol' prodigal roommate? Get your punk-ass on in here."

As he closed the door behind Walton, he continued, always up for a chat. "Speedo got all uppity earlier 'cause he saw one of my T-shirts that was crispy with my essence from a night of makin' sweet love to some Skinamax. If ya ask me nice, I'll let ya shit in his drawer while he's gone."

Walton took a seat in his old chair with a smile. Though it reminded him of his days as a Cherry, he couldn't help but remember that Benamy was ETS'ing in a matter of months. "I think I'll take a rain check on that, Hoss, but thanks. Espinoza's gonna be my roommate when your monkey-ass gets paroled. I'd hate to piss off the guy I'll have to share a shitter with."

Benamy took a sip off his Mountain Dew and reclined on his bunk while he watched Brittany Spears dance around on MTV with the mute on. He asked about the exchange with Sergeant Gage that he had caught pieces of through his door.

Walton filled him in, then let a mini-rant go. "Can you believe this bullshit? They're now tellin' us what fuckin' doors we can use! We're preparing to go to God only knows where, we're entrusted with weapons that could fuck up a humpback T-Rex, and yet we can't even have more than a six-pack in our fridge! They want to know why we drink? I'll tell ya why. 'Cause drinkin' is the only think that helps us make it through another fuckin' day of this bullshit!

"You know, Ben, I like to think there's a threshold for how stupid they can make the Army. I like to think that it'll get to a point where they say, 'Well, that there's just about as gay as we can get it,' then it gets to start over and maybe make some fuckin' sense. I swear, I feel like I'm livin' in *One Flew Over the Cuckoo's Nest* or some shit. It's like the Army could fuck up a wet dream it wasn't even in."

Benamy ashed his cigarette into his perpetually full ash

tray, unruffled by the unfairness of life. "Hey, man, don't be knockin' wet dreams. It's like masturbation without all the work."

That night, Walton went out drinking with some of the platoon and took a cab back from the bar with Bing. As they entered the barracks, they sang *Family Tradition* as loud as they could and pounded on anything that would make a noise.

Once they made it to the second floor, Sergeant Gage charged out the dayroom, exclaiming, "Hey! Hey, you two! You better keep it down or I'll call the First Sergeant!"

Something snapped in Walton.

"I GIVES A FUCK!"

He thought of his run-in with Gage earlier in the day and the oppressiveness of barracks life in general. He decided to attack. "You call him, Gage! Call him! You call him and tell him to get his fuckin' ass down here, and you tell him Specialist Thomas by God Walton and Sergeant Bing will be here waitin' on him!"

Walton noticed Bing had backed his play and had taken a seat at the CQ desk with his arms crossed defiantly. Bing yelled, "Yeah, that's right! Get that motherfucker on down here! *Gawwddaaamn!*" The last he exclaimed like a crazed hillbilly.

The cockiness dissolved from Gage's face. "Look guys, I don't want any trouble. It's late and people are trying to sleep. You need to keep it down."

"That's all you had to say, Gage," Walton replied, suddenly feeling reasonable. Honor had been satisfied. "We're relatively civil folk and like to be treated as such every now and again. Let's go, Bing." Bing got up and did a drunken cartwheel as he walked down the hall. They had not yet begun to drink.

The next morning, half of Second Platoon stood around the CQ desk with Sergeant Heslich and Daniels, who were now on duty. Rebellion was in the air. Someone's stereo blasted old school country music while they ate McDonald's take-out, and a feeling of anticipation filled the barracks. It was nine-thirty AM and Walton was still drunk from the night before.

PFC Brickham, with his quasi-Mohawk, looked over from his hash-browns at the stairwell door and yelled like a kid at Christmas. "Jesus! Jesus has come with the keg!"

PFC Castor, who had the misfortune of having Jesús as a first name, pushed a dolly holding their unauthorized silver idol.

Without planning it, Second Platoon began drinking with a reckless vengeance, and soon caught the whole company up in their bacchanalian hysteria like a match to a powder keg, kicking off the four-day booze-athon that would go down in the history of the platoon as The Black Hole Weekend. Fraternization and platoon rivalry went out the window as everybody drank with everybody. A small handful of wives and girlfriends soon materialized, setting off the soldiers' Estrogen Radar, and causing them to circulate around like sharks in a feeding frenzy in anticipation of an opportunity to corner one of the women into a room.

Time took on a fluid quality, and everyone devolved into debauched four-year-old versions of themselves. A group of them went knocking door to door seeking mischief, and one of their band (Mueller from Third Platoon) had bolted into the room of Bing, who had been fucking a girl. Mueller grabbed her panties from the floor, put them on his head, and ran off down the hall in triumph. Benamy grabbed Bing's busted fiddle and attempted playing it. Walton tried to talk the young woman into getting the girls with whom she dyked out to come up and give a class on Lesbianism. (Walton had three reasons for doing so. Firstly, the barracks was a perpetual sausage-fest, and he was sick and tired of being around a bunch of dudes all the time. He wanted to spend some time with a girl so bad he could taste it, even if she ate carpet. Secondly, he wanted to learn their tactics and techniques, 'cause knowing was half the battle. Lastly, he didn't believe that *actual* full-on lesbians existed in the wild; there were just girls who needed good lovin'. This applied even to the embittered, frumpy, middle-aged man-hater set. Walton didn't have time for problems, just solutions.) At one point, he stepped out into the hall and saw Sergeant Bronson passed out on the floor after smashing his stereo into the wall. He had Bajez and Opie carry Sergeant Bronson to his room as the squad leader called out, "You wanna hear somethin' funny? Come Tuesday, I'm in charge again!"

Hours later, Walton looked around to find himself in a party in his neighbor's room. Bajez stood on a chair and delivered a soliloquy from *Scarface*, accent included. Mueler leapt onto Sergeant Bronson's back (who had gotten a second wind), and the cherry of his cigarette touched Sergeant Bronson's shoulder. Sergeant Bronson casually set him down then slapped him full in the face. Mueler wobbled backward, then pulled back and threw a punch that landed on Sergeant Bronson's neck. They both laughed, hugged, and resumed drinking.

After keg stands, the proprietor of the establishment, a soldier named Grand, played The Hermes House Band's version of *Country Roads*, and everyone who had heard it while in Bosnia sang along at the top of their lungs and danced to it like prison inmates let loose at Woodstock. He replayed the song until all the new guys in the room knew the words. The song was one of the platoon's two anthems; the other being *The Ballad of Chasey Lain*.

Walton turned his attention to a beer-saturated ball cap on the floor, put it on his head, and danced about like a madman. He peered into the amber goodness in the red plastic cup, and suddenly felt like Buddha sitting under the

Bodhi Tree.

There was Enlightenment in his beer. There was more to the world—*to Life*—than just what he could see and touch. It was all right there, *somewhere*, he just knew it. He fumbled for some idea or design that he couldn't lay hold of but often lingered on the edge of his mind. It beckoned from just outside the periphery of his vision. He felt a compulsion that if he could grab it and bring it into focus, everything would make sense and he could live at peace with the world for the rest of his natural life.

His frustration with the intangible *Thing* within him took him further down into the quicksand. He lived and worked in a concrete cage. People barged into his room to make demands at all hours of the day and night. His hair was thinning. He felt claustrophobic. He wanted to fuck one, any, and all of the five girls currently in the barracks who had smelled like a magic naked summer when he'd walked past them. He wondered what he was doing with his life. He thought about home, but he knew he couldn't be there at this point in his life, nor did he feel ready for a wife and kids. He finally got tired of thinking and grabbed the euphoria in the air like a life preserver. He was going to start not giving a fuck like he was getting paid for it.

He failed, however, to see the masochism listed on the price tag. While he murdered his throat with the music he roared, he smoked cigarettes he couldn't remember lighting, and the ones he didn't ash into his beer, he put out on his arm. Had there not been so many people near the door, he would have started hurling bottles at it, or maybe start a mosh pit. Somebody inevitably would. The Barracks Party Gods were jealous and always demanded a blood sacrifice.

As he walked to a vacant seat, Walton noticed a bottle of cherry cold medicine, liberated it from Grand's shelf, spat out the dose cup into the oblivion on the floor, and began struggling with the cap. "Who wants to hit this with me?" he yelled. Several Joes raised their hands. "Then someone get this fuckin' childproof cap off! I'm so fucked up I can barely operate my chair!"

After killing a healthy portion, he handed it over to Brickham (who at some point had taken off his shirt and had started wearing his reflective PT belt across his chest), who in turn took a pull and passed it around.

Walton got a fresh cup of beer at three o'clock in the morning and noticed that half the people were gone, leaving the room with a palpable loss of momentum. However, from the sounds of *Sundown* and good ol'-fashioned rowdiness down the hall, the boys in Third Platoon were still giving it hell. They loved them some Gordon Lightfoot.

The voices down the hall erupted in a cheer and Walton figured they had probably talked a Cherry into getting hooked up to The Gooch Machine, and the bastard had just gotten a dose of some volts. The Gooch Machine was an instrument belonging to Sergeant Wagner, a team leader in Third Platoon. The apparatus was designed to stimulate muscle development by sending an electric current into the tissue via a node ending in a suction cup, similar to the one owned by Bruce Lee. Soon after its purchase, The Gooch Machine became a tool of much inebriated amusement as the soldiers dared each other to use it in places and on settings that they usually regretted. It had paid for itself in hilarity.

Sergeant Bronson emerged from the sink where he'd just finished sticking his head under the faucet. "Goddamn," he observed. "People are fallin' out like a Vietnam firefight."

"Yeah," Walton slurred. "We need West Virginia lesbians and a crick." He glanced at the keg and saw the wholesome-looking Snowball trying in vain to fill an imaginary cup. (Dechico had started calling Private Chrisner, *Snowball*, due to his paleness.)

Grand turned from his computer to Snowball and yelled, "Chrisner! What the fuck are you doing?"

The young private spooned the keg while blindly trickling beer through the empty space between his curled fingers. "I'm waiting for the foam to stop."

"But there's no cup," Grand remarked.

Snowball opened his eyes and looked around in shit-faced shock. "There was one!"

Walton admired Snowball's steadfast determination in the face of such insurmountable odds. It was the mark of a true champion.

He liked talking with the private. Snowball was from Alaska and would occasionally say things like, "You're as free as you want to be." Watching Snowball, he remembered how the two of them had been drinking together recently and discussing Aristotelian vs. Platonic thought. Walton had finally grown tired of the highbrow flavor of their discourse and said, "Fuck those guys. I'll tell you what really means a fuck: *women*."

Snowball had clanked bottles with Walton, and after taking a drink, he had then said, "Let me propose a toast of my own. There's this girl back in Alaska. Her name is Sally. She's one of those girls who'll hike miles right next to you, then fuck the shit out of you in the snow."

Walton had been all too happy to drink to that, and after downing their beer, he'd asked, "So what's the story on Sally? Is she your girl?"

"No. She's just a friend. But who knows? Maybe someday we'll hook up if the Fates allow. Or if they even exist for that matter."

"Who knows?"

"That's pretty much the basis of philosophy, right there," Snowball had mused at Walton's response. The kid had often seemed to have philosophy on the brain.

Walton had agreed in a noncommittal fashion, and after thinking through the beer for a moment had said,

"You know, if there's *Nothin'*, then humans should win The Most Tragic Creature in the Universe Award 'cause we're aware, and it doesn't mean a damn thing."

Snowball had laughed and told Walton, "You quote people and you don't even know it." The private's eyes had been closed for five minutes, but he'd still been functional.

They had then speculated on what it was that compelled Mankind to seek war and conflict. Walton had wound up just shrugging and chalking it up to the eternal quest for a good fight and some pussy.

Snowball had then had an insight. "You're right. I think we want that 'trial by fire.' We want to see if we'll have the nerve to drive on when we see our buddies die."

Walton's stomach suddenly lurched and it brought him back to his booze-fueled present. He announced, "Fuck, I think I need to go."

He got up to leave and the room spun in a way that made him uncomfortably happy. He noticed the private now fully passed out from his lost cause at the keg and he tapped Sergeant Bronson on the shoulder to point it out to him.

Sergeant Bronson smiled through bleary eyes. "I love to see my children grown."

Walton laughed as he went to the bathroom and threw up. Brickham patted his back and cheered him on. Afterward, Walton washed his face and retired to his room to ride out the spinning world in the dark.

A group of troublemakers consisting of giggling girls and crazy soldiers soon barged in, and he drunkenly declared "If you ain't a Camel Light or a lesbian, you need to leave!"

Thus ended the first day of The Black Hole Weekend.

Following The Black Hole Weekend, the drinking not only continued on the weekends, but actually picked up speed the closer The Battalion got to going downrange.

The Brass was at a loss to understand why, and this caused no end of friction between them and the lower enlisted soldiers.

"You wanted to see me, First Sergeant?" Walton said as he stood at Parade Rest in front of First Sergeant Nolen. He saw Sergeant Roper out of the corner of his eye at his desk in the CP (Command Post), and he resented the fact that he shared the room with the former team leader and had to breathe the same air.

"Yes, Specialist Walton, I do. I hear you went drinking with Specialist Grand this weekend."

"That's true, First Sergeant." Walton held the First Sergeant's gaze and wished that circumstances were different. He'd seemed like an alright guy and Walton hadn't wanted to piss him off.

"Did you leave him behind?"

"We got separated, First Sergeant. I figured he made it back to the barracks."

"I see. So what you're saying is that you didn't square away your battle buddy. What happens when we go to combat? Are you going to leave your buddy behind there too?"

"No, First Sergeant."

"Were you aware that Grand is underage? Why would you be a party to underage drinking?"

"Because I thought he could get away with it, First Sergeant."

First Sergeant Nolen shook his head. "You know underage drinking is against the rules. I say it every weekend in the safety briefings. Why shouldn't I give you an Article Fifteen?"

"You're well within your rights to do so, First Sergeant."

"If I did, would it compel you to seek counsel?"

"No, First Sergeant, I can take my lickin's like a man."

"So you're saying you're just going to pick and choose

what rules you'll follow. What will keep you from doing this in combat? Grand is underage and this conflicts with Army policy. Why did you go along with it?"

"Because I don't agree with the policy, First Sergeant."

First Sergeant Nolen looked he might explode. Sergeant Roper paid close attention to his computer. "I'm disappointed in you, Specialist Walton. You're dismissed."

Walton turned and walked away. He went back to prepping the platoon's communication equipment for an upcoming field exercise, and noticed Grand.

The younger soldier came over and said remorsefully, "I'm sorry, dude. Roper heard about the weekend and told the First Sergeant."

Walton tried to put him at ease with a smile. "It's alright, Hoss. You didn't do anything wrong. The Bad Man's gonna get His pound of flesh one way or the other. As for Roper, he's just a miserable piece of shit. It's what he does. It's his whole reason for livin'. Sergeant Bronson's always talkin' about how the Army needs a good Combat-Cleaning to get rid of the weak, stupid, and useless. Well, *that* fucker would be the first to go.

"Besides, you're a soldier in the goddamned infantry. You should be able to have a pint like a man without it bein' like tryin' to get into a speakeasy. Fuckin' savages."

The word was out. The Battalion was going to sunny Afghanistan.

A few months after The Black Hole Weekend, Walton sat with Sergeant Bronson in Brickham and Bajez's room. The two roommates couldn't have been more different, and whenever Walton visited them, which was often, he could easily imagine the theme from *The Odd Couple* playing in the background. Brickham was an athletic and extroverted soldier from suburban Arizona, while Bajez (recently dubbed, *Dominican Lou*) was shorter and in possession of the quiet dignity and easy charm of his native Dominican Republic. Sergeant Bronson had taken Lou on as a Cherry and made him a SAW gunner. Dominican Lou in turn was fanatically devoted to him and seemed to always be waiting for word from the squad leader to kill someone with one of the numerous knives secreted on his person, or machetes in his jeep or under his bed.

"I didn't like that briefing," Brickham said from his recliner, while Lou rifled through a men's magazine and Walton and Sergeant Bronson watched TV. "That video was fucked up." Over the year of training, Brickham had taken his position as senior gunner and ran with it. Aside from continuing to try to get away with wearing a Mohawk, he had shown himself to be a hard-charger and had made the rank of specialist.

"That didn't bother me so much as the general reaction," Walton said. "Seein' guys run for their life and gettin' fucked up doesn't seem like the sort of thing you want to get used to cheering over."

The Battalion had spent the morning in briefings about Afghanistan and what their role would be there. Most of the briefings had covered its history and the customs of its inhabitants, which of course bored the soldiers, causing zealous team leaders to rap dozing soldiers on the head with knuckles, and issue curses and promises of cruel and unusual punishment.

However, one briefing had brought applause.

A projector screen showed the black-and-white heat signatures of people in a compound as seen from a gun-ship flying overhead. Small white human shapes scurried about like characters in a video game while a trail of white dots chased them until they touched the human shapes, causing them to stop, bounce in inhuman-like movements, or disappear altogether. The pilot's voice was piped in for the play-by-play.

Walton had watched, and though he figured the men

the pilots killed were terrorists; the human equivalent of rabid dogs, and were to be put down without mercy, he was uncomfortable with the fact that many of the Joes had watched with eager eyes, relishing in the extinguishing of life like watching a porn star catch a cum-shot to the face.

He then realized he needed to quit acting so uppity because he wasn't above those feelings either. Deep down, he lusted for the same things as every other swinging dick in the room; they might find The Shit here.

Brickham shook his head. "It just doesn't seem right. Everybody's got a hard-on for killing and shit. Like that guy who gave the ROE briefing and talked about what conditions it was okay to kill a kid."

"Don't believe half those motherfuckers," Sergeant Bronson said. "There ain't a motherfucker here who'd shoot a little girl."

The sad things in his old squad leader's eyes made Walton hope that there were things that he'd never have to see. They sat quietly for a moment then he got up. "Well, I'll let you boys get on with your rat-killin'. That's me out. Me and Pace gotta make sure the boys put all the right shit on the duffel bags."

"How you like workin' for Sandlin?"

"He's great. I really like workin' for him. It's the squad itself…I'm still gettin' used to 'em. It ain't Second Squad."

Sergeant Bronson said flatly, "Well, I tried. Smokey wouldn't allow it. I'm an old man. Survey says: I'm afraid of change. But you'll like Sandlin. He's almost as lazy as I am."

Walton turned to leave, but paused. "You know, Sergeant, I found myself quoting you the other day. You know that Cherry, Vantassle? Well, he's in my team. I sat him down while the boys were workin' on his gear and said, 'You don't know your job. Pay attention to the others and do what the fuck you're told and you'll be alright.' I then told him he picked the wrong fuckin' time to be a Cherry and dropped the stats on him; you know, the one that says at least one from the company will die. I told him to not be the motherfucker that keeps someone from comin' home."

Sergeant Bronson grinned in a way that Walton wasn't sure if it was approval or something sinister. Knowing him, it was probably a bit of both.

As he walked down the hall, Walton shook his head at the workings of the tribe to which he belonged. His thoughts soon wandered over into anticipation of pre-deployment Leave, which was just around the corner. He had been planning on heading up to Montreal for a bit on a solo mission, then attending Lunchbox's wedding instead of flying back home.

Walton had heard good things about Canadian girls. He thought that getting into some mischief with one would be a fine send-off, just in case he wound up getting shot in the face downrange. As a team leader, he put his chances of catching lead as higher than most. A team leader was always on point during patrol, and they were at the head of a stack when clearing a room. That was also where the bad guys often were.

He needed to find Heinz. Supposedly, the kid had just visited Montreal on Pass. Maybe he knew of some whorehouses.

<u>Stepping-Off</u>

Walton could've sworn the building was laughing at him. He wouldn't have put it past the son of a bitch.

In the years since he'd been living in the barracks, he'd developed a love/hate relationship with his adopted home. Whenever he'd return from training in the field or from a deployment, the sight of it made him smile at the prospect of sleep uninterrupted by a guard shift, self-love in a hot shower, a beer, and what passed for privacy there. However, when he returned from a Pass or Leave, with the aftertaste of freedom and happiness still on his tongue, the barracks seemed a hell of a lot like a prison *sans* the razor wire and sodomy.

His shoulders sagged unconsciously as they assumed again the familiar weight of his own little world as he made his way through the steel and glass doors of the barracks. Leave was over, and it was time to return to duty. He took a deep breath and braced himself. He had less than a year left before he was out. He just had to hold on till May 2004.

Weeks crawled by, winding the soldiers up ever-tighter as the deployment and all the unknowns hidden within it stared them in the face. Infantry SOP's and traditions exerted their influence in maintaining continuity in the face of uncertainty, whether they were equipment layouts, PT, or drills.

In the middle of the chaotic last-minute buildup for the deployment, Walton heard a knock on his door around two o'clock in the morning. He had finally fallen asleep just minutes before the intrusion. He had been tossing and turning over the package he'd sent to Amy at the strip club a few days before. After the Amy Awakening, he thought of almost nothing else and hadn't been able to wait until he got to Afghanistan to send her the parcel.

Speedo yelled, "What!" and Walton remarked briefly at what an improvement it was to live with him. It was nice to have someone around who was near his own age. That, and Speedo was fond of *The Big Lebowski* and *Apocalypse Now*. After multiple viewings, the two of them would run into each other as they tended their Joes and trade quotes from them. Between that and comparing notes over girls (Speedo was thinking about popping the question to his girlfriend), their place in the Army food chain, and memories of Benamy's antics, the two were becoming friends.

A private murmured quietly through the crack in the door. "Sergeant Espinoza? There's a call for you at the CQ desk. PFC Chrisner's dead."

Walton imagined the young Joe climbing a sheer rock face as he had been doing on the weekends and figured it was appropriate that the mountain had gotten him. Snowball would've wanted that. "What happened?" he asked.

"Car accident, Specialist."

"Goddamn."

"Alright, I'll be right there," Speedo said. The private left and Speedo sat up in the dark at the edge of his bed. "I'll bet that fuck fell asleep."

"You're probably right." Walton remembered seeing Snowball fall asleep in damn near every class or bit of training. It had become a running joke, and everyone had made it a point to watch out for it and have him stand up if they saw him about to nod off. "That kid was narcoleptic like a motherfucker."

Walton found it somewhat ironic but fitting that the next day Dechico had put up his deceased roommate's name tape and a few pictures of Snowball in all his glory on the bulletin board. He remembered when those two used to fight like cats and dogs and had lobbied endlessly to move into other rooms (though to no avail). And yet, they had parted as friends.

When Walton walked the halls of the barracks he noticed how Snowball's passing had rattled many of the cocky young soldiers in the platoon. They had walked like the young; impervious to the wounds of life and certain of their indomitable powers over the world, but now they knew that if one of their strongest, smartest, and most promising could fall, then they could as well.

The platoon continued with the business of the day as they drew out gear and practiced room-clearing drills. There were side tasks, though. Some of the boys picked up an ice axe and had Snowball's name engraved on it. They placed it in the coffin with him. A detail had to be sent to pick up the Chrisners and escort them around the Post.

Eventually, the soldiers of Alpha Company went to the chapel in their Class-A's to say good-bye. Walton stood near the rear of the pews with the rest of the ushers while people talked about Snowball.

At the end of the ceremony, the First Sergeant stood at the podium and read the roll call.

"Private Alberto."

"Here, First Sergeant."

"Specialist Baker."

"Here, First Sergeant."

"Private Caliph."

"Here, First Sergeant."

"PFC Chrisner…"

"PFC Chrisner…"

"Private First Class Matthew Chrisner…"

Silence filled the chapel till it hung densely like an oppressive force that was almost palpable enough to be seen. All eyes wandered to the front of the podium, whether they wanted to or not, to the pair of gleaming black combat boots that rested in front of the M4 that stood barrel down with Snowball's K-Pot resting on top.

Taps played.

One Friday, a raft of promotions came down from on high, and with it came the time-honored custom of Blood Rank. Walton laughed as many of the former Cherries received their rank pins and had the breath knocked out of them by their elders. When he was awarded the pins bearing a corporal's chevrons, Walton felt a strong sense of pride at the spirit with which Sergeants Cade, Dobbs, Sandlin, Heslich, Pace, Espinoza, Feran, and Bronson pounded the rank into his chest. Punching the pins into the enlisted was one thing, but an NCO's stripes was another matter. They had initiated him into *their* ranks.

That evening, Second Platoon celebrated by hitting the bars then winding up at the apartment that Sergeant Sandlin and Sergeant Bronson had recently started renting together. A knot of NCO's sat around in the front yard while a bunch of Joes drank, rough-housed, and played catch with a football by porch light.

The football went wide and landed near Sergeant Bronson's chair. He stared into the eyes of the Joes who'd been playing with it and yelled, "You hit me with that ball and I'll stab a hole in it bigger than a Las Vegas hooker's pussy!"

"That sounds like some shit this guy back home would say," remarked Sergeant Wider. Over the train-up for Afghanistan, the mortars section had developed a stronger presence in Alpha Company, and their humor had made them an easy fit with Second Platoon. Sergeant Wider was their senior NCO, and like Sergeant Bronson, Sergeant Wider had made his bones as a Marine before joining the Army. He often came down to shoot the shit with his fellow Jarhead.

"He was this red-headed guy who was a tunnel rat in 'Nam for three tours," Sergeant Wider continued. "He was one colorful motherfucker. He said one time he was in a cave and he heard a *click*. He turned and saw a cobra looking at him. Next thing he knew, he was in daylight. Guy came back and went through three wives and is always getting fired and rehired."

He shook his head. "I'll tell you what. When we go to Afghanistan, I ain't gonna be a happy man. I'll be there because they started it, and I won't be there to win hearts-and-minds."

"Fuck a bunch of tunnels," Speedo snarled. "We can put a motherfucker on the Moon; you'd think we can find a better way to fight war."

"They'll never get rid of us," Sergeant Bronson said. "There's always gotta be someone to climb up some steep-ass hill to stick his head in some dark-ass hole."

Speedo looked around at the NCO's and the Joes in the yard and said, "Man, I miss Benamy. They need to send Ben back to us. That fuck made me laugh."

At the mention of his former roommate, Walton felt a twinge of sentiment, and though he was happy that Benamy had dodged a Stop-Loss, he still missed the bastard. "No shit. I can still see him runnin' around the woods, and shootin' at everybody with a makeshift bow and arrow."

During the last few times that Benamy been required to go to the field with them before he'd ETS'ed, he had embraced Short-Timer's Disease and had taken grab-ass to new levels. He'd gotten into character and went native at times, stalking through the woods and patrol bases like Mogwai from *Last of the Mohicans*. He'd threatened to put various soldiers in the platoon "under the knife," and told them that before he ate their heart they "would know that their seed has been wiped from the earth forever."

When he finished laughing, Speedo amended his previous statement, saying, "Yeah. But the way I see it, now that he's gone, that means I only got two years left. Besides, he'll be having a ball doing reenactments and going to college."

Speedo then smiled widely. "Oh man, this one time we were sitting around and he was looking through one of his musket catalogs and saw some shit made in Japan and I thought he was gonna lose it. Motherfucker said, 'You can't get a Revolutionary War musket made by a by a bunch of Slopes! Let me see a motherfucker show up to a reenactment with *Made in China* stamped on his shit!' I about lost it."

After their laughter subsided, Sergeant Bronson looked over at Sergeant Wider to talk Army politics. When he angrily mentioned an article in the *Army Times* discussing the promotion of the general who had been in charge of them during the Bosnia rotation, Sergeant Wider hadn't been pleased by the development either.

"I hate that piece of shit," Sergeant Wider declared. "He was a cock-muncher. Speaking of cock-munchers, though, there was this girl I used to fuck back when I was in the Marines. I met her at a club and went home with her. This bitch did it all. She asked if I'd ever went anal on a girl before, and when I said no, she busted out a jar of Vaseline and we went to town.

"Some kid woke me up the next morning, and I looked around and saw all these pictures of her with this chief petty officer. Anyhow, she made breakfast then knocked her kid the fuck out with a bunch of cough syrup then sucked my dick and gave me cab fare home. She did that for two months until her husband returned."

"That's enough to make a motherfucker never get married," Walton said as they laughed.

Sergeant Wider was on a roll and kept the sagas coming. "There was this other time when I met this chick from San Diego State University at Tijuana. I had my buddy tell her I was deaf from a mortar accident and was on my way out of the service, so we did sign language. We fucked every weekend for a month, and at the end I went to NTC (National Training Center).

"When we came back, we went to TJ. I ran into the girl down there and she was pissed because not only did I not contact her, but I was talking and everything. Somehow, though, I had this flash of brilliance. I told her I had been away for an operation and that I was recovered. She just melted and we started back up again. Eventually, we got in a fight and I told her the truth. She freaked out."

As the booze kicked in and the soldiers got rowdier, they moved inside to keep from getting a visit from the police. Sergeant Bronson, Walton, and a few other soldiers sat in the living room while music blared around them. The older man looked at the soldier he had taken from a Cherry to an NCO, who now sat brooding on his couch, as if he could see inside his mind. However, he still asked, "You alright, Thomas?"

Walton looked over at Sergeant Bronson with an intense drunken face, trying to hold back a rage that had been creeping up on him over the course of the evening in spite of their fun. The rage, and the power that he felt come with it, scared him. He was unsure if it was from the time he'd spent in the Army, or the fact that he was now halfway through his twenties, or if it was the result of some mysterious, visceral reaction or animosity he had with the world, like an animal that couldn't see the walls of its cage but knew they were there. Whatever the reason, there was a hidden fury that had been eating him alive since he didn't know when, and it had seemed to grow over the years. He'd been able to trust the booze to take the edge off, but at some point the beast had become impervious to drowning and had grown able to deny him his rightful childlike euphoria.

He composed himself and answered, "Roger, Sergeant. I just find myself feelin' . . . angry and . . . violent. When we were all at the bar earlier, I just wanted to start fuckin' shit up and beatin' the hell out of everything. And no one had really *done* anything to deserve it. Everything just annoyed the hell out of me and it felt like everyone was closin' in on me. It's crazy. I feel like I have to keep myself on a leash with both hands, but I don't really want to." His hands unconsciously flexed as though he were about to grapple with an enemy. "I want to cause pain to whatever is near me that pisses me the fuck off for whatever reason. Does that make any sense?"

Recognition possessed Sergeant Bronson's features along with an evil grin as Walton had talked. "I *know* that feelin', Tom," he said as he pointed to his head with the index finger belonging to the hand that held his bottle of beer. "I feel that feelin' every goddamn day of my fuckin' life. The trick is knowin' you can turn it on and off.

"You'll do fine, Tom. Just remember this feelin' you got in ya. You can use it, and make it work for ya. It'll make you a better corporal." He then got nostalgic. "*Corporal.* Now *that's* the motherfuckin' rank."

At long last the day came, and the soldiers finished the logistics of closing out the barracks and mounted the busses bound to the birds at the airfield. Second Platoon brought along the stray they had picked up to step in for Snowball. Private Tasker had arrived fresh to Alpha Company two days prior, and his Cherry-ness shined like a halo. Dechico wasted no time ragging on him for having never drank or gotten laid.

The Brass shook each soldier's hand as they boarded and Walton almost laughed out loud. It made him think of the whole *Good Game* ceremony children had to do in little league.

The 'Stan

Afghanistan in August is the geographic equivalent of trying to hump an angry, fat, red-assed baboon whilst sober. It's a commitment, and there's no good reason to try it in the first place, but if you did, it was best to try to adapt to the situation, get it over with as soon as possible, go home, and never do it or think about it again. It was result of Mother Nature's nasty three-way with the Sun and The Bad Man, and Afghanistan made it clear from the beginning that she was not your fucking buddy.

The steel cargo ramp of the C-130 opened into a foreign world of nuclear light, and once it lowered to the black iron skillet of the flight line, Second Platoon hoofed it out of the back. BOB (the Bright Orange Ball, AKA: the Sun) seemed close enough to touch, and a curse of some sort was on the tongue of every mother's son as they squinted their eyes behind their issued sunglasses. Sweat didn't last long enough to bead and died at it began, devoured by an angry sun.

The soldiers cooked alive as they walked a quarter of a mile in well over 120 degree heat under the weight of full-battle-rattle and all the gear they would be living with for the next six months to a year. Once they made it to a massive tent, an NCO immediately walked them through a barrage of paperwork, and after they finished the red tape, another NCO directed them to their tents. The buildings on the Post came from two different worlds. One species originated from The West in the form of tents sitting in neat ranks and files. The other was local, taking its color from the khaki dirt, and pock-marked from an old firefight more often than not.

Chaos ensued as The Brass demanded a never-ending stream of tasks to be completed at once, and the orders tumbled down hill. As soon as Second stowed their duffel bags under the plastic cots they would be sleeping on, Sergeant Cade began yelling for team leaders to distribute ammo to the Joes. Once that was finished, they reported to the flight line to practice entering and exiting Black Hawks and Chinooks (lovingly referred to as "Shithooks"). They stayed up half the night as team leaders helped their Joes re-sight the lasers and optical devices on their weapons while compiling accurate lists of each soldier's weapons and equipment and their correlating serial numbers.

The sun oppressed everyone and their only defense was to have a bottle of water on hand. Dust clung to everything, carrying with it a flinty smell, and insinuated itself into the mechanisms of their weapons and equipment, forcing them to engage in more maintenance than usual, and compelling team leaders into a heightened sense of vigilance over the cleanliness of their soldiers' weapons that bordered on obsessive compulsiveness.

Walton felt like he got his ass chewed every five minutes. Though he still felt possessive and proud over his first proper team of his own, he was half out of his mind from trying to juggle managing them, getting settled in, and adapting to his new squad leader's way of doing things. He felt like an overwhelmed outsider, and every time he put out one fire, another burned his ass.

"We seem to be having a problem following directions," Sergeant Sandlin said flatly outside the tent after their third day In-Country. He smoked a cigarette and stared at Pace and Walton with emotionless blue eyes under a thick mat of cropped black hair.

Sergeant Sandlin had been Benamy's team leader and mentor for two years, and Walton suspected that Sergeant Sandlin didn't like him and would rather have had Benamy helping him ride herd over his Joes. However, Sergeant Sandlin was the soul of professionalism and had been nothing but fair. Walton hoped to do right by him.

93

"Did I, or did I not, put it out that no one from Third Squad is to drink soda?"

"Sergeant—"

"Shut the fuck up Pace. It's a yes or no question. Didn't I put it out that soda is banned?"

"Roger, Sergeant," the lean lantern-jawed soldier answered.

Sergeant Sandlin continued to regard them icily. Walton hoped he'd never have to play poker against him. "Then why the fuck did I see a soldier drinking a goddamn motherfucking goddamn soda at the D-Fac (Dining Facility)?"

"It wasn't one of mine, Sergeant," Walton said defensively. "My boys are straight."

"It doesn't matter whose Joe it was. The fact is, I put shit out and it wasn't executed. Who's fault is that?"

"Ours, Sergeant," Pace answered.

"Okay, then, why aren't you guys doing your job? Do I have to follow around behind you and make sure you're doing what the fuck I goddamn say?"

"No, Sergeant," they replied.

"Then why are we having this conversation? I should be able to put some shit out and know that you guys are gonna make that shit happen. You guys have got to start taking charge of your soldiers. You've gotta start putting your foot in their asses. They should fear you. Look at that new guy, Sergeant Dobbs; he acts like a motherfucking team leader. You guys don't."

"Sergeant—"

"Interrupt me one more time, Pace. I'll smoke the fuck out of you." He held a pause to let the quiet words sink in. "See, this is the kind of shit I'm talking about. You need to learn when to shut the fuck up. I'm not interested in some hokey-ass explanations. I want to know I can put shit out and you guys are gonna make it happen. But you guys aren't there yet. I don't like doing this shit, but I see I have

94

to. If you drop the ball like this again, I will give you both a humiliating smoking in front of the Joes and all. Do I make myself clear? Alright. Now get the fuck out of here."

Pace and Walton went back into their hooch and retreated to their respective corners. Walton took a seat in his newly bought camp chair and returned to *American Pastoral* (one of the Amy books), and tried to forget the encounter. As soon as his hands touched the cover of the book his mind went back to Amy and the night she had given it to him. Did she think of him when she was in bed with The Vegetarian and close her eyes and wish he was the man holding her instead? Did she ever walk through her park and remember him next to her? He cursed himself for being a pussy and focused on reading.

"What'd he want, Corporal?" asked Gonzaga, looking up from his learn-to-speak-Portuguese book.

Walton shrugged and looked at the Puerto Rican soldier in his fireteam. "He was pissed 'cause Cook was drinkin' a fuckin' soda after we told y'all that shit was banned. He said if he caught anyone else with soda he'd humiliate us in front of y'all."

"That's fucked up, brah," said Fuan, another one of Walton's Joes, from the bunk on top of Gonzaga's. The big thirty-something Samoan dwarfed the small plastic and burlap cot. "Did you tell him we didn't do shit?"

"Yeah, but he wasn't interested. Look, if y'all see anybody from Sergeant Pace's team drinkin' soda, set 'em straight. I ain't crazy about catchin' a smoking for some dumb shit out of my hands."

Walton went back to thinking about Amy and was reminded of the briefing the night before. Lieutenant Howard had read aloud a report about the Afghan culture and had touched briefly on their attitudes to women. The report argued that women in the Afghan culture weren't without value. The opposite was true; the men put them on a pedestal, seeking to protect them with constant chaperonage and the development of the burkha to keep them from being eye-fucked by the lustful eyes of strange men. (Walton suspected those cultural mechanisms also served as a check on the female sexual instinct to use their pretty as a weapon to stir up trouble and get what they wanted. He figured all that restraint, when unleashed, must erupt in all kinds of fun ways once they let their hair down. Just like in that song *Behind Closed Doors* by Charlie Rich.) Haji (the locals) had a proverb:

What is the greatest thing in the world?
Your mother.
What is the second greatest?
The ground beneath your mother's feet.

He wasn't too sure about the whole gay thing they did, though. Evidently Haji had to save up a crazy amount of money to front to a woman's family if he wanted to marry her and if her family had no objections. Getting that kind of wampum together took years, and in the meantime, the poor bastard had no conjugal access to the gals, and in a pinch, made due with his buddies for intimacy, which was why a fair number of them went around holding hands. It gave new meaning to what it was to "take one for the team." When the LT had read that part of the briefing, Sergeant Bronson had interrupted by saying, "You motherfuckers that drink that Haji tea those fuckers offer you—just remember, every cup of tea you drink was made by a man who fucked another man in his ass."

His mind got caught up in reflecting over the differences and similarities in the two cultures, but mainly how they dealt with life and death for the rest of the evening. When the lights were out he lay awake listening to Merle Haggard on his CD player, and when Merle sang the line, "*And are we rollin' downhill like a snowball headed for hell?*" Walton thought of Snowball and wondered.

"So do you guys eat women out?" Sergeant Sandlin asked the 'terp a few days later. He rode in the back of a truck with Walton's team and a bunch of Hajis. Third Squad had reported to the HQ that morning for Haji guard, and was to spend the day supervising the bands of locals who performed work details throughout KAF (Kandahar Air Field) and ensuring they didn't try anything subversive.

"Yes, we eat de women," the small man said. He had the dark brown skin and features of his companions but lacked their style of dress.

"Bullshit," Sergeant Sandlin said with a laugh from behind his sunglasses. "There ain't no way in hell some bitch is gonna let you eat her out with a goddamn motherfucking goddamn beard like that. Say, how do you say, 'Your breasts are like buttermilk biscuits?' Whenever I go to a foreign country I try to learn how to say that. So far I haven't had that much success here. God, I miss pussy. We need a motherfucking goddamn whorehouse around here. Back in the States, I can like, *smell* those places." He then pointed to his nose. "Sarge is like goddamn motherfucking Tucan Sam with hookers, but in this country, not so much."

After the detail, the squad returned to the tent and Walton went to his corner to listen to music and read. His mind, though, was back in Montreal. Boots eventually entered his field of vision and he looked up to see Brickham, who gestured at his ear. Walton reluctantly paused *The Weight*, and removed his earphones.

"Hey, would you consider Sergeant Sandlin, Irish?"

"I guess so."

Sergeant Sandlin put an *I-told-you-so* look on his face. "See! And that's a college-educated man talking!"

"Oh bullshit!" Brickham wasn't buying it. "You are not Irish. You may be of Irish descent, but you're an American mutt just like the rest of us."

"The hell I am!" Sergeant Sandlin was openly enjoying winding Brickham up. He made fucking with Joes an art form. "I don't have any mud in the blood like *some* people. *Erin Go Bragh!*"

"What the fuck are you talking about, Sergeant?" The use of Gaelic had knocked Brickham for a loop.

"What do you mean, '*What am I talking about?*' half-breed?"

"Hey, it ain't his fault he's only half-Spic," Gonzaga remarked. The PFC relished any opportunity to stir up controversy and expound upon the supremacy of the Puerto Rican people. "Not everybody can be full-blood Puerto Rican like some of us."

"Full-blood Puerto Rican makes you what, a Sicilian?" Brickham wasn't having that either.

Walton grew weary of their race debate and grabbed his towel and hygiene kit. He flip-flopped to the shower tent, then stripped and hung his towel on the hook outside a vacant shower stall and closed the curtain behind him. He smiled at the hot water even if it smelled faintly of Shit Pond. He heard some National Guard POG's (Personnel Other than Grunts) in the neighboring stalls complaining about how the infantry didn't do any work. Walton shook his head, then tuned them out to better concentrate as he engaged in the deployed soldier's daily pastime.

As Walton reentered his squad's hooch, he noticed that they had finished with the topic of ethnicity and had moved on to something else. He heard Brickham finish a story, saying, "...and I was like, 'Oh goddamn!'"

Gonzaga laughed then said, "I got that beat. I walked in on my mom giving my dad head while I was on Leave. She had that deer-in-the-headlight look and all."

"Oh my God!"

"They're always doing shit like that. One time we were having breakfast and my mom comes in and she's like, 'Carlos, your dad broke it off in my ass last night,' and my dad just sits there like he's King Shit."

"Man, I'm fuckin' sucking," Gonzaga complained. "I gotta start doing more PT on my own. That run this morning smoked me." He shook his legs, one at a time, in an attempt to work out the stiffness and looked around the small circle consisting of Bravo Team as they stood in full-battle-rattle in the late morning sun. "How the fuck are they gonna have a fuckin' hour long run in the morning, then have us spend all day running and falling down in this shit? Why all the bullshit, Corporal?"

"Hell if I know, Gonzo. That fuckin' run sucked. Especially 'round Shit Pond. That shit ain't right." Walton removed a water bottle from his cargo pocket, poured some on his thumb, and snorted it to keep the inside of his nose from drying out and bleeding.

Sergeant Cade, the four squad leaders, and Lieutenant Howard approached. (Unlike the previous LT, Lieutenant Howard was an aggressive young officer from West Point who had played on its football team, and believed in having the soldiers train whenever possible.) Sergeant Cade's voice flew through the heat. "Alright, quit fuckin' standin' around and start training. This ain't no union."

Walton took his team about two hundred meters away from the gravel road and into a barren expanse of baked dirt. He gave the signal and they spread out into a wedge. After a few meters he yelled, "Bang bang!" to simulate contact, and they fell to the ground yelling out 'bang,' over and over like children at play. He followed the procedures of regulating the team's rate of fire, then bounding them across the imaginary objective. He then quickly checked each of his soldiers for the status of their ammo, communications, and equipment, and acted out calling in the ACE report.

Sergeant Sandlin came to Walton and said, "Just a second." The rest of Bravo Team drew near and the squad leader continued. "You guys look alright, but your bounding ain't aggressive enough. You ain't out for some goddamn, motherfucking goddamn badge and shit. This is what it needs to look like."

Sergeant Sandlin began off walking and looking around like he was on point, then yelled, "Bang!" and threw himself into the dirt like it owed him money. He simulated firing then jumped up, ran three strides, then pounded the dirt again and again.

After a few rounds, he got back up. "This is what I want it to look like. I know the dirt is like fucking concrete and this shit's heavy, but we either do it right, or we do it all goddamn day with Smokey and the LT yelling and breathing down our neck."

They ran through team level react-to-contact drills for two hours, then Lieutenant Howard cut them loose and they returned to their tents. After shedding their gear, many congregated outside to smoke and gossip in the shade.

"Hey, guys," said First Sergeant Nolen, having materialized out of nowhere with a genial expression which, from a First Sergeant, Walton found almost as unnerving as old First Sergeant Wade's blatant contempt. At least you knew where you stood with someone when they hated you. "You guys just get done training?"

"Roger, First Sergeant," a soldier answered. "We did react-to-contact on the team level."

"That's good." He shook his head with a smile. "Well, I guess the rest of The Battalion isn't working so hard. Some guy complained to The Battalion Commander that there weren't enough company competitions, so now I need some suggestions."

"Tell us who it was, First Sergeant, and we'll go kick their ass," Walton quipped.

The First Sergeant chuckled and looked back at the group of soldiers good-naturedly. "Serious, guys, I need

100

some suggestions."

"How about a Sleep-Off?" Walton offered. "We could take naps, and the first person to wake up loses. Or midget-tossing. I always wanted to try that shit."

The First Sergeant laughed quietly, but soon some of the soldiers began throwing out suggestions. Walton seized the opportunity to make his getaway. Two minutes later, he was reading and drinking Gatorade.

A half hour later, Carasquay put his head in the door and called out, "Hey, Corporal Walton, First Sergeant wants to see you at the CP."

"Alright, thanks, bud," he replied, then put on his DCU (Desert Camouflage Uniform) top, Boonie hat, and rifle, then walked to the CP. He opened the door to find First Sergeant Nolen waiting on him. He imagined the sound of a cage door slamming. "You wanted to see me, First Sergeant," he said at Parade Rest.

"Yes, Corporal, I do," he answered with a raised voice that seems incongruous with his earlier disposition. His sunglasses were off and his eyes held nothing but anger. "Tell me why it is that when I suggest something like a competition, you shoot it down when you should be supporting it."

"I thought some Joe suggested it, First Sergeant, that's why I joked about it."

"You always seem to be joking, Corporal," the First Sergeant shot back. "The promotion board was a joke to you and now being a team leader is a joke."

"That isn't true, First Sergeant," Walton said, amazed at the ghost of resentment he allowed in his voice. "I take leadin' my team very serious."

"Oh really? What are their names?"

"Specialist Fuan, PFC Gonzaga, and Private Vantassle, First Sergeant."

"How is it that your job warrants levity?"

"It just does. I try to find the levity in the situation,

First Sergeant. These guys are under a lot of stress, and when we ain't training I try to keep things light."

"You're a team leader not a stand-up comedian! You know, Corporal, I like you as a person, but I think you're a horrible combat leader and I don't want your Joes to turn out like you. Corporal, do you take anything in the military serious at all?"

"Roger, First Sergeant."

"What?"

"Bringin' my Joes home alive, First Sergeant."

"Oh, so that's it, then? Fuck the mission?"

"No, First Sergeant, the mission goes without sayin'."

"So what else, then?"

"What else is there, First Sergeant?"

"*Right there*, Corporal!" The First Sergeant yelled with a pointed finger. "*That's* the reason you should get out. You don't take anything serious. You're one of those guys who comes in to do some time and suck up some taxpayer money. You're dismissed, Corporal!"

Walton left the CP boiling. He entered the tent, set down his weapon, and tried to calm himself. Sergeant Sandlin looked at him from his cot where he lay hibernating and asked, "How'd it go?"

"Well, Sergeant, it turns out your Bravo Team Leader doesn't take things serious."

Sergeant Sandlin shrugged from the prone. "Well, his squad leader's the same way. What'd he say?"

Walton gave him the story and when he finished Sergeant Sandlin shook his head. "That's how the First Sergeant is; pro-Joe, anti-NCO. Don't let it get ya down. Just shrug that shit off. I'm sure you've got plenty more ass-chewings as an NCO." He rolled over and went back to sleep.

That night, Walton heard Sergeant Bronson and Dechico's voice through the tent wall and walked outside to catch up on things.

"Look at this motherfucker here. *Corporal Walton,*" Sergeant Bronson announced. He sat with his feet up on a giant wooden spool with a sun net rigged up on a pole running through the center of it. Dechico sat with him, and an MP3 player played the songs they drank to back at Ft. Drum.

Walton took a seat and began filling his pipe from a plaid tobacco pouch. "What's up, Sergeant? How're y'all doin' this evening?"

Sergeant Bronson sipped at a Dr. Pepper. "Well, let me see. It's hot, dusty, there's no beer or pussy, and I can smell Shit Pond. I guess I'm fucking outstanding."

"That's not what the CO says," Dechico remarked. "He says there's too much trim walking around."

As he lit his pipe, Walton questioned the truth of that statement. What kind of mystery math the CO had used to arrive at that deduction was beyond Walton's ken. He'd seen maybe two dames so far. Aside from the heat and dust, the absence of women was the next thing to try to get used to. At least in The Boz' there had been *some* women on Post. But in Afghanistan? No women, no Bosnian Lap Dances (having a female barber wash your hair at the barber shop), nothing. They were all gone. They had collectively Dear John-ed Mankind's ass with a lipstick message on the mirror, mounted their spaceship, and blasted off back to Venus or wherever the hell the Talking Heads said they were from. From here on out they existed only in porn and memory.

Sergeant Bronson exhaled a stream of burning Marlboro Red and looked at the young soldier from Rhode Island. "That's too bad for him, Ginny," he said. Sergeant Bronson put out his stub of a cigarette and lit one anew. He drew deeply off it, then looked back at Walton and said, "So what the fuck happened with you and the First Sergeant?"

Walton told him the story in the same fashion he'd told

Sergeant Sandlin. Once he finished, Sergeant Bronson's face carried an angry, dissatisfied cast. "Fuck him," he said. "In life, you're either a non-conformist or a yes-man. How'd Sandlin take it?"

"He was cool with it. He didn't chew my ass or anything. I almost feel like it bought me some street cred with him."

"That's 'cause Sandlin almost got in a fight with him at the bar when we were training at Ft. Knox. He hates bullshit almost as bad as I do. You remember when the First Sergeant caught all us squad leaders sleeping just after lunch and wanted to get rid of us? Well, when I was drunk that weekend I let myself into the CP and taped one of my combat ribbons on his door. Motherfucker didn't say shit after that. You know, I think I've decided to come outta here with a Silver Star or a Medal of Honor, even if I've gotta die to get it."

Walton thought of the circumstances surrounding the earning of those medals. He found himself lacking the requisite enthusiasm. "Don't you think that's a bit excessive, Sergeant?"

"Nah. Walton, I'm thirty-one years old. I've had a good run. There ain't a whole lotta shit I ain't done. I'm ready to die. Besides, it'll shut up motherfuckers like the First Sergeant, and my Old Lady gets two hundred and fifty G's."

"I think I'll just settle for gettin' out," Walton said. He thought of May 2004 and wondered what it would be like. The roads of his fantasies had begun to lead toward there more and more. He shook his head. "Goddamn, I can't believe I'm gettin' so close to my ETS date."

"Did you learn something?"

"Yeah. I guess I did. A whole lot, actually."

"Then it was worth it."

Less than two weeks In-Country, The Battalion had its

first shoot-out with Haji.

The day before they were wheels-up, a loud *boom* had torn through the morning silence of Third Squad's tent. It had come into being without warning and disappeared so quickly that Walton had thought he'd imagined it. He'd peeked his head out of his red and gold Haji blanket and looked around the dark tent with a suspicious eye. He'd guessed that it had probably just been a mortar round. No one had stirred and this had made him happy.

He'd been exhausted from the past few days of running and throwing himself into the ground alongside the rest of the platoon under the demon sun or in the hard interior of the airport terminal. As teams, squads, or as a platoon, they had practiced the fundamentals of war with critiques from the squad leaders, Lieutenant Howard, and Sergeant Cade. There had been whispers of the need for certain members of the leadership to meet with accidents, but none had the balls to follow through.

Lieutenant Howard's alarm clock had eventually sounded off and he'd hit the snooze. Though everyone had been quiet, many had been awake and had hoped that he'd stay in bed. When he got up after the third time the alarm went off, they'd groaned as they dressed into their PT clothes.

The platoon had assembled into formation and Sergeant Cade had broken them down into ability groups. Though he'd given them the option of selecting which group they'd run in, he'd refused to allow them to join a group that would perform below what he'd known was their ability. He would yell at any who made such an attempt to get-over. Sergeant Cade held a dim view of shit-baggery.

Walton had joined the slow group in the hopes of minimizing his chances of falling out. It was bad enough he'd often fallen out of runs as a Joe, but as a corporal it made the embarrassment even worse. When the groups had taken off, everyone had done so wearing their body armor and weapon. Walton had cussed while he ran. There had been no comfortable way to sport a Kevlar vest with front-and-back plates, and carry an M4 with a 203 attachment, and run.

They had ran on the gravel road that led around the perimeter of the Post and when it had curved to the right and they'd continued forward, he'd cussed under his breath some more.

Inside the curve had lain Shit Pond. Tall weeds grew out of the circular body of dark wetness that was the sum total of every person's excrement inside The Wire. It had almost looked innocuous, like an oasis under the morning sky as it sat calm and still with its monopoly of the only green vegetation on the barren Post, but when they'd run deeper into the turn they'd collided into the wind carrying the stench of a thousand sick assholes, it had all seemed so surreal to Walton that he'd thought he might laugh if he hadn't been gagging.

When they'd finished PT, The Battalion had convulsed in a cyclone of rabid activity from top to bottom. Lieutenant Howard had informed them that Special Forces had been fighting and taking casualties for three days and that the QRF (Quick Reaction Force; a rotating detachment of infantry on stand-by) had been activated. The Battalion would be going out the next day.

It had fallen to Alpha Company to land south of a place called Qasa in the Daychopan province, then conduct a movement-to-contact toward it in the hopes of driving enemy personnel into awaiting SF and SEAL ambushes. Alpha would then clear the town. After the briefing, the platoon got busy with equipment and weapons checks.

Walton sat near the open ramp of the Shithook as Second rode out into Indian Country. He watched the cool Afghanistan morning pass beneath him like he was flying on a magic carpet. He looked around at his companions in the bird with him and then out across the sky to the other Shithooks arrayed behind them in a wedge and felt potent. He knew that on paper he was just a bookish young man from Middle America, but in the Shithook with his platoon of natural-born, pure-bred sons of bitches next to him, he felt like he was in a war band of pagan gods out for vengeance and blood. He could barely fathom how this moment compared to a day of life back in the States consisting of eight hours in a cubicle then going home to watch sit-coms, and maybe rub one out to some porn.

The door gunner positioned at the ramp pulled his legs up, which had been straddling the .50 cal. mounted to the floor near his crotch, stood, and turned around to face Second. He held up all the fingers on both his hands and called out, "Ten minutes!"

The platoon repeated the call as the bird began to lower. The door gunner called out the warning at five minutes, then at last, one minute. Second rose up under the weight of their gear and grabbed on to each other or whatever was close to hand and bolted down. The Shithook hovered low to the ground and kicked up a vortex of dirt. The bird jumped lightly, then settled, and when she did, the word "*GO!*" soared above the chaos and they charged out of the Shithook into the dirty hurricane.

The soldiers fanned out as they ran and hit the ground. Shithooks landed around them, disgorging other members of The Battalion then lifted off to the sky, leaving them alone on the ground. They were in a valley, and all eyes looked to the mountain peaks surrounding them, each individual seeing shadows that could hide the man who ended his life.

Walton lay covered in a layer of fine dirt. He panted greedily through gritty teeth, out of breath from the thin air, exertion, and excitement. It was hotter there than back at Kandahar and he felt light-headed. He looked around and found his team was right beside him.

"Pick it up, Second," yelled Sergeant Cade, looking as stable as if they were just at a training exercise back at Ft. Drum, "and start pushing up!"

The platoon got on its feet then began the walk up to the peaks. The earth was covered with fine gravel and many fell in their efforts to get to the high ground. However, within ten minutes all were in position.

Walton had been expecting something akin to the Normandy invasion, or at the least an ill-tempered Hell's Angel's rally from the sound of the op-order, but instead the valley was silent as a tomb. So much for Operation: Mountain Viper. Time crawled by and though he knew he needed to keep his wits sharp, he felt complacency coming on. He looked around and noticed others letting their attention wander also, if only briefly.

The soldiers baked on the rocks for an hour, then pulled down into the valley and walked to the village. The harsh slant of the mountains tapered off into rock-walled terraces that hosted the most vegetation Walton had seen in Afghanistan outside of Shit Pond. A few lonely Hajis and their goats paused in their field labors to watch the long lines of foreign soldiers move toward their homes. Those at the front of the formation established an outer cordon around the village, letting no one in or out, and once it was sealed, others began the task of searching buildings and people.

Walton and his team spent all day laying in the prone on the outer perimeter of the city trying not to fall asleep. When the novelty of possible combat gave way to the reality that they were just making a show of force in a quiet farming village, the heat and boredom became a narcotic that blurred reality. They got lost in their thoughts, try as they might, and occasionally a head would bob over a weapon. Walton and his team kept each other awake but it required effort.

While the hours dragged on and Walton watched the same damn piece of Afghanistan in the white sun, he zoned out. BOB finally sank in the west as those tasked with searching emerged from the village and were absorbed into the cordon. When night was well under way, Second Platoon moved out on patrol.

Third Squad led the movement and Walton was glad Pace walked point. He knew he lacked the experience of Pace and despised the idea of embarrassing himself in front of the platoon. The night was dark and the moon was thin, thus dulling everything in the green light of the NOD's, and making land navigation a challenge.

Second Platoon marched through the night until they came to a rocky outcropping where they established a patrol base for a few hours rest. When the night sky took on lighter hues, Lieutenant Howard's voice broke the silence on the I-com with, "Alright, get 'em up." The platoon stood on stiff joints and finished their trek to the next village they had been tasked to search.

Initially, Walton was excited that his team would get to help conduct the search, however, he soon got over that. He felt dirty after touching the Hajis. They had no running water or anything remotely comparable to modern hygiene, and they smelled of the dirty goats that they spent their time herding. Their homes were made with thick clay and the doorways running through them were half the size of the ones in the States, requiring the soldiers to stoop under to enter.

Hours of searching took its toll, until the soldiers quit trying to stand up straight and went about with their tasks in a perpetual stoop as if the pharaohs had returned and had their asses out building pyramids on the back forty. They looked under Haji's rugs and mattresses, in the barns, and in every nook, cranny, haystack and shit-pile for weapons, ammo or incriminating paperwork.

While waiting to enter a compound, Walton made small talk with the 'terp. The conversation was politely unremarkable until Walton noticed a Haji male squat close to the ground like a frog during the lull in conversation and asked with a nod, "What's he doing?"

"He's pissing, man," the 'terp answered with his hands casually in his pockets as if everyone knew that.

Walton arched an eyebrow. "What, is he afraid he'll miss the ground?"

"No, he just doesn't want his genitals to be seen."

"Then what's that he's doin' now? From here, it looks like he's playin' with himself."

"No man, he doesn't want to touch himself because *it's* unclean. He throws a little dirt on the tip to soak up the piss, then scrapes it off with a stone."

Walton shook his head and went back to searching. Fucking Haji. Would he *ever* learn?

They finished at the village with no results and pushed off to the next one. As his body walked under the gear and heat on his way from Point A to Point B, his mind focused on the Hajis tending their vividly-colored Opium plants in their fields. His grandparents had told him stories about growing up picking cotton and working in their families' truck patches and how they had out-orneried The Great Depression in Oklahoma. (The consensus among them having been something along the lines of, "To hell with The Depression, we were here first!") He had worked in their garden as a little boy and could remember the feel of the damp dirt in his fingers and under his nails, and the release that came from pulling out a handful of the offending weeds that threatened the Good Plants, then stepping back hours later to see just how righteous that clean, well-tended earth looked.

He could see his Maw-Maw and Paw-Paw toiling out in fields like these (*sans* Opium), singing about Jesus and The Sweet-By-And-By, and wondered why Haji didn't do the same. Did Islam even have its own version of Gospel music? He figured they should. Any religion worth a damn had to have something to help sing away the blues associated with the mortal coil. If they didn't, he'd be half-tempted to get rid of his gear, go down to the Opium fields and show Haji a thing or two about some workin' in the sun. He'd go all Old School Okie on their asses. They wouldn't know whether to shit or go crazy. Their Allah would look down from Heaven and think, "Jesus! Those cheery Haji bastards are working their asses clean off." Maybe they'd even get more virgins come the Judgment Day. Though Jesus was hands-down the People's Champ, Islam had definitely found an acorn there. Motivation was important, and pussy had magnetic properties.

The march took several hours and though they got to rest by sitting in an over-watch position while others searched, Walton could tell people were beginning to break. Eyes lacked the sharpness they had just a day before, and faces were red, and lips, cracked. The soldiers shuffled rather than walked, and the weight on their backs seemed to grow heavier with each klick. They finished searching the village, then moved to the resupply point where they loaded up on water and stripped down a few MRE's (Meal Ready to Eat) apiece and stuffed the contents in their pockets for later. There was little time in the day to eat them.

That night, Walton sat watching the bit of Afghanistan in his sector and elevated his feet as best he could on the boulders of the patrol base in the rocky high ground. He was beginning to get used to the certainty that work as a team leader didn't end just because the platoon made a patrol base at the end of the day's march. He'd had to give his boys a hasty sector of fire, followed by a proper sector of fire complete with a sector sketch of the terrain, which he'd then had to push up to Sergeant Sandlin. Afterward, he had to see to their weapons, equipment, water, and food. At last came the rest plan.

He turned at the sight of Speedo out of the corner of his eye as his fellow team leader trooped the line. Speedo stopped abruptly at a soldier twenty meters away, who from the angle of his K-Pot, appeared as though he was diligently looking over the top of his rifle with his NOD's on. Walton couldn't make out the soldier's face.

Speedo set a hand on the soldier's back, causing him to flinch. "Tasker, you see those rocks out there?" he asked in a quiet but aggressive tone.

Tasker bobbed his head and replied with a quick, "Roger, Sergeant."

"That's good, Tasker." Speedo then dusted off the NCO scorn. "Because for a second there, you looked like you were fucking asleep to me!" He pointed out to Tasker's sector. "You know, Tasker, there could be some fucking Hajis hiding behind those rocks waiting for one man on the perimeter, just *one* man, to fall asleep so they can sneak up here, cut his throat, and kill the whole fucking platoon. You think about that."

As Speedo resumed his walk, Walton laughed to himself. He could almost hear Private Tasker's eyes straining with awareness.

Second Platoon moved out in the morning to secure the body bags loaded with the resupply of water and MRE's that the National Guard pilots had naturally dropped a klick away from where they were supposed to. The rest of Alpha Company linked up with them, then a few hours later they picked up, and each platoon moved to its individual objective in the mountains.

As Second climbed a steep draw, someone pointed out to the CO (who along with the Antennae Farm, had decided to accompany Second) the presence of a Haji watching them from the top of a nearby mountain. "Where's the 'terp?" the captain asked. "Have him get out the megaphone and call him down."

The bearded 'terp put the megaphone to his mouth and called out in Pashto. The Haji just stood there watching as though the platoon had dicks growing out of their foreheads. The 'terp repeated himself but drew the same response. The CO ordered a few mortar rounds lobbed over his head and Haji got the point and left.

They traveled upward for hours in a world of rocks; rocks that fell from some clumsy soldier hundreds of feet ahead walking on auto-pilot, rocks that rolled under their blistered feet as soon as boots touched them, rocks that had to be walked around or climbed over, and all seemed to reflect the hellfire and brimstone power of BOB. Soldiers began coming down as heat casualties and the medics hustled to tap veins and start IV's so they could continue the climb.

After their ascent, Walton sat behind a small boulder after giving his Joes their sectors of fire. He looked down at the valley beneath him and across it to the range of mountains that stood out in stark contrast to the powder blue sky. Lieutenant Howard said they had climbed to an elevation of over nine thousand feet above sea level. He thought the scene might be breathtaking in a rugged fashion if it hadn't been so exhausting. He fit the mouthpiece of his CamelBak tube to his cracked lips and drank down a few swallows. He heard footsteps and began to cuss preemptively.

Pace rounded a boulder and came to stand in front of him. "Hey, Walton, I need two of your Joes."

"What the fuck for?"

Though Pace had done an outstanding job of leading the squad since Sergeant Sandlin had become a heat casualty hours prior, Walton still couldn't help but be annoyed by the presence of his counterpart. He smelled more work.

"The CO wants a patrol to go up that mountain," he answered pointing to a taller, steeper mountain than the one they rested on.

Walton became livid. "What the fuck! My boys are played out, dude! We've been walkin' for days and now they want us to go scale that fucker? Fuck that!"

"They won't be *scaling* the mountain. They'll just be walking up that goat trail then getting a grid for the top," Pace said with gentle hand gestures to emphasize the ease of the mission. "That's it."

"*Riiight.*" Walton didn't believe in the existence of "that's it." He sighed and shook his head. "Alright. Fuck it. Me and Van'll go. When do we leave?"

A composite makeshift squad soon assembled of some of the able-bodied soldiers left in the platoon. Lieutenant Howard had Speedo walk point and he led them up the goat trail that wound up the face of the mountain. The trail was narrow and the soldiers spread out into a long single-file line consisting of Speedo's team of five, followed by Lieutenant Howard and the Antenna Farm of RTO's, and Pace's team of five in the rear.

Walton walked at the trail end of the formation, and by the time he began walking, the formation stopped again. Speedo's voice carried over the rocks suddenly. "I've got a man up front with a cell phone!"

Everyone in the formation loudly echoed the words, "cell phone!" and became tense with the knowledge that it was a common practice among the Taliban and Al-Qaeda to call in mortar rounds on soldiers with a cell phone. Speedo yelled again, saying, "He's got a forty-five!" They began repeating that, then he yelled on top of it, "He's got an RPG!"

Walton thought he heard Lieutenant Howard say, "Shoot the fuck!" but was uncertain because the moment changed like a light switching on in a dark room. The world convulsed, followed by small arms fire. As soon as he thought the words, *Battle Drill 1-Alpha*, Lieutenant Howard bellowed down at the frozen soldiers, "Get on line!"

Walton looked at the team in front of him and yelled, "Get the fuck up the goddamn mountain!"

Finally, he thought to himself. His very first firefight.

Rounds sounded off up the trail from Speedo's direction and from the friendly position behind them as the soldiers got on line and began bounding. They reflexively fell into the rhythm of shuffling a few steps, then setting down to cover the man next to them as they stormed up the perverse rocky incline.

Walton could hear a demand for a sit-rep from the CO over the I-com, and the LT promptly bark back at him to let him run his fight, but it was one of a thousand extraneous details saturating his awareness that he filtered out while mechanically trying to execute his responsibilities. He thought about the current rate of fire of the boys at the front of the formation and how long they could sustain it with the ammo they carried. Observing the terrain, he looked for the positions that he and each of the Joes would most likely use for cover as they advanced. Walton yelled for the private at the far edge of the team to close up his interval but to keep an eye on their flank, while he gripped his rifle like a desperate lover. From the corner of his eye, Walton saw the private comply, but he made himself focus on his sector while the shots continued to ring from the Hajis above them.

The firing suddenly stopped and plunged the world into a silence so eerie he almost wished the sound would return. The LT then ordered them to get to the top, which seemed forever-tall in an M.C. Escher's wet dream kind of fashion, because one of the Hajis had made it over and they had to get his ass before he disappeared.

Walton was retarded with exhaustion. He remembered Malone having once quoted Robert Dinero in an interview where the actor said, "If God exists, He's got some explaining to do." These words went on a repeat cycle in his brain.

Fear and fatigue played tug-of-war with his existence. His mind stumbled at the mystery surrounding the switch that had started the chain reaction of forces putting men like him and Haji in a fight with each other. He thought the man who could figure that out could rule the world.

He looked at every shadow and crack in his line of vision while keeping an eye on the friendlies. After the second false top, the LT called down to them to mark a spot near the crest with smoke rounds from their grenade launchers for the gun-ship to hit when it flew by. Walton and Pace tried several rounds of smoke from their 203's but the rounds just bounced off the stone and boulders, settling nowhere near where they wanted them to go.

While laying down and waiting for the strike to hit, he thought he'd probably cut someone's throat with his Leatherman for a re-hydration packet. They made water taste like it came from the ocean, but he couldn't imagine anything that would make him happier. He didn't want to move. He heard the gun-ship approach and imagined it shooting him by mistake and realized he didn't care and thought that knowledge should bother him. Sergeant Bronson had once told the squad back in The Boz' on the night before their first mission In-Country where they'd been ordered to seize a house allegedly used to train Al-Qaeda operatives that, "All you motherfuckers who've been wishing for a piece of the action are probably gonna get some, and I'll laugh at y'all when you do." The house had wound up being just a normal family's home (and it had disgusted the platoon to have been made to act on bad intel and come off looking like a bunch of jack-booted stormtroopers to the scared children) but that didn't stop his old squad leader's words from coming back to Walton with a handful of bone-tired enlightenment.

That night, Walton sat in his spot at the patrol base watching the mountain that had hosted the activity just hours prior. The air was cool and the stars were out in force, and there was an unusual sense of calm throughout the patrol base as he pulled guard at his position; like their cherry had been popped so the world wasn't quite as dangerous as they'd thought.

Walton knew this was a lie, though. They'd gotten off easy. The last rumor that had come down was that there were three Hajis killed in all. The word was that Dechico had zapped one in the head, Brickham had gotten one with the 240 Bravo, and the gun-ship had cut the other in half, though none of them had been eager to speak about it one way or the other. Second Platoon hadn't lost a soul.

Vantassle had walked over shortly after Walton returned from the evening debriefing and had given him a piece of hard candy. The gesture had meant the world to Walton and he thought that the enjoyment he found in the candy, after spending days being famished and dehydrated, must be what it was like to do Ecstasy or Cocaine.

While he sat on his rock nursing his candy and listening to the others swap stories of the things that had happened, he heard Pace utter the old cliché, "There's no Atheists in foxholes." From where Walton sat, God didn't seem to have a dog in the fight one way or the other. Because they had superior firepower, logistics, numbers, and tactics, they had won and the Hajis had died. If God existed, He didn't seem to figure into the equation.

Though he was proud he was with his platoon hunting the terrorists who had attacked his country, Walton felt on some level that it should have all been avoided at some beginning, whenever the hell that was. He remembered a scene from the *Mahabharata* where the god Krishna told the warrior Arjuna that the fight before him was his *dharma*—his duty—and that life was full of drama like war and conflict and that was just the way it was, so he needed to be a man, reach down and grab his nuts, and pull his

117

fucking weight. Blood made the grass grow. Walton tried to siphon some comfort off of that, but there wasn't much to be had. He soon changed his thoughts to Amy walking with a smile on her face and a bounce in her step. He imagined what it might be like to see her again. Being with her in Montreal seemed like a polar opposite universe from the one in which he found himself. He still had a hard time accepting the fact she'd been real.

The next evening, Brickham and Gonzo joined Walton as he re-took his seat near a boulder back at the patrol base. It had been another nut-buster of a day, and he felt like a bag of smashed ass.

"You guys see anything, Corporal?" Gonzo asked.

"Fuck no," Walton said wearily as he finished making old man noises while he settled. "That patrol was one spectacular of a waste of time. Ain't nothin' up yonder but BOB, rocks, and thin air. The highlight for me was seein' Carasquay talk to himself and listen to Sergeant Feran quote *Predator* the whole time. That was fuckin' awesome. He's really got that movie down.

"Sergeant Espinoza went down as a heat casualty and we were so high up they couldn't get helicopters up to him so they had to walk him down. That mountain we did today was higher than the one we had to fight up yesterday. This fucker was ninety-five hundred feet. We can put a man on the Moon, but evidently we can't make a helicopter operate in high-altitude. We were that high up. How funny is that?"

"What was the deal with you guys running up the mountain all of a sudden? Y'all took off like y'all were about Kirk-Out on someone up on that motherfucker."

"Kirk-Out? What the fuck's that?"

"You know, *Kirk-Out*; to fuck shit up like James T. Kirk on *Star Trek*. I guess they don't teach that shit in that college you went to, huh, Corporal?"

"No, Gonzo, I don't guess they do." Walton sighed

and looked at Gonzo. "Espinoza was on point and he said he saw someone at the top, so we had to get on line again and all that happy horseshit. I'll tell you what. Carasquay humped the SAW up the whole goddamn way. He's a fuckin' man." Walton topped off his CamelBak and took a long pull from it.

"And another thing," he said as he shook an angry finger for emphasis. "Those company FO's in the Antenna Farm need to learn to shut the fuck up. We were almost back here and one of those knuckleheads said he saw some stacked rocks, so the CO sent Sergeant Feran and me to check it out for mines or IED's. I bet we cleared half the goddamn nooks and crannies in this motherfucker." He took another sip and let the water sit on his cracked lips for a second. They had started bleeding again earlier. "Man, Haji can hide all the weapons he wants in this shithole. This ol' corporal's fuckin' smoked."

"That ain't no shit," Brickham agreed with a laugh while Walton aired himself out by flapping the opening of his body armor. "After having to hump the gun up this motherfucker, I'm done. I'll be pulling guard, and if I see a Haji, I'm gonna wave the motherfucker through. I'll be like, 'Go, Haji, but hey, keep it down.'"

Gonzo chuckled, and added loudly, "Hell yes! Ol' Haji could be hiding tactical nukes up in this motherfucker and I'd be like, 'Fuck it, you're good!'"

Evening fell with a violent orange sky the following night. Third Squad assembled near Sergeant Cade and the squad leaders while they went over last minute equipment checks. There was something ominous in the air, and the soldiers answered it by devotion to their weapons systems.

"You've got one of your knee pads on upside down," Sergeant Sandlin informed Walton.

Walton looked down and shrugged absently. He was too exhausted to expend the energy required to fix it. "I don't give a fuck, Sergeant."

Sergeant Bronson grinned. "Yep. He was trained by the best, alright. *Sergeant* Walton."

"Ha! I think you mean, *Corporal*. I'll believe I'm a sergeant when I see the paperwork."

Sergeant Cade tossed aside a spent cigarette. "You didn't hear? Your orders came in on the first of September. That's the day of your first firefight. That ain't some everyday shit. You should think of staying in."

Walton was deeply honored by his platoon sergeant's complementary tone, but that didn't stop him from saying, "I don't think so, Sergeant. This next summer, I plan on gettin' an apartment and being The Drunk Guy at the Pool."

"Hey Walton, come here," Sergeant Bronson said. Walton followed him a short distance away. "You know you're goin' out tonight with some reporters and shit, right? Don't let them do some shit to get you killed."

"Roger, Sergeant," Walton answered, unsure of whether to be grateful or afraid that he wasn't the only one feeling a spooky vibe.

They returned to the rest of the squad and Walton noticed that everyone seemed just as on edge as himself. He felt jittery and could see it in the eyes of others as well. The fact that it was his first night on point didn't help matters any. They didn't dwell on their darker thoughts for long, though, and the squad soon filed past Sergeant Cade at the choke point where he diligently counted every soldier that walked past him. When they returned, he would be there waiting to count them back in again.

Walton gave the hand signal for a wedge and his team spread out and passed it back. He steered them along a path that led to the back side of the mountain which they had been ordered to scout out and retrieve grid coordinates to.

He gave his suspicions full reign and stopped the formation several times to check crevices and shadows for anything out of the ordinary. He constantly tried to put his attention everywhere at once and saw something potentially lurking everywhere. After an hour, Sergeant Sandlin had Pace lead them up a hill to a cave they found to be empty. He then placed Walton back on point for their return.

As Walton neared the small point of flickering infrared light marking the patrol base, he noticed several stands of rocks stacked on top of each other. He had heard there were possible land mines around, but somehow the stacked rocks before him suddenly seemed more sinister than the ones from the day before.

A familiar silhouette began to come into focus in his NOD's. Sergeant Bronson stood a few hundred meters in front of them and waved for the formation to move left. Walton made the turn and stopped once he was back inside the perimeter and checked to see if his Joes still had all their sensitive items (issued equipment). He reported to Sergeant Sandlin who was speaking with Sergeant Bronson.

His former squad leader turned to look at him and shook his head. "You know why I was waving you off the path? 'Cause it's marked as a fuckin' minefield."

"They said somethin' about that over the net earlier," Walton said as he considered the turn of events. "When I saw those rocks it seemed too late to do anything about it but keep walkin'. And anyhow, we were almost back to the patrol base."

Sergeant Bronson wasn't finished. "That ain't all. I was up at the gun with Brick and he saw four motherfuckers up to something, coming over the hill as you guys walked around it. There's some hokey shit goin' on out here tonight."

Walton returned to his Joes who stood with the reporters in body armor. "Congratulations, gentlemen," he announced with a smile. "Y'all just successfully walked through a suspected minefield."

The soldiers and reporters looked at him blankly which only made him grin more. The photographer was the first to find his voice and asked, "Are you serious?"

"Yeah. The area is believed to be a fuckin' minefield. You know, for the kids."

The soldiers of Alpha Company burned their trash in the morning then set up into PZ (Pick-up Zone) posture. Soon the rhythm of the Shithook's rotors throbbed in the distance. At long last, the birds came into view. The hulking machines set down and the prop-wash caused a brown-out that darkened the sun and made dirt cling to eyes, noses, mouths, and every exposed bit of skin smeared with moisture. Sergeant Cade yelled, "Go!" and the platoon charged up and over the ditch they sat in, merged into files, and ran into the bird.

As they rode the flying steel back to KAF everyone looked giddy to finally be leaving. Even Lieutenant Howard had a smile.

Walton climbed to the top of the wooden range tower to get away from the platoon after he had gotten his boys re-qualified on their weapons. He liked the altitude, though it was slight, and it seemed quiet and more peaceful. He missed solitude. Having people around all the time made him feel anxious and burdened with having to perform a role to keep things going smoothly around him.

"Hey, Walton," greeted Tener around a hand-mike as Walton stepped away from the ladder. "What's up?"

"Not a goddamn thing. What's new with you, Hoss?"

"Hold on a second," Tener said as he held up his index finger then focused on listening to the mike. He then leaned over the rail of the tower and yelled, "COLD!"

All the soldiers below took up the call and ceased shooting while a familiar craft flew slowly overhead by the grace of God and a weary engine. The mail plane was on approach. The perpetual plume of black smoke billowed out of the back as it made its daily descent into KAF, and everyone watched, waiting for it to explode at any moment. Walton figured that'd be just like the fucking Army; have the shittiest plane possible fly in the only thing anyone gave a fuck about: the mail.

Tener continued listening to the hand-mike, and when the traffic stopped, he began again. "You know me, Walton, just chillin'. My Old Lady's been giving me shit about how bad our credit is. Man, my credit's so bad that places won't even take my cash. How's shit going with Third Squad?"

"Not too bad. I've got a good team and Sergeant Sandlin tries to keep the bullshit to a minimum. Pace is kinda annoying, though. Me and Brick saw him pick his nose and eat it the other day, and when Brick gave him shit about it, he denied it. What kinda motherfucker does shit like that?"

A bead of sweat began the long march down Walton's forehead. He wiped it away, and as he did he felt the grit of Afghanistan in his sweat like liquid sandpaper. He examined the residue of sweat and dirt on his hand then looked over at Tener. "Tener," he said, "I think we need to call up for more dust."

The platoon continued to fire until they burned up their allotted ammo. Afterward, the Joes policed up the brass and trash then walked back to the tents.

A week later, Second Platoon and a contingent from HQ rode Black Hawks out to the village of Kshatah Mil to conduct a VCP (Vehicle Checkpoint) in an effort to search local traffic for men on the Black List. Upon landing, the soldiers ran out into the darkness and collapsed into the prone until the birds were airborne, then they picked up and ran to their objectives along the major avenues of approach.

Third Squad set up east of the village and spent the night freezing and keeping watch while the headquarters element slept in their woobies (polypro blankets) and sleeping bags. They cursed BOB and praised him with the same breath until at last he rose, taking his time, giving only thin light at first, then bringing the heat they would later damn.

"Motherfuckers," Fuan cursed while he cast a disdainful eye at the headquarters crew as they crawled out of their fart-sacks and greeted the day. "That's some bullshit, brah."

"You're goddamn right! It is some bullshit! Hey, Sergeant, why didn't we get to sleep?"

"Just lucky, I guess, Gonzo."

Looking at Gonzo Walton felt a remnant of tension lingering from a come-to-Jesus meeting he'd recently had at the behest of Sergeant Sandlin. Gonzo had mouthed off to Sergeant Pace, and Sergeant Sandlin reiterated his position to Walton that he needed to get tougher on his Joes. As soon as the Gonzo situation blew over, Pace had called Brickham a queer, to which Brickham countered by telling Pace he was a moron. Sergeant Sandlin had interpreted the matter as a lack of *esprit de corps* between team leaders and had laid down the edict that until further notice, Pace, Brickham, and Walton would go everywhere together. Walton's suggestion of making a secret handshake instead, failed to change his mind.

Motion in the distance brought Walton back to matters at hand. "Holy shit!" he exclaimed with a nod in the direction of the rickety vehicle approaching. "It looks like the motherfuckin' Beverly Hillbillies are rollin' out for this one! This makes me think of The Dust Bowl, with my people all runnin' around tryin' to overcome adversity 'n shit." Fuan and Walton halted the vehicle while Gonzo provided security and Van searched the bearded occupant and his Haji ensemble of turban, sandals, and pajamas.

Sergeant Sandlin and Sergeant Wider walked up accompanied by the 'terp. "Ask him who he is," Sergeant Sandlin ordered the 'terp.

The 'terp began to ask questions and the Haji rambled.

"What the fuck is that guy doing, telling his life story?" Sergeant Wider jokingly asked. "I think you oughta shoot him for runnin' his mouth."

The 'terp turned back to Sergeant Sandlin and said, "His name is Mohammed. He is farmer. He goes to work his fields."

"Alright, he's good," Sergeant Sandlin answered. "Let him through." Mohammed mounted his ramshackle vehicle and drove away.

The scenario played out hundreds of times throughout the day with a variation each time. They stopped farmers, mechanics, local militia, and even several wedding parties driving tractors, trucks, and compact cars. The women were allowed to stay in the vehicles but the soldiers searched every man from head to toe.

Children gathered around and by midday a crowd had formed, ranging from the kids, to adolescents, to graybeards who sat across the road from the checkpoint. The children toyed with the soldiers at first; the same ones rode through the checkpoint over and over again on their bicycles so they could be searched, or they tried to sneak in and snatch something. Soon, some of the adults even began joining in the fun.

The soldiers made gestures for them to stay back, and complied with the doctrine of using the bare minimum of force to the letter. The Hajis took this as a game and knew within the first minute the soldiers wouldn't hurt them, and that they could get away with anything short of killing. The 'terp shook his head in disapproval and took action by throwing rocks at the offending Hajis, and making as if to give chase. They got the picture and kept a respectful distance, sitting in silence. Waiting and studying.

From children to old men, force appeared to be the coin that Haji respected above all others, and the wily bastard had a code all his own to govern its use. Empathy and understanding, and the permissiveness to which they led, eventually became weaknesses for those who held them too closely as virtues. Realizing this caused Walton see that the Third World Shitholes were strong in a way The West wasn't, and hadn't been since long before he'd been born (although he had to tip his hat to those boys from the backwoods and dirt roads. They "jest plain likes to fight," as a Civil War general had noted of those hailing from the canebrake). The West looked like a bunch of pussies next to them, having somehow made neurosis an art form.

Haji hadn't been tamed. He'd kept his traditions and culture. He'd kept his fucking *identity*. His village and his tribe meant the world to him, and he defied all comers to remain the sovereign lord over his domain. If you would have told him about things like Ricardo's Theory of Comparative Advantage, global civil society, or liberal intergovernmentalism, he'd have been pissed off for having his time wasted on such bullshit. He might have even shot you for it if he really felt like showing his nuts. (Coming from a long line of outlaws, settlers, rebels, and hillbillies, Walton had great admiration for stubbornness, and for people who cherished their roots and wanted to be left the hell alone.) Haji's people went after what they wanted and didn't apologize for it or try to saddle themselves with a bunch of self-righteous guilt or foolishness about "saving the world."

(Of course, as far as Walton was concerned, Haji and his culture were also fucked up like a soup sandwich. He was brutal, illiterate, broke as a joke, and smelled like five tons of petrified ass. Allah only knew what he did with those goats. However, he bowed to no one, and Walton begrudgingly respected him for it.)

Walton felt a kind of fear at their unapologetic ways, yet at the same time he wanted to emulate their fierce independence by ceasing to reign in the snarling things that were always there lurking below the surface and itched to call bullshit on the world; the tribal, caveman instincts within him, and the intuitive responses to the dissonance between reality itself and what people (like those in the media) merely *said* was true, the sum of which he felt he had to constantly restrain and over-compensate for by being "nice."

The more Walton saw of the world, the more he found the classical thinkers to be a damn sight more sensible than the modern eggheads who held totalitarian wishful thinking as a civil religion. Elements of the messianic illusion of *progress*; the Enlightenment-era hubris of human and institutional perfectibility, infected the entire spectrum of political, economic, and cultural thought, with every wannabe tyrant, power broker, and lackey engaging in moral extortion and trying to pawn off (or force) on the world their own version of what the Promised Land looked like. They didn't seem to realize that their shit had been done before way back yonder. Utopia was for suckers.

When he'd studied Ancient and Medieval History in college, there had been times when he had felt like he was reading about current events. Juvenal, for instance, had written things echoing what he'd learned as a boy in Sunday School or had overheard from the Old Timers pontificating at the gas station near his grandparents' house; "We are now suffering the calamities of long peace. Luxury, more deadly than any foe, has laid her hand upon us, and avenges a conquered world."

When times were hard and the world seemed to be against them, people maintained strong communities and held fast to discipline and solidarity, developing what Ibn Khaldun had called *Asabiyyah*. However, let them grow wealthy. Let them be insulated by hegemonic power and abundance. Then they'd follow after their capacity for pleasure and vanity, and the intelligentsia would justify it any damned way they could. (Walton was confident in his research methodology. At some point, he had embarked upon his own regimen of hedonism in the name of fitting in and "having fun." That something within him often protested aspects of this path was another matter.) Eventually, people in such circumstances grew addicted to novelty. As they did, they lost their edge and devolved into perfect savages. They ceased to cultivate humans. They became disconnected from the dirt. Their cities, which started as hubs to serve a growing people, metastasized into resource traps, then finally became ruins to be gawked at by tourists, and cautionary tales for any who'd stop to hear the lessons the dead had to teach about life.

Paradise was always lost, in the end.

In coming to dominate much of the planet and achieve widespread affluence on a scale never seen before, Walton thought The West had become a victim of its own success and had embraced self-castration. The rot of imperial fatigue gnawed at its core. The earth stank with it. It had taken something fundamental from its own people, and they had grown soft and decadent in the warmth of learned helplessness, making deals with whatever devil promised them everything without them ever having to pay or bleed for anything. Leaders pimped to the masses the promise of security without sacrifice and privilege without responsibility; not to their country, their neighbors, or even to themselves. So long as the words were pretty and their cage was shiny, people didn't give a damn who held the key. Western Civilization was no longer populated by the proud citizens of nations made sacred by generations of sacrifice, but by hucksters, consumers, and bullshit peddlers who had traded in their rugged birthright to hang upon a cross of modernity.

(Though Walton meditated on civilizational decay while he sweated and searched the multitude of Hajis, he had no intention of living a life without things like cold beer, hot water, modern dentistry, or pretty girls with shaved legs who smelled nice. He just thought The West needed to stop doing dumb shit. Given the merciless nature of history, though, he knew this wouldn't happen. Decadence was a part of a process that was irreversible. It would continue until newer forms of order took the reins. While the prospect of belonging to a proud civilization that prized nobler things like honor, wisdom, and beauty inspired Walton, he was bummed out that as a result of the glacial nature of such change, he wouldn't live to see the day. In the meantime, he thought he might do his part by trying to clean up his act a bit once he got out of the Army and finished traveling and sewing his quota of wild oats. He could get back to his roots. Act like he had some raising. He could build himself a cottage so far back in the woods they had to pump in daylight, and live a quiet life filled with growing things. There would be years of overalls, books, tinkering in the barn, and sitting on his porch of an evening smoking his pipe. Maybe there would be a shapely young woman who liked to laugh and sing, and wear those cotton dresses in the summer. Maybe there'd be children. In the days of decadence, tradition and improvisation could meet somewhere revolutionary.)

Second Platoon worked another VCP a few days later, this time in downtown Kandahar. The SOP remained the same; soldiers stopped traffic while others provided security and searched personnel and their vehicles. This time, though, the scale was much more daunting. They had been ordered to shut down traffic on the main artery of the second biggest city in Afghanistan.

The Afghans quickly showed themselves to lack any basic understanding of the concept of a line, and trying to get them to do so was like herding kittens. Civilizations clashed in a traffic jam. Walton stopped traffic in the eastbound lane, but in no time a vehicle from the rear broke out of queue and attempted to pass around. Walton stopped it as well, but soon a second line began behind it, and the process repeated itself until there was a row of lines going across the street, leaving him to marvel in awe at the presence of the most disorganized motherfuckers he'd ever seen.

The situation percolated even more as spectators gathered. They crowded in until they hovered near the soldiers, but scurried when pressed away. They didn't stay away for long, though, and soon had to be chased again.

The day was not without amusement, however. At one point, Walton noticed a motorcycle pull out of its place in line to turn around and begin driving away in the opposite direction. A car pulled out in front of it to do likewise, and the motorcycle crashed into it, sending the rider flying over the hood like an airborne Jawa. The angry Haji got up and traded insults with the driver, then picked up his bike and rode away. Walton almost pissed his pants laughing.

The circle of missions, training, and fighting boredom, began growing like a tumor in Second Platoon. Then one day, the hammer dropped.

"Hey, Walton, Pace; take your boys out for team training," Sergeant Sandlin ordered after PT and breakfast. November was around the corner and Afghanistan was actually cooling off. While many of the Joes welcomed the more bearable daytime temperatures, the more seasoned NCO's knew it meant that winter was coming and their monkey-asses would be out in it.

Walton stood in the middle of the training area near the junk yard, looking at his Joes in full-battle-rattle. He glanced up at BOB then shook his head as a lonely dust devil passed aimlessly by. This brought with it a moment of clarity. "Fuck this," he said. "Do y'all need any practice running and fallin' down?"

"No, I think we got that down, Sergeant," Fuan answered.

"That's what I thought. Let's go over to those conexes."

They ambled over to an area adjacent to the training grounds where empty conexes lay stacked on top of each other in long rows. They found an empty one and sat inside it and bullshitted for an hour and a half. When Walton felt that enough time had passed they walked back to the tents.

He sat down in his chair, and as he re-read the most recent letter from his parents, Pace took a knee near him and spoke lowly, "Did you take your boys out and train?"

"Of course. Why do you ask?" Following his lie, Walton ran a hand through his brown hair, enjoying the texture of it. Like most in the platoon, he had shaved it off before deploying on account of the heat, and it was finally long enough for a proper 3-2-1 fade. He liked that it made the effort to hide his beginning-to-thin scalp when it wasn't matted from his K-Pot.

"I didn't. I took my boys up to the PX and I ran into the squad leaders, Sergeant Cade, and the LT. They were fuckin' mad. Lieutenant Howard said he's gonna have a meeting later and deal with this shit. What do you think's gonna happen? Do you think they'll give us Article Fifteens?"

"Calm down, Pace. What can they do? Fire us? Smoke us? Yell at us? I wouldn't worry too much."

An hour later, Second Platoon stood in formation in front of the platoon leadership. "Take off your fucking sunglasses!" Lieutenant Howard commanded with contempt. He looked around at the platoon. "Why is it that I put out a simple order and it fails to get executed? I find Sergeant Pace at the PX. Sergeant Dobbs was at the MWR tent. I don't know where the rest of the teams were, but they sure as hell weren't at the training field."

"Sir—"

"Shut the fuck up, Pace, you're fired." The words struck like lightning. "That goes for all the team leaders. As of this moment, you're all fired." The platoon stood dumbfounded. Walton wondered if this meant that he got to be a Joe again.

"You're all complacent and I can't trust you. I'm restructuring the platoon. Sergeant Bronson, you've got First Squad, Sergeant Heslich, you've got Second, Sergeant Sandlin, Third, and Sergeant Feran, you've got the guns. Sergeant Bronson, pick your Alpha Team."

Which is how Walton wound up sitting in his chair in the new First Squad tent and holding the counseling packets of the Joes of Bravo Team: Bajez, Castor, and O'Falin. He looked around at the Alpha Team Leader, Sergeant Musen, whom he hadn't gotten to know yet, and his team consisting of Daniels and Opie. Mac and his gun team (Garno and Tasker) and Doc also shared the tent, but had to make do with a bit of space near the door.

After Walton settled in, he stepped outside to see if there was anyone to loiter with until dinner. As soon as the door closed behind him, he saw Sergeant Bronson smoking a cigarette alone. Upon seeing Walton emerge from the tent, the knowing evil grin took hold of Sergeant Bronson's face.

Sergeant Bronson ended the silence by simply saying, "Welcome home, motherfucker.

The Winter of Discontent

Sergeant Bronson kicked Musen and Walton's cots and said, "Get 'em up and get 'em packed." What followed was a tent full of soldiers trying to jump out of their asses. They loaded up their assault packs and went over weapons and equipment, replaced batteries and pressure switches, and distributed frags and smoke.

They spent two days on stand-by until they finally got the go-ahead to mount the C-130's that flew them north to Bagrum. The Brass billeted them in a large open building next to one of the D-Facs, and they practiced room-clearing drills, performed weapons maintenance, and at times stared out at the towering snow-peaked mountains that stood like titans on the horizon. The rumor going around was that they would be flying up there and running ops for a few weeks. Haji liked to do his fighting in the warm weather and hole-up in his mountain villages near Pakistan for the winter. The Battalion would be going after him.

Sergeant Bronson, Walton, and Musen sat on cots as First Squad gathered around after the op-order for NCO's. Walton had looked at Sergeant Bronson's notes as the leadership had gone over a host of unpleasant details, and found Sergeant Bronson writing down the words, *"They're going to get us all killed because they're all stupid."*

"So what's up, Sergeant?" Castor asked Walton as he approached.

Walton grinned and said, "It's the mission of the damned. Ain't none of us comin' back from this motherfucker."

"*Sarge*...I'm coming back," Sergeant Bronson announced confidently over his cup of coffee in spite of his earlier reservations. "I like my apartment, and if you're with me, you're coming back too. Sarge is all about using the Sergeant Major as a bullet-stopper. *'We need you to assault, Sergeant Bronson.'* Fuck you! Eat a dick!"

The squad leader looked around, and once he was satisfied everyone was there, he began. "Basically 2/87's been engaged up north so we're goin' there to snatch up a bunch of Taliban/Al-Qaeda leadership. It's gonna be cold and wet and we're gonna be at high altitudes. We're gonna be walkin' up mountains where the people who live there haven't seen a conventional military force since the British in 1898, except for the Australians who stayed long enough to say, 'Fuck this.'

"The people there are supposed to resemble us physically and they farm trees. To combat inter-tribal tree theft, they plant anti-personnel mines they stole. To hear those Brainiacs at the op-order talk, be prepared to see every weapon known to man in the past hundred years.

"Supposedly, this is the biggest thing since Haiti. They got SEALs, Rangers, Delta…Carasquay thinks they might even have *Star Trek* gettin' in on this motherfucker. Check it out though; these people wear flip-flops and burn poop for God's sake. Don't get all freaked out by this shit."

While Sergeant Bronson explained the details of the upcoming operation, Walton thought about what the First Sergeant had said to the NCO's at the end of the op-order; "This mission is one hundred percent planned by officers, but it will be one hundred percent fought by our soldiers, and it will be one hundred percent led by us. This is the biggest event I've ever seen. The benefits of the success of this mission are immeasurable, just as the consequences of failure are immeasurable. If we must lose a man, let it be from something we couldn't control."

Later, Walton tried to quit staring at the ceiling and get some sleep, but it was slow in coming. The smells and sounds of hundreds of sleeping soldiers packed into one building filled his senses and gave him comfort in the fact that they were all still alive.

He thought of his home and family in the same way he used to pray when he was a little boy and summoned the faces of all those he loved. He wondered how they were and what it might be like to see them again.

As his mind wandered down the path that led to sleep, a thought touched his brain like a bitter aftertaste on his tongue. It had been months since he had written to Amy.

She must've forgotten about him. Or maybe it had all just been an act. Getting men to believe in the fantasy of the spell she cast over them was how she made her living. She had probably just been humoring him as a lonely soldier far from home whom she had taken pity on like a lost dog. She was no doubt cervix-deep in the fun and excitement of being a part-time professional object of desire/full-time force of nature. Or maybe she and The Vegetarian had worked things out. The last thing he felt before sleep embraced him was loneliness.

Alpha Company flew out with the rest of The Battalion the next evening to land near a village held by 2/87 who jeered at them under their breath because The Battalion had flown out in Shithooks like a bunch of fucking champions while 2/87 had ridden trucks. The Battalion picked up and split off into companies and platoons who spent the next few days walking blisters into their feet, burning in the sun, and shivering in the dark.

It rained the second night out and Dominican Lou spent his twentieth birthday under a damp poncho hooch freezing with the rest of the platoon. He quietly sang *Happy Birthday* to himself and Walton thought it was one of the most hysterical and simultaneously sad things he'd ever seen. An Uber-Joe with a golden soul like Dominican Lou deserved a pile of pussy and all the Johnny Walker and steak he could handle, and Walton wished he could've provided it for his Joe's special day.

Walton was on point and not sure what to do about it. Sergeant Cade and Lieutenant Howard had positioned

First Squad at the head of the formation and Sergeant Bronson had put Walton up front. He was glad to be getting more experience, but he was still nervous about fucking up. Sergeant Bronson was right behind him, though, and the two scaled rocks all day like lizards, looking for accessible routes for the rest of the formation.

Though he wouldn't admit it to anyone, the more Walton was on point, the more he found that he liked it. With the distractions of the modern world replaced by the possibility of violent death with every step, he felt like the hours of vigilance and anticipation (and fear) he spent up front sharpened something in him. Ancient instincts lying dormant perhaps. Being on the hunt with his tribe…there was a *rightness* to it all that appealed to some fundamental aspect of his masculinity in a way which he found both thrilling and liberating.

The Bad Man, however, was still at work. During a patrol break, Walton set his assault pack down with the intention of resting against it. The assault pack was having none of it, and immediately began to roll down the steep hill as soon as Walton turned his back on it. It started slowly at first, and Walton scrambled after it with his arms outstretched, yelling, "NOOO!"

The assault pack sensed his desperation and picked up speed. It bounded from one rock to another. Walton could only watch impotently until it settled on the ground below. He stood there looking down at it for a second, feeling disgusted and betrayed. He cast his eyes toward the heavens and silently shook his fist.

"That was fucked up, Sergeant."

Walton turned to look at Lou sitting at his position next to a boulder with the SAW. He had seen the whole thing. "Yeah, Lou. That was fucked up. I'll be right back. Shit." He sighed and walked down the hill under the eyes of his Joes and some Haji kids sitting on their roofs in the distance. He figured that was about par for the course.

When at the bottom, Walton half-heartedly kicked his assault pack for being a dick, and then put it back on. He looked up the steep hill and went through a litany of profanity. He spent five minutes climbing up to be greeted by laughter, cheers, and clapping from his Joes.

He smelled cigarette smoke and turned around to find Sergeant Bronson grinning. He asked, "Are you sure you want to get out, Tom?"

Walton gave him a dirty look.

Second Platoon picked up shortly thereafter and resumed their march. Their path gradually narrowed to goat trail on top of an irrigation dyke that hugged close to the mountainside. Sergeant Dobbs lost his footing, fell, and broke his ankle. The platoon shifted gears and retrieved him, loaded him onto a skedco, and carried him through the broken terrain to ground open enough to facilitate the medivac bird.

They spent the better part of the next day walking eight klicks then halted. Lieutenant Howard walked up to Sergeant Bronson and pointed to the highest peak in a nearby ridge commanding the view over a river. It stood like a giant among the high ground, ugly and raw, carved and broken with sharp angles that bred shadows which devoured light; a natural monument built not to the handiwork of God, but the Devil. As he pointed up to it he said, "We've got to set in an over-watch up there."

Sergeant Bronson strained to look up at the peak, shading his eyes with his hand. He turned to look at Lieutenant Howard angrily. "You've gotta be fuckin' kiddin' me, Sir."

"No, Sergeant, I'm not. Your squad, the team leaders with the 203's, and the gun teams are going up there."

"That's some bullshit, Sir! Charlie Company's already puttin' soldiers up there, and it's almost night. Those boys are gonna get fucked up tryin' to climb that shit in the dark."

"Then you'd better hurry."

Sergeant Bronson grit his teeth. "Musen, Walton! Get 'em the fuck up and get your asses on the road!"

The trek up began with a bridge made of rope and ancient wooden slats. It swayed slightly from a faint breeze and the skittish soldiers crossed it one at a time. There were more gaps than boards, like the broken teeth of a homeless man, and with each soldier the bridge-contraption moaned with agony, causing Walton to wish he could get the go-ahead to shoot it and put the poor thing out of its misery.

At the end of the far side of the rope bridge, rough-hewn blocks wound up the mountain like stairs and within the first five minutes of the climb, the mountain staircase earned the name Stairway to Hell. The soldiers paused occasionally to give a moment of rest to leg and back muscles that ached with fire. Lieutenant Howard's voice blared out of the I-com every few minutes to tell them to hurry. (Walton turned his off.)

As a lone Haji scampered past them on his way to his home near the top, Walton observed, "That's one anti-social motherfucker to live up on top of a place like this." He wiped the sweat away from his forehead with the back of the beat-up black flight glove on his non-firing hand. The other never left his pistol grip.

"Haj ain't fuckin' around, that's for goddamn sure," Sergeant Bronson said after taking a sip from the mouthpiece of his CamelBak, and stretched. "I'll say this for him. He's a hard motherfucker. What gets me, is think about the effort these motherfuckers put into building some shit like this, and they still ain't figured out running water yet." He looked at Walton questioningly, then they both shrugged and began again.

They caught up with the stragglers from Charlie Company and pushed past them to the peak. After negotiating with the owner of a house there, Lieutenant

Howard placed the soldiers on the edge of a cliff overlooking the valley. The LT was giddy at the advantage the over-watch gave them, and his pride at what they had accomplished infected the soldiers.

Cold came with the darkness, but the LT and Sergeant Bronson started a small fire that flickered below the over-watch, concealed by the house and the surrounding wall of its tiny courtyard. The soldiers greedily lay around it when they were allowed to sleep, while those on guard watched the valley and waited for someone to kill as they huddled together to try to keep from freezing. As they pulled security, they passed the time by talking quietly to one another about the lives they'd live when they were back in the real world.

The night passed peacefully, and in the morning many were angry that they had gone through the effort of climbing to the top and hadn't even had the chance to shoot at anyone. They climbed down as the sun rose and continued their movement until they arrived at the company patrol base located near the river.

As they arrived, the I-com opened up with Sergeant Wider's voice saying to his fellow former Marine, "Happy Birthday, Jarhead."

"Yeah, it was the best fuckin' one yet," Sergeant Bronson replied dryly.

Sergeant Wider laughed over the net. "You know, on the Marine Corp Birthday you're either fucked up drunk, passed out in a gutter, or sitting on a mountain freezing your ass off."

"That ain't no shit, brother."

Sergeant Bronson replaced his I-com back into its pouch, then looked at Walton and ordered, "Come with me." Walton followed him until Sergeant Bronson halted at a bend in the river. He pointed nearby, saying, "I need you to build a rock bridge right here."

Walton looked at the current and furrowed his brow

with a muted but heartfelt, "Fuck. Roger, Sergeant." He glanced upriver hopefully. "Do you think I should push upriver some and try to find a shallower spot?"

"No. Build it here. We're gonna use it to get to the PZ either today or tomorrow. I'll get you some men."

The detail began trickling in and Walton started them on a human chain to carry the heavy rocks to the river. The current swept the stones away, so Walton waded into it to make sure they were seated properly. Brickham joined him, and after forty-five minutes the two stood shoulder to shoulder in the water as they set rocks in place like bricks. Walton slipped while pushing toward the middle of the river, the current protesting their efforts by carrying off the basketball-sized rock in his hands. The chill of the water took the air from his lungs, forcing him to fight to breathe until he righted himself. Others joined in the attempt but it became apparent it would take a long time to make a bridge suitable for the company to walk over. They continued building.

The First Sergeant came to stand on the bank and watched them work in the frigid waist-deep water. He shook his head and called out, "That's enough. Stop what you're doing. We'll find another way. No sense in drowning to build a fucking rock bridge."

Brickham and Walton splashed out of the water, soaking wet with chattering teeth. Dechico stood by the bank, and when the two neared, he nodded his head in approval and said with a grin, "Proper."

BOB soon clocked out for the day and night passed quietly save for the occasional rip of sound from Specter gun-ships opening up on enemy personnel five klicks away. Walton looked up at the stars that sparkled above the river, rocks, and sleeping soldiers, and smiled at the sound. He wasn't sure what the gun-ships were shooting with, but whatever they were using made them sound like what he imagined dinosaurs would have and he pondered at how a sound can mean death for some and comfort for others. The world was wild and she would not be tamed.

"Here, Tom, have some coffee," Sergeant Bronson offered in the morning as he approached Walton's position.

"Thanks," Walton said as he smiled at the gesture. He took a sip and handed it back.

Sergeant Bronson sat down on a rock, taking the cup back, and had a drink. "How's your shit?"

Walton nodded at his drying clothes laid out upon the ground. "They're still damp, but serviceable. I did burn a hole in the crotch of my pants, though, when I was drying them on the burn pit. So I'll be sportin' polypro pants underneath to keep my junk civil till we get back to Bagrum."

"Well, it'll dry when BOB gets his shit together," Sergeant Bronson said as he appraised the gray dawn. He then looked over at Walton, who sat with matted hair and a dirty face in his wet weather pants and jacket, and wrapped up in his woobie. Sergeant Bronson shook his head with a grin. "I wonder what your mama would have to say about you now."

"Best she don't know. She don't exactly cotton to the idea of her boys falling into these sort of circumstances. Still, it's kinda fun, though."

The squad leader handed the metal canteen cup back to Walton. "You know, you oughta meet my wife one of these days. Compared to her, I'm a saint."

"That'd be a trip," Walton said as he held the warm cup. "I have a tough time imagining you domesticated. Lou said it looks funny on ya."

"You'd be surprised. I'm actually pretty mellow around her. I really don't even drink around her."

Walton tried to picture the salty bastard who had been his mentor for over three years in a quasi-normal home life, but had a hard time doing so. However, he figured if

141

anyone deserved a happy home, it was him. "So what's the story on us leavin'? Is that still happening today?"

"No. Did you hear that shit last night? Well, the motherfuckers who've been runnin' from us for the past sixty-five klicks ran into a blocking position held by the Secret Squirrels or some shit. Haji didn't do so hot last night."

"Well, fuck him," Walton said with a shrug. "I reckon he had it coming."

"Yeah. You know what's funny? Sandlin and Feran gotta go back up Stairway to Hell. That's fuckin' awesome. You know, when we get back to KAF, I'm gonna eat five bowls of ramen and sleep for two days."

Alpha Company picked up the next day and walked to the PZ. Within a few hours the Shithooks extracted them and carried them to Jallalabad where they performed weapons maintenance, shat and beat off in the porta-johns, and napped under the shade of makeshift tents consisting of their DCU tops hanging from the muzzle of their rifles. The leadership even turned a blind-eye to the Joes as they rat-fucked the more choice selections of MRE's, provided they rendered up tribute to their team and squad leaders. Once the priorities of work were finished, they rested away the hours waiting in the sun until other birds took them back to Bagrum.

"Goddamn, you fucks bought a lot of CD's," Walton said the next day as he sat down on his cot after making a hot chocolate run to the on-Post coffee shop. Lou sprawled out on the cot next to him and two PFC's, Percy and Shipley, sat on the ones across the aisle divvying up a stack of CD's between them.

Percy gave a big, blonde, ear-to-ear grin. "Guess how much they cost? Nothing! That's why I go nowhere without my black man." He rubbed Shipley's head affectionately like a genie's lamp.

"Look here, I could die tomorrow for a country that's

142

fucked me my whole life. Do you think I'm gonna pay for some AAFES shit, here of all places? Oh hell no," Shipley said as he waved a hand in a dismissive gesture.

Lou opened an eye and looked at them. "You know, my dad always used to say, 'When you're making something, you need to add something stolen, no matter how small. It adds something extra.'"

"See? Goddamn Dominican Lou understands."

Walton looked at them with a tired humor. He didn't approve of them lifting stuff from the PX, but he didn't want to narc them out to their team leader. Anyhow, apart from capers of petty larceny, they were outstanding Joes in the field, and that was what mattered. "Whatever. If you fuckers get caught, though, that's on y'all's ass." He did a double-take. "Wait a minute. We got a Jew, a black guy, a Dominican, and a white guy. I'd say we've got the makings of a very fine joke."

"Almost got him!"

"What the fuck?" Walton turned toward the commotion and saw Dechico chase after a mouse with single-minded intensity.

Sergeant Bronson looked up from an issue of *Perfect 10* that was making the rounds as he lay on his cot. He barked, "Dechico come here!" Dechico drew near sheepishly and Sergeant Bronson stared at him. He then rolled up his magazine, sat up, and swatted the Joe's head with it. "Don't be fuckin' around with that mouse! You might jinx us and fuck up our karma. Maybe we'll all get captured and get treated like that. Now sit the fuck down."

"Don't worry about jinxing us, Dechico," Sergeant Sandlin countered with grin. "It's called the food chain, bitch. If you don't like it, get the fuck out!"

The Shithook bucked wildly as the pilot tried to steer her close to the top of the terraced hill, days later. The steep angle of the terrain made landing the helicopter impossible, and those closest to the ramp watched the tip

143

of the rear propeller nick into the terraces. Second Platoon stood looking out the back, poised and waiting on the word. The bird settled in mid-air for a second, and at the command of the door gunner, the soldiers jumped out of the back, hit the ground, and pushed down the terrace to make room for the next falling Joe. Within fifteen minutes, LZ Goose was riddled with three-man positions pulling security all around it.

As night fell, Sergeant Bronson climbed up the terraced hillside to the position he shared with Walton and Sergeant Feran. "Hey, y'all want to hear something funny? First Platoon got dropped up in the snow line."

Sergeant Feran laughed. "Yeah, well, they're all hardcore. A little snow ain't shit to them." Sergeant Feran was a soldier from the state of Washington, and he had transferred to their unit prior to the deployment. His curmudgeonly disposition caused him to assimilate easily into Second Platoon.

"You know what kills me?" Sergeant Bronson asked rhetorically, "They spend all this money to fly us out here to get this fuck, *Faqirullah*, or whatever the fuck his name is, and they just set us outside the village and have us wait. Now you tell me; if you're a motherfuckin' terrorist mastermind or some shit, and the Army drops a battalion of motherfuckers a klick away from your home, and they just sit there, what the fuck are you gonna do? You're gonna pop some motherfuckin' smoke that's what."

Sergeant Bronson took out a cigarette from the pack in his plastic travel soap carrier, lit it, shook his head, and mumbled over it. "We're gonna spend the night freezin' up here, then tomorrow we're gonna go down there and search and not find shit, when we should start combing that bitch *right now* to find his monkey-ass." He removed his K-Pot and scratched his head.

Night dragged on in an effort not to die. The cold bit through the thin part of the sleeping bag they'd been allowed to bring, and the heat of a few months ago seemed like a dream. Walton walked a circuit around his position to keep his feet warm and imagined what he'd do when he was back in the States and out of the Army. He sang songs in his head until his turn at guard ended. He approached Sergeant Bronson, and as he prepared to wake him, he heard his voice say, "I'm up, Tom."

"Roger, Sergeant," Walton replied, then began getting ready to rack out.

Sergeant Bronson sat up in his own bag with a sincere, "Fuck this bullshit," and put in a fresh Combat-Dip of Copenhagen.

"Sergeant, I like to think you and I are reasonably intelligent men," Walton grumbled from inside his sleeping bag. "Yet, here we all are, on a mountain, freezing, and about to search a place for people we know are gone. All because someone said so. We should all be rulin' the world, not freezing here."

"Just remember this when you're out," Sergeant Bronson's disembodied voice said in a hushed tone as he could be heard getting up. "I'll tell you one thing. You'll appreciate shit like showers and beds a whole lot more."

Walton lay on the ground and shivered like a dog shitting peach seeds. He didn't think he'd been this cold in a long time. Winter in The Boz' had been bad too, but in a different way. Old Second Platoon had often been out in it, and during one particular road march, Walton had been so mad at the world over the situation that the anger behind his thousand-yard stare had drawn the attention of Oversnach. After a brief discussion concerning their miserable circumstances, the tattooed soldier, who had walked next to Walton like red-headed Zen in a set of BDU's or the Tao with a rucksack, had laughed amiably and said, "Your convictions are honorable. Put down the stone."

That was what he needed to do; put down the stone.

Walton tried to quiet his mind by breathing deeply, but the effort never lasted long and soon gave way to his imagination.

Life would be a lot easier if it were a ZZ Top video, he thought to himself. The Bearded Ones (and the mustached drummer) would magically appear on the frigid hill in bum-fuck Afghanistan and give him the keys to a funky red hot rod with three chicks in it. Music would ensue. He'd drive away a hero with his tarts to a sexy-assed world of classic rock and sunny beaches. There he would dwell in a magnificent thatched hut that came with clean white sheets on a big damn bed and bright-eyed naked girls smiling and squirming all over each other. With Amy thrown smack dab in the middle of them all just for good measure. Maybe he'd even get one of those cool guitars that spun around. When he was out of the Army, maybe he'd grow himself a righteous, patriarchal beard...

Sergeant Feran nudged him two hours later. "Hey Tom, it's time for your shift. Say, Mulane's over at the next position and he just told me a joke; what's the difference between Michael Jackson and acne? Acne doesn't come on a boy's face till he's thirteen."

The Battalion converged on the hillside village of Aranus before dawn and they began a systematic search. Men were separated, then searched and questioned by the male soldiers while a small group of female MP's searched the women. They spent the day walking up and down the mountain and talking to one Haji after another. All told the same story; Faqirullah was gone.

After the day's activity, Walton sat with Bravo Team on the roof of a building pulling security down into the valley below, and eating handfuls of Haji bread that the leadership purchased off the locals. He rolled around in his mind the memory of the first building he'd searched in the tilted village that clung tentatively to the mountain. The sprawling home was said to have been Faqirulla's.

Walton had stood at the front of a stack with his team behind him and pushed through the open front door into a long hallway lined with doors and crannies. As they'd begun their search, a part of his mind had been wound up with fear, wondering when they would find a bearded man with a rifle in his hand, hiding behind something and waiting to take as many soldiers with him as he could.

Though most of the rooms had been accessible, there had been a few that had been locked, and Walton had needed to kick them open. He found that he liked kicking them open, and it had soon taken on the form of secret addiction. He'd savored the feeling of exerting himself over the object and the sensation of it snapping open under his boot, then flowing into a room the instant the door yielded to him, right into the face of what could be death; either for him or the men they hunted. There was nothing like it.

As Walton had left the empty compound, he had mused that he may have just walked through the home and touched the things of a terrorist. When darkness came, First Squad led the long line of tired soldiers back across the river and up the hundreds of thigh-high terraces to the sprawling battalion-sized patrol base.

They crossed back over the river in the morning, through the maze of the village and along the mountainside to the PZ six klicks away. Walton passed a team from Bravo Company as they left the perimeter and when he heard the song they sang and clapped to, he laughed loudly and made it his mantra for the march.

Allah, Allah, you're so fine,
You're so fine you blow my mind,
Hey, Allah! Hey Allah!

Back at Post, Sergeant Bronson gave the order, "Get them to fuckin' chow," and Musen and Walton sent their soldiers to the D-Fac. The servers had almost broken down lunch, but they remained open for the returning soldiers who hadn't found their quarry.

The squad moved in like a pack of dirty cavemen and hunched over their trays, raising their eyes only to unapologetically eye-fuck the two female soldiers who still sat drinking coffee. The women were with a male POG who looked uncomfortable near the disheveled, smelly soldiers. The POG had correction on his tongue but he thought better than to say anything and they soon left.

Upon returning to KAF a few days later, there was little in the way of downtime. Between the ammo layout, the power failure, running laps around The Wire, and the platoon being stuck on QRF again, Walton toyed with the idea of ending it all in a hail of gunfire with The Bad Man's minions like Butch and Sundance or throwing himself in front of one of the Shit Trucks that trolled the porta-johns on Post. His most recent annoyance was to be tasked with giving the Joes a class on the M4. As he sat listening to Waylon Jennings and thumbing through the M4 manual, he missed being drunk.

Sergeant Cade suddenly stuck his head in the tent and yelled, *"Irene!"* The squad cussed collectively and got on their gear, swearing that Sergeant Cade needed to stop watching *Black Hawk Down*.

"Musen, Walton, get 'em over here," Sergeant Bronson ordered after an eastbound Shithook ride. The two walked off in separate directions and returned with their soldiers. "Look, gentlemen, some fucked up shit went down here. When we go up that hill and secure the site, I don't want to hear any snivelin' or cryin'. You need to reach down, grab your nuts, be a fuckin' man, and do your job. Understood? Walton, take your boys up front. Musen, you got trail."

Walton left the patrol base and his team automatically broke into a wedge behind him. They continued on for a few hundred meters, then tightened into a file as they entered the village. He led them across an irrigation ditch and walked onto the main road of the village where the inhabitants sat on walls and in the dirt with their nerve-wracking blank facial expressions as they divided their attention between the soldiers and the reason the camouflaged men had come.

Walton scanned his sector as he walked, but his eyes kept returning to the bright collection of reds, blues, and greens that lay on the ground in silent conflict with the drab colors of the world around them. Small round shapes bulged under the vivid blankets with an occasional smear of blood striking out from under them. He wondered why the sight didn't bother him.

He continued walking past the veiled gore of the scene, and at the pock-marked building across the road from a collection of silent Hajis, Walton halted. He set his team in positions around the road and the rest of the platoon completed the cordon.

"Some fucked up shit went down, here," Sergeant Bronson said again as he joined Walton after spending twenty minutes with the leadership while they questioned locals. "Some pilot bitch was flying an A10 and opened up on some guy on a motorcycle from a mile away who was supposed to be Taliban. The guy got away but she shot one man, a teenager, seven little boys, and one little girl by accident. Sandlin looked under the blankets and said one of the kids had been cut in half."

"Damn," Walton said, thinking there should be something better to say.

"Yeah. Fuck it. Anyhow, the village elders said the guy's gone, but they've seen him armed and know his house is right there. You and Musen are gonna take your boys and search it while they get some CSI motherfuckers to look at the bodies."

First Squad spent the next hour rifling through the owner's belongings. They found several AK47's, ammo, frags, RPG rockets, and even a novelty photo of the owner with Osama Bin Laden. Once they finished, they searched it again then joined the platoon in searching the rest of the village. They worked into the depths of night.

"Hey, Sergeant, check this out," Dominican Lou called out from across the darkened storage shed.

"What is it, Lou?" Walton asked as he drew near the white glow of the soldier's small Maglite.

Lou flashed the light at a wooden box, and said in a conspiratorial tone, "There's a bunch of money and shit!"

Walton observed the wad of out-of-date Afghan bills for a long moment. "Looks like Haji Monopoly money."

"Can I take some, Sergeant?"

Lou's toothy white grin made Walton think of the Cheshire Cat. "Motherfucker, I already let you snatch a set of brass knuckles."

"I know, Sergeant. I can't help it. I like to steal."

Walton frowned in thoughts ending with the words, *Fuck it.* "Alright, Lou, but just take a small bill. And get me one too."

They exited the shack and Walton noticed Private Tasker walking into a building to help a team search. He was struck by how much the young soldier looked like a little boy, and it reminded him of his youngest brother back home. The sight of Tasker, appearing so out of place under all his weapons and equipment as he walked among the dead children, made Walton feel hollow until anger seeped out, making, *"I fuckin' hate Afghanistan,"* the words he'd go to sleep to.

"Man, I'm getting fucking tired of running all the time. I'd like to put on some mass," Brickham said over his breakfast.

"I've been sayin' that for years now," Walton replied.

He looked down at his skinny frame and felt the embarrassment he'd carried in his pocket since he couldn't remember when. He looked at the others in the D-Fac and was willing to bet he could tell which ones were infantry and which ones weren't; POG's being the ones with the time to go to the gym. He shook his head, wondering when they had all become a bunch of goddamn twelve-year-old girls. "Still, I'd rather do sprints than run all over the fuckin' Post like we did when we first got here. You know, I'm really proud of Lou. He has a tough time with this shit, but he keeps pluggin' away. You don't hear about that shit in the States, though."

Brickham scraped the bottom of his bowl of instant oatmeal and gestured with his spoon. "Did you see Lou's latest issue of *Playboy*? They had motherfuckin' Kato Kaylen sitting around and chatting at the goddamn Playboy Mansion. What the fuck did *he* do? Meanwhile, we run all over Afghanistan and our water smells like poop. What the fuck?"

Walton laughed and tossed his napkin onto his tray. "Fuck it. I just keep remindin' myself I got less than six months left. Unless they put a Stop-Movement down on us, I'll be back in the real world in February. Provided of course, I don't get shot in the face."

"Yeah, good luck with that. Are Dechico and Dobbs still going back?"

"Last I heard they were. How's shit back on the homestead?"

Brickham shrugged. "It's alright I guess. My wife might be going to Iraq and that pisses me the fuck off. Having my wife in a combat zone...God! But the rest of the familiy's okay. It's definitely another world, though. I got a letter from some people at my parents' church who said, 'Wow, when you get back from Afghanistan you must have all kinds of neat stories.' What the fuck? I can just see me having milk and cookies with these people saying shit

151

like, 'Oh yeah, we went to this one shithole where we fucked this one guy up with the gun and my buddy put one in another guy's fuckin' nugget.' Those people back home are living in a whole other fucking world."

In the quiet pause that followed, Walton suddenly overheard a bit of a conversation between Percy and Gypsy (AKA: Specialist Gedespie from Second Squad) who sat nearby. They were discussing an alleged rape case in California, and according to them, a woman had gone up to a man's room, had sex with him, and then later falsely accused him of rape.

The twenty-one-year-old, one hundred and fifty pound Gypsy remarked dispassionately, "That is why the only safe sex you can have is with a prostitute."

Percy laughed so hard at his statement that it sounded like he might have a seizure. When he could finally breathe again he declared, "She's a scandalous bitch and should be shot in the face!"

A girl in a pilot's uniform walked by, and Walton tastefully eye-fucked her with a smile until she passed from view.

He and Brickham soon left the D-Fac tent, and after throwing out their trash, they ran into Heinz and Ericks. At the sight of them, Walton grinned and asked, "What's up fellas?"

"I think I'm losing it, Sergeant," Heinz answered. "I need to be able to go to the gym on my own. The only time I get to go is when the fucking POG's are there, and they just stand around at the weights and fucking talk."

"I like it when chicks work on the medicine ball because I imagine I'm behind them and having sex with them," Ericks said in his clipped, collegiate manner.

Heinz turned to look at him angrily. "What the fuck did I tell you about using proper English 'n shit?"

"Oh, I'm sorry," Ericks replied, then began moving his hips back and forth with his hands out in front of him. "I meant, 'I imagine I'm fucking them in the ass.'"

"That's better." Heinz lowered his eyes, looking dejected. "I think I'm losing my will to live. I don't even beat off any more."

Walton slapped him lightly in the face then pointed his finger at the soldier in mock umbrage. "I don't ever want to hear those words come out of your mouth again! Ever! You're a goddamned infantry soldier! You need to beat off *at least* once a day whether you need to or not. That's probably your fuckin' problem."

"Remember this: rich whores are always lookin' for someone to use to piss off their daddy," Sergeant Bronson sagely advised while a contingent of Second Platoon watched a bootleg copy of the Paris Hilton sex tape during a game of *Axis and Allies*.

As Tasker positioned his armies in Africa, Sergeant Feran turned to Percy (who eyed the bank), and said to the soldier, "Percy, if I catch you extorting money, I'm gonna take you outside and set you on fire!"

While Percy convulsed with laughter, Dechico shook his head. "What the fuck is with that laugh? You should have heard this fucking guy when the safety inspector checked out the tent and told Sergeant Bronson we'd have to move the water resupply away from the back door because it was a fire hazard. Sergeant Bronson told the guy, 'You know we're in a tent, right? We have the technology to cut ourselves out if we have to.' It took forever to shut this kid up after that."

"Hey! I've been told I have a very endearing laugh."

"That's right, Percy, you keep your head up," Brickham encouraged. "Women like a guy that can laugh." He looked over at Dechico. "Why aren't you playing with us, you dirty Wop? It'll expand your mind."

"I already expanded my mind. It's called Ecstasy."

"That green shit makes me feel like I'm watching this

with my NOD's," Castor remarked as he viewed the boudoir grappling on the TV. A mischievous impulse then noticeably seized him. He tilted his head toward Doc, who sat next to him, and announced loudly, "Everybody knows Puerto Ricans are the fucking shit-bags of the Hispanic race!"

Doc's eyes widened theatrically. As a Puerto Rican, to get shit from a California Latino was more than he could bear. He took Castor's bait and thus reignited the latest front in the never-ending ethnic ass-grabbery. Doc demanded satisfaction on behalf of his people. "No way! Sexy Ricans are head and shoulders above you peasant Spics!" A tirade of Spanish ensued.

Gonzo looked up thoughtfully from his boys in China. "You ever notice how there aren't any horses around? Rambo must've killed all the horses in Afghanistan. I haven't seen any. If they do, they're probably like those cows in the villages. All emancipated and shit."

Walton almost shat from laughing. "You mean *emaciated*. That'd be like Lincoln issuin' the Emaciation Proclamation, and all those kids in Ethiopia with flies on their faces bein' emancipated."

Tasker paused from deploying his forces to ruminate over the issues at hand. "Dude, if we had horses I'd have them carry all my AG gear and 240 ammo. I'd be like, 'Thank God!'"

Sergeant Bronson directed his attention to the Cherry. The younger soldiers had taken to calling the squad leader *Psycho Dad* at times and Walton had the impression that he secretly relished playing the role of the paterfamilias. "Tasker, there is no God. The sooner you get that through your fuckin' head, the better off you'll be. Percy, where was God for your people sixty years ago?"

"Tasker, we so have to hook you up with The Yeti when we get back," Dechico added while watching Miss Hilton with a bored expression. He finally lost it and yelled, "God, I miss pussy!"

Sergeant Bronson turned next to the Italian. "Y'all don't hook him up with a fat chick his first time out, Ginny. You'll scare him of pussy. A word of advice, though, gentlemen; don't try to get some ass your first night back. You'll just embarrass yourself. Feel on some titties, eat some pussy, then go to bed."

As the game wore on, Walton watched his platoon laugh and tease each other with the openness reserved for siblings. He could not imagine such camaraderie and freedom of discourse among as disparate a group in the civilian world. The PC Thought Police would have denounced them on national TV for "hate speech" and tossed them in the gulag until someone apologized and kissed the ring of whatever community had been offended. Then there would be the smug entreaties about the need to "open up a dialogue," and to "have an honest discussion in this country" about whatever was the fill-in-the-blank media-driven cause of the moment, or some other bit of cockamamie horseshit from the progressivist totalitarian field manual. If it was really significant, they'd even get a bunch of ornamental people to weigh in on the twenty-four hour news networks to help "raise awareness."

Walton thought about his ETS date with bitter sweetness. He was going to miss these fuckers.

When it ended, Walton returned the DVD to the Second Squad tent. As he passed Sergeant Feran on his way out, he wished him a Merry Christmas. His holiday greeting was returned by the NCO who promptly yelled, "Yeah, ho, ho, ho. Go spread some Christmas Cheer, ya fuck!"

The Trouble With Haji

Walton sat in the back of a truck as the small convoy lurched through the ferocious dust storm just outside Kandahar. He readjusted his dust scarf to keep from getting The Dirt Lung and dwelled on the day before.

Second Platoon had returned to their tents after a few days of running patrols and VCP's to find their mail waiting on their bunks. On his cot was a package from Amy Dauphin of Toronto. Seeing her feminine handwriting on the box had made him feel like he'd been shot. But in a good way.

He'd opened it to find a novel by a Canadian author and a letter explaining that she'd had enough of The Vegetarian's philandering and had left him. (Amy had written that with the help of one of her stripper friends, she'd loaded up all of her worldly possessions and had attempted to just disappear. She'd almost gotten away with it, but The Vegetarian had arrived just before she'd handed in her key, thus foiling her plan and prompting a five-day break-up. While the prospect of a couple of petite off-duty strippers, no doubt wearing faded cut-offs and white tank-tops, glistening with sweat, and carrying boxes of books down the stairs had made for an amusing mental image for Walton, there was something about her attempted Vegetarian Escape Gambit that bothered him. He was happy The Vegetarian was no longer an obstacle in his campaign, but the stealth of it, and the premeditation and passive-aggressiveness of the act, had left him with a feeling that disturbed him in a way he couldn't define.) She'd quit stripping (praise Jesus!) and had gone back home to come of the Stripper Closet and mend fences with her family. She was considering going on a trip to India and Thailand with some friends, and had extended an invitation for him to join her. She'd also sent her email address and told him to write. He hadn't been the same since.

By the time the dust storm abated, the trucks stopped outside a small village. After searching the compounds, First Squad was sent out to recon the surrounding hills while Doc treated a sick woman. After fifteen minutes, O'Falin called out, "Hey, Sergeant, I think we've got a cave."

Walton called in O'Falin's find to Sergeant Bronson, who then ordered him to check it out. Walton set Domincan Lou and Castor behind a group of rocks near the mouth of the cave for cover fire, should the need arise, and took O'Falin with him up around the flank. The two burst into the cave and found nothing but a narrow pocket of space with a few smaller sub-caves that were no more than two feet tall at their openings, one of which tapered off even smaller as it went deeper into complete darkness.

"Two-One, this is Two-One Bravo," Walton reported. "The cave is clear but it's got a crevice I'm gonna check out."

Sergeant Bronson's reply crackled through the I-com. "Wait a second." He made his way to them, stuck his head in, and assessed the cave. "Can you fit?"

"Yeah. But I'm gonna have to get shed of some of this shit," Walton answered as he shucked his K-Pot, LCE, and body armor.

"Be careful, Thomas."

"Roger, Sergeant. I'm Short-Timin'. You ain't gotta tell me that."

Walton turned on his pocket-sized Maglite, and with his rifle pointed forward, slithered on his belly into the depths of the cave. The roof of it occasionally scraped against his back as he maneuvered forward. He imagined it collapsing on him with every inch he advanced. When at last he found the end, it was empty save for a few shiny food wrappers.

Going backward proved to be more difficult than going forward, and he forced himself to breathe while trying not to think about how much it made him imagine being buried alive. He decided when he got back to KAF, the first thing he'd do was to email his mom and remind her to have him cremated if things should ever go wrong. He'd spent enough time in the dirt.

Later that afternoon, Second Platoon passed through downtown Kandahar on their way back to KAF. Sergeant Bronson, Lou, and Walton visited a school and had tea and raisins with the teachers as the rest pulled security. Afterward, Walton sat in the back of the truck and watched a gaggle of children materialize from out of nowhere and make greedy gestures with their hands while Castor jeered at them after the fashion of a Latino comedian First Squad had been watching on DVD.

Walton soon noticed a small cluster of shyer children in the back of the group and saw a little girl watching him. He continued to survey the crowd of children but still felt the stare of the little girl. He turned to give one of his own, thus beginning what seemed like the First Annual International Staring Contest. The trucks started up, and as they began pulling away the little girl finally broke into a bashful smile and waved to him. Walton waved back with a grin and prayed that life would treat her kindly in the "new" Afghanistan.

"Look, gentlemen, there ain't no shame in my game," said Sergeant Major Brooden, one of the sergeant majors from HQ, to the group of soldiers from Alpha Company who were set to leave the Army soon. The re-enlistment briefing was over and Walton felt like someone had just tried to sell him a used car.

"I have to tell you all this shit, 'cause we have to play the game. I don't care whether you re-up or not, but a real warrior would stay in. America's in trouble. They ain't gonna come out and say that shit back in the States because it would scare the shit out of people, but it's true. The Army's under-strength, especially the infantry, and needs good soldiers. They'll take new ones, but they'd rather have seasoned veterans. That's the reason behind this push to get you guys to re-enlist."

The Sergeant Major continued to talk about the virtues of re-enlisting, but Walton ignored him. He thought about the apartment he would be living in next summer. He was dedicated to the dream of being The Drunk Guy at the Pool. He'd be the Oklahoman equivalent of The Dude, living a life untroubled by the petty concerns of Man. Amy would come down regularly to visit, and between her and the perky neighbor girls, his life would read like a letter to *Penthouse*. (At least, until he left to travel the world. After that, he figured he'd be ready to rusticate.) When the Sergeant Major felt he had adequately checked the block, they went back to their tents.

That night, Walton lay wrapped up in his Haji blanket and woobie listening to Elvis sing *Peace in the Valley*, as was his custom. His mind drifted and became lighter as he floated toward sleep. As it did, his cot shuddered violently and he saw Sergeant Bronson standing at the foot of it. Walton started mumbling curses and began looking for his boots.

Second Platoon mounted the trucks a few hours later. Walton climbed up into the back of one near Mulane, who like Walton, was a recently-promoted sergeant, though he had burned up his Cherry days in the Korea deployment. They both occupied a similar position in the hierarchy and shared a love of hating the Army. They also had made it a habit of calling each other by their first names. They found the practice of doing so to be a pleasant form of rebellion against the Army's hard-on for impersonal bureaucracy.

"What's up, Ed?" Walton asked as he took a seat.

"Livin' the dream, Tom, you know me."

"They catch you while you were sleepin'?"

"Of course. Goddamn, I love this place!" Mulane was also a certified Sarcasm Instructor. "Fuckin' Army."

"Did you hear anything about what we're doin'?"

"I don't fuckin' know. They didn't tell us shit. Just that someone got fucked up at some place called Qulot and we gotta check it out."

"Wahoo n' shit. Ever forward." Walton was less than enthusiastic.

They passed camel herds, Bedouin camps, villages, and Hajis of every description under the steel-colored dawn. The terrain changed from the flat of Kandahar to mountains and even an occasional creek. Soldiers began feeling the call of nature and they pissed into water bottles and threw them out. Sergeant Musen exceeded the standard by standing and pissing out the back of the moving truck.

After three and a half hours, they set up outside an AMF (Afghan Militia Force) compound. They stopped traffic and set up a protective cordon around the trucks.

"Walton, Musen," Sergeant Bronson called out after deliberating with Lieutenant Howard, "Get the fuck over here. Alright, two non-governmental officials were killed here, so we're gonna check it out. I don't like this one. There's too many fuckin' Hajis with the AMF runnin' around armed. Sarge could have a bad day here. Keep your boys spread out and make sure they're actually pullin' security and not just daydreaming like they usually do. Let's go."

First Squad walked down a side street to the compound in a staggered file on each side of the road, and several hard-eyed Hajis watched them with AK-47's and in various states of what passed amongst them as a uniform.

The air was dead, as though an invisible force had turned off all the sound, save for the footsteps of soldiers and the occasional creak of their gear. Walton made eye-contact with one of the bearded soldiers who squatted frog-like atop a wall that ran along the road. The Haji shared the same lazy look of his companions, yet something in his eyes made Walton wonder if the Hajis felt the same tension as their American counterparts.

A strange electricity saturated the air of the ragged compound. Walton flexed the thumb in the flight glove of his right hand as it lay tensed upon the safety selector of his rifle. A bead of sweat dared to annoy him by inching its way down his face like a wet snail till it dangled off the tip of his nose, but he refused to wipe it with the thought they just might have to eat a shit-sandwich at any moment.

Second Platoon entered the courtyard and fanned out to pull security on the surrounding buildings. Several Toyota Hiluxes and compact cars were parked along the far wall with a small white car lying a bit away from the others. Bullet holes scattered randomly throughout it and the windshield spider-webbed around bloody holes like a deranged game of connect-the-dots. Two AMF soldiers carried a covered body from one building to another, and Lieutenant Howard and the 'terp entered the largest building in the compound with an AMF commander.

Sergeant Bronson and Castor tried to talk with one of the soldiers with the aid of a 'terp. The squad leader gave the AMF soldier his sunglasses, lending a comical air to the bearded man. The atmosphere immediately relaxed and they began to pass the time chatting via 'terp.

A general entered the courtyard and the lounging AMF soldiers suddenly straightened up. The commander, Lieutenant Howard, and the 'terp followed behind. The LT came to stand near Sergeant Bronson, who filled in as the platoon sergeant while Sergeant Cade recovered from a broken ankle.

"The AMF said some locals shot these guys up," Lieutenant Howard informed. "Their commander wanted to send some of their soldiers with us when we go to check out the scene, so I said, 'Fuck it, why not?'"

They exited the compound and headed to the trucks. A Hilux loaded with AMF soldiers followed close behind, reminding Walton of the good 'ol boys in pick-ups back home. They spent the afternoon driving down the long stretch of highway, while stopping every so often to talk to a local. The sky eventually darkened and they turned around to check on one last village before they returned to KAF.

The convoy rolled past a large citadel that dominated the horizon next to a valley and a collection of earthen buildings below. Minutes later, the loud *boom* of an explosion sounded off along the road.

Having spent months getting inoculated against the fear of Afghanistan's random noises by way of deep immersion, Walton thought nothing of it. Then the convoy stopped. He looked out the back and noticed a group of Hajis standing in the distance with the air about them of mischievous little boys in the middle of a neighborhood prank. One carried a spent RPG launcher. Something passed among them and they scattered like cockroaches. The moment carried a surreal quality that Walton found hysterical and he laughed.

"Get the fuck off the truck!" Sergeant Bronson bellowed as he appeared at the tailgate. The comedic stylings of Haji held little sway over him.

The trucks immediately spewed soldiers. They ran to get cover and set up security around the convoy. Second spent the next few hours shivering in the cold as evening came on while Lieutenant Howard and the squad leaders talked. The AMF took charge of looking for the Hajis who had shot off the RPG, and Second Platoon drove on to an abandoned gas station where they set up a patrol base and froze in the dark until morning.

When BOB began to peek his head above the horizon, The Loneliest Haji in the World walked toward the gas station down from the mountains. Upon seeing the platoon of Americans in his path, he turned without pause and walked back in the direction from whence he came.

By midday, Second Platoon returned to KAF and began the business of cleaning weapons and re-packing for the next mission, whenever that was to be. Once the weapons and equipment were straight, then they would be allowed to eat and get cleaned up.

"Man, I'm so hungry I betcha I could eat a can of Crisco," Tasker proclaimed to the tent with his Kentucky accent as he squared away his gear.

"I bet you won't!" Castor jeered.

"I bet I could! My mama used to make biscuits with lard."

Walton imagined the young man's mother making biscuits from scratch and it reminded him of his own mom. On weekend mornings, she'd quietly sing hymns and old songs while she cooked a big breakfast for the family in the sun-lit kitchen. His dad would periodically come in to get a cup of coffee and to sneak a piece of bacon or a kiss, and maybe indulge in some shameless flirting. Walton made a mental note to write to his folks. "It sounds like you got a good mom, Tasker."

The young man turned with an unaffected smile that made Walton feel a thousand years old. "I do, Sergeant! My folks are real strict, though. One time I lipped off about somethin' my mom fixed that I didn't like, so she made me do the cookin' for three weeks."

Sergeant Feran walked in and sat near Sergeant Bronson's bunk and told him, "Your boys don't have radio guard tonight. We got it. We have to listen for a call to get our shit on to get briefed to go someplace on vehicles that don't exist." Logistics had been growing

163

strained from the op-tempo, and the quality of transportation had been diminishing over the months. Sandbags as floor armor for the humvees and trucks was the norm.

Dominican Lou shook his head. "Our platoon just got in and we already have to pull radio guard? Why do they insist on fuckin' with us?"

"It's 'cause they don't have anything better to do," Musen answered. "We should chip in and get them Xboxes or something."

Walton laughed and couldn't help but agree. Nothing good came from The Head Shed. He suspected that all that coffee and PowerPoint must do something to their brains. Couldn't they just read or beat-off like normal soldiers? Then again, Musen also regularly stated that he was aiming to get a Purple Heart on account of the perks. With a guy with those kind of dreams, you had to be careful of his insights. Walton wished him good luck with it. As for himself, he wasn't crazy about getting shot by some fucking rag-head. He just wanted to get out in one piece. That, and see Amy ASAP. It was important to strike while the iron was hot.

Sergeant Bronson coughed and snorted grotesquely, then spat out a wad of corruption into his spit cup. He spent a moment considering his handiwork and observed, "Goddamn. That ain't right. I think that's got gravel in it." He shook the cup from side to side and continued his reflections. "You ever just sit and think about how much dirt we have in our bodies? Think about it. Everything we do involves dirt. We run around and do PT in dirt. We eat in dirt. We shit in dirt. We sleep in dirt. We're gonna get back and be sweatin' dirt for a month."

"No doubt," Walton said. "I want to know who the fuck's in charge of decidin' where the wars are held, and kick them in the nuts. Fuckin' savages. They probably couldn't find their asses with both hands with the lights on. Hellfire, back in the day they got to have wars in all the cool places like, Germany, and France, and what-not. You can't tell me the Allies weren't balls-deep in a bunch of European Juice Boxes. Bright-eyed, big-titted, blonde Krout chicks, or sexy brunette bitches with tight bodies, wearin' garters and corsets and all speakin' French...

"And what do we get? War in one of the shittiest, hottest, driest countries on the planet, with the worst food, and weirdest motherfuckers livin' in it. Good job, Army! Way to be a dick."

Sergeant Bronson nodded sadly. He became bored with the cup's contents and turned on the TV to find a documentary on AFN (Armed Forces Network) about Hollywood stars who had entered the service.

"Could you imagine goin' clubbing with Private Elvis?" Walton asked rhetorically.

"You know he got all the pussy," Sergeant Bronson agreed. "I'll bet motherfuckers fought over who got to be his wing-man. You know Private Elvis had on his A-Game."

Tener approached and Walton announced, "Look at this motherfucker here."

"Hey, Walton." Drawn by the moving images on Sergeant Bronson's TV, Tener turned and observed, "Man, we've been here for four months and I don't think Psycho Dad has rearranged his shit except when the safety inspector came by."

Sergeant Bronson didn't bother looking away from his TV. "Tener, I'm a middle-aged white man. Survey says: I'm afraid of change. What're you up to, man?"

"I think I'm gonna kill Sergeant G. He's driving me up the fuckin' wall."

"Fuck that dude. I wouldn't rely on him to scratch a dog's ass. Hey, do you have that huntin' game?" Some of the Joes had gotten the squad leader playing video games.

He found that shooting digital deer helped him cope with The 'Stan.

"No, I gave it to someone from Second Squad and he lent it out. Motherfucker's Uncle Tomming it and shit."

Alpha Company assembled a few weeks later and began loading up for a mission to downtown Kandahar. The weather was getting warmer and Haji had finally come down from the mountains. One of them had been feeling fancy and had thrown a grenade through the window of an MP humvee, blowing the arm off the soldier who had picked it up and saved his buddies by throwing it out. Alpha had been sent out to investigate.

While Walton waited for his soldiers to mount their truck, First Sergeant Nolen yelled out his name. "Walton! When are you leaving?"

"I don't know the exact date, First Sergeant. Last I heard, I'll be leavin' next month to start clearing."

"Not anymore!" said the First Sergeant as he laughed. "The Stop-Movement just came down. You ain't goin' anywhere."

A blinding wave passed over Walton as he took a seat, leaving nausea and the words, *fuckin' goddamn Army!* in its wake. Score one for The Bad Man. The truck began to lurch forward and Walton called back to him with a piratical grin, "That's fuckin' great! I pray a Haji fucks up so I'll get a chance to shoot someone!"

The convoy stopped at an abandoned amusement park in the downtown area; an odd bit of Western junk in the middle of a Third World city. They dismounted and set up a perimeter.

Walton heard laughter as he fumed over his misfortunes, and turned to see the squad leaders standing several meters away. They grinned as he approached.

Sergeant Bronson was the first to speak. "The First Sergeant said some shit about you." There was no mistaking the shittiness of his grin. "After you said you were hoping to shoot someone, he said, 'Hey, Sergeant, keep an eye on your Joes with this Stop-Loss business. We don't need them going crazy.' I said, 'Walton won't do shit. He knows I'd fuck him up if he did.'"

"I figured you'd be pissed," said Sergeant Sandlin. He was enjoying this too.

Sergeant Feran laughed outright. "See, you might as well just re-enlist."

"Fuck that noise, Sergeant. I'm gonna get out of the Army or die tryin'. This is some fuckin' bullshit! Goddamn fuckin' Army. So what the fuck are we doin' here anyway?"

"Show of force and askin' questions. A bunch of bullshit," Sergeant Bronson murmured over a cigarette. "Some of the Hajis have a case of the ass over the new constitution. These people don't realize their constitution fuckin' sucks anyway 'cause the motherfuckers who wrote it don't go out to where all the Hajis stand by the side of the road and shoot at each other just for fun. Holy shit! Did you see that?" he asked in astonishment as he pointed off in the distance. "That's a Haji with fire in a bucket! You're a hard-up motherfucker if you gotta carry around fire in a bucket."

They closed down the perimeter within an hour then set up a VCP. After that, Alpha Company drove the streets of Kandahar on platoon-level patrols. The city percolated with odd scents and sights from hundreds of tiny shops selling everything from meats to carpets. Lieutenant Howard let them buy Haji bread and they dismounted and walked around eating the warm, flat bread that vaguely tasted like grass, while watching doors and windows.

They made a stop just outside Martyr's Circle. The squads not watching the trucks provided personnel security while Lieutenant Howard and Sergeant Bronson questioned the locals through the 'terp.

A little boy just out of school approached Walton as he stood and brooded. The little boy stopped right in front of him, looked up with a smile, and then waved. With his fledgling English the boy said, "Thank you, soldier."

Walton stared silently at the little boy for a long moment. He was ashamed of himself for being such a selfish piece of shit. He could hear his mother's voice say to him, "You oughta be horsewhipped." The tension within him fled, and he returned the boy's smile, suddenly no longer as angry and bitter as he had been. When he found the words and was at last able to speak through the lump in his throat, he simply replied, "You're very welcome."

The little boy's smile somehow became even wider and he waved again before turning to walk away with his red backpack bobbing behind him and not a care in the world. Walton remembered one of his younger brothers having a backpack like that long ago.

They continued their patrol, and soon other children came to gather around Walton and his team, drawn by the novelty of the soldiers in their neighborhoods. He didn't like them being so close; his unit's presence could inspire an attack that could get the children hurt. However, the threat level appeared low enough that the leadership didn't order them to disperse the kids, so Walton let them tag along while they walked back to the trucks. He remembered what it was like to be a little boy, and knew that if he had been their age, he'd have probably shat up a perfectly good pair of He-Man Underoos at the prospect of looking out the window and seeing what appeared to be a bunch of action figures come to life. He recalled the hours he'd spent as a boy saving the universe from the forces of evil with the help of his toys and wondered, *"What Would Optimus Prime Do?"* His older brother instincts kicked in and he made it a point to try to talk to the children in a way that made them feel like grownups.

While Walton tore off a chunk of some more freshly-baked Haji bread, a boy walking next to him asked, "Do you like our bread?"

"Yes, it's very good."

"What is your bread like?"

"It's different," Walton answered with smile as he handed what was left of the Haji bread to the boy, who then mimicked Walton by tearing off a piece and passing the rest over to his friends.

While he walked and talked to the children as the Haji bread made the rounds, Walton was almost happy. He thought he'd email Amy about all this when he got back to KAF. She'd probably get a kick out of it. He then began rolling over in his mind again the contents of the last email she had sent him a few days prior, making a meal out of her every word. He looked West toward where he imagined her day would soon be born.

Walton sat cleaning his M4 outside the tent on account of a soldier on the other side of Post having shot himself in the head due to an accidental discharge. How being outside could minimize the chances of future accidents made no sense to Walton, but he guessed The Brass had to do something to make it look like they were doing something.

He stewed quietly in his anger and frustration while he listened to Frank Sinatra's *Reprise: The Very Good Years* in his headphones. The album was one that he could listen to all the way through, and it never failed to make him happy. He needed a hit of something to lift his spirits, and outside of Amy in something skimpy, he thought The Chairman was just the sort of go-getter for such a mission. The past few weeks had been unimpressive to him. Time passed slowly like old people fucking, and he was ready for the storm of malaise to break.

Due to the action at Qulot, The Brass had ordered a firebase erected there which had been quickly dubbed, *Firebase Purgatory*. To sustain its heaters and generators, fuel had to be brought in regularly, which had meant that someone had to pull security on the shipments, which meant that Second often had to go out on convoy duty

There had been a bombing in Kandahar, so Second Platoon had been sent out to the fringes of the district to make a show of force and ask questions. Sergeant Sandlin's humvee had rolled onto its side when the narrow path it was on had collapsed. They'd provided security throughout the day and Walton found the Hajis of that village to be some of the most annoying and passive-aggressive ones he'd seen. That night, the wrecker almost destroyed a building when trying to get the humvee out, and the soldiers had cheered as it fell.

A few days later, he'd had to run back to the tent from the Post barber shop because three soldiers from Bravo Company had gotten shot at the firebase at Dey Rah Wu, and Second Platoon was to have gone out. The Battalion wound up sending Charlie Company instead which had suited Walton just fine.

Dominican Lou had fallen out of a squad run and had taken a swing at Daniels, who had been trying to help push him. Castor had yelled at him to keep up. Sergeant Bronson had then steered the formation to the airfield and ordered them to roll around in the dirt before continuing the run.

Afterward, Walton had taken his team aside and said, "I figured out what our team's problem is: *me*. I've been lazy and indifferent. Lou has some things to work on, and when we finish this Qulot business, I'm gonna start helpin' him. God knows I need the extra PT. Castor, I've been cuttin' you slack as my senior specialist, but it ain't your place to yell at my Joes, it's mine. O'Falin…I don't know what your problem is. You're just weird."

Second had gone on a hearts-and-minds mission to some rural villages for the medics to administer health care. The Hajis continued to refuse to get in anything resembling a line unless physically forced to do so. Many of them had tried to sneak through multiple times to get free stuff and complained about having to wait.

Senior-ranking people asserted their authority. The Sergeant Major had yelled at the squad leaders from Bravo Company because the soldiers who had just been shot hadn't been clean shaven. Lieutenant Howard threatened counseling statements and worse due to PT fall-outs (of which, Walton had been one), and the First Sergeant complained about the wearing of flip-flops near the tents. He also reminded them of the need to take a weapon when going to the latrine, and the prohibition on female visitors due to the infamous Sexual Predator. The Sexual Predator (known also as The Balaclava Bandit) had been conducting sorties into female tents, and with his face hidden by a balaclava, ran down the rows of cots grabbing their boobs while they slept, then hauled ass out the door before they could mount a defense. The Sexual Predator struck like lightning and remained at large.

It had rained for days on end.

By mid-February, Alpha Company had spent two days searching the citadel near Qulot which was run by the AMF. Questioning had revealed that one of the AMF soldiers had been running guns for the Taliban. Many of the soldiers had whispered about the corruption of the AMF and the prospect of having to fight them, as well as the possibility of an Afghan civil war between the various military factions.

Second's turn at the Qulot rotation came, and they had spent their days stringing concertina wire at Firebase Purgatory and filling up sandbags for fighting positions along the perimeter. At night, they'd crowded into tents to sleep on the floor while the 'terps and non-infantry personnel had ample room and cots. When outside The Wire, they'd gone from one village to another and every Bedouin camp in-between, rolling up on them like the platoon was in a John Ford movie. One such foray had revealed a mountain riddled with Taliban and Al-Qaeda caches of rockets and rounds for recoilless rifles and mortars.

"Fuck it, let's just steal a humvee."

For Walton, it was time to rebel against the machinations of The Bad Man. A little anyway. He and Brickham had been silently eyeing The Wire at KAF as they returned from breakfast and toted around the day's portion of stir crazy.

It had been like this in Bosnia. During one of their rare days off back then, Walton and his old buddies from his days as a Joe had sat at one of the patio tables at the coffee shop on Eagle Base when Sergeant Sandlin and Sergeant Bronson had stopped by to harass them. After Sergeant Sandlin had expounded upon his lascivious designs regarding the cashier and told them they hadn't lived until they'd fucked a bitch who had Chlamydia, Sergeant Bronson had taken a sip from his cappuccino and his eyes had focused with vision and purpose.

"Shit," he'd said miserably. "I'll tell you fuckers what. By the end of this week, I'm goin' over The Wire. Y'all notice all the fence they got up around this motherfucker? It ain't to keep Bosnians out. That shit's to keep us in. You're in fuckin' jail, gentlemen. Fuck this bullshit."

Sergeant Bronson had been right, and his words returned to inspire Walton like the disembodied voice of Obi-Wan Kenobi. The Army had filled the crawling days with busy work, and now it was time to give something back.

Brickham and Walton walked to the motor pool and picked out a cargo humvee. Walton fired it up as

Brickham took shotgun, and they drove it back to the tents. Within ten minutes, it was loaded with Joes. They drove past the gate then went a half-mile down the road to the Haji-Mart.

The Haji-Mart was a rag-head flea-market where Haji and Joe played capitalism under the eye of BOB. Bearded men with their turbans and Haji clothes sat near rugs, jewelry, knives, muskets, and bootleg DVD's, all trying to draw attention to their wares. Walton settled for a few bills of old Iraqi money with Saddam Hussein on the front. Amy would no doubt enjoy the novelty.

Once they returned the stolen humvee, Walton played a spirited game of *Halo* with the boys and returned to his tent. Sergeant Bronson stood as he taped up the handle of the battle-axe that Dominican Lou had picked up for him at his request. He looked up briefly and greeted, "Hey, Stop-Loss."

"Hey, Sergeant," Walton replied as he set his rifle on his cot and collapsed into his camp chair. He dusted off his copy of *The Wind-Up Bird Chronicle* and opened it to the Montreal postcard that Amy had sent in her care package, which he now used as a bookmark.

In his mind, Amy had somehow gotten inextricably linked with the idea of books, and though Walton wasn't sure how he felt about that, he didn't fight it. They'd developed the habit of writing quotes from books they liked at the end of their emails, and when he quoted Mr. Murakami's work, her excitement at reading lines from one of her favorites had him scouring the small cardboard library he had set up next to his cot for The Next Great Quote to try to impress her with. Their correspondence had become a fun mental exercise for him.

"Keep makin' jokes," Walton challenged to his squad leader. "If they go all Darth Vader on this po' boy and change the deal on my ETS date and involuntarily extend me, you're gonna wake up one day and find my ass gone.

I've just about done my time." Inspiration struck, and he decided to do a little in-squad political wrangling. "I'll take Lou with me and we'll go to the Dominican Republic and start up our own revolution and go fuck up some *Haitianos* or some shit. Years from now, the men who fought alongside us will have children who'll ask them, '*Papi*, tell me of the *Revolicion*,' and they'll be like, '*Mijo*, I rode with El Dominicano and El Gringo when we cast the *Hatiano* into the sea.'" Lou perked up from his book at the prospect. If Dominican Lou hated one thing above all else, it was Haitians.

Sergeant Bronson raised an eyebrow and said lowly, "You know you ain't gonna go AWOL. You know I'd find you."

Walton allowed himself a cocky smirk. "And how do you propose to do that?"

"Think about it, motherfucker. You're gonna fuck around and write your mama and that shit's gonna have a return address on it. All I gotta do is show up and pull some, 'Excuse me, Ma'am, I'm your son's old squad leader and it's really important I talk with him.' Tell me I won't find you."

"That's exactly what I'm tellin' you, Sergeant. I'll be like, 'I'm sorry, Mom. From here on out we're communicatin' by motherfuckin' message-in-a-bottle!'"

Walton sat watching the late afternoon wind play with the dunes. They looked terrible and oppressive with their barren slopes and rises that stretched from one horizon to another, yet beautiful in that same way as well.

The desert mesmerized Walton. He felt as if he couldn't look away from it and saw it have a similar effect on the other soldiers. If you stared at it long enough, the unending sun-bleached khaki met the deep spectrum of blue in some infinite faraway place. It had a gravity to it that tugged you gently but relentlessly toward The Holy

Point like a siren's song, and in your deepest cells you just knew that it secretly pulled the whole world along as well, whether it knew it or not, with the slow inevitability of destiny.

The village that First and Second Platoons had searched during the day sprawled quietly behind him, silent in contrast to the violence of a few days prior.

Some NGO's had flown out in a helicopter to scout out a place to build a school for the local children and someone had shot them for their troubles as they had been preparing to leave. When the soldiers had arrived there had been blood on the sparse grass.

They had searched every room, questioned every male, and had detained more than a few, but none had proved to be solid leads. Walton had doubted they would find the culprits. Having initially gone to college in the hopes of becoming a pediatrician, he deeply respected those who wanted to do right by children, and was saddened by the loss of life. However, there was something about that sort of business that had struck him as meddlesome. Nobody liked it when someone pissed over their fence.

He believed in the old adage, "The hand that rocks the cradle rules the world." He'd speculated that NGO's in a warzone would've no doubt laced their instruction with Dewey-inspired "progressive" pedagogy and Western ideas in an effort to capture hearts-and-minds. Going into a village in foreign country, and teaching their children different ways and ideas, regardless of intent, was asking for trouble. Using a classroom to separate children from the culture of their parents was a form of kidnapping.

Walton took a sip off the water bottle half-full with powdered Gatorade. He re-read the letters from his brothers in his mind, then thought of Amy. She had told him in an email that she'd decided to stay home in Toronto instead of visiting India and maintained that her invitation still held.

She had mentioned that she was considering enlisting in the Canadian forces and signing on as a medic due to her drive to help others and the competence she'd felt from successfully handling a few tough situations during a stint as a lifeguard, as well as aiding people hurt in a car accident a few summers back. She reasoned that it would only be for two or three years, and in addition to the money and training, she would get to catch a deployment.

She'd said she looked forward to hearing his thoughts on it, and he couldn't wait to tell her that after hearing all about her quasi-feminist fears of being locked away in a cage, to enlist in the Army was a flagrant symptom of insanity. Was she out of her fucking mind? He would have to find a way to talk her out of it, but he'd have to be careful. She gave him the impression she didn't cotton to someone telling her how the cow ate the cabbage, and if they did, she'd do the opposite just to spite them.

At his request for her to tell him more about her life back in the world (and provide him with a form of escapism into a happier reality), she'd written of the Salman Rushdie/*Lord of the Rings* kick she'd been on, that she sang loudly to her CD's when no one was at home, and weekly smoked pot with her brother while watching *Fear Factor*. It also looked like she might be landing a job at conventions introducing people in English and French and wouldn't even be taking the cocktail dress off or anything. She'd wished him well in Indian Country and told him to come home soon.

Captain Cordova walked in front of the formation consisting of all the NCO's of Alpha Company. They stood in sweaty PT's and looked like murder. "Men, you're probably wondering why the op-tempo has been so high. The reason for that is that I have volunteered you for every mission that has came down . . ."

Walton quit listening.

The CO finally dismissed them and Walton wandered back to the tent with a brain full of blues. Outside the hooch, he noticed Shipley smoking a menthol and he looked at it greedily. He wanted to be that relaxed.

Shipley smiled sympathetically. He seemed to sense Walton's need find refuge in Nicotine. "Hell yes, Sergeant Walton wantin' a motherfuckin' cigarette. I feel ya, playa."

"Thanks, pardner," Walton said with appreciation as Shipley handed him a cigarette and lit it. "Fuckin' CO. What'd you guys do?"

"We ran around the airfield. What'd they have y'all do?"

Walton shook his head in disbelief. "CO ran us ten motherfuckin' miles. We made it a point to fall out repeatedly, but that's beside the point. Fact is, the motherfucker does that shit, then tells us he's volunteered us for every mission that came down the fuckin' pipe."

"Oh hell fuck no! We should stab that motherfucker when he comes out of the shower. Fuck him."

Sergeant Bronson entered the tent then came back out grinning triumphantly with a cigarette of his own prepped to burn. His eyes darted to Walton's cigarette. "Well. They finally broke ya, I see."

"Yeah."

"Welcome to The Dark Side, Tom."

The Shithook flew through the night and Walton was almost glad to be out on a real mission again. Between the piss-ant VCP's, re-supply runs, and tent drama, it felt good to do something worth the effort. The darkness of the bird's interior had a peaceful way about it that lulled most to sleep. Walton found sleep evading him so he put his Amy and post-Army fantasies on replay and watched the craggy land fly under.

They lowered and went through the ritual of repeating the minutes till set-down then when the order came, they ran out. The extra mortar round in Walton's assault pack fell out (there was little room for anything other than the packing list) and he scrambled to snatch it back up. They maintained a perimeter until the bird lifted off, then they picked up. The shit-bird pilots had set them in the wrong LZ. Again.

In the morning they walked down into the village of Siblay. Second and Third Squads provided the outer cordon while First Squad handled the interior. Sergeant Musen's team assisted the ANA (Afghan National Army) in searching the houses while Walton's pulled security on the males as they sat outside the mosque and awaited questioning under the stare of a donkey who brayed every so often.

Hours crept by as Lieutenant Howard and Sergeant Bronson used the 'terps to ask every man in the village the same questions. Eventually, Sergeant Musen's voice came over the I-com, saying, "Two-One, this is Two-One Alpha, I got something."

A half hour later, Sergeant Musen escorted two Hajis with flex cuffs on their wrists and sandbags over their heads to a low wall near Walton's position and sat them down. "One of these fuckers is Haji Mohammed," Musen said. "The other is Gullah Nabi. They were using aliases but we found a document in one of their houses from the Taliban saying they had protection. The LT found out they were lying about their names and got mad as fuck. We found their names on the Black List so we PUC'ed (Personnel Under Custody) them. You got 'em?"

"Sure."

"Hey Sergeant," Castor called from his position. "Check out this donkey's dick! Fucker's been hard almost all fuckin' day." Castor brayed in imitation of the donkey. He'd been staring at it as though the donkey's cock held the secrets of life and death and would jump off and sing and dance at any moment. "That's probably Donkey for,

'Hey, I'm horny, somebody jack me off. Pleaassee!'"

Sergeant Bronson's voice came over the I-com. "Hey, Walton, come here."

Walton left the Hajis with his Joes and squatted near where Sergeant Bronson, the LT, and the 'terp sat helmet-less with a spry but grave Haji who looked older than God's dog as they drank tea with him. "Do your boys want any more tea?" Sergeant Bronson asked.

"No, we're good."

Walton turned to look at the withered old man again. He sat hunched-over, his gnarled brown skin standing out against the pale gray of his beard, and though his tone was shaky, he gripped his walking stick with a strong hand. Walton shifted his attention back to his squad leader and asked, "So what's the story on Papa Smurf?"

"This motherfucker's eighty years old," Sergeant Bronson said with a nod at the old man. "He was Mujahedeen back in the day. I got the utmost respect for any motherfucker who'll fight Russian tanks on horseback. And win."

Sergeant Bronson continued listening to the old man's narrative in a courteous manner that Walton had never seen on him before. When the old man finished, Sergeant Bronson reverently extended both of his hands to the wizened fighter and said, "Tell him, 'Thank you very much,' for his time." The 'terp translated and the old man took Sergeant Bronson's offered hands in his own, then got up and left.

"He say anything worthwhile?"

Sergeant Bronson topped off his cup and leaned back against the wall. "Not really. He hates the Taliban, though. He said he used to lead a cell back in the day that was made up of the men of his village and they'd hooked up and ran ops with other Mujahedeen against the Soviets. When they finished with the Russians, he and others like him urged the Mujahedeen to put down their weapons

179

and go back to their old lives, but fuckers like the Taliban kept theirs and acted like bandits, and pretty much fucked up the whole goddamn country. That's a cool motherfucker."

Walton watched the ancient warrior shuffle back to his place among the others, and supposed he could understand why Sergeant Bronson had made it a point to show so much respect to him. The old man's brand of Haji seemed like a better version than the ones the soldiers now chased. Not that the old man was no doubt the cruelest swinging dick there. He just had style, though, and that was something.

"What about the Dynamic Duo over there?" Walton asked as he hiked his thumb back to the detainees.

"They're going away," Lieutenant Howard answered curtly. "Fuckers were lying. They had their name on a letter of protection from the Taliban and were also on the Black List. That's good enough for me. Hey, Sergeant Walton, Sergeant Musen is doing another search of the village; why don't you ask these guys questions again."

"Roger, Sir." Walton removed his helmet in keeping with the others and took a seat. Sergeant Bronson and Lieutenant Howard picked up and moved into the shade of a neighboring building, leaving him alone with the 'terp. "Lou, send me over one."

By the time he questioned his third Haji, he was almost as bored as the 'terp. The fourth Haji was as unremarkable as the others but Walton observed the forms; "What was his name? What did he do? Where was he from? Who did he farm for?"

"He says he doesn't know."

Walton's head jumped up, and his eyes set upon the Haji. "How the fuck can he not know who he works for?" He remembered his dad's blue collar devotion to his job. For over twenty years, the old man had come home muddy from working on water lines. He was a man with a family to feed. There would be no way in hell Mr. Kenneth Paul Walton wouldn't know who his boss was.

"Tell him I think he's lyin'." He growled quietly, leaving a heat in his voice that he didn't remember adding. He took a deep breath, scratched behind his ear, and in a calmer tone, began again.

"I can understand wantin' to protect his employer and that he's got to provide for his family, but tell him if he doesn't start answering my fuckin' questions—here, tell him to look at those guys over there. Tell him if he doesn't start answering my fuckin' questions, he's gonna piss me the fuck off and we're gonna take him away with those guys in our helicopter and he won't see his family for a long, long time." The 'terp had said the peasant Hajis were scared shit-less of helicopters.

Walton watched as the 'terp translated and the Haji became afraid. He looked at the small man and suddenly felt ashamed of himself. He was just another bully threatening violence against a weaker man. This wasn't what he wanted. He was disgusted at the game they played, yet a part of him stirred at being in a position of dominance. He pushed the navel-gazing impulses down, focused on his responsibilities, and listened to the 'terp. The man *was* hiding something. Maybe something that could cost the lives of others.

"He says he works in the fields of that man there," the 'terp said as the peasant's finger pointed to the man who had been serving them tea all afternoon.

"Why did he lie?"

"He says he was afraid he would lose his work."

Walton furrowed his brow and tried to adopt a sympathetic face to put the worker at ease. "Let me talk to his boss."

The 'terp called the man over and the Haji took a seat. Walton nodded politely, then remembered the Haji briefings and respectfully said, "*Al salaam alaykum.*"

181

He waited for the Haji to finish the traditional greeting formula, then he turned to the 'terp. "This man owns a lot of land and has a lot of people workin' for him, doesn't he? Ask him if he knows or has heard anything about the Taliban hidin' weapons around here. Does he know if they've been doin' anything around here, lately? Make him understand we don't want to hurt him, but anything he or his workers know could save people's lives and help us get rid of the Taliban that keep fuckin' with them."

The 'terp and Haji conversed in Pashto and when the 'terp was satisfied, he looked back at Walton. "He says the Taliban stole from people on the road here last summer."

"Find something, Sergeant Walton?" asked Lieutenant Howard as he and Sergeant Bronson approached.

"Nothin' spectacular yet, Sir. This Haji lied about workin' for that Haji, who's sorta this Lord of the Manor/Pa Cartwright motherfucker 'round here," Walton informed as he pointed his finger at the respective participants in the drama. "That Haji said the Taliban was doin' a bit of highway robbery in the area last summer, but that's all I've gotten so far."

"Hmm. That's old, but it's something to push up." He looked around. "I think we're about done here, anyway."

Second Platoon left with their two suspects in tow and climbed back to the top of the hill they had stayed on the night before. Those on guard repeatedly questioned the Hajis throughout the night as ordered, and the soldiers did so with a seriousness and intensity that Walton had seldom seen on them. (Lieutenant Howard also had ordered that a team leader be near the detainees at all times to ensure they weren't abused by over-zealous soldiers.) Walton couldn't remember when they'd been so alert at a patrol base. The Hajis reeked of fear and sat stiffly as they muttered answers to the soldiers from inside the sandbags covering their bearded faces.

First Platoon picked up Second in cargo humvees the

next morning and took them back to the company's patrol base. Second refitted, then pushed up to clear a nearby mountain range that soared high above the valley. None of the soldiers were the least bit excited at the prospect of the climb that suggested a rerun of Daychopan.

It took them an hour to cross the farm land of the valley to the base of the foothills. The Platoon split up with Sergeant Sandlin and Sergeant Heslich and one of the gun teams on the ridge to the east, and Sergeant Bronson and the other gun team to the west, and within another hour, both had made it to the crests.

"Hold up, Walton."

Walton stopped and wandered back to Sergeant Bronson. "What's up?"

Sergeant Bronson pointed to the tip of a nearby peak. It ended in an unnatural rock formation and ANA soldiers crawled over the boulders near it. "That ANA guy with the RPG is gonna blow that fighting position up there. We're gonna hold up and watch him."

"Cool." Walton produced a pack of Marlboro Reds as he sat on a boulder (he had tried for Camels in honor of Benamy, but no dice) and lit up.

"Let me get one of those off you."

Walton handed the pack and a lighter over as Sergeant Bronson took a seat next to him, then went back to admiring the view of the valley below. The mountains offered up a Spartan beauty under the hard blue sky, and the thin green vegetation that skirted the weak river cutting the valley floor reminded Walton of the seams on the back of a woman's stockings. "There's a lot of yonder up here," he said.

"Yeah. Motherfucker could definitely lose himself that's for damn sure."

"You know, Sergeant, it's a shame they got so many fuckin' minefields and terrorists and shit livin' here. This place ain't half bad in some spots." He took a deep drag, and though he still hated the taste, and didn't like it nearly as much as his pipe, he enjoyed the act of smoking while at rest. Smoking cigarettes was a whole different animal whilst sober. "Fuck it. So, how's it look with those two cats from yesterday? Think they're for real?"

Sergeant Bronson shrugged, then coughed and spat out a batch of phlegm from his readily available supply. When he finished inspecting it with his boot, he went back to taking in the scenery as well. "Looks that way. You know Sergeant Johns from Scouts? He said some shit the other day that made sense. Morale's been so goddamn low because we've been doing so many missions that always wind up with us drivin' Haji into Secret Squirrels waiting up the trail, and Joe doesn't ever get to see the Haji he's chasin'. Like we're the wing-men that get the bitches wet, but the Special Ops gets to take them home and smash their guts. Joe doesn't ever get to see the results at this level. Maybe now that they know what it's like to actually *catch* the bad guys, things'll be different."

Walton figured that added up. Since the Al-Qaeda Hajis were largely hidden, the only way to engage them was to smoke them out. The Hajis, though skillful and fast, were only a hit-and-run force and The Brass sent infantry units off to bird dog them from their hiding places since there was no way the Hajis could match their numbers and firepower in a stand-up, knock-down, drag-out fight. The fleeing Hajis would unknowingly walk into the ambushes set by the Special Friends who were inserted by air and had heaps of support. In the end, it worked, but for the Joes on the ground, they felt like they were forever going after their quarry and never had the satisfaction of sinking their jaws into them. Until now.

The ANA's movement caught Sergeant Bronson's eye and a glimmer of enthusiasm crossed his face. "Here he goes."

The ANA soldier fired three rockets and missed each

time. Sergeant Bronson shrugged in disappointment and they picked up. The mountains to the east began to flatten out until the soldiers on patrol met the valley while those in the west continued on.

An hour and a half later, Walton came upon several familiar markers on the trail. He pulled out his I-com and said, "Hey, Two-One, this is Two-One Bravo. Looks like we may have mines up here. I got stacked rocks."

Sergeant Bronson's response was fast in coming. "Well, I guess we'll find out. Short-Man's got to walk his mile."

Walton sighed and lit up a cigarette. As he walked, he mused to himself what a pain-in-the-ass war it was sometimes.

The shadows grew longer as they walked and Sergeant Bronson grumbled over the I-com intermittently to Walton for his speed or choice of path, and to Sergeant Cade for their continued movement in general. When the order to return came, they pushed down into the low ground to begin the walk back.

The valley floor was flat and cool, and when they returned to the fields, a breeze caught the grass and Opium poppies as a lone Haji called the faithful to prayer. The reedy chant pulsed from beat-up speakers and filled the whole world with the sound. The soldiers continued their slow walk, their shapes and gear making them stand out as a vulgar interlopers in the strange place, yet the dust and stale tang of old sweat that clung to them endowed them with something that would never completely wash away or allow them to be again the men they had been at far away homes. The moment struck Walton as foreign and surreal, yet comforting.

Once back at the patrol base, they integrated into the perimeter and went about the priorities of work. Everyone looked busted and even Lieutenant Howard smoked a cigarette. Getting to spend his rest period by just sitting in the shade with his back against a wall and his K-Pot off had made Walton feel like he'd won a prize. He tried to not smile at the prospect of getting to use a toilet again.

The soldiers burned their trash in the morning, then assembled into PZ posture. The Shithooks thundered into the valley to pick them up, and the pilots made the birds dance through the valleys on the way home, making fierce love with the aggressive terrain by doing "The Map of the Earth."

The ride was ecstasy for Walton and he felt content and safe in a powerful way that reminded him of going on trips with his parents as a child in their '77 Buick. He looked at the sparse angles and curves of the belly of the bird like a lover. He adored the Shithook and the way she always came into a dangerous place to bring him and his friends home. She wasn't pretty, but she was dependable, and Good Lord how the girl could cruise. He didn't sleep on the way back, choosing instead to enjoy the ride.

They spent the next day back at KAF in preparation for the next mission. They cleaned weapons, changed batteries, and built a sand table representing a village of a place called Miam Do. Alpha Company was to fly there and attempt to seize Taliban/Al-Qaeda collaborators and search for their caches. To hear Lieutenant Howard talk, it could be the real deal (a sentiment they seemed to repeat at every op-order, though Walton sensed again the same vibe that had saturated the night patrol after the firefight at Daychopan. The Bad Man was near).

After the briefing, some of the soldiers tied two dung beetles to a stake in the middle of a shallow pit for a fight to the death. Sergeant Bronson tried to make it more interesting by setting a knife between them, but the beetles failed to catch on.

That night, Dominican Lou stopped Walton as he was about to enter the tent after dinner. His dark face was worried, and his eyes were drawn inward toward some secret place. He asked to speak with Walton privately, and when he was satisfied that no one else was around, he asked conspiratorially, "Hey Sergeant, can I ask you a favor? It's something kinda personal."

Looking at Lou, Walton immediately got a bad feeling, and wondered what kind of trouble his soldier had gotten himself into. He figured the little klepto must've stolen something again, or stabbed some POG. However, seeing the rare traces of fear on the younger soldier's face caused Walton enough concern to want to try to put him at ease. "Sure Lou. I can't make any promises, but if I can help you, I will. What's wrong?"

"Nothing's wrong, Sergeant. I was just wondering . . ." Lou looked away from Walton for a second, then his brown eyes grew intense when he brought them up again and said, "If we get into The Shit like they're saying . . . well, if I get shot in my balls or my dick, will you shoot me, Sergeant?"

"Lou, I'm scared of that too, but c'mon—"

"Please, Sergeant! I wouldn't ask just anybody. If I get shot and can't use my dick, I don't wanna fuckin' live! Just put a bullet in my head. Please, Sergeant."

Walton imagined the fight that possibly awaited them and how something like that could happen so easily. He wouldn't want to live like that either. "Alright, Lou. I'll give ya my word. *If* you get shot in The Business, and *if* I think I can get away with it without them nailin' my ass for it and sendin' me to jail, I promise, I'll . . . I'll put an end to your pain as clean as I can. Cool?"

Lou lit up and stuck out his hand to shake with his team leader.

The next morning, Walton sat near the ramp of the Shithook and thought about his job. He summoned in his mind the maps and satellite images, and visualized making his way to his squad's target building. He eventually tired of it and just enjoyed the moment with a private smile. He

187

wondered how many more times he'd get to ride in a Shithook, but he decided to save that melancholy for another day. He let his mind linger on Amy instead.

The Shithook sat down and Second Platoon bolted out of the back, breaking off into four-man teams as they ran. Walton suddenly noticed that certain features hadn't made it to the briefing; such as the fact that the village had been built on top of hill that was a damn sight steeper than the intel had said. Whatever speed the wedge-shaped formations had built stopped as they reached the base of the hill like they were hit in the back of the head with an invisible hammer.

After an inner tirade of raging profanity, Walton crested the hill then ran to the corner of the nearest building. A Haji knelt nervously with an older model cell phone, and Sergeant Bronson yelled from behind, "Leave him, push on in!"

Bravo Team stacked behind Walton outside the entrance to a building, then flew inside. They began aggressively clearing rooms until they at last found the G-Spot: a room filled from floor to ceiling with rockets, mortars, and cans of ammo of every description.

Sergeant Bronson posted a soldier for security, then First Squad moved on until they'd secured all their target buildings, all the while finding small arms and occasionally something bigger. The Hajis had even hidden weapons in their mosque. "Two-Six, Two-One, my shit's secure," Sergeant Bronson reported into his I-com, announcing that they'd seized the foothold into the village for the rest of unit

As Walton later pulled security on the corral of males sent to the center of the village by Sergeant Sandlin's blocking position on one of the roads, he could see Sergeant Bronson standing with the LT and one of the bearded Special Forces soldiers as the hirsute man in body armor angrily questioned a Haji by way of a 'terp. The

188

word was that SF had lost a man a few days ago, and the men who had killed him were supposedly in the area.

The LT conferred with Sergeant Bronson quietly for a moment, and the squad leader nodded and turned to approach Walton. He ordered him and Private Steves from the engineers to accompany Lieutenant Newman (who worked as Alpha Company's Executive Officer, or "XO") with the ANA soldiers who would be conducting a continued search of the village.

The intensity of the mission mellowed into a more methodical pace as the ANA went about their tasks under the supervision of their Marine platoon sergeant counterpart who chatted with the XO. Walton kept an eye roaming around but allowed himself a smile at the ANA soldiers. They had a Laurel and Hardy physicality about them that he thought comical.

They pressed on from building to building and when the sun was high, the XO stopped them and they had MRE's near the mortars squad, who lounged about in a field. They spent twenty minutes eating and filling their CamelBaks with water, then resumed their search.

Small arms fire seared the air and time stopped. Haji had decided to show his nuts.

The XO yelled, *"Get cover!"* and they ran behind a low wall and looked out into the small trees surrounding a compound in the distance.

Walton moved in a crouch, trying to look for some semblance of a muzzle-flash to locate where the shots were coming from while staying behind cover. He called in to Sergeant Bronson to give a sit-rep but no one answered. Shots fired again with a staccato aggression that was the equivalent of auditory rape. Reality took on a fluid quality and thought was a vague concept. The moment devolved them back a million years.

The ANA pushed out toward the compound and established positions in a wide arc. The XO rose, released his hand-mike, and said as though he were Iron Mike come to life (Iron Mike being a giant statue which stands like a graven image devoted to the pagan god of infantrymen outside of Building 4 at Ft. Benning), "Sergeant Lanagan from Third Platoon is down. Let's go."

The XO led at a fast trot into the direction of the shooting with Walton and Steves behind him in a small wedge. With every round fired from the compound, Walton winced inside as they ran, just knowing one would find him and put him in a world of mangled torment he couldn't imagine. He was terrified. The shots continued and the XO picked up their pace, leading them into it without hesitation.

Walton suddenly saw First Squad and a collection of other soldiers arrayed in a perimeter around the front of the compound, lying on their stomachs or huddled next to nearby walls in the vicinity of the Antenna Farm. Sergeant Bronson and Sergeant Cade stood next to a doorway at the head of a small stack fighting enemies inside, and Walton broke away to join them.

He rushed through the perimeter, and as he passed a group of soldiers, one fell violently to the ground a few feet away from him. He remembered the soldier was a sergeant from the engineers named Dern. He had given them a class on C4 a few months prior. A few of the soldiers drew close to see his condition, and Dern mumbled, "My head's ringin'." The part of Walton that was still able to think wanted to laugh at the sergeant's luck at having survived a head-shot.

Walton pushed up toward the stack and suddenly his blood was hot. He had been at the rear of the formation when the fight at Daychopan happened and hadn't seen much, but this was different. This was in his face. This was why he'd joined the Army. This was a scrap to run to with his platoon—his tribe—right in the thick of it, fighting their guts out. This was a fire roaring hot enough to burn away the bullshit that had been spoon-fed to him to stunt his growth in the name of setting him free. This was the smell of bullets breathing, and the dry Afghanistan air drinking the fresh wet blood from the last thought of the newly dead Haji lying on the ground. This was the altar where he could pay for everything he'd ever loved. This was death making life real.

Sergeant Cade and Sergeant Bronson threw frags and fired into the entrance with a methodical vengeance as he reached them. Seeing his senior NCO's in the front of a stack and doing a team leader's job embarrassed him. Throughout his enlistment he had always known that he wasn't the soldier he should be, and now other men were doing the fighting a man his rank should be doing.

He grabbed Sergeant Cade's shoulder and said, "Sergeant, I'm a team leader. I should be the one up front here." He couldn't believe he was spouting that sort of bullshit. He immediately knew he should've thought of something better to say. If he hadn't been scared shit-less, he'd have laughed at his melodramatic punk-ass. He needed to quit watching so many fucking movies.

Sergeant Cade looked around with a hard face that betrayed how much he wanted to stay there in the front of the fight, then pulled back to better use his experience to help co-ordinate the details that meant life or death for the whole platoon and not just a fireteam.

Walton pushed up to Sergeant Bronson, who turned to look at him briefly. A nearby team leader from Third Platoon said worriedly, "We've gotta get Lanagan out!"

Sergeant Bronson moved away from the doorway with calm, but heated precision, and gestured to the body on the ground with his muzzle. "If that Haji moves, put two in his ass," he ordered.

While trying to remain covered by the wall to his right, Walton divided his attention between the bloody Haji sprawled in front of the compound entrance and a closed wooden door standing just inside it, looking for anything resembling a threat. He did not like that door being at an angle across from him. It put him in a possible Fatal Funnel (a sector in which an enemy could fire from a choke-point, like an entrance. The area covered by such a sector resembled the conical shape of a funnel, with Haji at the apex of it). However, if he lost sight of it, Haji could possibly come through it and get the drop on them.

Walton was now up front. His thoughts lacked words. There was only the wound-up terror and anticipation of something coming through the door. It caused his imagination to overlap with his awareness, and they bred a twisted hope that something would, just so the fight would hurry up and be over and the excruciating tension would stop. Every nerve that held him to the doorway screamed with fear that the next round would find him and he'd die here in this shithole country at the hands of a man he'd never even met, or that he'd fail at his job and cause someone else to get killed.

Sergeant Bronson returned and placed a steady hand on Walton's shoulder while he continued to pull security. "Alright, Tom, you're gonna go through this doorway and hang a right. We'll be right behind ya." The man was a rock.

"Roger, Sergeant."

Walton stepped into the compound entrance with O'Falin, Sergeant Bronson, and Sergeant Cade (who had jumped in again, unbeknownst to Walton) right on his heels. He hung a right, going through the open doorway like he had through hundreds of others in the past three and a half years, and moved toward the corner in front of him. As he button-hooked left to move to his point of domination while scanning his sector, he stopped short. O'Falin read his movement, and paused in his advance along the left wall also, ceasing further movement into the room. Walton never seen a scenario quite like this.

He crouched in a small courtyard. Of the walls that framed it, the ones to his left and right belonged to two structures of indeterminate depth, and each had a closed wooden door at the far end, thus covering half of the courtyard with two potential Fatal Funnels. Sergeant Dern's dome-shot proved Haji was shooting from covered and concealed positions. Like doorways. Therefore, it behooved him to keep himself and his team out of all of these fucking doorways if he could avoid it. He wondered if it was possible to be more scared. The world seemed to be made out of doorways.

His first heartbeat inside the courtyard became his second. The years of instruction flashed through his brain, telling him to stay out of a Fatal Funnel, and now here were two covering each other. If he continued to advance to his point of domination, he'd be covered by the door to his left. O'Falin would advance to his own point of domination along the left wall and would wind up covered by the door on the right. Half his team would be potentially covered, and if one of them went down, it would be a goat-rope trying to get the bastard out. Even if neither one of them got zapped, the small courtyard would be cluttered with them going back and forth breaching and clearing with their back exposed to one door for at least as long as it took them to clear whatever was on the other side of the first one they went through.

To stack his team on one door, regardless of which one, would allow them to be covered by the opposite door like sitting ducks, and they could all wind up getting killed. If he did get through a door, he still would only be taking two other men with him into one of the mystery buildings (holding who knew what), leaving one guy behind who would be responsible covering their backs, with an untold number of possible Hajis on the other side of the unopened door who could pop out at any time. Once they started trying to clear the buildings, their single team could get over-extended real fast.

The second heartbeat passed as he groped for a way to adapt. If an additional team was brought up then they could each stack on a door and breach them at the same time. That way, at least one team stood a good chance of making it into one of the buildings and would hopefully be able to pinpoint where Lanagan and Haji was. From their current foothold in the courtyard, whoever was in charge behind them could then keep pushing supporting teams through and not lose momentum.

"Hey, Sergeant," Walton called out, "I got a door to my left and right, but I don't see Lanagan. We're gonna need some more people to help clear this." He looked nervously from one doorway to another, expecting to hear shots at any time.

"Get outta there, the ANA's gonna push through," Sergeant Bronson said.

Walton turned and moved out, then he took back his position at the compound entrance near the dead Haji. O'Falin crouched across from him, pulling security into the opposite direction, back toward the courtyard they'd just left.

"Shouldn't we be farther out of this doorway, Sergeant?" O'Falin asked.

"I'd like to be, but if we pull back farther we can't see those doors," Walton replied with a scant nod toward the wooden door angled across from him, and to the courtyard entrance on the other side of the wall next to him.

"We really need more guys."

Walton grinned while staring a hole in the wooden door in his sector, expecting it to open at any time. "You know The Battalion; a day late and a dollar short." From the periphery of his vision, Walton saw O'Falin return the smile.

Walton's hand suddenly flew back at the whim of an

unseen force that ripped the air with a familiar ringing sound in his skull. He found himself on his back, saturated with confusion, wondering what was going on. An odd sensation lay in his hand, like he had touched an electric fence or cut his hand deeply with a knife.

He brought it to his field of vision and saw his right hand hanging at an unnatural angle, limp, torn, and bloody, gaping with ragged holes through his flight glove and up to the middle of his forearm. "Oh shit, I've been shot!" he said as the pieces fell into place.

Someone was trying to kill him.

Walton was immediately, blindingly, wordlessly, overwhelmed by how helpless and fragile the body was which held him to reality, and as he noticed his own gore, his shell seemed both suddenly unfamiliar while at the same time stirring up a tender affection, as if it were an old friend whose every intimate secret was known to only him. His awareness became a brittle millennia of terror that *this* may be the very last moment he'll ever have; that for him it could end right there in the Afghanistan dirt and he'd be swallowed up by the greedy black void that loomed among the ringing lead and he'd finally find out if God was real or not. He felt closer than he had ever been to satisfying the ache to *know* and finally be at peace with either *Nothing* or *God*. Even if the teachings of his youth turned out to be true and there was such a thing as eternal damnation from which there was no appeal, and he was bound there, it would be worth it if only to have the satisfaction of knowing the truth of the mystery.

And yet, Walton was exulted to the point of stupidity with relief that he was still alive however precariously. Time yawned out into the infinity before his birth and after his death, threatening to reclaim him at any second, and the humility that came with the knowledge of this broke Walton's heart with thankfulness for the gift of his life. The fact that he had been fortunate enough to exist at all had been a wild act of grace. It was enough to make his soul cry out in the hope that whatever had allowed him to come into being would be there to catch him when he made his leap into the dark.

The conscious portion of his mind discarded the thought of returning fire with his now useless hand, and sought to figure out a way to grab his rifle slung across his chest with the left hand and shoot at the faceless man shooting at him. As his brain groped for a way out of his predicament, other thoughts skimmed across the periphery as it grasped with a greedy reflex to force Death to pry his greatest moments of life from its fingers; he was a little boy on a family road trip, sitting in the back seat of his parents' car with a read-along book next to his middle brother who would grow up and join the Navy. He was ten years old again and quietly sang to his newborn youngest brother as he rocked him and fed him his bottle, feeling like his heart would burst. He was in Montreal and could hear Amy's laugh and feel her hand in what was left of his own.

His existential struggle seized him as a formless yearning that occurred within the space of an instant while his body fumbled around awkwardly trying to get its shit together as Haji kept shooting. Sergeant Bronson materialized over him out of nowhere, dragged him away from the doorway, and immediately began bandaging the remnant of his hand with the aid of the team leader from Third Platoon.

"Not so tight," Walton chided. "I don't want to lose my hand."

Sergeant Bronson spoke while he wound the cloth, not bothering to take his eyes from it though shots still rang viciously behind him. "Motherfucker, I know how to put on a pressure dressing." His familiar gruff tone made Walton want to laugh.

Sergeant Bronson and the soldier from Third Platoon

eventually shifted their attention from his hand to the wound in his upper arm. Walton wondered when he'd picked that one up. He hadn't felt anything. How many times had he been shot? Haji was one sneaky fuck.

As they worked, Walton quickly raised his left hand to his teeth, bit the frayed fingertips of his surviving flight glove, and pulled it off. He stuffed the old dusty black glove that smelled of Afghanistan and had been mended over the years with bits of dental floss, into his cargo pocket with a grin. Al-Qaeda may have killed one glove, but he'd be damned if he'd give the fuckers the satisfaction of claiming both of them. He'd had those gloves longer than his Joes had been in the fucking Army.

They soon finished, and Sergeant Bronson looked Walton in the eye. "You good to walk?"

"Roger, Sergeant."

They helped Walton to his feet, then Sergeant Bronson pulled him close without taking his firing hand from his M4, and spoke into Walton's ear above the shooting and yelling, saying, "Don't worry, brother. We'll get this motherfucker. I'll save you an ear." He then turned around toward the doorway, raised his rifle to the high-ready and began firing into the compound.

Walton turned with his rifle dangling from its torn sling. A soldier took it, telling him the CCP (Casualty Collection Point) was at the mortar position, and Walton began to walk toward it with his hand elevated to stem the blood-loss.

The CO stood at the corner of the building with the Antenna Farm, antsy at not being in the fight. He stopped Walton with concern in his face, and asked as he looked for symptoms of shock, "Where are you, Walton?"

"I'm in a fuckin' firefight, Sir."

A staff officer looked at him and asked, "Are you alright?"

Walton looked at the staff officer, then shifted his eyes

197

to his raised wounded hand, then redirected his gaze back to the officer. He didn't bother to say anything.

Captain Cordova looked at the staff officer and said, "Get a detail and take Sergeant Walton to the CCP."

The detail spread out and escorted Walton back to the mortar position. The shots continued behind him, and his mind swirled. An extraneous thought found it comical the way the detail of soldiers ducked at the sound of the shots, as if they thought they were Neo from the *Matrix* and could dodge a bullet traveling faster than sound.

Walton became ashamed. He was leaving while the fight was still on and his squad put their lives in a doorway. He should have done things different. It ended like this? *Through* the door? Walton had to give Haji points for thinking outside the box on that one, but shooting a guy through the fucking door just wasn't very sporting. Sometimes Haji was a real dick. Walton felt an impulse to turn around, but let the nonsense pass, cursing himself for being a fucking moron. He was now Combat-Ineffective and would be about as much use to them as tits on a bull.

As he neared the CCP, the fight began to seem miles away rather than just mere meters and he smiled. In spite of the shame, he was giddy, which in turn only made him feel even more guilty. He'd survived. It was finished. As long as a strays stayed away, he'd be going home and never have to wear a uniform again. He'd be able to get clean and sleep. *Sleep.* He felt tired and wanted to rest.

He kept his hand elevated as he walked, and the creeping fears percolated; of losing his hand, or that one of the rounds that pulsed through the air he breathed would catch him in the base of his spine and paralyze him, damning him to a wheelchair until he died, or that another would find his cock or balls and render him unable to make love to a woman.

He passed the First Sergeant, who knelt near the open field and smiled with a thumbs-up as he said, "Alright

Okie!" Walton returned the gesture and was happy that he'd seemed to have redeemed himself in the First Sergeant's eyes. He took a seat near Sergeant Dern who looked around with wobbly vision as he rested, and while a medic went to work on his hand, it occurred to Walton that his legs were pointed toward the fight. He continued to imagine getting shot in the taint or his genitals. That would totally blow ass. He decided he was too tired to shift his position and took his chances.

He could see the compound in the distance and the soldiers scrambling around it like ants. War was so fucking...*weird*. He was safe (more or less) while the rest of his platoon was still in The Shit. *The Shit;* it blew his mind how people could fight so hard against strangers. The world was crazy. He looked down at his hand and chuckled. He remembered Sergeant Wider telling them during one of their drinking sessions, "If we go downrange, and start taking rounds, and you can hear them, don't worry. It's the ones you *don't* hear that get ya." That was no shit.

The medic began to go right to work with the IV needle, but had difficulty getting a good stick. After his fourth failed attempt at starting an IV, he cursed in frustration.

"You're doing alright," Walton assured him. "Just calm down." He looked at his hand and feared the pain that would be coming. "Say, when do I get Morphine? I'm afraid I'll run out of shock."

"I'm supposed to start the IV first."

"C'mon, I won't tell," Walton said with a conspiratorial wink.

The medic barked a laugh that seemed to alleviate a bit of the tension. "Alright."

While the medic injected the Morphine, Walton saw Sergeant Feran pass by with a gun team. He looked over at Walton and yelled, "Big Dub!" with an encouraging smile, then continued toward the fight. Walton smiled back and waited for the Black Hawk. Within minutes it arrived, and the First Sergeant directed him inside. Walton entered, laid down on a stretcher, and the door closed behind him.

The bird lifted, and one of the two medics within pounced onto Walton, straddled his pelvis, then leaned in close and began cutting off his gear and DCU's. The soft humanity of the medic's face looked out of place against the harsh confines of the olive-drab bug-shaped flight helmet—HOLY SHIT! A FUCKING GIRL!

A girl was cutting his clothes off.

He found this arousing, yet tried not to think about how nice it was to be touched by a girl, even in a clinical setting. He wondered what color of hair she had under that goddamned helmet. She looked like a brunette to him. Then again, maybe she had one of those long, lush, chestnut-colored situations. Women's hair was really fantastic when you thought about it. He imagined he could play with a woman's hair—just her hair—for hours. The girl's face had been caressed by the Afghanistan sun, creating a warm healthy canvas for her freckles. While she went about her tasks with the gravity and economy of movement of a samurai, Walton had to restrain himself from reaching up with his fingertips to play connect-the-dots with her freckles. He bet her skin was soft like cool liquid silk. He forced himself to focus, figuring he needed a hard-on like he needed another hole in his sorry ass.

She got near his pants and he halted her. "I should warn you, Miss, I don't wear underwear."

Her freckled face smiled with something between a happy leer and a warm business-like smirk under her big-assed helmet, and she replied, "It's okay." She continued to cut, but left him a DCU fig leaf to cover his hydraulics. Afterward, she placed a wool blanket over him and began the IV that the medic had been unable to complete.

"Hey, pardner," Walton called over to the other medic, "could you go in the big ammo pouch on my LCE and get out my camera and take a few shots?"

The medic smiled and took some pictures. Walton then had the two medics pose together and used his good hand to take a few snaps of them as well. They were good people and they ran a squared-away bird.

The Black Hawk carried him to KAF where an ambulance took him to the infirmary. His awareness was clouded, and the only thought that seemed to hold was the memory of the way Amy had looked on Canada Day as she'd smiled and walked next to him with her red blouse and the navy skirt that had artfully displayed her stems. She walked through his mind like a dream until he finally lost consciousness.

He woke with half his arm wound up like the business end of a giant Q-tip. The first thing he felt was a queasy sense of fear. "Excuse me," he asked a matronly nurse. "Did y'all take my hand?"

She smiled down on him and patted his shoulder. "No, baby, you still have it."

"Thank you, Ma'am." Walton rested his head back down on the pillow and grinned, near to tears. He was officially The Luckiest Motherfucker on Planet Earth.

Sergeant Major Brooden approached him along with a few others he didn't recognize. "Hello, Sergeant Walton. How are you feeling?"

"Alright, I guess. How's my platoon? Did we get any more casualties, Sergeant Major?"

The Sergeant Major's face became a fraction more grave. "Yes. We lost Lanagan and Espinoza. Desilva caught some shrapnel from a frag."

Walton's eyes widened. "Espinoza? Are you sure, Sergeant Major?"

"Yes. I'm afraid so"

"How'd it happen?"

"Sergeant Lanagan was shot in the head, but you probably knew that. Sergeant Espinoza went down shortly after you. His squad went in on another attempt at retrieving Sergeant Lanagan, and his team was up front. He was shot up from the waist down and bled out."

Walton laid there floating in an odd detachment, wondering if it all was real. "What about the rest of them? How're they doin', Sergeant Major?"

"They've shut down for the evening and will stay put until morning. We're gonna send some shit in and level the place. They found a number of the guys we were looking for and several caches all over the place. It looks like you guys found an actual Al-Qaeda cell. You guys did good." He looked Walton over with concern. "Is there anything you need? Did you need to call your folks?"

"That would probably be a good idea."

Someone produced a cell phone and he dialed the number. "Mom? Hi, it's Tom. Look, Mom, I don't have much time. I've been shot. No, I'm okay. I'm not sure what'll happen. Yes, I'll let you know as soon as I know. I love you. Bye." He pressed the end button, thinking he'd probably just killed his mother. She'd sounded like she was on her way to work. He'd heard cars in the background and her voice had cracked as she told him she loved him.

He gave the phone back and shook hands with the Sergeant Major, then got up to find Desilva. He looked down to see he was wearing a tie-dye T-shirt, donated courtesy of the Red Cross, and he abided in its awesomeness. After finding the younger soldier and checking on his wounds, Walton went outside with him to smoke a cigarette and ask out about Speedo and Lanagan.

Walter Reed and the Countess of Montreal In-Exile

Walton sat at the window of the shuttle bus and watched the Washington Monument pass by under a midnight sky. The world was speckled with lights and activity and he regretted that the first sight of his country had to be one of modernity. The neon, and the concrete, and the billboards; there was something about it all that seemed foreign and garish.

However, he was home. And he was high. He smiled at the hazy feeling of the Morphine and surrendered to the sense of floating that the shuttle offered. There were other wounded soldiers with him and they talked about their injuries and how good the States looked and what they were going to do first, but he didn't listen to them or even care about the fact they existed. He just wanted to float.

The shuttle stopped outside of Walter Reed Army Medical Center and he got off. He wore the track pants and sweater that he'd received in Landsthul, Germany (the latter he'd had to cut up to get his hand through). He could feel the cool of the pavement under the thin disposable slippers and found the sensation very appealing. He was tempted to open up the box of complementary Girl Scout Cookies in the Red Cross plastic bag, but decided it probably wasn't the best time for it. He really wanted those Tagalongs, though.

A nurse welcomed him to the hospital and directed him to a lab where an X-ray technician took pictures of the bony pulp of his hand. Afterward, he walked to another room where a tall young doctor with glasses had him sit, and then began cutting off the dressing.

As the doctor removed the layers of cloth, Walton smelled the clammy combination of disinfectant and wound that came from his swollen hand. When the doctor freed the last layer of bandage and moved to throw it away, Walton began peeling yellow strips from off of the wounds themselves.

"You've done this before?"

"Yes, Sir," Walton answered. He winced as he continued to pull the strip away from the gash. "This ain't my first rodeo. I used to help my nurse clean my wounds when I was in Germany." He then remarked with a grin, "Didn't hurt quite this bad, though." Of course, he supposed he just might not have noticed on account of the nurse from Germany having been so cute. She had given a mean sponge-bath. The spanky, brown-haired slip of a girl had no earthly business being single, and Walton had offered up a prayer of thanks that they still cranked out Wife Material every now and again.

The doctor finished removing the yellow strips himself then cleaned the wound. After he redressed it, he said, "Let me see your bicep." Walton complied, and the doctor lifted the sleeve of the sweater to expose two lines of torn skin, both running lengthwise across Walton's upper arm with stitches crossing them like train tracks.

"Those stitches should be ready to come out," The doctor observed. He produced a small pair of scissors and went about cutting and removing them. As he worked, he told Walton, "I know it looks like the scar cuts through your muscle tissue, but with time and scar massage, you'll have a normal bicep again. You could even do weight training and make it as big as you want."

"What about the hand? Will I get to keep it?"

"It's still too early to tell. Dr. Jones will see you soon and he'll assess the wound and decide what to do next. You will probably have a debrisment in a few days where we'll go in and clean it up from the inside some more."

A nurse took him to a room where she started a fresh IV and left him to sleep. He drifted off, but four hours later another nurse came in to wake him up to take his vitals. When she did, he struggled not to throw something.

A few days later he sat across from his family for the first time in over a year. It felt odd being around them at first. He heard himself speak to them, but it seemed like it was someone else using his voice. However, this didn't stop him from appreciating the way his brother Mike had gotten a Pass from the Navy and turned the hospital room into a party, even going so far as to smuggle in a *Playboy* and some books. His other brother Joseph looked taller than he remembered and had begun growing his first beard. His mother caught him up on family gossip, but his dad just sat there staring at his son's hand.

Walton was soon on a bed in Pre-Op. He absently listened to the doctors explain the details of the procedure they were about to perform, and warn him of the usual possibility of death and infection. When the anesthesiologist injected the knock-out juice into the IV, Walton smiled. He would soon be enjoying a nice break from the world.

He stood near the ramp of the Shithook as she lowered to the ground like a giant beast outside of Miam Do. The prop-wash blasted the dirt on the ground and the bird danced under his feet like a boat on water. She touched down and he heard, "Go!" He sprang forward…

And was restrained by a nurse. He struggled against her, but as he looked around, he finally ceased. He was on a gurney, staring up at the ceiling with people and lights all around. Words like confusion and fear didn't exist for him, just their meanings. He didn't know what was real and began to cry.

Reality eventually found him and he calmed down despite the insubstantial feeling of the world around him. He missed the oblivion, but he resolved himself to his surroundings. He looked down to find a grotesque collection of rods and pins drilled into the bones of his hand and forearm.

"What's wrong, honey?" asked his mom as he lay back in his room, hours later.

"It hurts." He saw his mother's brown eyes take on a pained, knowing expression and he said, "Could y'all please leave? We'll talk tomorrow, if that's alright."

There was a look on his dad's face that Walton hadn't seen since his mom had almost died in a car accident a few years prior. "No, Son. We want to stay."

"Kenny, he wants to be alone," his mom said gently, and Walton almost smiled at his mom's uncanny grasp of hospital etiquette. She knew more about hospitals than she would have liked. "Son, we'll come back tomorrow." They hugged him and left.

Walton pressed the call button as soon as they were out the door and waited. No one responded. The pain blocked out everything, and went into the core of the mess of his hand and wrist, evolving and picking up intensity with each second. It somehow managed to be sharp and dull at the same time. He closed his eyes and pressed the button again in vain.

Time slowed down to a long infinity and the ache that gored into his bones violated his mind as if the doctors were still boring into his hand and arm. He writhed slowly away from, then back toward his elevated arm in a futile effort for anything resembling comfort. It was the worst physical pain he could remember. He made low guttural noises in anger at a world where such pain was possible. Again and again, he pressed the button and tried to breathe.

An Age of the earth came and went before a nurse stepped in, her dark skin contrasting with the bright pastel scrubs. "What's wrong, baby?" she asked comfortingly.

He croaked with a pained voice, "It hurts, Ma'am."

She recited the litany. "On a scale of one-to-ten, ten being the most intense pain you can imagine, what is your pain rating?"

"'Bout an eight or a nine."

"I'll go see what the doctor has for you."

She left and returned moments later, wasting no time in injecting something into his IV. She bore an apologetic expression and said, "I'm so sorry. They forgot to schedule any follow-up meds for you after your surgery and you caught us at shift change. This won't take long to take hold." She smiled at him and patted his hand. "I'm Ms. Burmingham and I'll be your nurse for tonight. If you need anything just press the call button. Okay?"

He smiled with hope at the liquid that coursed through the tubes leading to his hand.

For the next few days, Walton faded in and out of sleep. Every now and again he shot a glance at the wound-vac that drew corrupted fluid from his wrist. The nurses continued to annoy him by checking his vitals every few hours, but most were pleasant, so he chatted and flirted with them when they came around.

He had forgotten just how good women smelled. It made him want to put his hand on them when they got near him with their crisp white uniforms. However, when they moved the things on his bed-tray to set down medicine or a bit of equipment, he had to restrain himself from yelling at them. The bed-tray was *his*, and they had no right to disturb his things so carelessly. When his IV beeped, he would almost lose it completely and want to break whatever was near, and from the corner of his eye, he wondered why his mom looked like she didn't recognize him.

She sat in a chair next to him and watched the small TV that hung from an arm above the bed. Walton had made it a point to spend a portion of each day watching the news, or reading a paper or magazine to catch up on the world. He also wanted to keep his mind busy so he didn't wind up sitting around and feeling sorry for himself like the clichéd "wounded vet" that seemed to be a staple of modern war movies. His mother, however, couldn't be bothered with listening to a bunch of eggheads rattle on about "how they have a magic solution for other people's miseries," as she put it, but she loved her boys, and had learned to put up with Walton's tendency to rant over current events long ago.

He'd noticed a reoccurring argument that kept insinuating itself into many of the media pundits' narratives that disturbed him; namely, that the wars downrange were the result of Christians in rural states. The assertion that people like his parents were to blame disgusted him, and as a man who'd been wounded in his country's service, it felt like a slap in the face.

Having spent the first nineteen years of his life deeply involved in the Church, he had never once heard in a prayer meeting, worship service, or even on a Wednesday night business meeting, anything whatsoever about putting the Middle East to the sword. No deacon had ever made a motion for the congregation to pressure elected officials to have the U.S. blow up Muslims. No preacher had ever said that he felt like The Lord had laid it on his heart to make the streets flow with the blood of the nonbelievers. No youth minister had ever told them that the greatest thing they could do for God was to kill Haji.

That there were adults who made a good living manufacturing such rubbish, and didn't get fired for passing off such a shallow analysis of international affairs, was beyond the pale. They needed First Sergeant Wade in the worst way. They were ate up with The Dumbass. None of this really surprised him, though. People like his folks had been one of the country's preferred whipping-boys since before H.L. Menken.

What Walton did remember from those years in the Church was a lot of people who were barely getting by, scraping together what money they could to donate to orphanages for children they'd never even met. Or they'd occasionally get together a group of volunteers to travel to some impoverished village on a mission trip to build a clinic or a bit infrastructure to help out the poor.

As far as the Middle East was concerned, Walton had the impression that the churches he'd grown up in had more or less adopted the foreign policy of the Governor from *The Best Little Whorehouse in Texas*, who'd said "that it behooves both the Jooz and the Aye-rabs to settle their differences in a Christian manner." Other than a loosely-defined commitment to Israel, that was about as far as they went. Of course, there was also the constant praying for peace. No doubt in part because it would be their sons fighting in whatever war got cooked up; they were among the few remaining segments of the population that still believed in sacrificing for America.

Their yeoman ancestors, with their toughness, high degree of religiosity, and community-centered norms and values, had been handy to have around for whenever country had needed people to till the dirt, settle the frontier, bale hay, pick cotton, mine coal, turn bolts, work railroads, and fight wars. However, their decedents in the brave new world were to be fitted with a yoke of shame, and to be unofficially branded as trash or vilified in their own home. They were to be fed a steady diet of dissention, entertainment, and dependency infrastructure lest they maintain some semblance of backbone and self-reliance. Didn't the silly Proles know that the modern nation-state was now just supposed to be a market of "human capital" and not a sovereign country of citizens?

Looking at his mother, he wondered if their loyalty wasn't misplaced. Given the tone of the bigots who wrote articles and mocked those like his family, who had been born and bred in "flyover states," and made them into the cause of all that was wrong with the U.S. and the world, he didn't think such "elites" were worth the blood it took to keep them safe and prosperous. While he still sympathized with the Church in spite of his many questions and uncertainties, he no longer valued turning the other cheek as he used to. Sometimes you ran out of peaceful compromises. Some people just had to be fought. Tooth and claw. The trick was figuring out who it *really* was that deserved the ass-kicking.

His mother interrupted his brooding. "Germany sure looks pretty," she said as AFN ran a commercial featuring European Posts. "Did you get to see much of it?"

"No. I was in the hospital the whole time." He didn't tell her about the wifely brunette with the sponge-bath skills. "They lost my records then had us all laid out in the entry way on our stretchers when we were leaving and there were all these kids and families lookin' at us like we were in a freak show. When they finally did get us on our way, they drove us on the roads that I don't think have been repaired since World War II. It was almost funny to see all us mangled up soldiers gettin' all tossed about and groaning."

She shook her head in a way that made Walton think he probably shouldn't have said anything. "I can't imagine. I'm pretty impressed with the hospital here, though."

"I was too, until last night," he said flatly as he recalled the night before. "That was horrible. Ms. Burmingham was great, though. She hooked me right up."

"Well, Ms. Burmingham just made a new friend."

They spent a moment watching TV, then he said from a need to converse, "I feel bad. Maw-Maw called last night and I got pissed and told her not to call me here. That I was wore out and that I'd call her. It ain't right to talk to your grandmother like that. I think the drugs must make me cranky or somethin'. I feel sort of...*angrier* than I remember. And it's like, all the time, it seems. Mom, your boy's turnin' all Dr. Jekyl and Mr. Hyde on ya," the last he said with a smile to try to put her at ease. "I should call her and apologize."

"It's okay, Son. You've been through a tough ordeal."

The phone rang and they looked at each other. He picked it up, expecting to hear his grandmother. "Hello? Hi! How're you doin'?"

"Who is it?"

He turned and smiled in a way that made him look as though he hadn't been shot. "It's Amy!" he said as he covered the handset. He entertained the notion that it was almost worth going through that whole experience if only to read the urgency and concern in her email after he'd told her, and to hear the eagerness in her calls.

His mother beamed. She wanted grandchildren and didn't care how she got them. "Well, you tell Miss Amy I said, hi! I'm going to go get a bite at the cafeteria. Do you want anything?"

"No, Ma'am. Thank ya, though."

Walton closed his eyes and saw Amy's face while she asked about how he felt, and told him how much she'd wanted to hear his voice. Hearing her somehow amped up the voltage on the caveman-ish feelings that crawled around inside him. He liked how powerful he felt with the growling thing within him. The bullshit was gone on some level and the world had gotten so simple that he could hardly contain himself. "I like your voice too, darlin'. It's the highlight of my day. Say, have you been drinkin'?"

"Yeah, I drank a little," she said with a faintly perky slur. "I just got back from a funeral for my great-aunt and everyone got really drunk. I sat and drank Scotch and listened to my dad's British cousin talk about how he used to say he was a member of the Rolling Stones so he could get girls to sleep with him. He's awesome."

"I'm proud of you. It's still daylight and you're tipsy. God, I wish I was there. I'd get drunk with you and we'd break shit. It would be fuckin' awesome."

"It would be, but I don't know about breaking things."

"Are you kiddin'? It's the shit. Here, break a glass right

211

now and you'll see what I mean."

The line went silent, then an eruption of shattering glass filled the phone, followed by their wicked laughter.

A man with the rank of captain and the air of repressed hilarity looked up from the paperwork on his table with a smile and greeted, "Hey, Walton, how's it goin'?"

"Not too bad, Sir." The Occupational Therapy Center was dim and quiet, in stark contrast with its usual raucous atmosphere. "This place ain't the same on Saturday."

"Yeah, it's a bit more relaxed. Hey, you changed your pajama pants."

Walton looked down at his second pair of flannel pants and shrugged. "It had to be done. I could smell myself and that ain't ever good."

The captain wrinkled his nose. "Yeah, I didn't need to know that. Did you bring a CD? Ah, the Stones. Excellent choice." Captain Vertain loaded the CD player, and waited patiently to begin. When it did, he sneered rakishly and silently played air guitar. After the first few riffs, he then returned to the table and began the ultrasound massage on Walton's hand to break up scar tissue.

"Man, with nobody here I feel like I can cuss again," Walton confessed. "I've been around my folks and the nurses for so long that I hardly talk because I have to censor myself."

"It's totally cool to cuss here on Saturdays," Captain Vertain said as he moved the wand in a clockwise motion on the wound. "Watch, I'll cuss right now." He then looked up commandingly at the empty room and yelled, "SHIT!"

Walton shook his head in a frantic fashion. "Aw man, don't say, *shit*. I had a horrible episode last night. You know how Morphine constipates you? Well, I hadn't shat in like, two weeks."

"Jesus!"

"Exactly. At first, I figured me and my body could sort this out on our own and avoid havin' to deal with the embarrassment of bringin' in a third party. Call me old-fashioned, but I really don't cotton to the idea of people foolin' around with the workings of my ass. I'd just take the stool softeners, wait, and let nature take its course. As time went on, though, I began to have my doubts. I wasn't in pain, but I figured after two weeks this could become a health issue. Who needs that?

"Anyhow, I ring for the nurse to explain my situation and get some relief, and since I've had a semi-regular diet of porn since I was like, twelve, I was naturally hopin' for some cute little doe-eyed bubbly thing that wouldn't compromise my pride too much if she handled my ring-piece. It'd be embarrassing as hell, and it wasn't exactly my idea of how to spend a Friday night, but I'll take gettin' touched by a chick over not gettin' touched by a chick, any day of the week and twice on Sunday. Might even be kinda kinky. It'd stay just between me, her, Jesus, and whoever does the laundry 'round here. After all, there was this one NCO in my platoon from Michigan, Sergeant Sandlin, who was the most awesome-est dirtiest dick dog you'd ever hope to meet, and he said a chick once surprised him by stickin' her finger in his ass when he was in mid-hump with her, and he said he'd never came so hard in his life. He said it felt so good that he was tempted to do it to himself one day when he was beatin' off, but didn't, because that was just him being a good Catholic.

"But *noooo*, they send in a *dude*. A fuckin' dude! In walks this big damn male nurse I've never met before who says he's Nurse Smith, and he's carryin' a suppository that looks like one of the Lone Ranger's silver bullets. Half a month's worth of shit in my intestines and I'm feelin' okay, but the second this motherfucker walks in with somethin' he's supposed to put in my ass, I'm suddenly sick. I ain't gonna lie; at this point, I'm kinda freaked out.

I've got myself a bait-and-switch on my hands, Hoss, like you ain't ever seen.

"I told him, 'Look, I've never had one of those before and I'm not sure how it works,' and he explained that it goes in the ass and breaks up the shit, then a half-hour later, you're in business. I asked if I put it in, or if he does, and he replied that it didn't matter, but that if it didn't go in far enough, we'd have to try again.

"Sir, if you'd have put a gun to my head a week ago and told me that you were gonna kill me unless I got a suppository in my ass forthwith, but I could choose whether it would be me or a stranger who inserted it, I'd have told you to go piss up a rope, I'll do it my goddamned self. But now that I'm findin' out that if I ain't a first-time-go I have to go through the ordeal of doin' it all over again, I'm startin' to have second thoughts. I could just see me spread-eagled on my hospital bed with one arm covered with all these rods and pins and IV's 'n what-not, and the other halfway up my ass tryin' to plant the charge. Then, only to find out afterward that I had to repeat the process. I thought about it for a bit, then decided to swallow my pride and let a professional do it. 'Get it right the first time,' and all that. Like I know how far up my ass I'm supposed to go with that thing. I've read Field Manual 7-8 cover to cover, and I assure you, there ain't nothin' in there on breach-loading an asshole.

"I had to roll off onto my side and bare my ass, and I'm embarrassed as hell. I'm embarrassed for me, 'cause shit ain't exactly goin' according to plan and now I've got some strange guy who looks like he plays professional football about to put somethin' in my ass and I really ain't crazy about my life at that point. After being shot, that kinda thing is just addin' insult to injury. Literally.

"On top of that, I'm embarrassed for Nurse Smith. He seems like a good dude. He ain't hurtin' anybody. He probably got into this gig to save lives and help people and maybe hump some nurse chicks. All that shit they put in the brochures. But you know they've got this poor bastard out changin' bedpans, and havin' to clean up God knows what, and dealin' with freaked out soldiers havin' crazy dreams, and I don't know what-all. If that ain't enough, he's gotta make the rounds puttin' shit-bullets in a bunch of dudes' hairy assholes. That's a tough row to hoe. I ain't ever had to deal with that sort of thing, but I've changed my share of diapers, so I think I understand that this kinda shit can really fuck with your day.

"To try to hold on to some shred of my dignity, and out of respect for our mutual humanity 'n all that happy horseshit, I figured I'd make small-talk. You know, like that sort of a situation wasn't weird at all. 'Wit is the denial of suffering,' says the Freud.

"So we began talkin' about his previous experiences in administering Silver Bullets. All of a sudden I thought he was tryin' to put a model train set up my ass. I just about climbed up the motherfuckin' wall tryin' to escape. It was traumatic, ya see. Fortunately, it took only a split second and he said he thought he got it in far enough.

"I kinda felt violated, you know? Seriously, we have global wireless communication systems facilitated by satellites in a geosynchronous orbit IN OUTER FUCKIN' SPACE, but we're still puttin' stuff up people's asses to help them shit? Fuckin' savages!

"Anyhow, soon I feel the shit brewin'. I call him back in and he unhooks me from my IV so me and the Jungle Gym I've got drilled into my arm can go drop a deuce.

"So I'm there on the shitter with my PJ's around my ankles, three gunshot wounds from an AK-47, a Silver Bullet up my ass, and two weeks' worth of compressed shit headin' for daylight, and I swear, I had to have been dilated to like, a twenty, or somethin'. The situation was backfiring on me in every conceivable sense of the word. I'd try to let it out, but then it all tried to come out at once, and I thought I was gonna rip my fuckin' O-Ring. Like I don't have enough goin' for me already.

"On top of all that, I'm makin' weird noises whether I want to or not. This beast is a DEFCON-1 level growler. And it's mad as hell. It *wants* to fight, I can feel it. God only knows what someone would've thought if they'd passed by. I'm in there wrestlin' with this thing, and gruntin', and bearin' down, and I'm gettin' light-headed. The Lamaze Breathing ain't gettin' me anywhere. Trouble is, I know that if I let myself pass out, then it'll get the drop on me and do somethin' horrible. Maybe remove my organs while I'm unconscious and sell 'em on the black market.

"But then, I'm also goin' through this and I'm laughin' my fool head off. Partly 'cause toilet humor was always hysterical to my brothers and me, but also 'cause I'm thinkin', 'This is what I get for laughin' at Sergeant Sparn.' He was one of my old platoon sergeants and he had to go around with a feminine hygiene product in his asshole on account of a boil. We saw Doc pull it out once and reload a fresh one, and the whole damn platoon almost died laughin'. So there ya go. If there's a moral, I guess it's, 'What goes around comes around, so be careful about laughin' at people havin' to have stuff done to their ass, 'cause you could be next.' Then again, maybe there ain't a moral. Maybe The Bad Man is just a dick.

"So anyhow, I'm in the shitter havin' a significant emotional event. The situation is getting out of control. I then thought, 'Hey, I'm a sergeant, I should be tactical about this. Maybe with a little courage, discipline, and patience I could squeeze it out into passable chunks. Attack the shit asymmetrically. Divide and conquer.' But that just pissed it off. And anyhow, the contractions were killin' me. 'There is nothing more powerful than a shit whose time has come.'

"Eventually, I had to give the Suppository Devil his due. A piece, no, an Ass-Asteroid like a VW Bug finally entered the splash-down phase and I had to double-over and grab the handicap rail like I was givin' birth in the shitter.

"Now, I gotta admit, Sir…I was kinda curious about the fruit of my labors. You know it had to be huge. It certainly felt like a monster. Like a Toilet Kraken. But that could've been a subjective analysis. Maybe it was normal size, but had been hard like a stone and my body hadn't been prepared for that kinda threat level.

"But, I also kinda *didn't* want to know. There's some things that ain't healthy for the human mind. Like maybe if I dared to peer into the bowl I'd wind up lookin' into the face of evil. 'Look not behind thee…lest thou be consumed.' That's what my Bible says.

"In the end, I figured the best thing to do was clean up, flush it, and get the hell out of there before it decided to come after me. You know, like in a battle drill; 'Shoot, Move, and Communicate.' As mean as it was, I wouldn't have put it past the thing to have vengeance in its heart and try to launch a counterattack.

"By the time I come out of the latrine, I'm punchy. Gettin' shot was one thing, but now I'm stackin' trauma on top of trauma, and I feel like a broke-dick dog. I barely had the strength to wash my hands. Finally, I made it back to bed, closed my eyes, and just tried to put the whole ordeal behind me. No pun intended.

"I swear, Sir, after havin' to pass a Lincoln Log like that, I don't see how chicks and the gays can handle anal sex on a regular basis. That sort of thing can't be healthy in the long run. You watch, in fifty years there's gonna be a lot of old people runnin' around with fucked up assholes."

From behind a plate of chicken strips, French fries, and a Cherry Coke, Walton surveyed the people in the D-Fac alongside his trusty IV-on-wheels while carefully avoiding eye contact. People saw a wounded soldier sitting alone and felt compelled to join him. He appreciated the gesture, but it always left him feeling sad.

While sitting in the same chair a few days prior, a kind elderly man had asked to sit down and Walton had given him a smile and offered a chair. As the old man chatted with him, Walton had got caught up in his story.

The old man had ran away from home when he was seventeen, had been drafted into World War II, and went into communications, at one point even working for Patton. He had married, gotten out of the Army, and earned a degree in Art History. Together, he and his wife had quietly loved each other through the decades as the world changed. His wife had been diagnosed with Alzheimer's and it had taken her away from him three years ago after it had slowly killed her mind. He'd told Walton that he had just turned eighty-nine years old, and a week ago he had been asked by the authorities to surrender his driver's license. He'd come to Walter Reed to see his doctor. Walton's heart had gone out to the old man as he'd thought about how heavy and oppressive his loneliness must be.

He soon lost interest in the world of the D-Fac, and replayed in his mind the conversation he'd had with Amy after he'd watched *To Catch a Thief* the day before on the classic movie channel. They had almost burned up a phone card talking about how cool it would be to live in the south of France like Cary Grant had and the things they could do there. Inspired by the channel's line-up for that week, he had then told her all about the virtues of *High Noon* and sang her the theme song over the phone.

Lost in his musings over Amy and the possibility of life as an expat, Walton let his guard down and didn't see the woman with the grey-flecked blonde hair until she was already at the table. She gave him the smile that women reserve for children who remind them of their own, and said, "Hi. I noticed you were alone and I was wondering if

218

I could join you?"

Walton repaid her with a smile of his own and said, "Yes, Ma'am. That'd be nice. My name's Tom."

"Mine's Leanne. It's nice to meet you, Tom," she said as she sat down. "I have a son named Jonathan about your age. He was in Iraq." Like the old man, Leanne would ask him questions and answer his own, and sometimes they even managed to find a laugh.

However, as the conversation continued, Walton picked up more pieces to work with and noticed something that seemed peculiar. Though she had said she *has* a son, everything else about him was in the past tense. He then realized what it was she wanted.

"He's gone, isn't he, Ma'am." It wasn't a question.

Walton then saw one of the saddest smiles he swore he'd ever seen in his life. Looking at her face, he saw Leanne as a wide-eyed young woman living in the world-changing moment of just finding out that she was carrying her very first baby and *knowing* life was intimately connected to her and growing within her as the product of her and her husband's love, and that it completely depended upon her for its survival. He saw the months of pregnancy that wouldn't end, the first time she held him, the late night feedings, the joy of his first steps, the heartbreak of sending her young Jonathan to his first day of Kindergarten, and the pride of seeing him go to proms and graduate from High School.

She had probably felt that pride again when his drill sergeants had awarded him the infantryman's Blue Cord he'd earned at Ft. Benning, but it must've been laced with the fear of the possibility that he had set his feet on a path that would put him in danger. Living with that, and trying to hide it for his sake, had no doubt gone against her every instinct as a mother, but she had done her best.

Beneath her pride in her son, Leanne's face bore the haunting sorrow belonging to those who have poured their very soul and life's blood into their duty of doing everything they could to see another life grow strong and healthy. And then had lost it forever.

"He is. We just lost him a couple of days ago. He died from wounds from an IED in Iraq."

Walton did his best to swallow emotions for which there were no words and said as reverently as he could, "I'm sorry, Ma'am."

"It's alright, Tom," she said bravely. She looked down at her plate, seeing things Walton wanted to stop imagining. "He was a good man. A good soldier. My husband and I are just happy to have had him in our lives at all, even if it was just for a little while." She looked back up at him fervently. "He died protecting his country. I have to believe that."

Lounging at a table in the bar at the Malogne House, the outpatient hotel on-Post reserved for wounded soldiers and their families, Walton drained his beer with an almost orgasmic expression and wallowed like a pig in shit at how good it was to taste booze again. It was another one of those little things that made it feel odd to be back.

April drew to a close and he wished he could speed up the healing process. The days had become a dull endless cycle filled with therapy, formations, boredom, and soldiers spilled out of a walking horror movie, the monotony of it all leaving him feeling like he was getting absolutely nowhere. The doctors refused to be anything but vague when he asked them when he'd be able to take Leave, which only served to make him more irate. He looked around at the soldiers in the bar with their families and their prosthetic legs and arms, and eye patches, and livid scars, and he took solace in the fact that things could have been a damn sight worse.

He thought about the soldiers' lives. They had been babies once. Like Leane's Jonathan. They had been children and teenagers with hopes and dreams, and had been through variations of the same frying pan as he had been (and worse, from what he saw of many of their wounds). He wondered how things would play out for them. He was awed by how many still had so much fight in them. They were magnificent sons 'a bitches. A guy who could go around without a leg or half his face after all hell had broken loose and had taken a chunk of him with it, but still kept his head held high, inspired Walton. Haji didn't have shit on them.

Still though, the sight of them left him wondering what it was that they had bought. No doubt they had fought for their buddies and their platoons the same as him. Battles were sacred, and they belonged to those who'd fought them. However, they had bled in those battles as the result of orders that ultimately had tricked down from on high. In the grand scheme of things, what was the significance of what went on downrange? What did it all mean?

Something was wrong. It wasn't merely the wounded and the hospital; it was war, and that was to be expected. But the country, the world…the whole spirit of things was shot through with vileness and confusion. He couldn't put his finger on it, but he sensed its presence nonetheless.

The more Walton thought, the more he wasn't sure what the hell it was they were doing. He didn't know anyone in the national security establishment personally, and he was aware that there was a hell of a lot going on above a sergeant's pay grade, but it seemed to him that coming up with a coherent strategy was really kicking their ass. He had no problem with the U.S. coming down on terrorists like the fist of an angry god. It behooved America to keep its Pimp Hand way strong. However, fighting an open-ended war on multiple fronts as a part of an effort to flip the Middle East for its own good, just over a network of Haji's who'd gone off the reservation, struck him as excessive. Walton believed that further destabilizing foreign countries by trying to overthrow their political, cultural, and economic structures was a good way to make a bad situation worse. He didn't think The Brass had thought that one through. It was like no one read the classics anymore. As Sun Tzu had written, "There has never been a protracted war from which a country has benefitted." Fucking savages.

In every op-order he had been to there had been things like a statement of the commander's intent and a list of their objectives. That made sense. If you were going out on a mission into Indian Country, you needed to know what the hell it was you were supposed to do.

Evidently, the people in charge didn't have to do that. One of the biggest things that pissed him off about the "War on Terror" was that there didn't seem to be a clear objective. How could you score without a goal? None of The Brass, military or civilian, really talked about what victory was supposed to look like. Whenever they tried to, they sounded like a bunch of privates trying to explain why they were all fucked up; they didn't really know, but they were willing to gamble that if they just kept talking, the words would eventually start making sense.

And what the hell was it that had given Haji such a case of the ass in the first place? There were as many explanations as there were eggheads. It wasn't like no one had seen this thing coming. Haji seemed to have been pissed since those Libyans had tried to fuck with Marty McFly back in the Eighties. There was too much that didn't make sense. He needed more intel. Then again, maybe Alexander had been right. You didn't try to untie some knots. You had to cut them. But how did you know which ones to cut? Knots had a funny way of becoming nooses.

Walton shook his head. The world could kiss his Oklahoman ass. He had books to read, a girl to chase, and beer to drink, dammit.

He slowly ran his good hand over the cover of *A Year in Provence* in the spirit of a caress. Amy had spontaneously sent it in a package two days prior. Her hands had touched the novel when she'd put it in the box she'd filled with books, chocolate, and warmth.

He loved getting books from Amy. They whispered something to him about her. Something intimate. He devoured them as soon as he got them. He'd make a day of reading them. He'd throw the candy and books into his assault pack and read them one after another on a bench in the sun, or under one of the trees outside the Malogne House which had begun to bloom. They were more than books. They were windows to ideas and feelings running through her mind. Reading them was an act of sensuality. Having her books in his hands and in his brain, was a way of having her.

He opened it to the card he now used as a replacement bookmark which bore the quote from Tennyson, "*Come, tis not too late to seek a newer world*," which she had used to write him a note in her buoyant penmanship. He boiled to get out of the hospital and see her.

Though their affair was temporarily on the back burner, they still enjoyed each other's conversations, and Amy had become something more than just a potential bedmate. She'd unknowingly helped hold him together through the worst of the past six weeks of his stay in the hospital with the ever increasing intimacy and fun of her regular emails and almost nightly phone conversations that often spilled over into the small quiet hours.

The phenomenon between them had gotten to the point where Walton found it difficult to relate to the other wounded soldiers there. He would often pass through the melancholy wards with a swagger and his IV-on-wheels to read her words in an email. Hearing her voice say, "Hello," never failed to cause a sense of clarity fall on him, and like Saul on the road to Damascus, he felt how powerful and terrible it was to be confronted with the sorrow at the knowledge of just how lost you had been.

With each seemingly ordinary word that ranged from her mother's kitchen redecorating strategy, to which people from any time (historical or fictitious) she'd want to have a dinner party with, her grandparents' romance, or the fear of winding up like the people who walked through their passionless uninspired lives with the lights off inside, she left him with the impression that beneath it all, she was fighting a hard uphill scrap to overlook a lifetime of disappointments and cynicism, and was genuinely trying to open up to him. (While discussing life and whether or not it meant anything, she'd mentioned having read somewhere that it boiled down to finding something to do, and having someone to love who loved you back. Walton thought that was as good a medical prescription as any.) She may have even been listening when he'd tried to explain to her why joining the service was perhaps not what she was looking for.

He imagined what it would be like to be a normal guy. Seeing Amy would just be a matter of buying an airline ticket. He wouldn't have to put in for a Pass or ask permission from anybody.

Walton gripped the bottle and came back to the real world. He cursed himself. Merely wanting something meant nothing. People in Hell wanted ice water and biscuits but that didn't mean they got them. Dreaming like this was stupid and childish. Like his Grandma Gladys used to say; "Put what you want in one hand, shit in the other, and see which gets filled fastest." He was in the hospital and he wouldn't be out until he was better and the Army said he could leave.

He looked at the erector set sticking out of his hand and arm. He hated his wounds. They were holding him back. He wondered what it would be like to rip the hardware out right then and there. He imagined the pain and the iron-tingle of hot blood, and was unsettled by the fact that on some level he *wanted* to feel just how bad it would hurt.

He took a long swig of his beer. He began to read and thought that he should give Amy a call before he went back to his room and had to listen to his roommate snore.

He stood in formation the next morning and resented that the Army insisted on dragging him out of bed just to stand in a line. If he didn't, they would drop the paperwork to take his money and/or rank.

The chaplain gave the Word of the Day and it was all Walton could do not to tell everyone to take their accountability formations and words of encouragement and go fuck right off. He would much rather just get on with his life, thank you very much.

The Med-Hold platoon sergeant took charge and Walton got ready to leave. "One last thing," the platoon sergeant said officiously. "We need some soldiers to clean out the Sergeant Major's office. We can do this the easy way or the hard way. Do I have any volunteers?"

Walton itched to bitch-slap him with his good hand. He fantasized about grabbing the NCO by the throat and slowly crushing his windpipe until the life bled out of the idiot's eyes. He looked at the broken soldiers around him and wondered if the man had lost his fucking mind. You couldn't swing a dead cat without hitting some Joe who was either missing a body part or had some form of hardware running into his bones. One soldier even had an indention in his head where he was shy a part of his skull. Walton realized he may dislike having to hang around the hospital when he was an outpatient, but he absolutely hated the Med-Hold side of the house.

His hatred kept him company as he made his way to Occupational Therapy. He'd decided to get there early and work on painting his ceramic lighthouse at the arts and crafts table until his appointment. He was mad at having been "encouraged" to participate, knowing that if he didn't it'd probably raise a red flag with the staff or social workers. He saw it as busy work, but knew Thucydides had been right; in this world, "the strong do as they will and the weak suffer as they must." In comparison with the mindless bureaucratic might of his Uncle Sam, he was weak, and so he would yield until he no longer had to.

A group of soldiers in civilian clothes sat at the table painting their lighthouses with a woman who looked to be in her forties or fifties. As he approached, the woman looked up from her own work, smiled at Walton, and got up to stand near the collection of lighthouses in various states of completion.

They exchanged pleasantries and then she turned to look over the ceramic cache. She stopped at one and said as she carefully picked it up, "Here we go. This one is yours isn't it?" When he replied that it was, she stopped to appraise it. "I really like what you've done with this so far," she remarked with enthusiasm, and after he thanked her, they spoke for a few minutes about technique and color, and how he envisioned the finished project.

He took a seat and began painting a blank spot of stonework on his lighthouse. As he worked, his anger continued to gnaw at him. It switched its target to his lighthouse, arts and crafts, and life in general. Here he was painting a damned ceramic lighthouse when there was a world full of things to get into out there, and a girl up north who could lose interest at any minute. He was wasting his time! With each brushstroke, the rage pulsed.

Walton looked up and surveyed his fellow inmates. His eyes met with those of the woman who led the arts and crafts table. She smiled, and in it was all the warmth, and openness, and patience that anyone could hope to see in a human being. It was free of the sickly condescension of pity or need for recognition. It simply *was*.

As her look of acceptance and compassion washed

226

over him, he struggled to return it, realizing he had to fight through facial muscles contorted as he was inside. When he finally managed to do so, the tiny network of wrinkles behind her glasses deepened, reflecting a lifetime of blessing the world with such smiles.

He returned his eyes to his lighthouse and devoted every ounce of discipline he possessed to not well up any more than he was already starting to. While he had been pouting like a little bitch and feeling sorry for himself, the artist could have been anywhere else doing whatever she felt like. Yet here she was with a bunch of busted up soldiers in a hospital in a part of DC where local thugs got into shoot-outs with the gate guards, and she was volunteering her time to encourage the war-torn to develop their own ability to create beauty. There was a lot that was heroic in what she did.

Walton was humbled beyond measure as he resisted the urge to weep from gratitude that she cared so much for them. What made it even harder was that she was not alone. A woman volunteering with the Red Cross had recently wheeled around a cart of books on his ward. He'd been angry and wound up tightly that day also, and had been short with her to the point that his mom had looked at him disapprovingly. The woman had let his tone slide right over her (though it had still sunken a barb, leaving him feeling ashamed at the flash of hurt he'd seen on her face), and she had then asked him about his favorite authors. The next day she had returned with a stack of books she'd raided from her husband.

Mick Foley, Melissa Etheridge, and Connie Stevens had stopped by his room when they'd made the rounds visiting the soldiers. When the professional wrestler had said he admired the toughness of the wounded, Walton had been quick to inform him that the man who'd fought his heart out in the *Hell in a Cell* match was every bit as salty as anyone on the ward. Melissa Etheridge had brought an Earth Mother vibe in with her and it had made him wish the two of them could sit on a porch together and talk about life. He'd known Connie Stevens from watching a bit of *Palm Springs Weekend* with his mom (it was one of her favorites). Though time had faded her Technicolor youth, it had been powerless against her allure. Walton had easily imagined having once stopped traffic.

The Fisher House had paid for his parents' plane tickets and had provided them with a room at the Malogne House for free so they could be near him. Churches and classrooms had "adopted" him while he'd been deployed. They'd sent him care packages and letters of encouragement, and told him they had been praying for him and hoped he'd be safe and would come home soon. His case manager continually tried to move heaven and earth to take care of him. There was, and had been, so much uncompelled Good directed at him from a thousand different directions that the grace of it all hurt.

Walton felt a powerful love seize him; for the artist volunteering to help with their arts and crafts; for the Red Cross woman who had brought him books he hadn't deserved; for groups like the Fisher House; for entertainers who visited not for publicity, but because they gave a damn; for the people worshipping in churches, and the school children and their teachers; for his doctors and nurses, and for all those who simply cared and tried to do something nice for others. Their kindness and strength reminded him of all things he'd been losing faith in. It gave him hope that for all the wrongness, all wasn't lost.

That was the America he'd been taught to honor as a boy. *Those* were its people. *They* were worthy of love and sacrifice. The politicos and uppity blowhards, they were just parasites who were good for nothing but stirring up dissention and attacking the very people who made their world possible. And though such parasites were loud, so loud that the earth seemed utterly polluted with their noise and the darkness they peddled, their punishment was that they had to go through their lives as themselves. They lacked the capacity to see and treasure the silent grace of good people. They were the living dead.

The love grew into a ruthless sense of protectiveness. With it came a new and cleaner version of anger and contempt, directed not just at the military bureaucracy or the various other thorns in his side, but at the ugliness that had hit him in the face the second he'd returned to the States and offered a Death by a Thousand Cuts courtesy of the media. The cheap idolatry it pushed was a pretender culture that had been pasted haphazardly over the true one; the one that still stood for things, and was tended and handed down by a remnant of Americans who seemed to be made out of heart. They deserved a country that still cherished them.

Walton closed the door behind him and sat in front of the psychiatrist, Dr. Janik. Walton was suspicious of psychiatry. He thought it had many compelling insights to offer, however, he objected to it posing as science. He also thought its practitioners all too often served as modern day witch doctors in the service of various interests. However, he did like nice, squared-away people, and his Shrink was just such a person.

Dr. Janik was a gray-haired man of an age with his parents. He had the gentle manner that Walton had come to associate with the hospital staff, but there was a *presence* to Dr. Janik; a calm awareness that suggested to Walton that even though he was trying to appraise his patients' feelings and behavior, whatever he found would be filtered through a sense of loyalty toward them. For all of that, it still seemed odd to Walton that men like Dr. Janik and old First Sergeant Wade could be from the same Army. The Shrink hadn't made him to do push-ups once.

He even permitted eye-contact. First Sergeant Wade would have killed a Joe and buried his ass out in the Ranger Rocks for that sort of thing. The old man had gone to great lengths to cultivate discipline and good morale in Alpha Company.

"Hello, Walton."

"Afternoon, Sir."

"Do you know why you're here?"

"Not really, Sir."

"Well, your social worker was concerned about you. She said you've been looking withdrawn lately."

Walton shrugged with a smile. "I suppose so. I ain't gonna jump off any bridges or anything, though."

Dr. Janik laughed. "I didn't think you would. You know, what impressed me the most about you was that you have a pluckiness about you. Now, though, you seem a lot more quiet. Is something on your mind?"

Walton saw an opportunity to gain some leverage and an ally and took it. "I guess a lot of it has to do with gettin' Leave," he replied, and suddenly wished he didn't have to talk. He resigned himself to the fact that Dr. Janik was a genuinely good man who was there to help him. "My life is sorta on hold right now. I'd like to make plans for Leave, but I can't because no one wants to give me a date I can lean on. Meanwhile, I have to stand around in those stupid accountability formations for outpatients. We have four a day, you know. They're wastin' my time, Sir."

Dr. Janik nodded. "They used to not have those but some soldiers were getting drunk all the time and missing appointments."

Walton leaned forward like a compressed spring. "Yeah, but I ain't that kinda guy. I make all my appointments. I want out, and it seems the fastest way is to play ball." He paused, looking down at his flip-flops.

"Also…it hurts to know I'll never be a hundred percent again." He met Dr. Janik's gaze again and the words spilled out. "The guy who said, 'Time heals all wounds,' was full of shit, if you'll excuse my language, Sir. No matter how much I heal, I'll never be completely better. My body is about the best it's ever gonna be and it'll only get worse until I die. And that's just a fact."

"That's a hard thing to know," Dr. Janik said with a sad, knowing smile. "Sounds like you're dealing with things that most twenty and thirty-year-olds don't have to deal with. Most people don't learn that stuff until they're my age. When I climb the stairs, my knees kill me, and I think, 'Damn, this sucks. I'm getting old.'"

"Yeah, that's it." Walton swallowed a lump in his throat. *Old.* "You know, my folks came up recently. They told me about my great-uncle who's goin' through Alzheimer's. I think maybe the day will come when they won't recognize me. Then there's the business of them calling and tellin' me things like, 'We sure are glad you're okay! We're just so happy The Lord had His hand on you!' I appreciate their sentiment and all, but what about Espinoza and Lanagan? They only want to give God the good credit, if He exists at all, meanwhile there's this world full of ugliness and pain."

Sadness and anger tried to overpower him in turns. Walton fought to gain control over himself by focusing on his breathing as he felt the doctor's eyes upon him. It was all bigger than he was.

Everything changed. He couldn't hold onto anything, even his own body. Everything he could dare to know, or have, or love, he would lose one way or another, regardless of his best efforts. It was simply a matter of time. He gave his head an abrupt shake and forced an affable expression. "Sorry, I'm ramblin'."

"No, you're fine," Dr. Janik said in a reassuring tone as he leaned forward. He gave a damn and couldn't keep it out of his voice. "Tom, those are all valid things you feel."

Walton felt like the fracture inside him was visible and

231

hoped Dr. Janik didn't press the issue. To break down in broad daylight in front of someone would just be embarrassing.

Something passed across the psychiatrist's face, and Walton thought the man understood.

"So, what are your plans after the Army?"

Walton sighed with relief at the doctor's deft change of subject. "I think I'm gonna travel 'round the world."

"Ahh, that sounds like a hell of a lot of fun. How long are you planning to be gone?"

"I don't know."

The feeling of relief passed and Walton wanted to stop talking. However, he feared that silence would only draw more attention to himself. There were things going on inside him that he needed to explore and work out on his own. He was afraid the Army would probably try to anesthetize them away with drugs and want to hold onto him even tighter than they already seemed to.

"I'm not too sure I belong here anymore." He gave himself a mental thumbs-up for his ability to make his voice sound firm and in-control, with just enough vulnerability to make the storm inside him sound like a mild thing that would casually pass. He would give them enough to know he was "self-aware," but he'd be damned if he'd give them all the goods. A fella had to keep something for himself.

"Just talkin' to most people on the phone makes me feel like an alien. Things seemed simpler when it was just a matter of trying not to die and lookin' forward to goin' home." A wave of guilt threaded through his mind. He hadn't even killed anybody; why was he such a pussy about this shit?

"A lot of soldiers feel that way. You know, the last time I saw you, you were reading *Gone With the Wind*. Are you still reading it?"

"No, I finished it." He grinned shyly as his negativity

faded a little. "I have a friend in Canada who sent me some books. She kinda has a penchant for modern Canadian literature so I've been gettin' a taste of something new."

The nurse left Walton alone in his new room a few days later after the latest in the battery of surgeries attempting salvage his hand. The room was dark, and he was relieved that he didn't have a roommate in whom he had to pretend an interest. He liked it better when he could enjoy the isolation by himself. Sometimes the staff would round up who they could into groups to talk about their experiences, the result of which resembled the Monday morning after the fall of Troy, and it just reminded Walton of how ugly the situation was.

He felt it much more dignified to just zone out solo, and his rapidly developing sense of entitlement gave him the green light. He was tired but could not bring himself to sleep or watch unremarkable television, choosing instead to look at the street lights that glowed with a blue halo outside his window.

He felt wrung out. Body and soul. In the vague lucidity that had been dawning since he'd awakened in Post-Op, he could still feel the hazy melancholy of the anesthesia washing through his system. He pressed the button on his Morphine regulator to give him the allotted dosage and he wished it wouldn't restrict him from having another for a half hour or so. He felt an impulse to see how much he could get in his blood. He missed oblivion. He wanted to be consumed by it.

Shortly after the anesthesiologist had injected the goods in Pre-Op, he'd felt it take hold of him and he had wanted to laugh as he'd soaked up the sensation of being gradually overwhelmed into nothingness. He'd grinned like a kid at Christmas at the prospect of becoming comfortably numb. They had told him that a part of him would be aware during the procedure but that he wouldn't remember the pain. He'd reveled in the magic of those words. *Not remember the pain.*

Once in the operating room, the nurses and the anesthesiologist had been cheerful in a way that had been contagious. They had asked if he had any requests for music for them to play while they were getting him ready. Creedence Clearwater Revival soon came softly out of nowhere and he'd smiled as they had put warm blankets on him. He'd wished that he could've stayed in that moment with the bliss and the freedom from the tamped-down lightning that melted his brain during his usual waking hours.

The doctor had entered at some point and had begun to go to work. He'd grabbed the fixator by the rod that ran parallel with Walton's forearm and had flung it to the side to begin work. Walton had watched his limp arm fly demonically in a long, fast arc under the efficient hands of the doctor and he'd been horrified at the sight. He'd asked them to wait until he was completely out, then he'd swallowed the shame that had pulsed through him at hearing the shadow of panic in his voice. Things had faded soon after, but in no time he woke crying in Post-Op, inexplicably and wordlessly broken-hearted by the fact of his existence.

Thoughts returned to him as he lay alone in the darkness. They reclaimed his mind and caused him to compulsively press the button on the Morphine regulator again in vain. He knew full well it wouldn't yield a dose for another ten minutes, but that didn't stop him from trying.

What was it about the drugs? What was it that made them better than the booze, and porn, and all the other substitutes that he'd grabbed hold of to fill the sense of waste? Perhaps it was because they stopped the part of his brain that thought, and wished, and knew deep down that there was something better than what passed for living.

Fuck the world.

In his drug-induced delirium, he reflexively reached out for a lifeline and picked up the phone, listening for the dial tone to see if he had any messages from Amy on his voice mail. The phone was silent.

Rage took him as he specifically remembered telling the nurses about his room change and requesting to have his phone activated. He feared Amy had called and he'd missed it. The room seemed to grow darker and the solitude more oppressive, as if what dragged him down inside had found a way to escape, and now sought to crush him from outside as well. It had gone in for the kill by removing the only connection that permitted him a way out of his shit life. He smashed the corpse phone unrelentingly into its cradle over and over, wishing and hoping that if he hit it hard enough it would bleed.

The noise attracted a nurse who appeared in the doorway with the stance of an angry mother, hands planted firmly on her hips. "Sergeant Walton, what are you doing?" she demanded with a faint Jamaican accent coming from her dark face.

His eyes held their anger, and though he tried to be polite, his voice came out as a hard growl. "They didn't turn on my phone like I asked 'em to, Ma'am!"

"I'm sorry to hear that, Sergeant, but there's nothing to be done about it now, and breaking the phone certainly won't help." She was having none of his bullshit, but there was concern in her tone. Both qualities made Walton like her enough to not want to give her any more trouble. She went on to ask with a hint of Jedi Mind Trick, "Why don't you lay down and go to sleep?"

"Because I can't!"

"Would you like me to bring something to help you rest?"

He wanted to kiss her full on the mouth. "Please?"

Walton answered the phone by his bed at the Malogne House and bolted fully awake at the jubilant drunkenness. Fuan and Dechico were on Rear Detachment at Ft. Drum, and they were calling to let him know The Battalion was coming home. The next day, Walton bought a plane ticket for the weekend and prepared to go off the reservation.

"Holy Shit! Sergeant Walton!" exclaimed Gonzo.

"Hey Gonzo," Walton replied with a smile as he took a seat on the CQ desk. "What are you doing here? I figured you'd be comin' in with the rest of the guys."

"They sent me back a few weeks ago for Pre-Ranger. What about you, Sergeant, are you back for good?"

"Goddamn! Motherfuckin' Sergeant Walton!" yelled Dechico as he approached with Fuan. "What're you doing here?"

Walton wondered when they had painted the walls blue. "I came to see the boys return. Y'all don't tell anyone, but I'm kinda AWOL right now. Just for the weekend, though."

Dechico grinned. "Proper."

"So what's the deal with y'all? You had your knee surgery yet?"

"Fuck no. I've just been pushing Cherries around and painting the fuckin' walls." He then elbowed Fuan, who stood with a few tender-looking patches on his face. "Fu here's been healing after him and Carasquay accidentally almost blew themselves the fuck up while they were searching a fuckin' room with lit cigarettes that turned out to have a bunch of gunpowder and shit for IED's in it. Here, check this shit out…"

After a brief tour surveying the changes in the barracks, they wound up at Dechico's room, where a fridge full of beer awaited Second. Dobbs joined them and they began drinking like it was going out of style.

"Hey, brother, you don't know how bad me and Dechico wished we were there when you guys got into it at Miam Do," Dobbs said as he leaned back against the futon.

Walton shrugged. "Fuck it, man. What's done is done. Y'all did your time."

"I know," Dobbs replied with a face that looked in on itself. "But sometimes I feel like Espinoza took my place. I think sometimes it should've been me instead."

Walton groped for words. "I had a lot of buddies who ETS'ed before we deployed to Afghanistan and a lot of them wished they had been there too. It just wasn't in the cards. Besides, there's always gonna be some fight somewhere."

He got up and retrieved a fresh beer, trying to think of a way to put his fellow sergeant at ease. "You know, Dobbs, I used to be intimidated by you when you first came to the platoon. You were all Alpha Male and shit. Especially with the Joes. A lot of the NCO's used to use you as an example."

Dobbs left his reflections and a clarity possessed his face. "I just didn't want there to be any confusion about who was in charge. I didn't want them to get killed by some Haji over some stupid shit."

"I know what you mean." Walton grabbed a nearby towel and wound it around his head like a Haji turban. "You know, it's funny, at one point, I actually found myself hating Hajis. I know they're people and shit, but I resented the fuck out of them, their culture, everything."

He flexed the muscles in his jaw and remembered one night in the hospital when he had watched the news with his mom. There had been a story of a little Afghan girl who had just lost her family and her legs to a land mine. He had then recalled the story of a young Japanese girl named Sadako Sasaki who had died on the threshold of adolescence from Leukemia brought on from the effects of the bomb on Hiroshima. From her bed in the hospital, she had embarked on a heroic attempt to try to make one thousand origami cranes in order to be granted one wish by the gods. Paper had been scarce, but that hadn't stopped her. She'd used whatever she could fold, and when people found out, they'd mailed paper cranes to her. She had once said in her all too brief life, "I will write peace on your wings and you will fly all over the world."

Walton had suddenly seen the faces of all the smiling children who had waved at him while on patrol and had made him proud to be a soldier and a human being trying to protect their lives and what innocence growing up in a war zone hadn't already stolen from them.

In that moment, he'd known that somewhere out there, one of them had just lost her world. Not only would she never again kneel to pray, or run, or jump, or climb a tree, but when she became a woman she would also never know what it felt like to feel her husband's legs entwined with her own, or to walk to a crib to pick up her baby. She would never hear her parents' voices again. The world had robbed a child of something beautiful, and it had become a shade darker with the loss.

No matter how righteous the cause, how important the need for justice, or how glorious the triumphs, modern war meant children being broken and killed. And there was no way to protect them all.

"I hate them, Mom," he had said as he'd watched the TV; not with anger, but rather sadness, because he'd known it was true. "I don't hate them for fightin' us. I'm a big boy and we're at war and that's how it goes. But they started the firefight in a village with a bunch of women and children around. I even heard they had a baby in the compound where they fought us. Someone told me that after we dropped a JDAM on the place it had been buried under the rubble. When they went in to pull out the bodies they found it. It was alive, but they think the concussion may have made it deaf. A *baby*, Mom. Who starts fights around their women and children?"

At that point he broke down in a way he hadn't around her since he was a child. Tears smashed the dam and fell violently, not only for the nameless little girl in the news story, but at the *something* inside him that had died when he wasn't looking and had left a hole where a demon supernova lived in its place. "I didn't want to hate anyone, Mom, but it's there…I don't understand it."

Walton adjusted the turban, devoured his beer, and grabbed another. "When I was at the airport, I actually found myself wantin' to search anyone who looked remotely like one. They paged some 'Mohammed' guy and I almost went for my Black List."

Dobbs stared off angrily toward the same feeling. "Fuck a Punjabi. I hate those fucks."

Dechico played their old drinking music and they lightened up, then beat the hell out of the furniture. Gonzo and Fuan got too drunk to function and went to their rooms. Dobbs sat with a thousand-yard stare playing Toby Keith's *American Soldier* on repeat in the dim, broken room, and Dechico left to use his cell phone.

Walton took leave of them and called Amy on the pay phone. He left a drunken message in which he wished her the best of luck at a film festival where she volunteered for the week. He then walked back to his room to go to bed.

A private slept in Speedo's bunk. Walton wondered if he was in the right room. The confusion passed with the realization that his old roommate wouldn't ever be coming back. Speedo and Lanagan had died far from home months ago. They had made their exits, leaving an empty stage where two young men had been.

Standing in the doorway, he saw the paper he had taped to the outside of his wall locker. It had been a warning for the Cherries who would be billeted in their room while they were deployed. Walton laughed at the memory of writing it with Speedo. It read:

239

Dear Shithead,

You may be living in our room until we return, but know this: if our room is altered in any way, shape, or form, we will smoke you until you are shitting blood and seeing the fucking Easter Bunny. Go ahead and think we're playing.

Yours fucking truly,

Corporal Walton

And

Sergeant Espinoza

PS: Piss us off after a foreign deployment and we'll fucking kill your sorry Cherry ass.

He opened his locker for the first time in almost nine months and removed the plastic baggie taped to the inside. He broke the seal and pulled out an envelope with the words, "Mom and Dad," written boldly on the front in his old penmanship, which was to have been found by the soldiers who would have cleaned out his locker had he died. After tearing it open, he removed the two Death Letters and re-read them. One was to his parents. The other was to Amy.

Walton stood outside Cold Storage the next day and watched Alpha Company ground their gear as though they were just returning from a field exercise and not their turn in the current war. He walked in their direction and spent five minutes shaking hands and back-slapping until he was greeted by a voice outside of his peripheral vision that he hadn't heard since Afghanistan.

He turned to look at his squad leader with a grin. To Walton, the man always seemed as if they'd just thawed his ass out from WWII. "Sergeant Bronson. How the hell are you doin'?"

"I'm livin'," Sergeant Bronson replied. "Come here." Walton followed him a few steps away from the formation. "So what's goin' on with you?"

"Not much. Just holdin' down hospital beds for the

most part. They had a fixator in my arm and when they took it out there was so much blood it looked like they blew up a small dog. Aside from that, shit's been dull. What about y'all? What happened after I left?" Walton had heard the details of how Miam Do had played out from numerous second and third-hand sources, but he wanted to hear it from Sergeant Bronson.

A fierce light entered the squad leader's eyes. "Sarge put some rounds downrange, that's what the fuck happened. Smokey had to pull me back. The ANA pushed through and lost three guys. The XO, me, O'Falin, and a few others went in through the roof and got Lanagan out. Heslich's squad got sent in and Espinoza was up front. Haji shot him through the door like they did you. The rounds hit his ammo pouch and fucked him up. Desilva got hit by shrapnel from a frag. Here, I got something for you." He rifled through a pocket in his DCU top and produced a string of pale blue beads matching the one tied around his wrist in defiance of the regulations. "This is a gift from Mr. Kudah Nahr of the Miam Do Valley."

"Who's he?"

"That's the man that shot you. I took them from him when we dragged the bodies out. I thought you'd probably want to keep them."

Walton later looked over the crowd in the bleachers at the gym for familiar faces, then heard his name yelled by a voice originating from a person he'd only seen in pictures, but who had indirectly determined the emotional climate of the world he'd lived in for years.

"Mrs. Bronson! It's nice to finally meet you!"

"It's good to meet you, too!" she replied with an exuberant New Jersey accent. "I'm sorry we didn't get you the stripper-gram. Jim said to get you one, but I couldn't find any for the life of me. I decided to get you the candy gift basket instead. Was it okay?"

"Yes, Ma'am. I'm gonna fool around and get fat off it."

After a brief conversation, he took a seat with Dechico. Fifteen minutes later, The Battalion marched in. Tall and proud. When the band played *The Star-Spangled Banner*, Walton got goose-bumps. Though he had respected the national anthem in a passive way growing up, after having spent the past four years sweating and bleeding alongside American infantrymen, the song meant much more.

While some of The Brass talked briefly, Walton located Alpha Company, Second Platoon. He smiled with pride for them and the things they had done, and how he'd seen complete strangers get forged into a tribe willing to kill and die for each other. He remembered when he was a Cherry and Sergeant Sandlin would randomly stare him down in the hall and how Sergeant Bronson had called him "New Guy" for the first six months. He remembered the feeling of being a twenty-three-year-old Joe and going on his first deployment with men who at some point became his brothers; returning to watch a whole new crop of Cherries fill the ranks and go downrange, then come out the other side as battle-tested soldiers.

He watched them standing on the gym floor in their DCU's, then noticed himself in civilian clothes. It dawned on him that the distance between him and his old unit was more than a few meters. They would continue to perform the tasks of infantry soldiers while he never would again. He was a part of a Second Platoon that was passing. He still looked forward to his freedom, and he hoped it would one day come, but he still felt a sadness from the knowledge that he was near the end of something that he had come to treasure in a way that he'd never be able to explain to those who had not lived it with him.

The Brass eventually released The Battalion and Walton shook himself from his blues to congratulate them and get roaring drunk.

"That Night in Toronto..."

Walton was soon to discover that Canada in the summer is the greatest, most magical place on Planet Earth.

The day he'd been waiting nearly a year for had finally arrived. After enduring the ritual of airport security he boarded a north-bound plane. (As the officer had swabbed his splint for traces of explosive materials, Walton had been pissed. Having performed hundreds if not thousands of personnel, equipment, and vehicle searches, he thought that such measures were not only ineffective, but unworthy of the land of the free and home of the brave. To say they were a dog-and-pony show would be an insult to both dogs and ponies. That the same country which had been home to men the likes of Daniel Boone and Neil Armstrong could fall prey to a cowardly siege mentality made Walton feel sad and betrayed. The longer he was back in the States the more he felt like the people running the joint needed to have their nuts spanked in a not-nice way. There was only so much mendacity that a people should be asked to tolerate.) As soon as he made it through Canadian Customs, he threw his bags in a limo and gave the chauffeur the address, unable to sit still. He savored the feel of the leather and was glad he'd taken Amy's mother's advice and had gone the limo route. He was amazed that the rate would be comparable with a taxi. These thoughts were short-lived, though, and dwindled next to the anxiety of seeing Amy again. The chauffeur could not drive fast enough.

After a half-hour of fighting the Toronto traffic, the black sedan pulled in front of a two-storey brick townhouse in a cozy suburban neighborhood. He paid the man in the foreign currency, and as the chauffeur helped him with his bags, he heard a familiar female voice yell,

"Tom!"

He looked up to see Amy. She bounded out of the front door and off the porch like a shot, straight into his arms. They hugged each other tightly and smiled as the limo drove away. Walton looked into her eyes and went blank. He was content to just stand there and grin while she looked at him. "Wow, you cut your hair," was about all he could get out.

"Yeah. I went drastic when I came back here after all the drama from Montreal went down," she replied as she touched her hair tentatively. "I cut it way too short. It was one of those textbook girl things, I suppose."

Walton shook his head. Amy had trimmed it just a bit shorter than Marilyn Munroe's in *Gentlemen Prefer Blondes*, and the similarity of appearance and animal magnetism between the two women didn't help his concentration one whit. He had noticed from watching her move through Montreal that she had intuitively mastered the feminine art of exuding cuteness and sexiness at the same time. Yet seeing her in her mother's yard, in blue jeans and a yellow T-shirt, she seemed to possess more vulnerability around the smile in her eyes, and it wordlessly wrenched him, drawing his every impulse toward her. It made him want her more than he had in memory and fantasy. He hadn't been prepared for that. "No. It's nice. I think you look pretty," he said, feeling suddenly like he was shit-witted.

Amy smiled and grabbed his assault pack. As she shouldered it, her unrepentant femininity appeared outrageously incongruous with the olive drab bit of military gear. She said with enthusiasm, "Come on, I'll show you your room. Not that you'll be needing it, but we'll put up a front."

She led him through the house and up the stairs where they set his things in the guest room. Afterward, they settled onto the back porch where she poured wine and turned up the volume on the living room stereo so that the music carried outside through the open patio door.

He shifted excitedly toward her in his seat at the patio table, lost in his overwhelmed senses, and beaming like a damned idiot. "My God, darlin', you sure are a sight for sore eyes."

"Thank you. You haven't changed a bit. But no, I'm all sunburned as hell. I look like a lobster."

"Does it hurt?"

"Not much. It's kinda past that stage. God, I can't believe you're finally here!"

He looked at her. She sat with her feet folded under her in the patio chair, her whole being dedicated to simply being happy. "You're tellin' me. I've thought about nothin' else for so long it ain't even funny."

The two drank wine and swapped tales of strip clubs and Second Platoon. They laughed and smiled, and the words didn't seem to matter as much to Walton as the feeling of sharing that coursed through them. They killed off the bottle, then left to go out on the town.

She took him on a walking tour of her part of the city; through the tree-lined streets and over a viaduct where she pointed out the safety nets that the city had put in place to prevent people from killing themselves. They walked and talked and she led to a park so thick with green that Walton's eyes almost rejected it.

There they watched the sunset, framed by Toronto skyline, and when Walton sprawled on the grass, Amy rested her head on his stomach and he reveled in the warmth and closeness of her. He wanted to draw her near and touch the face he'd seen in his thoughts for so long, but the fear of scaring her off and making her angry restrained him. He wanted her, but he knew that sometimes people bit off more than they could chew, and he neither wanted her to feel obligated to follow through on the pact she had made with him in Montreal, nor to be something she regretted.

When the sky turned dark, Amy led on to her brother's apartment in search of weed. He was gone, and after passing a bit of time with his roommate, they walked back to her mother's house.

"Do you ever watch *Buffy the Vampire Slayer*?" she asked as they rounded the corner to the moonlit suburban summer street of her mother's neighborhood.

"Huh-unh. I know of it, but I never actually sat down to watch an episode."

"Oh my God!" she exclaimed as she grabbed his arm, "You have to see some! *My claim to fame was to maim and to mangle, vengeance was mine...*,'" she sang, then suggested, "Let's go watch it in the basement." Once at the house, they settled on the basement sofa and drank wine while Buffy fought the forces of evil. Fifteen minutes into it, she suggested they change into their PJ's and watch it in the upstairs guest room.

Walton laid on the guest bed in his board shorts, T-shirt, and splint, and soon thereafter, Amy entered in a matching red tank top and shorts set. The mysterious power in the contrast between the bright red cotton fabric and her fair (and in some places, sunburnt-pinkish) skin made Walton suspect that he had arrived at the summit of his mortal existence. She started the tape and snuggled up next to him. Minutes later, she began lightly scratching his stomach. His blood heated with ache and he whispered lowly, "Keep that up, darlin' and you're gonna make me forget my manners."

She looked up at him and grinned defiantly. "Promise?"

"I mean it." He was a chain near to breaking. "Don't start somethin' you won't want to be around to finish."

Her smile deepened wickedly and she continued the light scratching with a brazen dare in her eyes. Walton at last cast aside thought and they kissed without restraint, pulling their bodies close together.

You've never seen a guy so happy to be in bed with a girl in your whole life.

Walton woke in the morning with a smile and drew toward Amy as they lay in her bed under the orange duvet from Montreal (the squeakiness of the guest bed had sparked too much hilarity for them to remain there so they had relocated to her room). He gently pressed his body against hers, caressing her while she slept, then kissed her lightly on the shoulder and settled. A line from an old Lee Marvin movie came to mind; "Certain women have a way of turning boys into men. And others for turning men back into boys." He figured there were also some women (like the one in his arms) that could do either, depending on their mood. He needed to watch his step.

He looked around the room at the books on the shelves illuminated by the sun peeking through the curtained windows, then at the girl in his arms. If he'd ever met a girl that ought to come with Cliffs Notes, it was Miss Amy Dauphin. She was a pistol. She was pretty yet intrepid, and didn't fail to amuse him by how easily her mind could jump the tracks from talking about things like some esoteric theme in French literature, to an anecdote about her girls back at the strip club, or her days spent getting her hands dirty tree-planting with the Forest Service. He ran through the months of all the words she had written and spoken as he held her, and permitted his smile to grow till it bordered on laughter.

Eventually she stirred, lifting her head sleepily, and then turned toward him. Walton encompassed her with his arms and they smiled at each other as though they had all the time in the world.

Looking in her eyes, he saw a warm sexy contentment, (this tickled his vanity, whether the display was real or staged) but what was more, a wildness percolated through all the other traits the girl exposed to him, and rather than feeling threatened by it, it inspired him to want to draw more out of her. This wasn't just a girl; this was an accomplice. He must be bold and charismatic to earn her company. He felt free to dare to be a man in a way that he never had before.

Walton reached up to guide an errant lock of hair away from her face and touch her cheek. She had the softest skin ever. He angled his mouth away from her a bit so as not to nuke her with morning breath, and said, "Mornin', darlin'."

"Morning," she greeted. "Are you hungry?"

They idled in bed for a long while then got up. While he showered, she threw on his white button-up shirt and cooked a quick breakfast as she sang more songs from the *Buffy the Vampire Slayer* musical episode and a few from Liz Phair. Afterward, they ate and chatted about what to do with their day.

When Amy finished showering and getting ready, they stepped outside and were immediately confronted by the sight of two little girls playing with a jump-rope in the driveway, along with what Walton assumed was an imaginary person. They let the rope go slack and looked up. "Hi, Amy!" they said with grins punctuated by the occasional shy glance at Walton.

"Hi, girls! How're you doing?" Amy was a living smile.

"Fine!" they answered simultaneously in a sing-song voice. The two bounced nervously from foot to foot, as if they were so full of energy that to stand still would violate the rules governing the Space-Time Continuum, causing the universe to collapse.

"Girls, this is my friend, Tom."

Walton exchanged pleasantries with the girls, then asked on a whim, "Is it all right if I jump in on y'all's game of jump-rope? I haven't jumped-rope in years."

The little girls were caught unprepared for a twenty-six-year-old man's request to jump-rope. They looked at each other, then at Amy, and after she nodded

248

they decided to play along. After a thorough deliberation between the little girls as to which jump-rope song would be the most appropriate for a boy, Walton stood between them and they began to make the rope dance while they sang a sassy chant about race cars to keep the cadence.

He didn't last long. After his third failed attempt, he stopped to watch Amy kneeling next to the girl in front of her as they laughed.

There was no Army. There were no First Sergeants, or fireteams, or responsibilities, or broken men missing limbs. There was just the laughter of little girls in the morning sun with the smell of dew still on the grass, as if God had just made the Earth. This was a lost world where things that should be, *were*. Anything of beauty was possible here, leaving him feeling as if he had strayed down the rabbit-hole. He stood dumbstruck and in awe of his life; that he could jump-rope with children and listen to their innocent laughter, and later, he could share a bed with a lovely young woman who was as warm and spirited as she was cultivated and offered more than just empty groping in the night that left one feeling lonely and ashamed when the act was over, or wondering when the coast was clear to sneak off. He had the world on a string.

They bid the girls farewell, then stopped for coffee and walked to Kensington Market. They made a detour along the way at Philosopher's Walk, and Walton couldn't pass up the opportunity to take a picture of Amy under an inscription on a building at the college that read, *The Truth Shall Make You Free*. They crossed a street while she sang *Sex and Candy* and Walton paused at the sound of another song that came over a loud speaker through the open door of a store. He stopped in front of it and listened. "Holy shit, the Stone Poneys! Dude, I haven't heard this song in years."

"What is it?"

"I don't know the title. Listen; '*You and I, travel to the beat*

249

of a different drum, honey can't you tell by the way I run, every time you make eyes at me. Whooooaah...' After he finished singing the line he said, "Sorry, I'm a dork," with a smile out of an attempt to transform his mania into humor. "My Shrink says recurring flashbacks of old songs is one of the symptoms of Post-Traumatic Stress Disorder. Pay it no mind."

She laughed and he wished he hadn't heard the song. He felt a wave of pain at the thought of the weekend ending. They had both been careful not to talk of plans and commitments and a relationship, but after ten months and two weeks of her gaining more and more of a place in his mind, he found he didn't give a damn about the thought of being trapped or bound to someone, and this knowledge surprised him.

Walton remembered how when he was in High School, his dad used to constantly give him grief about why he never brought any girls around, till it became almost a vaudeville routine with them. When his dad began firing up the inquisition, Walton would reply that he liked having money and freedom, and having girlfriends around cost a man both. (Though in truth, few had ever seemed interested, and though it made for a lonely time in school, he was ultimately happy about the results. He'd felt the world pull at him in a way that out-yelled the stormy torrent of hormones.)

His dad would play the jolly, great-souled, dirty old man, and parry with, "Aww Son, everything's better with a little bit of female companionship," or the variation, "Son, one of these days you're gonna wake up and be a lonely ol' man." He would then go in for the *coup de grace* with the prophetic words that had returned to haunt Walton since Canada Day; "Tom, one of these days, you're gonna find a girl, and you ain't ever gonna want to turn her loose." For Walton, it had sounded as much of a curse as his father had meant it as a blessing. He now realized his dad had

250

been right. (Ken Walton seemed increasingly so, the older Tom got.) He wanted this precocious young woman's company as much as he wanted the freedom to leave the Army and go ramble abroad. He'd find a way somehow, but that was a thought for later.

"And how are things going with your Shrink these days?" Amy asked.

"He's fine. A real good man. We have some pretty crazy conversations sometimes. Oh! We were talkin' books a while back and I mentioned the Margaret Atwood you sent. He even wrote *Oryx and Crake* down on his notepad and jumped on Amazon to check it out. That's the sort of impact you have, kid. Money can't buy that kinda influence."

"Yes, well, we aim to please, darlin'," She said in an attempt at his Okie accent. She then returned to her own, saying, "See! The publishing houses should start sending me royalties. I'm gonna open up the American marketplace for Canadian literature!"

With his best Sean Connery impersonation he said, "But of course, dear." Relapsing into his normal voice he then asked, "How's things with *your* Shrink?"

"Not bad. I sort of enjoy the whole therapy thing, actually. Despite the fact that I spend my time trying to analyze the doctor. Or trick him. It's sort of counter-productive. I really don't think he's very effective. Just the other day I sat and listened to him go on for half an hour about how the country's going to hell and how we need to be more like the Americans, and how I should vote Conservative in the upcoming election this summer. I was like, 'I'm paying for this?'" She then made a *c'est l'vie* look with her eyes and sang with jovial twang, "*Sometimes it's hard to be a woman . . .*"

That afternoon, they ate on the patio of a French restaurant where she snuck away and paid for dinner. When she returned, she did so grinning victoriously at

251

having beaten him in getting the check. Afterward, they left to catch a movie, then she led on to one of her favorite bars where they took a seat on a couch and she insisted, "You've got to try a Cactus Cocktail! They've got tequila, rum—a bunch of stuff. They're great!"

A waiter came to take the drink order and after she gave it, Amy asked, "What happened to the pool table?"

"We had to get rid of it. It was lop-sided."

"Awww. Still, it was fun to play on."

The man returned with two large carafes and Walton paid him. He took a careful sip. Then a not-so-careful one. "Damn, that's good."

Amy nudged him in the ribs with an elbow, then leaned into him and lingered there. "See, aren't you glad you came here?"

"But of course."

"*Be oui.*"

"What's that mean?"

"It means, *'But of course.'*"

"I think I like it better in French."

"French is fucking awesome. That's one thing I miss about Montreal is how the Québécois have French everywhere. They even act French. They tried to secede, but the rest of Canada won't let them. They still have a political party, though, and that's their platform."

"I can respect that. Kinda makes me think of Texas. We Oklahomans are sworn to a Red River blood feud with the Lone Star State as a matter of principle, but I admire the hell out of Texas's proud tradition of tellin' the rest of the country, 'Fuck y'all!' You know, I never really cared much for French, but after Montreal, I found I kind of liked it. I think when I get out I might have to visit Paris. It'd be all *Moulin Rouge* 'n shit."

Amy's eyes widened excitedly. "I love that movie! When it came out I'd walk around the streets crying after I saw it."

Walton began *The Elephant Love Song* and Amy quickly joined him for the female parts. They lost track of the time as they worked their way through other songs and the rest of the Cactus Cocktails. After a duet of *Danny Boy*, they ordered more drinks and sang whatever else came to mind, not giving a damn about the raised eyebrows of passers-by.

They left and walked the quiet Toronto streets hand-in-hand. The route Amy led them on required them to jump over fences occasionally, and the fact that she not only managed to do so in a long, brightly-colored, cotton summer skirt, but went up and over with a grin, impressed Walton to no end.

At one point she stopped an approaching man walking his dog, and full-on launched into *The Terrier Song* from *The Kids in the Hall* as she petted the animal. The more he got to know her, the more Walton suspected that Amy was absolutely, positively, shithouse in love with all Creation. Especially children and dogs. When in her stripper phase, she'd sometimes worked at summer camps for kids (almost like a superhero with an alter ego), and she'd told him at length all about her reunion with her childhood dog Sabrina, who was now blind and living at her father's house in the country. Though she hadn't seen the dog or her family during her days of living wild in Montreal, after Sabrina smelled her old friend she'd whimpered until Amy had picked her up.

This had prompted a phone discussion on the nature of unconditional love and whether or not it was possible among people. Amy had doubts, at least with the possible exception of the parent/child bond, but Walton refused to throw in the towel on love just yet. He'd grown up around the old-fashioned kind, and hoped he'd get his hands on some one of these days.

After she finished petting the dog and getting her fix, Amy practically glowed and bounced on her toes as she walked, causing Walton to fervently pray that Amy Dauphin would have babies someday. Lots of babies. Babies who grew into young'uns who ran all over the place with superhero capes made from bath towels, and did things like excavate the garden for buried treasure with crayon-drawn maps marked with big-assed red X's, and spoke a barrage of languages to any varmint they could get their hands on. Walton could see Amy's future minions fighting large-scale make-believe military campaigns out in the yard with sticks and BB guns, and competing for things like who got to sit on her lap, or who got to be up front in the canoe, and who got to pick the next story she'd promised to read to them.

He was convinced that not only would she take motherhood to a whole 'nother level, but that someday the people of Earth would need her offspring. The fate of Mankind was at stake, and this young Canadian girl held the key to salvation. The warp-drive engine, cold fusion, the cure for cancer, the future of the arts and architecture; they no doubt resided in her womb.

Walton angrily shook his head in an effort to "get aholt" of himself. His mind divided itself between the cynical part of him that saw these feelings ignited within him as nothing more than hormones and the trite stuff of a thousand bad songs and movies, while the other part wallowed in the moment and the effect Amy had on him and said to hell with how silly happiness seems to those who aren't happy. Walton had never been this happy before, and now that he was, he didn't care who knew.

Later that night, they lay wrapped up in each other's arms trying to maximize their skin-to-skin contact. They took turns playing songs on her CD player and occasionally drinking from the green water bottle which seemed to have the miraculous quality of appearing at Amy's whim regardless of wherever they were, as if she had up and decided one day that the laws of physics no longer applied to her.

When he played *Moi Lolita* (one of the songs which had been popular on the European MTV station while he'd been in Bosnia) from his drinking music, her eyes popped open. When it finished, she reached over him languorously to play it again, promising to email him a definitive translation.

She then played The Hip's *Bobcaygeon*, and as soon as the opening chords quietly struck the room, the song began to burn into his mind. The intimate tone and feeling it elicited seemed to understand and meld with what passed between them as they held each other in the dark. He knew that from here on out, whatever happened, he would forever associate it with Amy. This would be their song. It left him indebted to the band as if they had written it just for the two of them. He immediately decided he'd take a bullet for the band if the need ever arose. He thought fervently in the tone of the presidential candidates, "I'm Sergeant Thomas P. Walton, and I approve of The Tragically Hip."

They continued to pass the late hours reading each other excerpts from the books on the shelves in her room, touching each other, and sharing thoughts in hushed words meant only for the ears of themselves and God.

Walton watched her breathing slow and become more regular until sleep finally took her and he was left holding her body as it lay dormant in his arms. He laid there, holding vigil over her sleeping form, silently keeping watch and slowly gliding his fingertips over the soft creamy skin of the waist, hips, and thighs of his human treasure; just enough to feel her body with his good hand, yet he carefully made his touch delicate enough so as not to wake her. He smiled at the recognition that he was still pulling guard. But this time over *her*.

While he caressed her, he wiggled the fingers in his splinted right hand as her head rested in the cradle of his arm. He was happy that it looked like there was a good chance he might get to keep the hand after all, but with it as it was he felt handicapped. During their hours abed he sometimes reflexively moved to touch her with it only to remember that it was useless, thus prompting him to try and stop himself before she noticed and perhaps became uncomfortable. (Though when he'd told Amy about it, she'd just smiled and acted like it didn't bother her in the least, saying in a lecherous tone that the rest of him worked just fine. She was a team player like that.)

He'd tried to get by without the splint, but since the skeletal structure of the hand was held to his wrist by a single pin that only allowed him to comically flop it about, he put the contraption back on for good. The white sheath of plastic covering his arm nearly up to the elbow served only to remind him of just how far away from Amy he really was, and would remain.

The smile faded to a frown as the darkness crept back into his mind. He had jumped out of planes in Airborne School, and had walked point in Afghanistan for Allah knew how many klicks. He had been through too many suspected minefields to want to remember, and had run to where men had been trying to kill him and his buddies. However, as badly as all of that had scared him, none of it had terrified him like this girl. What was happening to him?

He held her just a fraction tighter, and in doing so, committed one of the cardinal sins of his life. For in those dark hours spent holding her while she slept, he was completely unaware that with that simple gesture of tenderness he had entered a minefield of a different kind, though no less dangerous, that could lead to the further corruption of his feelings for her and chain her with the burden of becoming another one of his potential addictions, or what was worse, his savior. As a student of history, he should have known the weight of the fate that men tended to put on the shoulders of those whom they expected to save them.

In Afghanistan, it had been so easy for him to plug her into the fantasies of freedom that he'd used to burn up the months of boredom, stress, and loneliness; the daydreams of sharp clothes, lush digs, and no-strings fuckathons on the regular with every woman who was up for it once they'd consummated their affair. Although at some point in the hospital she had become the brightest part of his world, they were both still governed by the unspoken rule that their momentum led to this weekend, and beyond that, *Terra Incognito*. Walton had thought he'd have no problem sleeping with randoms while saving the best of himself for the on-going international affair with Amy until he left to ramble and sample the brothels and seductresses of the world. Walton was a great respecter of professional craftsmanship, and figured the gals who worked in the erotic arts in places like Bangkok or Paris practiced things that most domestic twenty-somethings didn't know how.

Even then, he'd imagined meeting her in some far away city to drop some *Kwisatz Haderach* technique on her that he'd learn and take her to some new brain cell eradicating height, or returning to Canada to resume wherever it was they'd leave off. The way she'd seemed so fun and boundary-less, yet hadn't said a word about continuing past this weekend, had led him to believe that was the sort of thing was in her repertoire and wouldn't offend her. He had supposed she'd have her fun, and that he'd be alright with that. He just wouldn't ask questions to which he didn't want the answers. It had all seemed so simple.

Holding her, he then remembered Aliz. Though he hadn't fucked her during those nights in Budapest, he had felt a connection between them that had seemed real in spite of the fact she had been a prostitute. He hadn't been naive enough to think anything would come of it (or have any desire whatsoever to be Captain Save-a-Ho), but those first few months afterward, there was nothing else he could think about, it seemed, but her.

Looking at one of his buddy's pictures from Pass a short time later had pulled his head out of his ass. In the photo she had been bent over a pool table with a grin, a pool cue, and an NCO from another company right behind her, who would later fuck her every orifice as if their lives depended on it. The soldier had told Walton all about it one drunken night (though he'd thankfully been ignorant of the infatuation).

Aliz had taught Walton that he was not special.

There had never been a woman really *in* Walton's life before. At least, not like this. There had been a brief winter of dates and evening explorations with a girlfriend in his fogged up old pick-up back in High School, and the occasional drunken exchange with bar floozies, strippers, or foreign prostitutes, but nothing that could fundamentally change him and what he wanted as Amy had done.

For as long as he could remember, he had been on some single-minded quixotic quest or another, whether it be ideals, God, or the right to call himself a man. Now, here was flesh and blood, and it was maddening. Fear of intimacy made Amy his nemesis, and yet the desire to have it with her alone made him hold on to her for dear life. She brought to mind the idea about men and women being halves of a whole, and with her, he felt . . . *completeness*. This didn't take away from her humanity (or his), but rather, brought out its very essence to him. What he really liked about her wasn't just the way she looked or lit up a room, or her thoughts and opinions, or even because she seemed to like him (although those were all stellar). It was the mysterious place all those came from, the invisible spark of Platonic *Amy-ness*, out of which all those things bubbled that compelled him.

And yet, it made him sad and almost angry that like Aliz, he had nothing unprecedented or special to give or do with her that some man hadn't already lavished upon her with abandon long ago, the relics of which now rested in the white cedar chest at the foot of her bed. These women and their goddamned boxes, he thought painfully; they're like little mass graves under beds and in closets all around the world.

When he had given her the Death Letter from his wall locker, which his brothers would have been tasked with taking to her along with his CIB (Combat Infantryman's Badge) had he died, she had then opened the chest to retrieve the first letter he'd sent to her. He had been honored that she had kept it, but he had caught a glimpse of other letters, mementos, and pictures from her past.

He could imagine the other men; the men before him who had left the contents of the chest as they had passed in and out of her life. Walton felt the interlopers' presence in Amy's bedroom as if they were voyeurs haunting from the past come to compare their sweaty midnights with Amy against his.

He'd be expected to be okay with them. If he really cared about her, the story went, it wouldn't matter what she'd done or who she'd done it with. If he "felt threatened," even for a second, it was just a testimony to his insecurity and his "fragile male ego." The shaming language was right there in his head thanks to pop-culture. What a neat trick that was.

"You are going to be such a good husband!"… "You're going to be the best dad!" That's what girls told Walton. He hated it when women said things like that to him. The unspoken meaning of the backhanded compliment was that guys like him (who often made the mistake of being openly nice to girls) were only valuable as a fallback option for when women wanted to have babies before their ovaries gave out. In super-duper paratrooper terms: *"If their main didn't open wide* (bad boys), *they had a reserve* (nice guys) *by their side."* With a man like him they were safe. They wouldn't feel like they had to worry about being abandoned or cheated on. Until then, though, the girls wanted to try to use their tight young asses and non-yet-sagging tits to see how high they could trade up. Their youth—their most beautiful and fertile years—that magic hour was reserved for use in the sexual arms race for the panty-saturating men who all the other women *really* wanted. Men like Walton were to wait for leftovers. They were to be there at the end of the penis extravaganza on bended knee to give a ring and their undying love to a woman who didn't really want them in the first place.

Yet there he was in bed with a girl he'd met in a strip club, and as lost as a bastard on Father's Day. There had to be a lesson there somewhere.

Though he had more conflicted feelings about Amy than he knew what to do with, Walton was thankful that he had met her that night in Montreal. He thought she might just be the same kind of crazy as him. There was something about her. He wondered if this was his chance to finally get out from under the goddamned feeling of unending adolescence. The world didn't need another Drunk Guy at the Pool.

Was this just another affair to her? A summer novelty or future anecdote to compare with her friends' liaisons over drinks on a Girls Night Out? Another impulse purchase in the world of sexual economics that will be out of style when the fall collection hits the stores? Another face in the parade of hook ups that fade with each year into a hazy residue of memory? Maybe this connection he felt was all just a bunch of participation mystique in his head. The park, holding hands, the phone calls, and the all too innocent invitations to the basement; these were moves in a game she could probably play blindfolded.

Walton wanted to *have* her in some way no man ever

had, and make her feel the depth to which she had carved her name in him. A species of narcissism whispered in his ear, twisting his feelings without his knowledge until the tainted sum of them reached out and found its mate in the animal turbine the war had woken. He was in too deep. He briefly clenched his jaw, stilling the primal impulse to connect with her, to dominate her, to grip her body, her beauty, her magic…he wanted…

Forcing himself to just caress her was one of the most intense acts of willpower in which he had ever engaged. He took a deep breath to clear his mind. A name flashed. *Kudah Nahr.*

Had he ever had to deal with this sort of thing? Walton doubted that Haji ever got this wound up over a skirt, but who knew? What *had* his would-be killer's life been like? Had a woman on the other side of the world wept alone on a thin mattress in a corner of a baked dirt house when she'd found out that he wouldn't be coming back? What had made them enemies?

The war. Walton remembered the firefights and how bizarre it had seemed for the two sides to devote so much intensity and so many resources to fight each other, though they were complete strangers. Him and his buddies, Kudah Nahr and his cell; they were merely cogs in a pitiless machine run amok, shuffling along on a busted chain of causality.

Somewhere in the Beltway, a tyranny of Ivory Tower eggheads had probably thought all this was going to be a hell of a good idea. ("We have statistics and charts and everything! Just wait till you guys see our PowerPoint presentation!") Walton was sick of "experts" and their intricate fucking plans, which oddly enough, always seemed to demand more coercion, more sacrifice, more centralized bureaucratic control, and that the Proles should just shut up and bend over. That strategy wasn't even original. The West's Brahmins failed to grasp a fundamental truth that hairy-legged, knuckle-dragging infantrymen had known since the dawn of war; "The best laid plan goes to shit once the first boot hits the ground."

He wondered how a country these days went about getting rid of its intellectual and cultural elites. America and the world had been through enough.

The era seemed marked by leaders in almost every field of endeavor who failed to understand that being in charge meant more than just telling people what to do or how to think. It meant loyalty to your own, and giving a damn about what things were like on the grunt-level, and being willing to give your life for the lowest-ranking private in your team if you had to. Leadership demanded that a man never gave an order that he wasn't prepared to carry out himself. That he had to fight like hell to try to rise above his flaws and hold himself to a higher standard than those under his charge. (Walton had been all too aware of his own short-comings as a team leader, and had struggled with them. However, he'd seen the genuine article in action, and had admired it when he did.) A people's greatness was won by action, not policy papers. Deeds not words. Even the dumbest Joe knew that.

Walton mused that if he ever needed any proof that the Brainiacs shaping national policy had never served as enlisted personnel in a line unit, he just had to pick up a major newspaper. As a sergeant, he had the utmost respect for Joe's capacity for jackassery, however, the current state of affairs was beyond even his ability. You had to have a lot of people with a lot of higher education operating over a long period of time to fuck up the world to the extent that it was.

He focused harder on his breathing then finally found his way to the bright side of the half-full glass. He lightly kissed Amy's sun-burned shoulder. Fuck the world and the horse it rode in on. She might have things she wasn't proud of, but God knew he did as well. He had no business being uppity about motes in people's eyes.

The gravity of the Bible Belt drew him back to thoughts about grace and redemption. Maybe for them it *really* didn't matter. Maybe none of it did. Maybe what was important was that the crazy parts of their lives were getting farther away in the rear view mirror every second, and he should be a man, grab his nuts, and quit sniveling. She was here; *here*, at last, with him now, this girl he felt he'd always been looking for in the back of his mind, quieting the silent aching void that had compelled him to scan the face of each woman he passed until the night before Canada Day. He'd found her, and they were embarking on a new phase of their lives, however tentatively. From here on out, it was simply a matter of finding a sunset to ride off into.

When morning came they took their time in leaving for the day. They read the newspaper while eating at one of her favorite restaurants, and the waiter glanced at her in a flirty way that made Walton want to sock him right square in his fucking mush.

After breakfast, they continued on to a cemetery where she watched the squirrels with great enthusiasm. She led on to a section that had been landscaped to look like a Japanese garden. They sat on a bench and she said, "I love this place. You probably think I'm crazy bringing you to a cemetery, but it's so beautiful here. You know, if I was dead, I'd totally want people sit and lean against my gravestone, and hang out and smoke a joint."

"No, I don't think you're crazy, Amy. It's peaceful. A bit odd, I'll allow, but peaceful."

Walton's obsessive melancholy from the night before returned and grew until it became something that lodged in his throat and now tried to choke him. "Amy, I've got a proposition for you," he said slowly. "I'd like us to have an affair."

"Isn't that what this is?"

263

"I mean for more than a weekend. I know we live in different worlds...but...I'd like to see more of you. You can see who you want," (he didn't mean that part at all, but said it as an attempt at sounding cosmopolitan and not needy), "but I want to hear from you and be able to visit you like this again."

Her smile slipped into thought, and she looked off into the world where he suspected she kept the fears, conflicts, uncertainties, desires, and all the other chaotic things she was trying to put a brave face over and learn to rule. Here was where she kept the life she had left and the upside-down-ness she still felt inside from breaking free of it. Here was where she paid the price for her near-decadent vivaciousness. Here was the glimpse into the threshold of the room in her soul that she had only spoken of, and to witness it first-hand frightened him.

This part of her wasn't the glamorous ex-stripper, or the cheerful free spirit. This doorway written on her face led to a dark, destructive, wild place that seemed to scare even her, (though he doubted she'd admit that to him) and for now, it was a room into which she could not allow him or anyone else to enter. The sight of this left him wondering how much he really knew about her.

Watching her, Walton was reminded of a horse riding lesson he'd once had. The mare had been docile and accepting of his lead initially, but when he'd started exercising her in the corral that morning she had been restless and pent up, itching to run at full-tilt right from the get-go. He had gone about putting the mare through her paces, then he at last let her go at a full gallop. She had bolted so hard that he hadn't able to hold on to her with his novice abilities and she had thrown him ass-over-teakettle.

Walton had hit the ground like a sack of shit, laughing at the mare's hard-to-contain morning volatility and seeing her wild nature come out after all the repetitive discipline of the riding lesson. It had made him like the horse all the more, and he'd been eager to get back on her as soon as he could get up off the ground. He'd felt like he had learned more about the mare in that moment than he had throughout all the stable preparations and time spent in the lesson up to that point. It had occurred to him later that to understand a thing when it was in the throes of its wildness was to understand the thing itself. He didn't think Amy would cotton to being compared to a horse, but the two did seem to have their similarities just then.

The sight of this newfound part of her failed to deter him, however. In an odd way, it plucked a chord he understood all too well.

The moment and its reflections lasted for the briefest of seconds. The clockwork of wheels turned in her mind as they had in Montreal, and when she had processed her thoughts through to conclusion, she then nodded her head suddenly, the smile returning like a sunrise and she turned to share it with him, saying, "Okay." Her usual Devil's-little-sister demeanor returned and she said "Here, let's go," with a wink.

They got up and walked to a park where they paused at a jungle gym out of nostalgia. While Amy puttered about on the bars (Walton mused to himself with a smirk that you could take the girl out of the strip club, but you couldn't take the strip club out of the girl), she picked up on the dark undercurrent still dominating his mood and asked with concern, "What's wrong, Tom?"

Walton furrowed his brow and clenched his jaw, trying to think of a way to explain something he didn't understand. His emotions changed shape and he felt like he was back in the Shrink's office as the near-hysteria within him reemerged. With the fingers of his splinted hand, he gripped the rigid plastic framing it until it gored into his flesh. He drank in the pain and aggression, wishing there was someone shooting at him so he could run and try to kill them.

A million thoughts vied for attention in his mind. He lived again in the firefight at Miam Do. He remembered how alive he'd felt; the residual lust from the thing deep inside him that had wanted to be a part of the chaos, while at the same time the rest of him had frantically prayed to any god who would listen for it all to stop. He could still feel the cold weight in his hands of his old M4, and hear the familiar metallic clicks it had made when he'd chambered a round and switched the selector from safe to semi; the small force of its recoil as he squeezed the trigger and put a round downrange. He missed the Shithook and the loud comforting hum she made that sounded like a mechanical lullaby as she devoured miles of barren land beneath his platoon while taking them to or from a place of danger. The sight of tracer rounds careening burning paths through midnight like the brutal livid gods of lightning bugs. The feel and sound of a wooden door exploding open under the unrestrained force of his boot. The flinty arid taste of Afghanistan breathed through his brown dust scarf in a blinding storm of tan and gray—

And yet he also remembered the broken shapes of children under the blankets in that nameless shithole village, and the soldiers missing their limbs and faces in the hospital. One soldier at Occupational Therapy had been confined to a wheelchair while his parents watched him and silently mourned the dream they'd had for their son who wasn't yet old enough to buy a beer. Then there had been the story an anesthesiologist had told him before putting him under about a man not much older than Walton, who had not only just lost his arms and legs, but had been blinded and rendered deaf from an IED in Iraq. The doctors had also had to carry the unimaginable weight of telling the man's condition the young wife who had come with their three children to visit their soldier.

The ugliness of what he had briefly glimpsed of war

and its rotten afterbirth set him on fire and he wanted to yell till his voice died at the knowledge of just how goddamn fragile, and short, and precious this fucking life was, and how no one else around him could hear the clock mercilessly running out.

Opinion-shapers liked to trot out glib terms like PTSD that were nebulous in shape, as if part of a veiled effort to pathologize and dehumanize those who'd had the audacity to go to war on behalf of a country that no longer gave a damn about its own people, and then return with unquiet hearts. Walton refused to see himself as broken or sick. The real disease was this bullshit culture where everything you did was just a drug to make you forget that you were dying. War, though, woke you up to reality; you were alive and it all hung by a thread. After having learned that lesson in his guts, Walton didn't want to ever go back to sleep. Even the rage was better than that.

With Amy there was LIFE, and a direction forward that led out into a future worth fighting for. He wanted to grab her, throw her over his shoulder, and carry her off to a place where Man hadn't yet brought his madness; to make her feel all the joy and beauty that ever was and watch it play across her face, wringing every drop he could from this accidental gift of existence and the dumb luck of having met her.

He collected himself and looked at her as he tried hard to make a believable smile. "I think I've got the Black Dog like you said in one of your emails. I think about life sometimes and get angry. Happiness never seems to last, you know? I once read a quote where some guy referred to a period of history being 'nasty, brutish, and short.' I kind of wonder what the point is. There's so much pain and ugliness. You know, it's funny, I can't imagine myself livin' past thirty, and I don't think I really want to."

"No!" Amy snapped at him with an angry expression, and Walton was immediately glad it looked like she didn't have anything to throw. She didn't strike him as the type to get violent, but she was a woman. And with them, you just never knew. "You have to live past thirty! What kind of nonsense is this? I mean, sure, life sucks sometimes and all good things must end, but there's still more good things. Tom, are you sure you're okay?"

"Of course," he said with an attempt at a grin. He really needed to get his shit together.

She nodded and climbed down. When she neared him, she extended her pinkie. "I'll tell you what, Tom. I'll make a pinkie-swear with you, right here and now, that if you promise to live past thirty, I won't join the Army. Deal?"

Walton's artificial smile became real. He took her pinkie with the one on his good hand.

They returned to the house to watch the movie *La Femme Nikita* and nap a bit, then went to her mom's church where her choral group performed in a musical. Afterward, they walked to a bar on Bayview where they had pizza and beer while a cover band played AC/DC and Creedence like they meant it.

After drinking and singing along to classic rock anthems for a few hours, they headed back. Walton changed into his board shorts in the guest room, and when he entered Amy's room he found her sitting on the orange Montreal duvet with her legs folded to the side beneath her, bathed in the soft incandescent flicker of candles. A large thin book lay on the bed next to her and the faithful green water bottle sparkled like a great emerald jewel in the window sill. *Bobcaygeon* spun again, and Amy turned the alarm clock on the nightstand around to face the wall behind her; she had stopped time, allowing Walton to live in that moment forever.

He laid down next to her and touched her hip with his fingertips, gently making the pale blue silk of her chemise caress her bare skin underneath. "You sure look pretty, darlin'," he said lowly through the lump in his throat.

The light gleamed in her bold happy eyes, shining brighter to Walton than the candles resting on the window sill and nightstand. "Thank you, *darlin'*," she returned. "You look quite dashing too."

Amy and Walton yielded to the stillness of the moment as they locked eyes. The smiles on their faces grew in warmth until she said, "Here, let me show you something." Amy opened up her High School yearbook, and the gesture of her sharing even more of her world to him scared him, yet made him want to stay even more. Hell, it made him want to put his jeans back on, knock on Ms. Dauphin's door and swear a blood oath to her that he would henceforth take care of all of her yard work and light automobile maintenance *in perpetuity* on the sole basis that she had given birth to Amy.

The next morning, he sat at the kitchen table while Amy and her older brother Charles went to work on a belated Mother's Day breakfast of crepes.

"So what do you think of Canada, Tom?" Charles asked.

Walton savored the simple intimacy of drinking coffee with Amy and her brother in the kitchen. There was something magical about a home when the people in it liked each other. It made him look forward to being out of the Army, and it took the edge off his nervousness at trying to make a good impression with Amy's family. He half expected someone to pull a shotgun on him at any second and start asking him about his "intentions." "I like Canada a lot. Growin' up, I was kinda prejudiced against it 'cause all the third-rate comedians are, but I'm really impressed. It's clichéd, but everyone is laid back in a way they aren't in the States. Y'all are so free up here."

Charles smiled into the crepes batter. "We like it. It's very Shire-like here. I think it may have a bit to do with all the pot we consume. Speaking of which, I brought a few joints, Amy. Kate said you had been looking for some.

Anyhow, as you know, Tom, a lot of our Baby Boomer culture comes from Americans who dodged the draft. A lot of them smoked pot as well. So it's kind of a part of our national identity. In fact, one of our former prime ministers, Jean Chrétien, joked over the issue of decriminalization, '*I'm gonna have a joint in one hand*," Charles imitated in a thick French-Canadian accent, "*and de money for de fine in de udder.*"

Walton laughed, and Amy shook her head with a smirk and quipped, "I know so many people who smoked pot with Trudeau."

They continued to compare and contrast their countries while Amy just watched with a smile and occasionally threw a primer into the conversation. They were joined by Ms. Dauphin and relocated to the table.

Walton felt conspicuous as the outsider but they all went to great lengths to make him feel at home, even going so far as to pull out an atlas and have him point out where he was from. Ms. Dauphin soon threw down the gauntlet by threatening to make them all sing *Oklahoma.*

As a proud Okie, Walton was game to belt out the anthem, but didn't want come across as chauvinistic, so he modestly declined. However, having been born of people who belonged to the land (and the land they belonged to was grand), he greatly appreciated the gesture.

After the meal, Ms. Dauphin left on errands and Walton smoked the first joint of his life with Amy and her brother. He asked Charles his patented Three Movies Question. Charles then engaged Walton in a forty-five minute conversation over movies (Charles opted for Kenneth Brannaugh's *Hamlet*, *The Chungking Express*, and *Last Night*, along with a few others as honorable mentions) and was articulate in his diction on subjects like the virtues of viewing *Lawrence of Arabia* on seventy millimeter film to a degree that made Walton feel a kinship with him and hope he'd get to sit down with Charles again.

Charles eventually left for work, and Amy paused from showing Walton how to roll a joint from the scant makings she kept in a cigar box with Frida Kahlo pasted on the lid, and took a seat on his lap like a human cat.

Walton took a sip from the white wine they'd been drinking, and paused to look at the remainder in his cup. "Man. My drinking skills have gotten rusty. After this weekend, I'm gonna need to spend a day just rehydrating."

Amy nodded her head in agreement as she snuggled into him. "I haven't drank this much Scotch since I was a stripper."

He smiled and softly raked the back of her thigh. "I really like your family, Amy," he told her.

"Thanks. I'm kinda fond of them too. You've got to meet my dad sometime. I take after him on so many levels."

Walton pulled her closer. "Amy, you know how I'm always talkin' about travelin' around the world when I'm out? Well, I'd like to invite you to come with me. I hadn't ever planned on—or even wanted—to take anyone, but I think you'd be the perfect traveling companion. You're smart, funny, sexy, good with languages, and with the proper motivation I could see you stabbing someone in the brisket. At the worst, it'd be six months to a year of playin' tourist and seeing the bones of civilizations, and at best, it'd be the adventure of a lifetime. You don't have to answer now, but think about it."

The odd sphinx-like smile of hers reemerged. God only knew what it hid. "I'll think about it," she said. "And if I decide to go to Nicaragua and teach English for a month like my friend Cathy did, then you are more than welcome to visit for as long as you want." The Sphinx Smile then turned absolutely wanton. "When do you need to leave for the airport?"

"Not for an hour."

They looked at each other and hurried upstairs.

Walton sat on the airplane playing *Bobcaygeon* over and over. (Amy had snuck the Tragically Hip CD *Phantom Power* into his assault pack. He had given her his copies of *My Friends Are All Going to be Strangers* and *Kill Two Birds and Get Stoned.*) He casually raised the back of his hand to his face and inhaled the faint scent of her that still lingered there, the same way her face and voice clung to his mind. Leaving her to return to the Island of Misfit Toys at Walter Reed hurt worse than anything he could recall.

Blast Radius

"FUCK!"

Through grainy eyes, the spidery red digits of the alarm clock on the cottage nightstand read six thirty-five PM. It was now apparent that killing the whole six-pack earlier in the day had probably been a bridge too far. He should've at least had the presence of mind to set the alarm. Either way, Walton was already five minutes late.

After setting the world record for brushing his teeth (now was definitely *not* the time for bad hygiene), Walton grabbed his keys and flip-flops and dashed toward the rental car, barely pausing to lock the door. There was a threat at work, and he was growing feral from an intrinsic need to eliminate it.

He turned the key awkwardly. The new cast made everything a bit more difficult. When the engine came alive he put the spurs to her. He had been thinking and drinking all afternoon over a way to save the situation, wearing a hole in his brain and heart as he'd sat overlooking the most picturesque setting in the history of Canadian Cottage Country; the very sort of place they would've went canoeing. He saw Amy everywhere he looked, and when he blinked, she was somehow even etched on the inside of his eyelids.

Since those first weekends together, their lives had evolved from touching to overlapping. Amy's initial skittishness about the blossoming anomaly between them had faded each day. In the beginning, Walton had figured Amy had developed her flirting skills as a mechanism to draw people in and make them feel safe while she maintained control and kept her real feelings close to her vest. This had led him to wonder whether her feelings toward him were real or not, but he had resolved to step out on faith and tread the path that advised, "A spirited filly needs a steady hand."

273

The strategy had paid off. Amy had begun to talk about the possibility of taking him up on his offer to go traveling with him and had offered suggestions about the places they could go. A small poster from the movie they had seen together appeared on her bedroom wall. She would occasionally drop anecdotes about things like how for a long time she'd carried around in her bag the first letter he'd sent her, and though it had taken her a while to get to where she felt like she could write him back, he'd been with her. She'd written in an email that when she'd gone to bed after their first weekend together, the sheets had smelled like him but it had felt empty. She'd gone on to write that her icy heart was melting, but followed with the warning for him to proceed at his own risk. According to her, "The pheromones don't lie…It's like someone's pulling the strings." They had begun to make their own history. Walton and Amy had plunged into the depths of something that had carried them off. He'd racked up the frequent flyer miles accordingly.

While sharing the buzz from a few Hoegaardens one evening, Amy had confessed a concern that long-distance relationships often weren't "real," and that in a perfect world he would have an apartment on the west side of Toronto, and she would have a toothbrush there, and she'd be able to stay over five nights out of the week and wake up in his arms and then have to haul ass just to be late for work because she didn't want to leave his bed.

Walton had stifled the initial irritation at hearing the vocabulary of pop-psychology directed toward their bond, then felt the twinge of the conflicting impulses of wanting to run from being the object of her affection, while wanting to draw her closer to the center of his world. As soon as she finished, he had words waiting, and let them fly with a stone-cold voice. "What if I told you that was possible?"

Amy reached out across their table to hold his

un-splinted hand. She leaned forward with an expression, that to be the recipient of it, made Walton almost want to die, just so that he could find relief from the excruciating joy he felt to behold it. But that was just the start. "If you could pull that off," she'd said, "I don't know; it would probably make me believe in God."

As soon as his plane was dirt-side, Walton had gone about his business like a man possessed. He'd gathered his Army paperwork, his resume, and college transcript, and made a nuisance of himself to the highest-ranking senator from Oklahoma he could find. He told the senator about the prospect he faced of wasting a year in Med-Hold and proposed a plan to make better use of his skills and time by transferring to the U.S. Embassy at Toronto. Walton wrapped himself in as much poise and determination that he could summon in order to seem like the very sort of young go-getter a senator would want to invest in. He went door-to-door borrowing cups of those qualities. He imagined having more, and then used that too.

At the end of his dynamic spiel, the senator said he thought that what Walton wanted was a great idea and that he wanted to help him any way he could, and that while he was kind of busy, he wanted to make this happen for him. Walton, the senator, and his senior aides then began discussing the strategy to make it real. While walking around the Senate Building after the meeting, he'd nursed a prayer for Amy to know that he was bound and determined to make his way to her and he'd do it by any means, and that if the good senator made this happen, he'd win the everlasting loyalty of a dyed-in-the-wool, thoroughbred son of a bitch who'd cut throats for him, whether Walton agreed with his politics or not.

When he emailed this to Amy, she'd replied (with a few choice French words he'd had to look up) declaring that she was "crazy in love" with him. That she had tied the word *Love* to him, and had been the first to mention it, had been a kick in the guts. He wasn't used to being so valued by women, and to see Amy reciprocate the wild yet certain feelings that raged in him, made him nigh shit up his back. She'd written that her heart was in her throat and that she'd go about her duties with him on her mind, like Franz or Simon from *The Unbearable Lightness of Being* (one of the top books in the Amy Dauphin required reading list). She, the Dreamer, would take Walton with her everywhere.

While Walton had gone about his regimen of Occupational Therapy and surgeries, and fighting and scheming his way through red tape, Amy had taken charge of her life as well, and sent it into a (somewhat) different direction from the strip club.

Shortly after they had begun keeping regular company, or at least, as much as two people can who live in different countries, Amy volunteered down at the Liberal Party headquarters and let slip the dogs of war. She was a dynamo at the office and had channeled her never-ending enthusiasm and energy into it with a will.

Amy's loyalty to her long-held political views, and her affection for Walton (who was a fire-breathing reactionary/neo-agrarian by modern standards), had created a contradictory set of mental circumstances. However, she was ideologically flexible and had risen to the challenge. She had somehow managed to fight for her Liberal-assed Canadian ideals while simultaneously championing the U.S., all the while making it seem like the most sensible platform conceivable.

One day someone at the office had been bitching about America and the diminutive blonde had let the bastard have it with both barrels, metaphorically speaking. When she told Walton about it over the phone she'd growled with all the command authority worthy of any NCO, "Don't fuck with my Oklahoman, man! I'll fuckin' kill ya, man!"

Amy and the Liberals had put up a fight, but that year

they were weighed in the scales and found wanting. She deftly changed gears and had taken a job as a *sous chef* at another summer camp, and though Walton hated that she'd be farther away from him for a few months, he had seen her going all Canadian Pastoral at her father's bucolic *bon vivant* residence and knew that she thrived in such surroundings. As cityfied as she seemed, she belonged in place where she could see the stars. It would do her a world of good.

The camp made her work ridiculous hours, but she'd still called every night in spite of him telling her she didn't have to, and she'd talked until she absolutely had to go in order to steal a few hours of sleep. On the rare occasion when he missed one of her calls, Walton had to try not to obsessively listen to her happy ADHD messages on the voice mail any more than four or five times. He did his best to be supportive of her, cheering her on when she spoke of her triumphs and new friends, and plotting with her on the assholes who stressed her out.

But the demon in him had not been idle. With nothing to do but heal and think during the daytime isolation of his parents' house on Leave, it had continued to scan the horizon for threats. It painted each guy she talked about into a potential lover, and every girl became the new friend who would convince her to run away back to the adventurous life of being a wild thing again. ("I hadn't planned on it. *It just happened,*" he kept expecting to hear her say some night.) The vain hope of being the guy who out-boyfriended all those who'd come before, returned, along with its old friend that underlay them all; the fear that his homely-assed self wasn't good enough to compete with her menagerie of ex-lovers or her secret wants and dreams.

In their last late night pillow talk phone call before he left for a weekend get-together with old Army buddies in New York City, Walton had put his foot in his mouth.

He'd been feeling poetic. His days didn't begin until he heard her voice, and he didn't want to do anything but pine over her and wait for her to call, and he told her this with a laugh in his voice and a smile. Amy had answered him with gentle enthusiasm, replying that he'd just have to use a little *Patience* and urged him to sing the Guns 'n Roses song along with her.

As she began whistling the familiar intro, he had felt a whim that he should say something to up the ante to further show the depth of his conviction. Girls went on forevermore with the jibba-jabba about guys not being affectionate or attentive enough, and he didn't want to lose Amy to neglect. He had said warmly into the phone, "No Amy, that's how I feel and there ain't nothin' you can do about it." The idiot had even smiled as he spoke the words.

A week of silence followed.

Brooding ensued on a promethean scale as he'd wondered what he'd done wrong. After he'd returned from the reunion in New York, the hours had crawled by as he obsessively watched the phone and his imagination made him its bitch. He had heard the old adage about hell having no fury as that of a woman scorned, and he had wished she would've thrown heaps of it his way just to let him know where he had mis-stepped. Anything would be better than her silence.

Her goddamned silence.

The anguish ate him alive. He'd driven all around his hometown in his truck listening to Willie Nelson, George Jones, and old torch songs. He couldn't sleep, and at night he'd climb up his dad's ladder one-handed and sat on the roof by himself, fit-to-be-tied. His brother Joseph, who had just graduated Junior High, would often come up and sit with him and listen like the solid gold wing-man that he was, or just share silence. Sometimes he would bring up a soda and try to cheer Walton up as though he were an amateur bartender. Other times, his mom would come out, look up, and ask if everything was okay. He'd tell her he was fine and she'd go back in shaking her head and muttering under her breath in a tone he'd doubted she used on the girls she taught in Sunday School.

His brain had tried to grind through the problem. There was a solution somewhere and he just wasn't seeing it. How had he gotten lost, and how the hell did he get back on azimuth?

He'd thought about how he'd always been the sort that women had deemed fangless and kept around in the Just Friends category. In his youth, in the name of trying to be sensitive to the feelings of girls he'd liked and "listening...*really listening*" to them, he had permitted himself to be subjected to the indignity of having to hear all about how some douchebag was doing them wrong. (As if he'd really wanted to hear about the guys who were railing the ever-loving shit out of those girls he'd secretly liked.) At the time, he'd wondered why a guy would be an asshole to his girl and why she would tolerate it.

He now knew better. He'd been deceived by a twisted culture that passed out shit and called it gold. It had poisoned his young mind with feel-good modern lies over hard ancient truths.

He'd once read somewhere that culture was "a series of survival strategies handed down from one generation to another." Looking back on a lifetime spent at the feet of movies, TV, and magazines, and how their narratives had often conflicted with the teachings of his family, the Church, and common sense, yet had always remained a step ahead of the game, ultimately shaping the dominant attitudes of the society in which he lived, he realized it had done him no favors. Pop-culture was psychological warfare, and the *anomie* it celebrated was the means by which the First World ate its young. Or rather, sacrificed its children to its gods. It was a theology of seduction; of pretty people selling things, and survival didn't figure into it. The intelligentsia had turned on their own people and set them up for failure. Thanks to the bullshit, The West had lost its ability to mate effectively.

As he'd gone from a child to a young man, Walton had been taught by the usual suspects that as a male, and like all other men before him, he was inherently evil, stupid, greedy, and oppressive. However, for him there was a chance for salvation. If he deferred to any who made a claim on him, and if he accommodated their wishes to standard, whether it was fighting a war, buying a product, voting for a politician, or mouthing the right words, then he could atone for the sins of his forbearers. If he gave, then he would receive. If he was "nice," then he would be loved and respected.

This was a lie.

The truth was that nature was merciless. If there was a Devil, then his fingerprints were on the whole damned thing. Humanity was no exception. The old ways; traditional norms and morals, they codified and enforced survival-oriented behavior. They fostered discipline. Whatever strategies and practices a people picked up that were contra-survival were foolish, and ultimately doomed to failure the groups who espoused them, while those who held strong to the fundamentals survived and out-bred their competitors. The end.

The world never had, or ever would have, a place for "Nice Guys." Men were the part of the species charged with carving humanity's survival out of an unforgiving world, and those who overcame the struggles life put in front of them did so by making it a habit of being tough. Sergeant Bronson had once alluded to this truth. While talking over unit politics one day, he had said of a soldier, "He's a weasly motherfucker anyways. Ain't no bitch gonna give him the time of day. Deep down, every woman wants a man that'll protect her, and that ain't him."

Women, above all else, loved winners. The more a man acted from a position of strength in his dealings with them, regardless of their bitching, the more they secretly fed off it. Women *wanted* to submit—they yearned to surrender—whether they admitted it to themselves or not, but only to a man who was stronger and more powerful than they were. A woman's vanity would not permit her to be bound to a pussy. Feminism was wrong as two boys fucking.

A "sophisticated" young floozie at a bar had once broken it down for Walton, though he'd refused to believe it. She had told him that "girls love a challenge. The guy who's always there for a girl, promptly returns a girl's calls, does whatever she asks of him; that guy, she'll cheat on. She'll want to go after the cocky guy who won't put up with her bullshit and maybe she can't trust completely around her girlfriends."

Walton had never hit a woman, but when the girl had told him that, he'd wanted to slap the bitch so hard her teeth rattled and had hoped she'd contract a hellfire and brimstone social disease. He had seen her as a card-carrying member of the Cunt Conspiracy. She was a living affront to every good woman he'd ever known. The idea of having to play the role of the popped-collared dick-head from an Eighties movie in that sort of a game, just so he could be wanted by a woman, made him want to vomit, and that most girls knowingly behaved like cunts made him contemplate a life of celibacy or renouncing his citizenship and moving back to Bosnia. Then again, maybe he could just remain in The West and save himself for the fucking of whores.

Sitting on the roof, it had occurred to Walton that the girl had been right after all. He'd figured he must've been too nice and "overly available" or some shit. He'd shown weakness and now Amy was running The Vegetarian Escape Gambit he'd always feared she would pull. Maybe if he'd have cheated on her with the fetching bit-tittied brunette girl shopping at the bookstore in DC who had been all too eager to give her card, unsolicited, to a wounded soldier and had asked him to call, perhaps then Amy would've stayed interested.

He'd mused with a sneer that if he'd kept the girl's card instead of throwing it away, went out with her, and had sex with her—the weird sex; like a Louisiana Tilt-A-Whirl, or a Mississippi Slip-'n-Slide, or if he'd really wanted to go for broke, performed "The Prestige"—then told Amy about it, hellfire, it'd probably make her want to get engaged. Fucking bitches and their head games. He'd once told Amy while he was holding her that she had cold feet, and she had replied in her jaunty manner with a kiss, "cold feet, warm heart."

What a crock of shit.

When the flashes of bitterness and anger toward her came, he'd choked them down guiltily with shame for not being understanding enough. He was jumping to conclusions, he'd told himself. Maybe he was being a moron and there was something *Feminine* at work that he wasn't seeing but was expected to know. He'd remembered the glimpses he'd caught of the quiet struggle in her heart and had thought he should give her the benefit of the doubt. Maybe she'd been dealing with some of the deep-down things that bothered her and she'd needed time to process them. She had sometimes gotten blue and went silent before when she couldn't bring herself to talk, and maybe that was what was happening now. Or maybe things had gotten too close for her and she had gotten scared and wanted to run.

Either way, if Amy had thought she could just turn heel on him as if he were some kind of goddamned…*vegetarian* without having to look him in the face, then she'd be very much mistaken. Walton had refused to be dealt with so flippantly. He'd decided to go Encyclopedia Brown on her ass and get to the bottom of things. He had helped hunt down terrorists, surely he could find a Canadian girl and suss out what the deal was. He'd kick this door open one way or another, Rhett Butler style. He'd kept the airline reservation from when he had made it weeks prior and flew up to the camp the day they had planned. What was to be a lovers' reunion had taken on the bitter taste of a confrontation.

As the rental car flew down the rural road shadowed by immense trees en route to the camp to pick Amy up after her shift, Walton could feel her in his arms as she had been earlier that morning. She had imploded, and the words she had whispered still rang in his ears.

She'd said she had done things in the past that she wasn't proud of and that she felt like she was "damaged goods." Walton had told her not to say such things about herself. That all that mattered was *now*. He'd thought about the influences that had encouraged her to follow a path filled with traumatic consequences. He'd wanted to track down the people behind those ideas and fucking destroy them.

They had groped for the cause of the breaking between them, and Amy's guard had been down enough to show Walton something he hadn't expected.

"I was so mad at you," she had breathed into his chest. "After all that talk about you not wanting to put me in a cage, when our conversation ended last Friday, you seemed like such a hypocrite to me. It was like, I'm under all this pressure and having to work these crazy hours, and on top of that you were making me responsible for your happiness, and it wasn't fair of you to put that kind of weight on me. I wanted to break-up with you and never see you again. But I didn't want to do it over the phone. I didn't know what to do.

"But when I saw you when you came looking for me in the kitchen, I remembered all the good times we'd had…"

As he'd held her, Walton had felt hurt and confused. He couldn't tell if it was cowardice, contempt, or that she just didn't give a rat's ass after all, but he couldn't understand how a girl could so casually leave the man whom she claimed to be in love with without even telling him to his face, let alone trying to mend things or fight it out. Amy had given two years of her youth to The Vegetarian, and he'd cheated on her, yet Walton's unforgiveable sin was telling her that he'd pined for her? In spite of his rooftop conclusions, the reality of it all still seemed utterly ridiculous. That a woman could change so fast and so thoroughly for such bullshit made Walton suspect that modern women were at heart just a bunch overgrown little girls who had traded in one set of Ken dolls for another. They lived in their own little world playing by rules that made sense only to themselves.

(He couldn't imagine his grandmothers or his mom and aunts having pulled shit like that when they'd been young. When those squaws had been on the warpath, they'd let their men know all about it. The women he'd grown up around may have come after their husbands with a cast-iron skillet, or said some cutting remark designed to make a man mad enough to punch a hole through a wall, but they didn't run from a problem. Walton's male relatives were notoriously ornery, and most had spent their first thirty years as hell-raisers; he imagined that a lot of times they'd had it coming. Other times, the girls might have just wanted to pick a scrap to mix things up a little. At any rate, the men had given as good as they got, often launching preemptive strikes of their own. They sometimes saw fighting as an important, if not fun, dynamic of their marriages. Walton's dad had often told him, "You've gotta keep a woman goin', Son," and his parents had been married almost thirty years. His dad's cousin had gone even further, saying that sometimes when his wife was out of line, a man had to "rattle that log-chain, Thomas Paul." There had been raised voices growing up, but there had been a lot of fun as well. And love. In fact, his grandmother was still pissed at his grandfather for having died of Leukemia almost twenty years ago. The way his Maw-Maw saw it, they hadn't finished growing old yet. Walton thought the whole fighting/making-up thing might be why he had a ton of aunts, uncles, and cousins.)

And yet, there were some things that he couldn't blame Amy for. Though he'd tried hard not to be, at some point he had become an emotional parasite. It was bad enough that he had to live with his own personal conflicts, but now he was forcing her to help carry them. This wasn't what he'd wanted, and if he didn't get his shit wired tight, *toot sweet*, he was going to fuck around and lose her forever.

He supposed he should be a bit more careful once they ironed this out, but he refused to apologize for wanting her so desperately. He was determined to defy, in his own private way, the spirit of his age which knew nothing but to bend knee to the easy, the disposable, and the new.

Life, and all its wonder, was cheaply valued in the global marketplace. A human being was seen as nothing more than a brief collection of atoms, and since the soul was not a currently quantifiable phenomenon, it was deemed not to exist, and could therefore neither be judged nor cherished. One person reaching out for another in the dark was relative to a lab experiment, and all of the passion, beauty, and magic fighting to make itself manifest were merely abstractions born of chemical reactions, eviscerated of all mystery.

Relationships in modern mating were just another form of consumerism; the sexual equivalent of musical chairs in which the winners sold out into limp marriages just to become breeders or to lock someone down before they became too unattractive. The pursuit of pleasure was held in higher esteem than the cultivation of love.

Love. He remembered a class in college where the professor had been discussing the nuances in the meanings of words found in Ancient Greek and Hebrew. Words like "love." The professor had put down his chalk, and after saying, "Let's chase a rabbit," he had embarked upon an account of loving his wife.

"The day we were married...boy, I thought we were *in love*," The professor had said intensely as he'd stared at the Old Testament class. "NOBODY had ever loved a woman the way I *loved* her!" He then drew down on them hard. "We just celebrated our Fiftieth Wedding Anniversary. Back then, we didn't know what *love* was."

For all its damned "liberation," sexual and otherwise, the era was woefully deficient in *heart*. Secret admirers were now stalkers. Romeo and Gatsby's asses would've gotten restraining orders. Cyrano De Bergerac would've been diagnosed with some chickenshit, two-bit, tin-horn disorder and put on Prozac. Guys like Kris Kristofferson and Johnny Cash would've been ignored. Motown would have never been invented.

But there was hope! He had heard it faintly in her voice earlier that morning despite her coldness the night before. It flickered too weakly to even talk about it around the volatile energy that Walton knew surrounded them, but it was there.

This misunderstanding was nothing. They'd go back down by the lake and talk. He'd charm the hell out of her yet and make her laugh with a grin and a wink at this silly-ass bump in the road, and when it passed, they'd be the stronger for it. He'd be all Burt Reynolds 'n shit, like ten motherfuckers. Amy had reminded him of the value of lightheartedness and he'd call upon that now to sweep her off her feet. He was going to square this situation away and not a damned thing would stop him. With both hands on the wheel, he drove the speeding car like a burning round fired downrange.

When he woke, he noticed the car was stopped at a downward angle and that there was blood, glass, and twisted metal everywhere. His thoughts were wadded in cotton. A woman in a Round Brown stood in the ditch with his car and pressed a plastic object to his lips as he sat restrained by his seat belt. She told him something about his having passed the Breathalyzer Test and that from the skid marks on the road he had been going at least sixty-five mph when he had come to the sharp unmarked turn. Walton couldn't have cared less because he now knew that he was officially SOL (Shit Out of Luck). He wished he was dead. Now there was no way that Amy wouldn't think he was crazier than a shithouse rat.

Though Walton possessed a vague sense of thankfulness that no one else had been hurt, his thoughts dwelled on her. He didn't want to see her, not like this, but he didn't want her to be waiting on him or thinking he'd turned passive-aggressive and had stood her up out of revenge. He asked the officer to tell Amy that he wouldn't be able to pick her up from work after all.

He came to again on a gurney with so many tubes sticking out of his body that he almost felt like he was back at Walter Reed, and if his thoughts were fuzzy before, they were now slippery and viewed from the bottom of a dirty pond.

He was surprised when Amy came in to the emergency room, and he immediately began drowning in a sea mixed with joy at seeing her, and the bottomless humiliation at her seeing him. However, watching her through his fractured eye-sockets, he couldn't have been more proud of the way she handled the sight of him. His face was mangled from the glass and crushing impact of the steering wheel, with drying blood matting his non-regulation hair and beard, and the ends of his front teeth shattered off at tiny angles, but you couldn't tell it from looking at her. He just knew she was gone.

She told him how brave he was, and that he wasn't a pussy at all as he joked about how much he winced as they sewed up the gashes in his face. She reassured him that doctors these days could do amazing things and that he'd probably barely even have a scar when they were through with him, which would be in no time. She held his hand. When he asked her to climb in next to him so he could hold her before they took him away, she even did that as well, despite the slurring drugged-out tone of his voice.

Regardless of the Morphine's best efforts, she filled up his mind as she laid next to him for the last time. He hated that he couldn't smell her through the nose that had been driven up into an Orc-like angle. No smell in all of the world had the effect on Walton that Amy's natural scent did. He had once asked her when she'd emerged in a towel fresh from the shower what perfume she wore and she had told him that she never did on account of her being allergic to them. He figured that made sense. At her core, Amy was a child of nature, and her body knew that her own fragrance was all she'd ever need.

When the time came to transfer him, though, she got up. As she walked to the door, Walton wanted to call her name like in a movie. He wanted to get up and grab her shoulders and spin her around and tell her that it was just a body and that he wasn't this *thing* he appeared to be. He wanted to show her that beneath the madness going on around them, the substance of their connection was right there below the surface waiting for them to reach out and hold on to it and keep it alive. He wanted to fix things.

But he was too broken. There were too many tubes and needles, too many drugs in him, too much blood lost, and no way to stop her without looking even more deranged in her eyes. He could do nothing but lay there and silently watch his world die.

She walked away and didn't look back.

"Looking for Space"

The young man stood in front of the cannon and grinned. He found it difficult to veil his embarrassment while surrounded by the relics of The Battalion's past and the cocky soldiers of Second Platoon. His eyes caught those of his old squad leader, whose mouth ended with the faintest of smirks, and continued to scan the room. The squad leader's posture was a more of a physical sneer than usual.

The soldiers of Second arranged themselves into a desert-camouflaged formation, and a colonel looked around the room to silence it with a stare. The young man didn't recognize the particular colonel (all officers above the rank of captain looked the same to him anyway), but he swallowed his grin and straightened up, squaring his shoulders like a switch being flipped, and came to the position of Attention. When the colonel had the reverence he sought, he began.

"We're here today to honor one of our own and present him with our nation's oldest medal; The Purple Heart. This award was commissioned by General George Washington for military merit, and today I'm proud to award it to Sergeant Thomas Walton for his actions, demonstrating the code we live by; of not leaving a fallen comrade behind."

Walton ceased to listen, and drifted off into a mental cocoon until his attention was needed. He remembered a quote from Napoleon; "Give me enough ribbon, and I could conquer the world." He saw again his old squad leader out of the corner of his eye, and after almost five years of working with him, didn't need to even wonder what the older man thought about the ceremony.

The colonel continued to orate, and though Walton was deeply honored, there was also something about it that felt very distant to him. He wished that he could just trade the colonel's praise for a set of Separation Orders and go his own way.

The colonel finished, clipped the medal on his chest, exchanged salutes with him, and backed away. Walton spent the next five minutes shaking hands in the foyer until only the squad leader stood in front of him. With a stoic, measuring look in his eye, Sergeant Bronson simply said, "Thomas." He held his stare for a moment, then shook Walton's hand. He ended the silence by saying, "Get the fuck outta here. You're good for today."

Walton let his restraint melt into the casual facade with which he usually approached the world at large. Out of an impulse for self-deprecation in response to being the center of attention at the award ceremony, he said, "Roger, Sergeant. Goddamn, it was tough to keep a straight face. They're makin' it sound like I'd single-handedly stormed Omaha Beach at fuckin' Normandy or some shit. All I did was forget to duck."

A hint of a grin cracked the squad leader's face but his eyes still carried the indelible mark of trials, revelries, and small glories left unspoken. "It was like that when they gave me my Bronze Star. But they don't do this bullshit for us," he said with a wry look as he nodded his head back toward the dispersing Cherries. "Take your shit and get the fuck outta here, Tom."

Once back in his room, Walton locked his door, threw his beret on the bed, and pressed a button on his laptop to fire up a random playlist. He opened a desk drawer, and while he absently tossed the medal into the ashtray in which he kept his spare change, the computer's tinny speakers bled out *At Last* by Etta James.

He flinched as though shot while a wave of surprise and memory suddenly coursed through his body like an electric shock. For a moment his good hand moved to change it, but he stopped and walked over to sit near the window instead; close enough to hear the song, yet far enough away to torment himself and not stop it.

He remembered. He'd heard the song at a bar on Staten Island while he was visiting old Army buddies from the Bosnia days. He had sat blissfully ignorant of the fact that meanwhile, hundreds of miles up north, Amy had been severing him out of her heart and turning him into nothing. He had watched ice melt into his Rum-and-Coke, seeing her smile in his mind.

"What're you thinking about?" Atnode had asked. Though the time that had passed since he'd been out of the Army had thinned Atnode's hair to the point of forcing him to shave his head, his defiant fuck-it-ness had remained alive and well.

"A girl."

"Ahhh. Fucking bitches," Atnode had observed with fervent cynicism. "You're thinking, 'I hate the cunt.'"

Walton had come to life, wild-eyed, as if erupting with pent up energy from a twenty-year coma and reflexively shot back with, "No, I love the cunt!"

Atnode had merely nodded and turned to share with Oversnach his thoughts regarding the sleek young barmaid who had just served them, while Walton looked back into his drink, wondering if the rest of the bar realized that his eyes were about to pop out of his head.

He *loved* her?

Walton had never uttered that word about a girl before. As he saw it, it was a personal act of defiance. (For him, the word was reserved for the woman who would someday share his name and carry his babies. This gave the word more power.) And yet, in that moment the world had turned and something had boiled out from the place inside him where the wordless things lived. He'd been terrified it might actually be true.

He could still see the way Amy had looked when he'd gone to find her at the camp after a week of silence. She'd

291

taken him down by the lake during her break from the kitchen, yet had kept a greater distance from him than she ever had before. The girl who used to run to meet him, to be held and kissed by him, and would occasionally attack him with passion, could hardly look him in the eye. The pain of seeing that had destroyed something within him on some level.

At the time, he'd been too numb to appreciate the irony that the petite young woman had stupefied him with shock worse than Mr. Kudah Nahr had when he'd come down from the mountains of Pakistan and riddled him with holes on the other side of the Earth. The crisp northern air had brought a hint of the autumn to come and kissed the cottony blonde hair that hung above eyes tinged with pity at the heart she was breaking. She'd forced a smile, and in an attempt to ease his pain had said, "Tom, it's like my dad always says; 'If you love something, set it free. If it comes back to you, it's yours, and if it doesn't, it was never yours in the first place.'"

The reckless joy that had once dripped from her Canadian accent was gone, and in its place was a cold emptiness that had faded the world. He had looked into the eyes of the lover who had become a stranger, and had wished he could make himself small enough to crawl inside her mind and try to find where the girl he had known had gone. In his vanity, he'd thought that he could somehow singlehandedly repair the breach. The next day, a car ride would prove him wrong.

But that was the summer and it had long since died.

He glanced at the drawer and thought about the medal. If he sent it to her, perhaps she'd speak to him. Surely it would elicit a response.

The idea came and he forced himself to crush it. Having spent the past six months sending Amy one sniveling-assed email, letter, and gift after another, he'd thoroughly established himself as a virtuoso of the pathetic. He had embarrassed himself enough. Getting wounded, dumped, and having his face and hand rebuilt had been hard, but that didn't give a man a blank check to go around acting like a jackass like he'd been doing. Besides, she'd probably just see it as another form of bribery or emotional blackmail and she'd be right. He'd made himself into a supplicant, and women had zero tolerance for that shit. He thought if he pushed her away anymore she'd probably fall off the planet. Maybe if he continued to give her some space, he could get his shit together and someday try to win her back.

The song swelled, and slivers of the last words Amy had written seeped out of Walton's brain like a lodged shard of glass; *"You are not the person I thought you were and that is not your fault...Please be man enough to let me go...My heart has been broken more times than you could surmise...I have absolutely no desire to share in your anguish. I have had a lifetime's worth of my own...And leave me alone. There's nothing left to salvage."*

Walton ordered himself, as a sergeant in the infantry, to pull his head out of his ass and have some fucking self-respect. There had been a cruelty to Amy. A jaded world had taught her long ago that in matters of the heart one either wounds or gets wounded. No quarter. And she believed it. He'd known this about her from the start, and had ignored it to his peril. He reminded himself that for all her smiles and warmth and talk of being "crazy in love," she hadn't even had the kindness to mail him his assault pack after his accident.

Walton wondered if there was ever a way to want and care for another without it becoming a burden to them or yourself. Was it ever possible to trust a woman without the secret fear that, given the right trigger, she'd turn on you when you least expected it, tear your world apart, and not feel the least bit bad about it? He now doubted it. Feminism had done a marvelous job of bringing out the worst in women.

As much as feminism gave Walton a case of the ass, though, he wasn't fool enough to try and lay all the problems of men and women at the feet of it. That battle had been old long before Aristophanes had written *Lysistrata*. But it did seem to him like a Pandora's Box had been opened at some point, and something very precious had been cheapened.

For him, this loss of value was evident in the fact that he'd met a girl like Amy at a strip club in the first place. He didn't hold it against her; The West suffered under a plague of advocates pushing self-destructive, bat-shit crazy agendas on impressionable girls for everything except impulse control and knitting. But since her, he'd learned a little about the true nature of "empowerment" in terms of sexuality, and the forces that seduced a girl onto that path.

During a recent check-up at Walter Reed following his latest surgery, he'd met an older woman over the internet. She'd been an executive in Northern Virginia and had been looking to have an affair before marrying her fiancé. The fiancé part had bothered him, but at the time Walton had justified participating in the betrayal by telling himself it was "found pussy." Someone was going to fuck her and it might as well have been him.

After a week of emails and phone calls, they'd met up at a hotel one afternoon. She'd left a key for him at the front desk and had been waiting, blindfolded, on the bed. (She had told him about her fantasy of being taken by a stranger in such a manner, and he'd been happy to oblige.)

Toward the end of their time together, after she'd asked if she could take the blindfold off and see his face, she had made the request for him to get a piece of paper which had been sticking out of the top of her purse. It had been a cashier's check for $1,500 with his name on it. She'd told him that she wanted him to keep it.

Walton had been floored. He'd refused without even

bothering to think, telling her that "money wasn't what this was about," and that he couldn't accept it. However, she had taken a tone that she'd no doubt cultivated as an executive and mother of two, and had told him that she'd insisted, and would be offended if he didn't.

While Walton had been amused by her brief attempt to display authority, given her prior submission throughout the day, he had acquiesced to her wishes. Watching her as she had lain on the bed, he'd seen the young girl inside her look back at him across the years and heartbreaks between them. She'd told him that she'd been happy to feel the kind of passion again where "sounds are sharper and colors are brighter," even if it was just for a moment, and that after their first phone conversation she'd decided she wanted to do something nice for him. She'd told him that she wanted to help him live out his dream of traveling around the world, and that if she'd been twenty years younger she'd have given him a run for his money.

After returning to his own hotel, he'd gone right back to being alone again. As Walton had washed off the smell of sex and *Chanel,* he'd sifted through the shame of being a party to unfaithfulness. He had sworn savagely to himself that he never would again. He'd been raised better. The woman had worn a ring that a man had loved her enough to give her, and with the hand it had sat upon, she'd touched Walton all over his body. She'd told him things; the story she'd painstakingly conjured to explain her tardiness to her fiancé, and how excited she was that she finally had an illicit story to share with her girlfriends.

At the same time, Walton had been sad that the woman had been devastated by her ex-husband in a way she'd never recovered from, and that her fiancé probably wouldn't ever really have her heart. It had seemed to him that sexual liberation was good for little more than turning out a world full of walking wounded.

However, he'd also grinned from ear to ear at the day's

worth of pleasure he'd found in the body of a woman who had been practicing at being a lover for decades. He hadn't had to apologize for, or restrain, the feelings inside him that had compelled him to dominate her and give and take whatever he'd wanted. In fact, contrary to feminist propaganda, she'd craved it to the point that seeing the response it had provoked in her had almost scared him. Some hidden ache within her had challenged him to yield more to his hunger as the day had played out, and it had demanded that she serve as the recipient of it. Seeing such passion come out in a woman had given him flashbacks to Canada, and there had been moments where it had felt like he'd been in the past and present at the same time.

What was more, she'd given him money. There had been something degrading about accepting it when lust was in play, yet it had been thrilling to his ego as well. By simply sharing with her his capacity for intimacy and the excitement of connecting with someone from the world of the opposite sex, he'd inspired enough ardor to motivate her to spontaneously give him four figures worth of her money. That was power.

Understanding this had given him what he felt was a new insight on Amy. She'd been made to be loved. She'd inspired fierce devotion from those around her and had lit up every damned room he'd seen her walk into. For a young woman with that kind of a spark, to figure out that she could make the world revolve around her for a moment and make money by sharing the sight of her body or the rush that came from being flirted with by her, had probably been like giving a monkey a gun.

At least that was how he'd felt at the end of the affair in DC; heady with power at the primal forces within him. Dangerous forces. He now saw how a girl could take up a crazy life and revel in the Faustian glamour of something like high-end stripping, then wind up lost before she knew it. The way Walton saw it, his quarrel was with those who'd twisted their minds with bad ideas and had made a virtue of corruption. He thought that under different circumstances, he and Amy could have been happy.

Regardless of his defense of her, he would never forgive her for giving him the happiest days of his life.

Looking out the window as the song changed, he watched a group of soldiers shovel snow from Alpha Company's formation area, their youth making his almost twenty-seven years feel ancient. Though hundreds of meters away, he could remember when he was a Joe, and imagined the soldiers no doubt bitching about the whims of weather, God, and sergeants, as if any of them gave a rat's ass from their lofty thrones about what a Joe thought.

In their hearts, Walton knew the soldiers were setting out to right a wrong or chase glory; "seeking the bubble reputation, even in the cannon's mouth," but in the grand scheme of things, they were just pawns in a game played by men who held power on behalf of an empire in the wild grip of decadence.

The naïve, all too damn young, Joes had been bred to spend their fleeting lives serving as wall fodder for people who held them, their homes, their attitudes, and their very identities in contempt; the Media Punditocracy, Think Tank Brainiacs, change agents, financiers, muckrakers, corporate vultures, and intellectuals who'd handed in their Communist badges for the cause of globalism, all of whom no doubt gave each other hand-jobs while talking about the importance of "making the world safe for democracy," or some such other bullshit you had to have a lobotomy or a PhD to believe. They had established a near-monopoly over words and ideas, and had turned the country—*his* country—into a den of thieves. The Left, the Right...they were both fucking savages. An entire caste of carpetbaggers on a global scale. He thought about the stern face emblazoned on his Purple Heart. This bullshit wouldn't have happened on George Washington's watch.

Betrayal.

Walton felt the old sneaking suspicion that the nation to which they had pledged their solemn oath had been prostituted out to something mysterious and wrong. Some idea or strategy that wasn't in the interests of actual Americans themselves. Pawns lived in the face of threats, and occasionally knew the game was somehow fucked even if the players didn't.

From his vantage point as an Okie who'd descended from stone-broke dirt farmers who once had fought on the losing side of a bad war, that seemed to be the way of things. Those who had the means and the want-to, hacked into the moral compasses of their people and seduced them into fighting on behalf of "the greater good" (as defined by their intellectual rigmarole). Once all the combatants were safely in the dirt, historians with social agendas would pronounce an official interpretation of the contest of blood which would neatly identify the good guys and bad guys according to biased political motivations, and then use it as a stick with which to beat opposing constituencies in the present.

Walton thought about America and her wars, and believed more and more with each passing day, that ultimately, many of the interventions upon which the service was sent were little more than militarized missionary work on behalf of the Carpetbagger Caste, bringing to the far corners of the earth a dose of That Old Time Secular Religion whether anybody actually wanted it or not. With gallows humor, he imagined that somewhere out there was an op-order with words typed in red ink saying, *"Go yea therefore unto all the world, preaching and teaching, baptizing them in the name of Democracy, Commerce, and Human Rights."* God have mercy on the heretics.

Not that he gave a damn for the crackpot conspiracy theories of the Tinfoil Hat Brigades; Walton had been in the military long enough to know that no one was in charge. However, he did believe that Dostoyevsky had been on to something when he'd written, "It was not you who ate the idea, but the idea that ate you." Walton figured that an idea had eaten The West a long time ago.

The self-appointed knuckleheads "framing the policy debate" and "setting the agenda" weren't really interested in security. Any Joe worth his salt knew that establishing security was merely the *first* priority of work. No, they were running the Long Con. For all the clever arguments tossed around and debated like theology among the gurus in the editorial sections of newspapers, academic journals, and on the Sunday morning talk shows, Walton was convinced that for the unblooded elites who held their leash, the military was a tool not for defending the U.S., but for making the world in their image. Marine Corps General Smedley Butler had been right.

Other instruments were more subtle but just as effective; schools and universities, the media, big business, lobbyists, NGO's, international finance, and the shallow Culture of the Lowest Common Denominator in which entertainment served the same function as religion, were all of inestimable value as well. (If it didn't make people want to spend their way into debt slavery or endorse a shiny new theory or program of theirs, it had no business on Prime Time or the newsstand.) They were conducting an ideological gang-rape of the world. Their loyalties were to influence and money. Power. They didn't give a damn for flesh and blood, or the connection to land. Or for the meaning of *Home*.

In the breathless drive to make the world rootless it grew more and more chaotic as a result, leading to an unseen precipice somewhere up ahead on the horizon. He could feel something in the air akin to the ominous tension that had sometimes loomed over a mission.

The Carpetbaggers and their useful idiots wouldn't be happy until they had "deconstructed" every standard, tradition, culture, belief, nation, community, family, identity, or shred of order, and filled it with their commoditized, globalized, *nothingness*. Maybe even instigate another World War in their continued efforts to chain the world to an empire of good intentions. Fucking savages.

Pride in one's country, pride in one's people, history, ways, and beliefs, was a valuable resource to be exploited whenever the Carpetbaggers needed the yokels and suckers to sign up, line up, and go fight wars. When they needed blood, they called it *Patriotism*. However, let those same yokels and suckers try to express those feelings in ways that didn't involve killing strangers, but rather sought to preserve and cultivate the strength, identity, and spirit of their homes, then The Powers That Be had The Talking Heads resurrect the specter of the long-dead Third Reich and trot out the clichéd shaming language with words like *Nationalism*.

Walton could almost hear the smug arguments of the bought-and-paid-for pundits and technocrats who would feel the status quo and their dreams of a compulsory universalist utopia threatened. They'd begin the intellectual lynch mob. "That's not *Patriotism*, that's *Nationalism*," they'd say. "You know who else embraced *Nationalism*? The Nazis. The Nazis were big into *Nationalism*."

The limits of their imagination were almost comical. Walton wondered how many times a day some nitwit compared something to the damned Nazis in order to keep the Proles in line. Were there no other Straw Men in their repertoire or dead horses to beat? It had been over sixty years since the Allies, consisting of men like Walton's steely-eyed grandfather, had handed the Axis their asses. Walton thought it was time for the world to move on and find new insults. (Then again, there were a lot of Talking

Heads beginning to compare dissenters to terrorists, so maybe they'd decided to mix things up a little.)

Of course, the Nazis had also borrowed from *Socialism* when building their monstrosity. The Talking Heads never mentioned that any more than they discussed the 60 million or so people who'd died under Stalin and Mao. (The blood spilled in the central-planning schemes of Marxist regimes, somehow having obtained a pass. Whatever their polarity on the Left/Right spectrum, Walton thought the Nazis and Communists both sucked.) The agendas pimped by the media were deemed enlightened and progressive, and opposing ones were evil, xenophobic, backward, bigoted, etc. Fucking hypocrites. Whores had more integrity than they did.

The next word would no doubt be *Isolationism*. As if the U.S. ever had, or could, tread that path. Eventually, they'd probably get around to *Fascism*, or whatever other *isms* they could think of that would establish the dreaded *Reactionary* frame to delegitimize the identity of the opposition.

Words like *Neutrality* or *Self-Determination* would never see the light of day, even though Walton thought they were wanted by most people all over the world; to simply enjoy the sovereignty of their homes with dignity, and neither have to fight wars not in their interests, nor bow to a confusion of supranational, intergovernmental, plutocratic master plans envisioned by faraway eggheads who'd never touched a shovel or sworn an oath that had cost them blood and sweat. And the Carpetbagger Caste hated them for it.

How he wished he had one, just one, of those fucking parasites present then and there. He wanted to feel one of their throats in the claw of his hand, or even better, to take them downrange. He eagerly imagined the look on their faces as a bullet or IED caught up with them and their flesh was torn and vaporized in one of the very wars or revolutions they'd helped conceive. Either way, the Joes could have it. He wanted no more part of Babel. The world could burn for all he cared. They'd gotten their last klick out of Walton.

An old idea from the minds of dead thinkers struck. As creatures of nature, maybe the species instinctively *needed* war and secretly hungered for conflict in its innermost being if left stagnating too long in the lotus-stupor of peace; demanded it like fall and winter followed spring and summer. Like death followed birth. If history was any judge, there certainly was an argument for it. (How the shitheads currently dominating the culture could embrace evolution through natural selection, and then with a straight face, still argue on behalf of the possibility of things like "world peace" or egalitarian castles in the sky was beyond Walton. That was the realm of fool's errands and Trojan horses. At least religion, myth, and common sense had the integrity to accept the hard truths about human nature. Especially the parts about folly and vanity.)

War; war in which a people's survival or way of life hung in the balance tested them. It sharpened them, defined them, and inspired them. It goaded them to be tougher, stronger, and smarter. War forced a people to give a fuck or perish from the earth. To be better than they thought they were, or else.

Whether he liked it or not (and he didn't), war seemed to function as a screening mechanism for human life. People were tribal organisms, and the victorious groups out-adapted and out-fought their competitors. They seized command of the lion's share of resources and had lots of babies who advanced on to the lightning round, and the losers withered demographically into historical footnotes. This level of conflict bound people together and purged a body of its bad blood or put it in its grave. War was the brutal birth pains of future order.

War also offered a glimpse of something transcendent. For all its ugliness, and the goddamned waste, and the haunting nature of violence that lingered long after the spilling of blood, even in a shithole like Afghanistan, for a brief instant, he'd seen men touch upon glory. Just the memory of having seen the soldiers from his unit, who were indistinguishable in appearance from any other men found on any street in the country, fight in some shit-assed dusty compound in the face of fear and death had humbled him. Walton had witnessed the Heroic emerge from within hearts of the men with whom he'd served. To see such a thing in the Era of Plastic was rare.

That Man might have some inherent nobility after all, failed to set Walton all a-quiver with joy. Modern war still drew certain types of men and then promptly culled them from the gene pool or dumped them back into a fat, dumb, and happy populace who couldn't give a shit less and didn't want them around. In doing so it either killed off or suffocated the very sort of men it needed most. The dynamic and the hard-charging; the brave and the bold who hungered after a challenge and were hell-bent on gambling with their lives. Or the responsible and the dedicated; those who were simply willing to sacrifice for their homes and the people they loved.

Sacrifice was honorable. But how often were the altars of the causes which demanded it? Walton supposed that once you cut through the bullshit they seldom were, and that far too many sacrifices were all too often in vain.

His attention shifted back to the soldiers on snow detail and he almost laughed. The would-be heroes had no idea they were going to wind up spending more time cleaning things than they ever would fighting. He thought that was a good thing. The do-gooder/mercenary schemes of the chattering classes and their masters were not worth one red drop of a Joe's blood.

Walton was suddenly caught up in the imagined spectacle of the entire United States Military standing tall in a vast formation before the Ivy League-trained cosmopolitans and multinational profiteers whose opinions dictated the actions of the service, and then some grizzled-assed NCO like old First Sergeant Wade declare with command authority, *"No! Fuck your orders!"*

Walton flexed his right hand. He'd found the cold of winter made it stiff. He continued watching the soldiers on the snow detail and realized that he didn't know them after all. *His* soldiers had left the Army or had been sent to other teams. Not even a year ago, he had been running like a bat out of hell from the back of Shithooks with trusted comrades and live ammo, getting in firefights, and kicking open the doors of known terrorists, and he'd never do any of that again. The thought of trying to find something in the world of malls and cubicle drudgery to match the raw potency of those experiences and fill the void they'd left with the life he had left to live, suddenly made him feel very tired and alone. And lost. He was invisible.

Roy Orbison began *Crying* and Walton closed the laptop with a sense of urgency, cutting off the song altogether. He figured if God existed, then He had one hell of a sense of humor. At least it hadn't been Dido. (*White Flag* would've nailed his monkey-ass to the floor.) He decided to take Sergeant Bronson's advice and get out of the barracks. Get some of that Upstate New York scenery. A drive to the bookstore for some coffee and loitering would hit the spot.

He clawed his way out of his now old-fashioned green and brown mottled uniform until he stood in the silence in his hairy skin and scars, naked as God, folly, and circumstance had made him for a moment longer than necessary, reveling in the simple fact that he was without clothes. He thought to himself; fuck a uniform. Whether it's some asshole in advertising on Madison Avenue or

Uncle Sam, they all wanted to put their name on you. They wanted to brand you like fucking cattle and condition you to be just like all the other drones; the shuffling masses of Abercrombie Zombies who lived out the spectrum of their lives based off what some douchebag wrote in an article. Fuck them and their uniforms.

He slid his feet into his shower shoes and slung his towel over his shoulder. As he neared the shower, Walton paused to look at himself in the mirror. The doctors had done far better than he could have hoped for.

The crash had been so damaging that they'd had to saw open his skull, and working beneath flesh of his face, repair his head from inside and out. When he'd recovered enough, he'd gone to the mall to buy a cap to cover up his shaved head and the seventy staples binding the scalp together. As he'd walked along the upper level, he'd seen a mother with her three or four-year-old son approaching. The little boy had been holding her hand as he'd walked next to her, and Walton had nodded and smiled at them. The sight of the mother and child had caused him to forget how marred his face was, but his obliviousness evaporated as they'd made eye contact with him. The mother had returned his smile kindly, but he'd seen in the little boy's eyes a child confronted by a monster. The little boy's terror had been so great that he'd let go of his mother's hand and hid behind her, clutching her leg.

Walton had thought he'd never heal. He'd been afraid that because of his face he'd been doomed to go through the rest of his life as one of The Unloved, but he had made his peace with the prospect. After several bouts of surgery, though, he almost looked normal. Almost. He still didn't recognize the distorted version of his old face. It was like looking at a stranger.

He ran his good hand over the foreign souvenirs of failure graven into his face, literally, carved into his skull, and kindled the contempt that silently taught him a merciless lesson every waking moment of the day and followed him into his dreams, giving him no respite. This face, this isolation, this world he now lived in; this was what came from being weak.

He couldn't blame the war. It was what he'd signed up for and he'd been lucky to get a small piece of the action. His time downrange had been one of the most significant parts of his entire life. War, like love (or whatever the hell it had been), had initiated him into one of the most ancient and universal mystery cults in the human experience, and the silent knowledge it bestowed upon him provided him with a sharper, stronger perspective through which to view the world around him. All in all, Afghanistan and Amy had been damned good training.

He could regret, however, and hate himself until his dying day for the unmanly way he had let his feelings control him. This was not how a man was supposed to be, he now saw, and he had the war and Amy to thank for this understanding.

Walton entered the bathroom and turned on the shower faucet. He felt the water temperature grow warmer against the flesh of his still-unfamiliar hand. The heat brought with it the realization that it was easier to hate yourself for being weak than demand of yourself strength. He was disgusted with his mind and knew he needed to grab his nuts and quit being such a pussy or he'd tear himself apart more than he already had. But how?

Naked and still, Walton struggled to think of a way to prevail over all the many flaws he despised within himself and the world. The toxic fury that raged in response to them became a desperation so powerful it caused him to explore a forbidden weapon.

He could kill them.

His mind formed a dream in which he could take all that ugliness, and pain, and failure, and weakness, and rage, and draw all of that vileness from out of himself and the world and give it human shape. If the darkness became a thing that could bleed, then it could die.

The impossible evolved and became more pragmatic. Since the enemy was in his mind, he could attack it where it lived. No Hamlet half-stepping or dick-dancing around. A bullet in the brain-pan, and then finally, peace. Or even better, in the heart. That way he could have some time to quietly savor the sensation of letting go like he did when he was going under before a surgery or as he used to when he'd laid down in his bed as a little boy after he'd had his bedtime story and said his prayers. Back then, his mom and dad would tuck him in and tell him they loved him, and he'd smiled from ear to ear as he had smelled the scent of the fresh cotton sheets his mom had washed and listened for his beagle to howl "night-night."

Death had almost got the drop on him at Miam Do, but if he chose this route, then he could meet it on *his* terms. He would be waiting for it this time. He would have the high ground. When his time came and he prepared to set down his burden, he would stare at the darkness in his mind's eye with a death's head grin, knowing that he would be taking his foe with him. His last thought would be one of defiance. Victory.

"I have absolutely no desire to share in your anguish. I have had a lifetime's worth of my own."

No.

There would be no victory for him in such a death. To think so would be to accept a defeat hidden in the fold of a lie. Amy had known that. She'd understood about the kinds of pain that could live in a mind, and had reacted to them by crafting a hair-trigger arsenal of weaponized femininity. His dumped-ass was living proof of that. The world had been feeding her *"Do as thou wilt"* bullshit since she'd been a little girl, and she'd suffered from where it led. And yet, in spite of her wounds, she'd fought, in her own way, to not yield to sorrow.

Her resolve to deny anguish a foothold had been a part of what had drawn him to her so strongly in the first place and now made it so goddamned hard to deal with losing her (if he'd ever really had her at all). Amy had been a beautiful, cold-blooded, unapologetic female embodiment of the will to live. God, how that girl could smile.

He put his towel aside, entered the shower, and let the hot water run over him. He forcefully kneaded the remnant of tendons in his hand to break up scar tissue as he'd been taught, then began increasing pressure until there was pain. He smiled sadistically. He might not be able to fight the stupid-assed Army bureaucracy, the bullshit-spinning politics in the news, or the Celebrity Cult; nor could he be proud of his brief flirtation with drugs or trying to satisfy the honest need for the feminine presence in his life with the *Sex and the City* clones whom he pretended to be interested in on dates he endured to save money on whores. (Though to him they all came from the same world that smelled of stale booze, latex, and cab fare home doled out from the guts of a leather wallet, all of which left him hating himself and feeling like he was cheating on Amy with women he didn't want to remember having fucked as he de-hookered wherever it was he was staying. Not that those feelings ever stopped him from starting the cycle all over again when he thought of her grinning welcomely on her back with a new beau in her Post-Relationship Hedonism Phase. As if their moment had never happened at all.) But he could sure as hell try to run from them. Memories, though…the important ones…

He understood now in his bones why his ancestors had headed west after the Civil War. A hundred and fifty years ago, when a man got tired of all the damned brokenness of his world, he could escape it by un-assing the AO (Area of Operation) and heading out yonder. Walton would have given anything for a frontier. Someplace that hadn't been tamed yet, where man didn't have to be small and could be a fucking *Man*. That had been one of the good things about war. He missed it and the way it had made his actions feel important at times. He missed the certainty that life had meaning. He wanted God; not mere faith in the face of silence as he'd had in his youth, but understanding; enough to still the ache that came from unrelenting sense that there was *more*, just beyond his grasp. *North*. He missed Canada in the summer. Was Amy well? She would be turning twenty-five next month. He imagined her life playing out over the years; the books she'd read, the places she'd go, and the home she'd someday have, complete with a husband, and children, and grandbabies, and all the little rituals and dramas that made life worth living. Growing old. Walton hoped her life would be long, and that she would have more happiness and laughter than she knew what to do with.

He let go of his hand and consciously willed his wrist to move with all his might until his arm shook from the effort, knowing full well that he'd never make it work again, but straining anyway. He vividly remembered the sensation of being able to manipulate it, but it remained still as if to taunt him. Walton felt imprisoned inside his scarred body and its unresponsive parts to the point of claustrophobia. He tried to breathe to keep from hyperventilating. Alone inside the tiny shower, the weight of his thoughts shattered the mask he showed the world of sales clerks and soldiers. He gnashed his teeth in a grotesque snarl and his shoulders racked with sobs as he lost his battle again, wondering what the fuck was wrong with him.

Shame at his weakness made his pain blossom into a seething rage, and like all of God's wounded creatures, he lashed out. The faceless wall in front of him became the avatar of his torturer and he punched it with his left fist. The wall remained unchanged. It was only himself that hurt.

The soldier wept. When it passed, he reflected how this sort of thing had become a regular occurrence with him. In the shower, on a walk, driving in his truck, when he was drunk, at night while he was trying to sleep; these waves of sorrow and anger came down suddenly out of nowhere like lightning, triggered by the most random things, and seizing him without mercy. He figured he was getting addicted to the pain and was embarrassed by how self-indulgent and pathetic that was. This was not how men like his dad and grandfather had behaved in their youth. America didn't put up with that shit back then. The country hadn't been built by men with tiny hearts who'd ran around feeling sorry for themselves. A man had to ruck up and drive on; he had to pull his weight or he ran the risk of dragging down the person to his left and right.

He remembered a sergeant at Ft. Benning who had been an instructor on the then-new Javelin weapons system. The sergeant had been a pure-bred 11-Bravo, possessing the old school masculinity of the men in the black and white WWII photos. He'd spoken with a commanding West Virginian accent that had often been shot through with humor, and Walton had always liked it when the man taught one of their classes. Sometimes during the breaks the sergeant would go outside to smoke and bullshit with the Joes in the class and he would dust off some outrageously hysterical story taking place Back-When-He-Was-in-Korea, or wherever.

One day, while discussing the differences between the Old Army and the New Army, Walton had seen something come over the NCO as he'd watched their group, the effect of which had given the sergeant's face a cast that had looked somewhere between pity and concern. The sergeant's voice had dropped in volume with an inflection that had carried with it a paternal quality, and he'd told them to gather in. The group had felt drawn into a conspiracy, and Walton and the other soldiers had eagerly anticipated hearing some bit of sage wisdom or infantry lore.

The sergeant had sighed wearily, then readjusted his BDU soft cap so that it rested in a more relaxed position. After staring sadly at them for a moment, as though looking into the future, he'd said, "Look fellas. Today's Army...well...y'all are a bunch of pussies. But that ain't your fault, ya see, 'cause America today is a bunch of pussies."

The shock of the insult had sparked something confrontational in Walton. He'd wanted to challenge the sergeant, but deep down he'd suspected there was some truth to it. He'd joined the Army, in part, out of a sense that he'd needed to pay his civic dues. He'd grown up under the protection and abundance of America, and he'd felt like he'd had a debt to pay that taxes alone couldn't satisfy. There had been something in the connection between himself and the country that generations of his family had fought and sacrificed for that had demanded a blood-price. Every civilization needed warriors to protect it, and he'd wanted to serve on the wall as one.

There had been another factor, though. He thought if he was to be completely honest with himself, one of the biggest reasons he'd volunteered had been because he'd thought the military was an enclave for masculinity. For tradition. He'd wanted to learn from soldiers who demanded that a man had to "Get tough or die."

Walton had wanted to be more.

For most of his life, he had been haunted by the feeling that something vital was being taken from him a little piece at a time and he'd hoped the Army could help him get it back. He'd thought it was one of the few remaining institutions where living by a code was still possible, and where the old words; loyalty, duty, honor, and courage, weren't used in irony or cynicism, but were used to dare a man to achieve something higher and more noble. It was one of the few cultural bastions trying to hold the fort against the Pussification of the American Male, and Walton had hoped that within it he'd find the means to purge himself of the bullshit and weakness that seemed to plague so many of the young men of his generation. Maybe even be proud of himself one day. At least that had been the theory.

Crying in the shower over things he couldn't change and a girl who he hadn't been man enough to hold on to was an affirmation of the sergeant's wisdom. As this knowledge confronted him, it dragged him to the edge of something; to some place offering a glimpse to a path that led to more than whining and clichéd emptiness.

His grandfather used to say, "We're a short time here, a long time gone." There was something profound in that. He was flesh and blood (and now bits of metal) bound to breathe only for a moment and then return to the dust and give back the life he'd been blessed with. Whether by the hand of Divine Providence or sheer dumb luck, he had survived Haji and his own foolishness. Any idiot could wallow in the ugliness and darkness of life, but to be able to find the glory, grace, and beauty in it demanded something. Some strength or vision which he desperately wanted. With tools like that, he could build his own damned world.

Walton scrubbed the tears from his eyes and straightened up his posture. He found himself grinning again like a son of a bitch. The Bad Man had tried and failed to take his scalp, and he lived to fight another day.

Fuck pain, fuck weakness, fuck shame, fuck excuses, fuck despair, fuck the darkness in his heart and in the world, and fuck being a victim. Terrorism, consumerism, progressivism, feminism, globalism, nihilism…*loss*…by God, he was going to live through this somehow.

Just to piss 'em all off.

Samuel Finlay served as an infantryman in Bosnia and Afghanistan. He enjoys reading good books, listening to old music, traveling, and sitting on porches. He was born and raised in Oklahoma.